MW01026052

INDUSTRIAL VALLEY

LITERATURE OF AMERICAN LABOR
Cletus E. Daniel and Ileen A. DeVault, Series Editors

BETWEEN THE HILLS AND THE SEA
K. B. Gilden

THE DIARY OF A SHIRTWAIST STRIKER
Theresa Serber Malkiel

INDUSTRIAL VALLEY
Ruth McKenney

In the LITERATURE OF AMERICAN LABOR series we bring back into print some of the best literature that has emerged from the labor movement and related events in the United States and Canada. We are defining literature broadly; the series encompasses the full range of popular writing, including novels, biographies, autobiographies, and journalism. Each book includes an introduction written especially for this series and directing the reader's attention to the historical context for the work.

We believe that the titles in the series will be particularly useful to students of social and labor history and American studies. Our hope is that, both individually and collectively, the books in this series will contribute to a greater understanding of working-class experiences in our culture.

LITERATURE OF AMERICAN LABOR SERIES

INDUSTRIAL VALLEY

RUTH McKENNEY

With an Introduction by

Daniel Nelson

ILR PRESS

Ithaca, New York

Copyright © 1939 by Ruth McKenney, renewed 1967.
Introduction by Daniel Nelson,
copyright © 1992 by Cornell University.
All rights reserved.

Library of Congress Cataloging-in-Publication Data
McKenney, Ruth, 1911–
    Industrial valley / Ruth McKenney; with an introduction by Daniel
Nelson.
        p. cm.—(literature of American labor)
    Originally published: New York: Harcourt, Brace, 1939.
    Includes bibliographical references.
    ISBN 0–87546–183–2 (pbk.: acid-free paper)
    1. Rubber industry and trade—Ohio—Akron—History—20th century—
Fiction. 2. Akron (Ohio)—History—Fiction. I. Title.
II. Series.
PS3525.A25573I5 1992
813'.52—dc20   92-2696

This new edition of *Industrial Valley* is designed by Kat Dalton.
The text, with exception of the front matter, is reproduced
from the original version, published by
Harcourt, Brace and Company in 1939.

Cover photo housed in the Amalgamated Clothing Workers of
America Records. Labor-Management Documentation Center,
Cornell University.

Copies of this book may be ordered through bookstores
or directly from

ILR Press
School of Industrial and Labor Relations
Cornell University
Ithaca, NY 14853–3901

Printed on acid-free paper in the United States of America
5   4   3   2   1

FOR RICHARD

CONTENTS

ACKNOWLEDGMENTS

The whole city of Akron helped me write this book. It is difficult to single out persons or organizations for special thanks—dozens of newspapermen, lawyers, rubberworkers, ministers, gave me invaluable help; nearly every organization in town from the unions to the rubber companies answered my questions and gave me information.

I am especially indebted, however, to the following persons and organizations:

The Akron Public Library and the head of its reference department, Miss Helen Purdham; the Akron Chamber of Commerce and its secretary, H. C. Atkinson; the Greater Akron Association; the *Akron Beacon Journal* and its publisher, John Knight; Walter Morrow, former editor of the late *Akron Times-Press;* the publicity department of the Goodyear Tire and Rubber Company.

The United Rubber Workers of America and all its Akron officials, especially Sherman Dalrymple, Frank Grillo, L. L. Callahan, John House, and L. S. Buckmaster; Robert Gamble and Eric Spitzer; Amos Murphy; Wilmer Tate; Reverend Noble S. Elderkin of the First Congregational Church; James Keller, secretary of the Summit County Communist Party; James S. McCartan; Allan Haywood, now head of the New York state Council of the Committee for Industrial Organization; and Howard Wolf, who gave me permission to use material from his book, *Rubber: A Story of Glory and Greed.*

Many people helped me prepare this manuscript for publication by checking data and suggesting additional sources. Of these, I wish to thank especially James Wishart, John Williamson, Joseph Gaer, John C. Carrington, and Bruce Minton.

INTRODUCTION

When *Industrial Valley,* Ruth McKenney's compelling account of class and industrial conflict in Akron, Ohio, first appeared in 1939, reviewers were pleased and puzzled. They were uniformly impressed with McKenney's skill as a storyteller and with her use of local color. They were less certain about what she had done. Was *Industrial Valley* a journalist's report from the front line of industrial conflict or a novel based on the experiences of Akron workers? Some reviewers treated it as imaginative journalism. Others, such as the critic Malcolm Cowley, heralded it as "perhaps the best American" proletarian novel.[1] An Akron reviewer despaired of any simple categorization; it was, he concluded, a "bewildering compost" of fact and fiction.[2] *Industrial Valley* is all of these things—it is about real people and events, but organized in the form of the radical novel and written from the perspective of the activist and social critic. A half century after its publication, it provides the modern reader with one of the finest (and most entertaining) introductions to the experiences and concerns of the depression generation.

Ruth McKenney (1911–1972) was born in Mishawaka, Indiana, and grew up in suburban Cleveland, where her father managed a factory. As a teenager, she developed a strong interest in writing and journalism and worked as a printer's assistant during vacations. While at Ohio State University from 1928 to 1932, she wrote for *The Lantern,* the student paper, and became a popular campus figure. "In rapid succession," she recalled, "I was a sorority girl, a riproaring communist, and a down your nose sophisticate."[3] She did not graduate, according to her account because she could not pass physical education, but more likely because of differences with *The Lantern*'s editors over the proper role of women in journalism.[4] After leaving school she worked briefly for a small-town weekly and was employed as a feature writer at the *Akron Beacon Journal* in October 1932. The next eighteen months would be among the most important of her career.

In 1932 Akron, Ohio, was a cross between Detroit and the Lynds' Middletown, an industrial city that retained many features of small-town life. Akron had grown faster than any other urban community during the 1910s as its principal industry, the manufacture of auto and truck tires, boomed. Because of Akron's increasing dependence on a single, highly cyclical industry, the post–World War I recession of 1920–21 devastated the city, bankrupting weaker firms and reducing industrial employment by 90 percent in less than six months. The city and its workers recovered in the 1920s, but the memory of that fateful period lingered.

There was good reason for anxiety. The recession had not reduced the city's dependence on the tire industry; indeed, as late as 1929 Akron plants produced two-thirds of all tires manufactured in the United States and employed more than half of all tire workers. Production, moreover, was becoming more concentrated. Three large firms, Goodyear Tire and Rubber, Firestone Tire and Rubber, and B. F. Goodrich, dominated the industry and the city's economy. Goodyear, which would become the central villain of *Industrial Valley,* had long been the nation's largest tire producer and one of the largest corporations, but it was far from omnipotent. Overextended, it had collapsed in 1920 and had been reorganized by outside investment bankers. This arrangement kept the local owners, led by the deposed founder, Frank A. Seiberling, at bay and created a legal and organizational vacuum that the production manager, Paul A. Litchfield, quickly filled. Litchfield, an outsider and technocrat, became company president in 1926. By 1932 he was the city's most influential citizen.

Litchfield was an imposing and controversial figure. An engineer by training, he emphasized production over sales and finance and used his company's enormous plants to push less efficient producers to the wall. In the late 1920s he negotiated a series of secret contracts with Sears, Roebuck that provided Sears with tires at bargain prices. These agreements kept Goodyear's factories working at capacity through the 1920s and benefited consumers, but they heightened competition in the industry and the sense of insecurity in Akron households, middle-class and working-class alike.

Litchfield's other controversial policies stemmed from his interest in labor reform. In the 1910s he introduced a series of welfare and personnel plans that made Goodyear a leader in employee relations and created a large cadre of devoted employees. Like other Akron employers, Litchfield was strongly anti-union; yet unlike many others he recognized the importance of the individual worker in mass production. In 1919 he introduced an Industrial Assembly, an elected body of employee representatives divided into two houses and empowered to enact legislation subject only to his veto. The Industrial Assembly was not a toothless company union: during the 1920s it gradually expanded its activities to include potentially sensitive subjects such as wages and hours. In 1926 it struck for a week to reinforce its demand for higher wages. In the early 1930s the Industrial Assembly was better prepared than most AFL organizations to confront the depression. It would be at the heart of the controversy that led to the great strike of 1936.

The Akron labor force was another legacy of the rubber industry's remarkable transformation. Before 1910 the city's working class was made up largely of German and Irish immigrants. The rapid expansion in tire production and the city itself required thousands of additional workers. Systematic recruitment efforts began in 1916. Workers from diverse backgrounds responded. Italian, Greek, Russian, and other eastern European immigrants filled jobs in construction, personal services, and retailing. Native-born Americans from southern Ohio, West Virginia, and other areas of Appalachia took most of the higher paying jobs in the tire and rubber plants. This division of labor reflected the rubber manufacturers' preference for young, powerful men fluent in English. To outsiders such as McKenney, the immigrants were invisible; the rubber workers, with their quaint country habits and speech, were the Akron labor force.

To accommodate the newcomers, contractors built thousands of large frame houses in a vast arc south and east of the downtown business district. During the boom years many families met their mortgage payments by renting one or more rooms to single workers. After 1920, when most of the renters disappeared, these outsize houses and their substantial debts added to the city's collective sense of insecurity. When employment and incomes shrank again in the 1930s, many homeowners could not afford to maintain their houses and south and east Akron became run-down. The notable exceptions were Goodyear Heights and

Firestone Park, model communities that the manufacturers had sponsored in the 1910s to provide superior housing for their most valued employees. The attractive, well-built homes of Goodyear Heights and Firestone Park, close to the plants and to parks, churches, and community centers, were striking evidence of the manufacturers' power to shape and manipulate their environment.

The boom and subsequent collapse of 1920–21 paralyzed local government. Akron teetered on the verge of insolvency throughout the 1920s, unable to keep pace with the need to provide basic services such as paved streets, expanded sewer systems, and additional schools. The problems of the school system became the focus of the Ku Klux Klan, which commanded a large following in south and east Akron through the early 1920s. Seemingly intractable problems discouraged most other potential leaders. Akron had a vigorous two-party system, but the victors in the often bruising battles that characterized local political life were frequently corrupt or incompetent. The mercurial Nelson Sparks and the bumbling Ike Myers, the mayors of the early 1930s, were typical of this group.

Ruth McKenney began her career at the *Beacon Journal* at an auspicious time. The collapse of the automobile business in 1930 and 1931 reverberated through Detroit, Flint, Toledo, Akron, and dozens of other midwestern cities and towns that were dependent on the vehicle industry. Production schedules were slashed and layoffs became common. To deflect the worst effects of the downturn, Akron manufacturers adopted a share-the-work plan that reduced virtually everyone to part-time employment. In the 1910s and 1920s Akron had been a place to make money. By the time McKenney began to report the affairs of the Rubber City, most Akron residents merely hoped to survive.

McKenney became an acute observer of the depression. She later wrote that she "had spent nearly a year exiled in Akron, Ohio collecting enough facts about rubber workers to fill six large file cases," but the truth appears to have been more complex and interesting.[5] Shortly after she was hired as a general reporter and feature writer, the paper employed James S. Jackson as a labor reporter. Jackson was very busy in the following years; his magnificently detailed accounting of the city's troubled industrial relations provided the raw material for *Industrial Valley*. But his presence also meant that McKenney had few first-hand opportunities to become acquainted with workers or their activities. She wrote a variety of human-interest stories, including a feature on women in aviation, but nothing on the rubber industry, the workers, or the rapid evolution of industrial relations that became the city's biggest story after 1933. Her newspaper account of the funeral of Alex O'Lari, a Communist who was shot by police while trying to prevent the eviction of a destitute family, was as close as she came to the subject that was later to absorb her attention.[6] Equally important, she apparently had little interest in learning more. Friends recall that she had sympathy for the unfortunate but no specific concerns.[7] The genesis of *Industrial Valley* came later, probably in 1936, after she left Akron.

If McKenney had been interested in industrial workers, unions, or radical politics, her friends and associates presumably would have known. She is remembered as outspoken, exuberant, witty, disorganized, and wholly unable to conceal her feelings. Her obsessions, she confessed, were writing, dancing, and eating steak. At least one of her escapades is recounted in *Industrial Valley.* With Earl Wilson, an Ohio State friend and *Beacon Journal* colleague who was also beginning a notable career in journalism, she enticed a group of local clergymen to accompany her and Wilson to a popular cabaret. She delighted in reporting the ministers' shock and embarrassment at the scantily clad entertainers and raucous atmosphere they encountered.[8]

At work McKenney was no less memorable. John S. Knight, the publisher of the *Beacon Journal,* recalled that he "sweated over her copy." The city editor remembered "plenty of mistakes of fact and spelling." A printer added that "she was nearly always inaccurate with her copy . . . and when the city editor got it edited . . . it looked like the map of New Zealand." But, as the editor admitted, McKenney had that "intangible something that compelled folks to read her stuff." In 1933 she swept the top prizes awarded by the Ohio Newspaper Women's Association. She was "as good a newspaper woman as ever covered a story in Ohio."[9]

In mid–1934 McKenney left the *Beacon Journal* and Akron. She later wrote that she took a job on a Trenton, New Jersey, paper only to discover that the staff was on strike. She soon found a job at the *New York Post,* perhaps with the help of Wilson, who had joined the *Post* a few months earlier. She remained there through 1936. McKenney returned to Akron several times in later years but was not present during the tumultuous developments that form the heart of *Industrial Valley.* She gleaned her knowledge from the *Beacon Journal* and from another source she became associated with in New York, the Communist party.

In 1936 McKenney wrote an essay on her Akron experiences entitled "Uneasy City," which the *New Yorker* published in its December 19 issue. Akron, she wrote, was "very grim." It was "dirty and ugly" and "smells like a rubber band smoldering in an ashtray." It had no theaters, art galleries, distinctive buildings, or attractive parks. Its officials were corrupt, its upper class supercilious; there were rumors that one of the Firestone daughters sent her laundry to Paris. But the wealthy and powerful were as uneasy as everyone else. Their formerly loyal and deferential employees, particularly the rubber workers who labored "like crazy people" in prison-like structures, were now rebelling, organizing unions, staging sit-down strikes, and persecuting nonunion colleagues. McKenney liberally spiced her account with worker dialogue. A sophisticate insulted a newly arrived West Virginian: "Ha, lookit, he's got one laig shorter than t'other, from walking around mountains." An angry East Akron resident threatened: "I aim tew tear the heart out of this here baster' who be the formain." A nonunion worker entered a tavern: "Kin it be you ain't got no union button? You r-a-a-t!"[10]

"Uneasy City" was well received and the *New Yorker* offered McKenney a position as a contributing editor. Because she would be paid only for what the magazine published, McKenney abandoned New York for an inexpensive home in Milford, Connecticut, which she shared with her newly divorced sister, Eileen. In Milford Ruth began a series of delightfully funny, self-deprecating stories about growing up in Cleveland that appeared in the *New Yorker* and then were published by Harcourt, Brace as *My Sister Eileen* (1938). The stories were popular and became the basis of a successful Broadway show in 1940. (Tragically, Eileen and her new husband, the novelist Nathanael West, were killed in an auto accident a few days before the show opened.) McKenney later became uncomfortable with her reputation as a humorist and insisted that she wrote the stories only to make money. They nevertheless highlighted her strengths as a writer: an ability to recount personal experiences in an engaging and humorous way and a sensitivity to the foibles of the middle class.

"Uneasy City" also attracted the attention of Richard Bransten, an editor of the Communist literary magazine, *The New Masses*. Bransten was the scion of a prominent family who had left his wife and son to pursue a career as a radical journalist. To obscure his past he worked under the name Bruce Milton. McKenney apparently did not meet him until 1937, when he contacted her to obtain information about the labor movement in Akron for a book he was writing. They met in Milford one Sunday in August and discussed the rubber industry and presumably much more. Twelve days later they were married. In the following years, Bransten served as McKenney's business agent and authority on social and political issues. On his recommendation she joined the editorial board of *The New Masses* in September 1937, contributed many personal and satirical essays to the magazine, and became involved in Communist party affairs. She and Bransten remained active in the party even during the Popular Front's collapse in 1939 and 1940, when most artists and intellectuals abandoned the party. In 1940 she wrote a widely circulated pamphlet urging the election of Earl Browder, the Communist presidential candidate. McKenney was the last of the popular literary figures of the 1930s to retain a link to *The New Masses*.

At the same time she wrote the Eileen stories, McKenney was busy on a larger, more serious book that drew on the material she had used for "Uneasy City" and reflected her new political associations. Under Granville Hicks, literary editor until 1939, *The New Masses* had promoted the proletarian novel, a genre that treated the strike as a symbol of liberation from oppressive conditions. Typically the proletarian novel was a story of industrial conflict leading to a climactic strike. The format provided McKenney with a framework for the material she had assembled rather haphazardly in "Uneasy City." McKenney's political perspective also led her to exaggerate the role of Communists in the Akron story, to imply, for example, that they were responsible for the formation of the international union in 1935 and for the settlement of the 1936 Goodyear strike. Most important, it affected her portrayal of the workers, the most obvious difference between "Uneasy City" and *Industrial Valley*.

In "Uneasy City" the rubber workers are figures out of "Lil' Abner"— crude, violent, and by implication contributors to the exploitative conditions that narrowed their horizons and thwarted their ambitions. In *Industrial Valley* they are occasionally identified as mountaineers or southern migrants but in most respects are indistinguishable from their northern neighbors. They speak conventional English, are rarely eccentric, and are capable of appeals to solidarity and brotherhood. A 1934 strike leader proclaims:

> If they lay a hand on one union man . . . they lay a hand on us all. If they bust this strike, they'll bust every strike. We're fighting, you guys and me, for the whole union movement . . . and the chance to hold our heads up like men.[11]

Whereas the dialogue in "Uneasy City" had conveyed an image of the worker as bumpkin or fool, the dialogue in *Industrial Valley* conveys a sense of the workers' moral superiority to the bosses and the bosses' minions.

In general, *Industrial Valley*, like McKenney's other works, is strong where she could draw on personal experiences, less effective where she had to imagine what people thought or said. Her portrayal of the city's pompous business leaders, inept politicians, and opportunistic shopkeepers—the people McKenney knew best—is the book's strongest feature. Her treatment of the workers and their leaders is less satisfactory. Apart from her comments on the rank and file, McKenney rarely mentions Sherman Dalrymple, the B. F. Goodrich local union—and later international union—president who was the most influential of the rubber workers, and John House, the leader of the 1936 strike. Instead she features men she had known, such as James McCartan and Alex Eigenmacht, leaders of the printers' union, and Wilmer Tate, the city's longtime labor gadfly and activist, who played peripheral roles in the events she describes. The result is an impression that the Goodyear strike was organized at the grass roots when in reality it was effectively organized from the top. The strike succeeded in large part because the CIO representatives, all outsiders, provided valuable assistance without compromising the authority or legitimacy of the international or local union leaders. McKenney thus captures the drama of the conflict but misses its significance for the labor movement of the 1930s.

Industrial Valley fittingly ends with a victory parade and the strikers shouting "We won! We won!" But a careful reading of the final pages suggests an important qualification: the workers won mostly in the sense that they avoided defeat. The Goodyear strike was a signal victory for the CIO, a prelude to other highly visible and successful union initiatives in 1936 and 1937, and a crushing defeat for the Industrial Assembly and company unionism, but was less decisive and satisfying for the United Rubber Workers, the Goodyear local, and Akron workers generally. In the following years Goodyear executives proved no less intransigent than they had been in 1935 and 1936. By the end of the decade they had beaten the local into submission in the Akron plants (and in most of their other plants as well) and had regained most of the powers they had lost in 1936. The other manufacturers were no less hostile. Firestone provided the long-term answer to worker militancy by agreeing to a URW contract in its Akron complex in 1937 and simultaneously moving production and jobs to southern, nonunion locations. All of the large Akron manufacturers had new plants in the South by the eve of World War II. War mobilization halted the flight for a few years and the postwar boom obscured it for a few more. By the 1960s, however, the pattern was unmistakable and by the late 1970s all auto and truck tire manufacture in Akron had ended.

The publication of *Industrial Valley*, when McKenney was twenty-eight, marked the end of the first and most important phase of her career. She had established herself as a humorist and an interpreter of social trends. In later years she continued to work in both areas. She produced two more books of stories about her sister and her family and a longer work about an uncle that were reasonably well received. An ambitious effort to write a fictional sequel to *Industrial Valley*, the proletarian novel *Jake Home* (1943), was less successful. Earl Browder, a prominent character in the story, summarized the reaction to *Jake Home* when he recalled that it was "awful, simply awful."[12] McKenney seems to have exhausted her most interesting material in *My Sister Eileen* and *Industrial Valley*. Never again would she have an experience comparable to the year and a half she spent in Akron.

McKenney's politics increasingly became an obstacle to her career in the 1940s. Her Communist affiliations closed many doors even after she and Bransten were unceremoniously expelled from the party in 1946 for siding with the then-discredited Browder. But her difficulties transcended her ties to an unpopular cause. She was never able to view her Communist associates and their experiences with the same reporter's eye that she focused on other people and events. At a time when personal accounts by ex-Communists were popular and commercially successful, McKenney was uncharacteristically restrained. Her autobiography, *Love Story* (1950), includes many amusing vignettes from the 1930s but only vague and unrevealing references to her associations of the 1940s.

Ruth McKenney was a fascinating individual, a capable journalist, and a natural storyteller who happened to be in the right place at the right time. That place and time was Akron in the 1930s. The result was *Industrial Valley,* one of the most readable and sensitive chronicles of an era. The republication of *Industrial Valley* makes this distinctive author and her special perspective available once more. Students of the cultural, social, and labor history of the 1930s will welcome the opportunity to renew their acquaintanceship with McKenney and depression-era Akron.

Daniel Nelson
Akron, Ohio
February 1992

1. Malcolm Cowley, "Collective Novel," *New Republic,* February 22, 1939.
2. *Akron Beacon Journal,* February 17, 1939. Also see Walter B. Rideout, *The Radical Novel in the United States, 1900–1954; Some Interrelations of Literature and Society* (Cambridge: Harvard University Press, 1956).
3. *Akron Beacon Journal,* October 9, 1933.
4. Mrs. Margot Younger Jackson. Interviews with author, September 11 and October 13, 1991. Margot Younger was a childhood and college friend of McKenney. She married *Akron Beacon Journal* labor reporter James S. Jackson in 1936.
5. Ruth McKenney, *Love Story* (New York: Harcourt, Brace, 1950), p. 13.
6. *Akron Beacon Journal,* October 18, 1932; *Industrial Valley,* pp. 40-44.
7. Mrs. Margot Younger Jackson. Interviews with author.
8. *Industrial Valley,* p. 159; *Akron Beacon Journal,* October 9, 1933.
9. *Akron Beacon Journal,* December 21 and 26, 1936, and February 28, 1939.
10. Ruth McKenney, "Uneasy City," *New Yorker,* December 19, 1936, 83-87.
11. *Industrial Valley,* p. 149.
12. Quoted in David A. Shannon, *The Decline of American Communism: A History of the Communist Party of the United States since 1945* (New York: Harcourt, Brace, 1959), p. 55.

INDUSTRIAL VALLEY

TO BEGIN WITH

The City of Akron, Ohio, lies near the center of the greatest industrial region in the world.

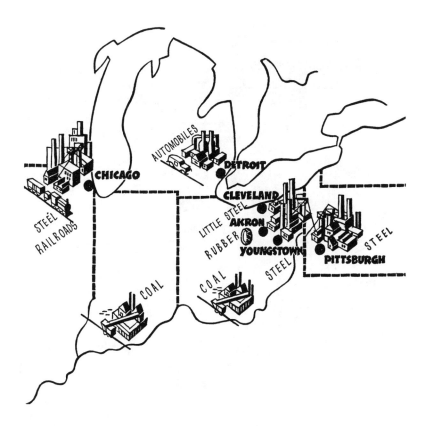

The town stinks and throbs and sometimes gets rich and more often goes on relief with Rubber. Rubber is the first and last fact of life to the people of Akron.

Akron is, quite by accident, very nearly a hundred per cent native-white town. Slavs and Poles and Hungarians work the furious blast furnaces of steel, but Rubber is milled and steamed and hammered into tires by big drawling mountaineers from West Virginia and Tennessee and Alabama.

1. *Total population:* 255,000.
2. *Total native-white population:* 212,000.
3. *Southern-born population:* 152,000.
4. *Foreign-born population:* 31,000.
5. *Negro population:* 11,000.

The World War made Akron, alone among the important industrial centers, an all-American city. Rubber boomed in 1914 and 1915 on the heels of the automobile industry. The rubber manufacturers needed cheap docile heavy-muscled labor at the precise moment when the usual European source of supply was being blown to eternity.

So every little hillbilly newspaper south of the Ohio River and east of the Mississippi suddenly bloomed with stirring advertisements urging the popeyed reader to leave the barren hill farms of his ancestors and trek north to riches and Rubber. Nearly sixty-five per cent of Akron's population was imported from the southern mountains.

The city is only medium-sized. It ranks thirty-fifth among American industrial centers. The town grew so fast, tripling its population between 1912 and 1920, that it swamped its own boundary lines. Greater Akron had a population of 89,000 more than the mere 255,000 the 1930 United States Census officially allowed the city.

Akron exploded from a bustling town into a roaring city, so its population is young and rawboned and hotblooded. Detroit alone is a younger city, younger by a fraction of a per cent. In Akron, eighty-eight per cent of the people are under fifty, and seventy-five per cent are under forty.

The town grew fast; now it has stopped growing. The people who live in Akron are young, but ten years ago, it was a younger town. Akron was, and is no longer, a boom-town.

These are details.

The main thing in Akron is Rubber.

This is a true story. All the dates, figures, street names, and incidents are exact. Only two names are fictitious. Job Hendrick and Tom Gettling, their wives and children, are actual people— but pseudonyms are used to conceal the identity of two families who play an important role in this story but must remain anonymous for reasons the reader will understand.

This is a true story of Akron, Ohio. It is also a true story of America's industrial valleys the country over.

BOOK ONE

JANUARY 1, 1932, TO JUNE 16, 1933

Parade

The unemployed of Akron paraded today. Early Saturday morning a rumor swept the crowded streets of East and South Akron. The story spread from one soot-blackened frame house to another: The Mayor will be handing out jobs at City Hall today for his new work-relief program.

Job Hendrick still lay in heavy sleep when his wife brought him the news. His gaunt face with the high cheekbones was collapsed and empty on the naked mattress. There were no pillows on the bed. Missus Hendrick had sold the pillows three weeks ago.

"Job," Missus Hendrick roared. "Hey, Josh, get up."

Job Hendrick let go of his sleep reluctantly. He groaned.

Missus Hendrick repeated gently, "Get up, old man. The Mayor is handin' out jobs."

Now he heard. He sat up yawning. His cotton underwear stretched across his broad chest as he sucked in the air and stretched.

"Gimme that overcoat," Missus Hendrick began briskly. "I'll try and give it a press, so's you'll look halfway decent—not like a bum."

Mister Hendrick scooped up the overcoat from the bed. Missus Hendrick had sold the blankets two months ago.

"How do you know?" he said, holding the overcoat in his arms and looking up at his strong big wife.

"Missus Gettling said Missus Howry told her."

Mister Hendrick got on his feet. He grinned at his wife, and as she reached out for the coat, he swatted her one across the buttocks. She laughed.

Mister Hendrick's own grin wore off slowly. His face was still contorted with the smile while his mind went back to its familiar treadmill: the rubber shops laying off, and the kids needing food, and what had a man come to when he didn't have a pillow for his head or a blanket to cover him at night?

3

Missus Hendrick was ironing furiously when her old man came down the creaky steps. Clouds of steam rose from the ironing board and Missus Hendrick's face was red with heat and excitement. The two Hendrick kids sat solemnly watching.

Liz junior spotted her father first. She squealed and ran to the doorway, catching him by his big solid thighs. "Pa, will you buy me a sled like what I didn't get for Christmas if the Mayor gives you a job?"

"Will you shut up about that sled!" Missus Hendrick said furiously. "The answer is 'No,' we got more important things to buy if your Pa gets that job."

Mister Hendrick rubbed his hand over his daughter's reddish-blond hair.

"I made you a cup of coffee, Job," Missus Hendrick said in a soft tone, as though she were ashamed.

"Where'd you get that?" Mister Hendrick asked heavily.

"Where'd you think? I borrowed it." Irritation played in Missus Hendrick's voice again. Her husband trod carefully as he went to the kitchen stove for the coffeepot. Liz was a good wife, he reflected, but lately she was always flying off the handle, enough to drive a man crazy.

When Missus Hendrick got her husband into his freshly pressed overcoat, she went to the door with him. The kids stood around to have their Pa kiss them and pinch their cheeks, rather thin just now for pinching purposes. Then Missus Hendrick laughed and gave Mister Hendrick a hug.

"Good luck, old man," she said.

"Yeah."

Job Hendrick and Tom Gettling tramped up the street together. They told each other that probably this whole thing was just some crazy idea of the womenfolks.

Tom skirted two kids dragging a spindly old Christmas tree to the curb for the garbage collection. "But I guess," he mumbled, "it was in the paper."

Job gulped. Mister Gettling carefully examined the gray sky, overcast with streaks of black rubber smoke. It made him feel funny in the stomach to see tears in the eyes of Job Hendrick, who was the sweetest second baseman he knew, even after ten

4

years in the shops, and about the best Number 12 tirebuilder in the business. Number 12 is a medium tire, but a mean one to get together.

"Jesus," Mister Gettling offered, "the smell is somethin' awful today."

Job was grateful. He sniffed with a great show of interest. "Ain't no worse than usual."

Tom did not argue. The rubber smell was never any worse and never any better. Mister Gettling and Mister Hendrick were veterans of the rubber smell. For ten years they had eaten, and slept, and made love with the acrid rubber stench high in the nostril and deep in the throat. Still, after ten years, Mister Gettling and Mister Hendrick gagged in the mornings when they first awoke and started smelling rubber as they put on their pants. Nobody ever got used to the smell.

"Anyway, it won't stink in heaven." Mister Gettling hoped Mister Hendrick would smile at the ancient pleasantry.

Mister Hendrick did not smile. He shuffled past the rows of box-like frame houses in silence. Tom tramped at his side, afraid to speak. They turned into Main Street.

Job Hendrick faced the main plant of The B. F. Goodrich Company. He knew the shape of every huge black iron gate. He knew the thickness of every thick brick wall. He could walk blindfolded among the smoke-blackened buildings and say which shop made Number 12 tires and which bleak six-story pile housed raw rubber. He knew how tall the three brick smokestacks stood to dominate the great expanse of dark brick and steel. He could pick his way like a careful cat among the maze of railroad tracks that ran among the buildings. Out of this solid square mile of gates and tracks and powerhouses, he could select the precise spot where the brown paper to cover the finished tires was cut to size. Job Hendrick had grown from a gawky mountain boy to a heavy solid man within those thick brick walls.

Job Hendrick knew the rubber shop. He knew it, and he hated it. The powerful black bulk, stretching up and down the street, and as far back as the eye could see, still, after all these years, made his heart heavy. He was afraid of it, really.

5

"Goddamned joint," Mister Hendrick muttered. "Looks like the West Virginia State Prison, only bigger."

Tom kicked at a cigar butt oozing out of the sidewalk slush. "Don't look like they're doin' much."

Job ran his practiced eye over the acres of dirty windows. He jerked his angular chin toward the three rows near the street which showed lights. "The truck tire is still up."

Mister Gettling sighed. "I heard they were only operatin' two shifts for a special order."

Job shuffled slowly up Main Street. He glanced into Joe's Hamburg Place, but he didn't see the two dicehounds shooting crap in the half dark, he didn't see Joe himself wiping shot glasses and passing the time of day with a former customer, now insolvent. He passed Dixie's Lunchroom, but he didn't spot Alec Browning, a Number 12 department man, trying to hit Miss Dixie up for some credit on a hamburg. Mister Hendrick was too sad to see anything but the black pile of buildings across the street.

"Rubber ain't the only business that's gone sour," Mister Gettling muttered.

Job eyed a pale dirty-faced whore who stood shivering in the narrow entrance of Pete's Hostelry, Men Only, Fifty Cents a Night, Private Room, $1.00. "Yeah."

Mister Hendrick and Mister Gettling tramped by Sunshine Drug Store noting through the mud-specked plateglass window that Old Doc was still doing a little business in tickets for the numbers game. The cold made them walk a little faster past a sign swinging in the wind, "Doctor for Men, Free Examination," past a thirty-cent lunchroom where a solitary customer was buying a bottle of under-the-counter needle beer.

When they could see the marble entrance to City Hall, Mister Gettling and Mister Hendrick hung back. They idled along staring at the bleak stone armory across the street, watching lawyers bustle up the sidewalk to the County Courthouse. They mounted the two shallow steps to City Hall. Mister Gettling swung open a heavy bronze-and-glass door and they stepped shyly into the dirty marble lobby.

Job spotted Joe Rummel standing in a little clump of men near

6

the elevator doors. He brightened. "What's doin'?" He spoke as though he were in church.

"Dunno," Joe whispered. "I just got here. We're waitin'."

Mister Hendrick stood very quietly. Every few seconds the big bronze-and-glass door swung open and more men shuffled across the marble floor. After their first murmured questions they waited, also silent, their hands limp and meek in their pockets.

Mister Hendrick elbowed his way right to the elevator door. He needed to be first when the Mayor called for job applicants. The crowd kept pressing him. They, too, needed to be first when the Mayor started taking down names. Mister Hendrick felt the warmth of Mister Gettling's body. He could feel Joe Rummel's apologetic breath on his neck.

Mister Hendrick was nearly knocked down by the rush of air and the bang of bronze hitting steel when the elevator doors suddenly opened before him. Behind Job, three hundred men crowded forward wordlessly.

"Lay off the pushing," Mister Hendrick mumbled. He looked straight into the eyes of a tall pot-bellied police captain. The police captain ran a finger under his collar, where it squeezed against his Adam's apple. He swallowed. He felt like wetting his lips but he tried not to, because he wanted to seem easy and careless, as though he met mobs of hungry unemployed storming City Hall every day of his life.

Mister Hendrick believed that the police captain was going to select the first men from the crowd and take them up to the Mayor. Mister Hendrick opened his mouth. He tried to speak. He meant to say, "Take me. Pick me out, for the love of God. I'm a good man and I need the work. I got kids. Oh, Jesus Christ, take me."

But Mister Hendrick was so scared no sound came from his mouth. He heard the captain's heavy voice only faintly. He heard something dim and far away about registration Monday. A phrase rang in his ears, but it had a ghostly sound like the roar from an ocean shell, "The Mayor hereby orders you guys to clear out and to dis-perse."

Mister Hendrick heard, but at first he did not understand. Mister Gettling pulled at his sleeve. "Job, Job, come on. We got to

7

get out of here." Mister Gettling grabbed Mister Hendrick's arm. "Job." Mister Hendrick heard the shuffling sound of men's feet moving slowly and patiently across marble floors. He followed Mister Gettling out the bronze-and-glass door.

The heavy gray mass of men dissolved slowly. In murmuring groups, the unemployed plodded away from City Hall, shrunk into their coats against the cold and the shame. Mister Hendrick took his place in this parade.

Lethe   *January 3, 1932*

People who had forty cents for a ticket filed into Loew's, downtown on Main Street, the whole day Sunday to see Greta Garbo suffer all, even death, for love in a film called *Mata Hari*.

Under a ceiling featuring stars and the Milky Way, surrounded by Moorish minarets, real oil paintings, and plaster oversized Roman statues, the audience sat impassive, watching Miss Garbo, in the role of a European lady spy, find regeneration through the Grand Passion.

News Items   *January 4, 1932*

Ed S. Rose, a Goodyear company policeman, was elected President of City Council. He opened the first session with a hearty prayer.

The Summit County commissioners, in an extra session of the Board meeting at the County Courthouse, cut the budget again and wiped out the post of the County Humane Officer. The County Humane Officer had charge of orphans, old people, the blind, and the insane.

Mayor C. Nelson Sparks announced that after Wednesday all racketeers and bootleggers in town would be arrested.

William O'Neil, President of the General Tire and Rubber Company, one of the largest of the junior-sized rubber shops in Akron, made a speech to the Akron Real Estate Board.

"Come out of the gloom of the Depression," Mr. O'Neil said, "and bask in the sunlight for a change. It's time we did more boosting and boasting." He reminded his audience that Akron had long ago been officially dubbed the "City of Opportunity" by the Chamber of Commerce.

Building permits in Akron last year totaled $2,076,667, a drop from $9,000,000 reported at the end of 1931.

The *Beacon Journal* congratulated Summit County for its falling marriage license record. The annual report showed that during 1931 the number of marriage licenses dropped to the lowest level in the past fifteen years.

"There are altogether too many people in the world now to subsist upon the opportunities it affords," the *Beacon Journal* wrote firmly, "and the ignorant and the unfit, having scarcely any other interests in life, will multiply and replenish the earth until we shall not know what to do with them."

Akron pastors made plans today at the luncheon meeting of the Ministerial Association to share in the city-wide campaign against Depression gossip. After a good lunch of creamed hardboiled eggs on toast, ice cream, and homemade cake, the ministers, representing both the polite Congregational and Episcopalian churches and the workers' churches, like the free Methodists and the unorthodox Baptists, listened to Dr. Roy Sanborn of the Akron Rotary Club make a speech.

Dr. Sanborn explained that the Rotary Club believed a great deal of the current trouble around town was caused by idle and vicious rumors. He said he thought the ministers could help a great deal by joining the "war" against gossip.

After his speech, it was moved and seconded and carried unanimously to set aside a special anti-gossip Sunday in Akron churches.

9

All the ministers went home turning over in their minds texts from the Bible that might be used to encourage men to stop talking about the Depression.

Death by His Own Hand   *January 15, 1932*

Gilbert Edgar, until yesterday a Vice-President of The First-Central Trust Company, Akron's only big bank, blew out his brains early this morning.

Mr. Edgar's death was an unexpected sacrifice to the cause of holding the big bank together through the dark days of the Depression. The men who had voted Mr. Edgar out of his job as Vice-President at the big marble bank got a nasty shock when they heard that poor old Gilbert had driven his car into a back road on the lonely hills of suburban Fairlawn and put a gun to his head. They hoped fervently that the suicide of an ex-Vice-President would not make depositors "lose confidence." First-Central could scarcely stand a run on the bank.

But the modest headlines in the papers did not disturb the 100,000 innocent rank-and-file depositors. The public could hardly know that First-Central, which represented a long series of bank mergers over the years, was now the classic house of cards, propped up by a huge R.F.C. loan and the grudging good will of the rubber companies.

Mr. Edgar, one of the many Vice-Presidents left over from the series of mergers, was thrown to the wolves to cut down operating costs at First-Central. The rest of the directors, Akron's leading businessmen, crossed their fingers and hoped that strict economy and a rise in real estate values would save the bank.

Mr. Edgar was Akron's first banker suicide.

The Silver Beaver   *January 15, 1932*

Paul Litchfield, President of The Goodyear Tire and Rubber Company, the largest rubber company in the world, was made a Silver Beaver today at a special ceremony held by Akron Boy

Scout troops. This honor came to Mr. Litchfield after fifteen years of devoted service to scouting.

School Days   *January 18, 1932*

Akron public schools opened again today after five weeks' forced vacation. The Board of Education announced grimly that possibly the schools could stay open until May 1, provided taxes proved sufficient to pay at least part of the teachers' salaries and buy coal for the winter months.

It was quite a triumph, opening the schools again. Outside the city limits, in what people called "the county," schools had been closed for weeks. In Akron, teachers had taken one pay cut after another. The superintendent, driven back from his plans for a modern school system, desperately announced in the papers that the "frills" had been blue-penciled out of school budgets. Kindergartens and cooking for girls and special classes for the subnormal went under the ax. Blueprints for new buildings were filed away and youngsters crowded into dangerously rickety portable schoolhouses.

Still, after all this, Akron schools teetered on the edge of closing, and closing for good. For the school superintendent and the harassed members of the Board of Education and the schoolteachers knew about "the duplicate cutting," but most of the people of Akron did not understand the bland slicing something mysteriously named the "duplicate."

Akron and Summit County's "duplicate" was, in plain words which neither of the newspapers in town troubled to print, the listing of all the property and its valuation for taxing purposes. The Mayflower Hotel, for instance, and The Goodyear Tire and Rubber Company appeared on the duplicate each with its assessed property value beside it. So did the little frame houses the rubberworkers lived in, and their assessed valuations.

When the Depression hit Akron, taxes seemed intolerably high to the men who held real estate for speculation, to the bank which had already foreclosed a lot of small property, and, naturally, to the rubber companies.

Of course, the tax rate could be cut some, but the Akron tax rate wasn't much higher than other cities of its size, and, besides, a tax rate cannot be cut in half. So the real estate men and the rubber companies took another tack. They pared down the valuation of all the property listed on the tax rolls on what they called the duplicate. One day the property listed for tax purposes in Akron was worth so many million dollars. The next day, after a brief announcement from the county auditor's office, it was worth ten per cent less.

On January 1, 1932, the duplicate was chopped for the second time, making a total cut of twenty per cent. This, gossips around town murmured, was only the beginning.

The outraged superintendent of schools, faced with bad tax collections, now had to contemplate a flat twenty per cent reduction in the always scanty school revenues. He ordered the schools opened, with the frank acknowledgment that he had no idea, what with the duplicate reduction going on, of how long they could stay open this year or how long they could keep operating next year.

Free public education was becoming a luxury in Akron.

Some Figures   *January 20, 1932*

Dog-license figures showed a shocking drop. Only 2,900 licenses for dogs had been issued compared to 9,000 licenses issued at the same time in 1931. About 6,000 dogs, apparently, had not been registered by their owners. County commissioners issued a stern warning that dogs without licenses would be picked up and killed.

Mayor Sparks announced that 9,200 men had registered for part-time work on city parks and streets. Only heads of families are being listed, but relief authorities fear that, even so, Mayor Sparks's figure does not begin to cover the number of unemployed wage earners in the Akron district.

Some 900,000 less street-car fares were collected in 1931 than in 1930, P. V. C. See, head of the Akron Transportation Company, announced in a dismal report that showed his business had dropped twenty-three per cent.

Major Economies   *February 6, 1932*

The Goodyear Tire and Rubber Company showed a net profit of $5,454,046 for the year of 1931, Paul Litchfield, President of the company, announced. This compared with $9,912,232 in 1930.

Mr. Litchfield's annual report spoke with manly frankness of rate cuts and the speedup. "Major economies," the President of the huge corporation wrote proudly, "were effected this year through wage reductions and in the increased efficiency of factory operations."

Up and down Main Street Saturday the annual Goodyear report was received with modest cheers. The rubber companies had been pulling such a poor mouth that lawyers, merchants, doctors, had been afraid the great corporations had been actually losing money. A five-and-a-half-million-dollar net profit for one of the worst years in the history of American industry was not, Akron's small businessmen thought, to be sniffed at.

But nobody in the great factory on East Market Street rejoiced about the five and a half million. The men on the tire machines spit tobacco juice and growled, "Ain't that tough, poor old Paulie got stuck with only five lousy millions."

Not many who worked in the dark red brick buildings noticed the part in the report about increased efficiency. A fellow up in the truck-tire department beefed a good deal about it, but the foreman told him to shut up, everybody knew he was a Red.

"So I'm a Red?" the big fellow bawled while the rest of the men on the shift looked hard at the floor so the foreman wouldn't know they were listening. "I suppose it makes me a Red because I don't like making time so hard on these goddamned machines. When I get home I'm so tired I can't sleep with my wife."

The foreman leered. "You probably ain't no good anyway."

The tirebuilder stood back from his machine and flexed his great arm muscles. "Nine years I worked in this stinking shop," he shouted for the benefit of his surreptitious listeners three machine-

13

rows over, "and now when I get home at night I'm so goddamned pooped out I can't eat my supper."

The orator paused, clamped down hard on his tobacco. "Of course," he continued, his voice heavy with sarcasm, "I got some satisfaction. It's sure good to know that my rate cuts and the god-awful way I work has kind of given a hand up to the good old Goodyear Tire and Rubber Company. Yessir, things could be worse. Five million bucks ain't so bad."

"Things could be worse for you," the foreman said. He was uneasy. He could feel the rest of the shift listening.

The tirebuilder scowled. "Yeah?" He turned back to his machine. Then he said loudly and very deliberately, "I ain't making much more than they pass out on relief. At least I wouldn't be bustin' my gut on some goddamned tire machine."

The foreman walked away fast.

High Wind   *February 12, 1932*

The teacher wished, with all her heart, that Roy Joseph would stop sniffling. Not, the teacher reflected as she sat waiting for the horrible bubbly sound Roy would inevitably make in about two minutes—not that it was his fault in the least. It was, in fact, a wonder that her whole class, the third grade at Mt. Hope School, hadn't died right off of pneumonia this winter. For, in spite of the tar the janitor had put in the cracks, in spite of the great wood stove in the corner, the portable schoolhouse was drafty.

The teacher was desperately glad it was Friday afternoon. Sometimes she went nearly wild, sitting in the little wooden school-house, feeling the cold from the frozen earth come through the thin flooring, watching the children start sniffling before her eyes. Sometimes, indeed, the teacher felt very indignant about the duplicate cuts that forced the scrapping of the school building program. The teacher kept looking at her watch and wishing it would be three o'clock.

The kids noticed the storm first.

"Miss Teacher," Roy whined. He had never learned her name. "Miss Teacher, it's gettin' awful dark."

14

The teacher glanced out the window. It was, as Roy said between his snuffles, very dark. The February sky was nearly black. The sound of wind, not the comfortable sound of whistling wind in trees, but the low roar of a strong fierce wind, broke around the flimsy building. The children put down their crayons and Roy, naturally, was the first to start whimpering.

"Children," the teacher snapped, to cover up her own terror, "put your crayons away neatly."

But her own hand trembled as she piled up the crayoned drawings on her desk. The low sound of the wind, a sound like a train rushing through a tunnel, filled the warm sticky room. The children sat motionless in their seats, watching the teacher with glittering fixed eyes.

Then Roy began to scream. The teacher followed his pointing small finger. The frame wall, at the corner where the stove stood, was bulging. You could see it move.

The teacher grabbed the edge of her desk so hard her fingers hurt. "All stand." The children clambered awkwardly out of their small wooden desks.

The teacher shouted now to be heard above the sound of the wind. "About face!" The children turned reluctantly, afraid to take their eyes away from the teacher. "March!"

"One, two, three, four," the teacher yelled, but she was drowned out in the fierce roar of the wind. The children began to tramp obediently out the door. Only the first ten or so, Roy among them, were past the doorsill when a thick sheet of rain fell like an explosion, and a clap of thunder and lightning broke all around the little portable schoolhouse.

"March!" the teacher screamed. But the children, the little ones, they were only seven and eight years old, broke their ranks and ran from the lightning and rain to the teacher's arms.

"March!" the teacher sobbed. She pushed the children with stiff hands, and together, in a huddled group, they stumbled out the door into the heavy rain. They were down the steps, just a few feet into the mud of the schoolyard, when they heard a cracking, tearing sound.

They turned, the small children and the teacher, and watched

15

·the flimsy wooden schoolhouse tremble on its foundations and then fall in a crumpled heap.

The teacher yelled "Watch out!", but her voice was lost in the thunder of the wind and rain. A flying brick caught the teacher on the arm, and she fell in the mud with a deep sound in her throat. A splintered beam struck Roy a blow across the shins, and he stumbled and sat down, holding his hurt legs in his small arms, crying hysterically in the rain.

Nobody, the newspapers said the next day, was seriously injured.

Buy, Build, Beautify! *February 23, 1932*

The Rotary Club, the Kiwanis Club, the Lions Club, and a group of other service luncheon clubs got their unemployment relief program started today with a big story in both papers and the áppointment of a "do or die" committee.

Acting on Mayor Sparks's announcement that the city could only furnish part-time work to 4,000 of the 10,000 heads of families already registered at relief offices, the service clubs began a make-work program for the remaining 6,000.

The slogan for the campaign was, "Buy! Build! Beautify! Help Akron's Unemployed!" Householders were asked to hire unemployed to build an extra garage, paint the front porch, dig a new driveway.

"People are going hungry," Richard Herberich, Kiwanis Club representative on the Make-Work Committee and scion of the town's leading real estate family, said, "and we've got to find means to fill their stomachs. They're restless from idleness, and we've got to make jobs for them to keep their minds at rest and their hands busy."

News Item *February 24, 1932*

A very large gray rat bit Phyllis Smith, aged six months, about fifty times as she lay in her crib early this morning. Doctors at Children's Hospital barely saved the infant's life.

Don't Hoard *February 25, 1932*

Akron citizens who had three cents for a *Times-Press* or a *Beacon Journal* were considerably startled to read a large advertisement urging them to stop hoarding their money.

The best people in town sponsored the don't-hoard-your-dollar-bills program, Akron's most spectacular anti-Depression campaign. President Hoover himself was the head of the national spend-now committee. Dr. George F. Zook, President of Akron University, was on the local campaign board, and so were the rubber executives and the heads of the big department stores.

The campaign started with full-page pictures of an honest day-laborer reaching down into a sugar bowl, presumably to take out his hoarded money.

"Idle money," the caption shouted in big type, "is crippling business, forcing men out of work, slowing down the wheels of industry, smothering the entire country's system of credit."

In more modest type, the advertisement declared, "Oh, it's easy for the average man to say, That's no problem of mine. I haven't a lot of money. But it is your problem. A ten-dollar bill withdrawn from circulation means a hundred-dollar loss to credit."

Late in the afternoon, mailmen delivered hundreds of posters covered with the same picture and the same cry, "Don't hoard." Main Street blossomed with the spend-now literature, and the hoarding-is-a-crime campaign was well on its way among a very surprised population.

Exx-traa! *March 1, 1932*

The faraway sound of a newsboy's voice calling an extra echoed tonight through Akron's streets, where already at ten o'clock people were yawning and making ready for bed.

At first the sound was very distant, only a nasal halloo and holler against the stirring March wind. But men in dirty frame houses, women sewing behind pulled-down green windowshades, kids still awake in their narrow beds, cocked their ears. For newspapers have extras rarely in Akron, and when they come after seven or eight o'clock, it means something really dreadful has happened.

So men went to their doors and women ran for their old house pocketbooks and kids got up and yelled, sleep still in their voices, "What is it, Ma?"

Slowly, from far away, the newsboy's cry grew stronger, until at last he appeared at the corner of the street, panting, running from one house to another, saying, "Paper, mister?" in a breathless automatic voice. Men cried in the darkness, "Here! Boy! Paper, here!" Under the street light the boy stopped for a moment to count the few papers he had left.

"Hey, you! Boy!" somebody yelled at him. The kid darted away from the pool of light to a porch across the street. screaming as he ran, "The Lind-bergh ba-by is kidnapped."

No Carfare   *March 9, 1932*

The thermometer stood at four degrees below zero. Elmer Snyder, thirteen years old, did not want to walk from his house up on Brown Street hill all the way downtown to Perkins School dental clinic.

Elmer's teeth were pretty bad, and his teacher in school had given him a slip to go to a free dentist.

"You be there, Elmer," she said.

"Yes, ma'am," he'd replied, but he did not tell her he had no carfare. He felt ashamed.

Elmer started to walk the three miles to Perkins School dental clinic, but the wind made his face numb and his chest felt caved in under his thin jacket.

When he saw a big car draw up for a stop light, he ran to catch a hitch. The car jumped forward just as Elmer grabbed for a hold. He rode a few feet, but his ungloved hands kept slipping. The car picked up speed, and the wind struck Elmer in the face like a steel whip. A truck lumbered into the highway from a side road. Elmer screamed. His small hands sprang open. His body plopped awkwardly from the automobile, rolled for a moment while he clawed the ice of the street.

Then the truck wheels, grinding and shivering with the smack of the brakes, closed over the child, blotting out everything human, leaving only an obscene pattern of blood and bones.

This Pinch   *March 11, 1932*

The *Beacon Journal*, Akron's leading newspaper, published an editorial which read, in part: "It is manifest that this pinch cannot abide forever and that in the long run it is going to be a good thing for the country."

Announcement   *March 18, 1932*

Mayor C. Nelson Sparks slapped his mahogany desk top with the flat of his hand and roared to reporters: "Even if I have to go to jail, I will divert $35,000 from the state gas tax collected here to feed families on relief. Men and women are starving in Akron."

Quiet Death   *March 20, 1932*

The Don't-Hoard-Your-Money campaign died quietly. Local sponsors of President Hoover's gigantic spend-now program came to the reluctant conclusion that nobody in Akron had any money to hoard.

Annoyance   *March 21, 1932*

The Suey Welch Athletic Club, one of the better-known and best-liked speakeasies in town, was raided by city police. Part of the furniture was smashed, the slot machines were taken, temporarily, down to the basement of City Hall, and the rather elaborate stock of locally distilled corn liquor and out-of-town rum and gin was confiscated.

When the place opened again, its address was changed and a

lot of its regular patrons spent two or three days tracking it down. Everybody, including the proprietor who had to pay a fine, was very much annoyed.

Housing   *March 24, 1932*

Mayor Porter of the suburb of Cuyahoga Falls beamed with pride as he announced that he had the solution for evictions in his town. He has wheedled, he said, the old cars from the now-defunct Cleveland-Akron streetcar line, and he will shortly install these worn-out car shells, minus their wheels and motors, on a vacant lot in the outskirts of his city.

Fifty-seven evicted families, Mayor Porter said, will be moved into these old streetcars, supplied with stoves to keep them warm, and allowed city water, from a near-by main, free.

Pedestrian-Poet   *March 25, 1932*

Orlando Nelson Potter, Akron's favorite eccentric, made a slight scandal in the radio station today. Mr. Potter, a white-bearded sturdy old gentleman, was famed as the champion pedestrian-poet of the United States. Although well in his seventies, Mr. Potter took little walks of three and four hundred miles every summer.

In the winter, he wrote poetry, collected newspaper clippings which he carried, pounds and pounds of them, in his overcoat pockets, and slept in the newspaper offices.

Interviewed over the radio, in a series of personality sketches of local characters, Mr. Potter was asked by the announcer, "To what do you attribute your good health and many years?"

Mr. Potter eschewed the typed statement he was supposed to read at this point, and speaking clearly and distinctly into the microphone, said, "To a good set of bowels."

Turning the Tide   *April 29, 1932*

The Firestone Tire and Rubber Company announced that several hundred Firestone employees, including those holding pivotal positions, had promised to buy a new automobile before July 1, "to help turn the tide of prosperity."

Food on Credit   *May 3, 1932*

Family Service Society, city relief organization, told Akron that its food supplies were now being bought on credit, all current relief funds having been exhausted. The city of Akron and the Board of County Commissioners joined together to fight for state aid after an issue of relief bonds was turned down by New York bankers.

"The situation is desperate," Family Service authorities stated.

Another One   *May 4, 1932*

Stanley Mikolajcsk, fifty years old, jumped to his death from North Hill viaduct early this morning. He was an unemployed rubberworker.

North Hill viaduct, a narrow span across the gulch separating downtown Akron from the city's North Hill section, was a favorite suicide leap. Late at night, or around dawn, people wanting to die came quietly across the bridge, and in the silence and shadows climbed the four-foot stone rail. They fell many hundreds of feet to be killed on sharp stones.

School's Out   *May 13, 1932*

A laconic announcement from the Board of Education followed a dramatic appeal by the Akron Teachers Association. The teachers begged to keep the schools open, pointing out that the children's school term was already many weeks short. They offered to work without pay if the city would provide light and maintenance for the buildings.

The Board of Education replied briefly that schools would close May 27, nearly a month ahead of time. Next fall, the Board added, manual training, home economics, and physical education would be dropped from the school curriculum. "We have no funds for continued operation," the statement said.

Bonus Army   *June 3, 1932*

A somber little crowd, mostly wives and children and newspaper reporters, watched Akron's section of the Washington-bound Bonus Army straggle out of town today. The eighty-five World War veterans, gaunt-faced, deep-eyed, climbed into five small rattling trucks and, waving ragged overseas caps, drove off, after several confused and slightly hysterical speeches, shouting, "First stop, Youngstown."

The Akron bonus-marchers left without even a day's food supply and only the haziest notion of what they would do if they ever reached Washington. No sooner had their worn-out old trucks disappeared down the main highway than a delegation of brother marchers from out West, hungry and broke, rolled into town. The local veterans' societies pitched in and supplied coffee, ham sandwiches, and gasoline to the two hundred strangers.

The newspapers and the decent folk of West Hill watched these bankrupt travelers uneasily. The *Beacon Journal* hinted mysteriously of "red activity" in the ranks of both the local and out-of-town bonus-marchers. But no public official stepped forward to challenge the ragged Washington-bound veterans, and the newspapers were content to talk darkly of "agitators" without naming names or demanding action.

For Akron, once the strongest Ku Klux Klan town in America for its size, had more organized veterans per hundred population than any other city in the United States. The ex-soldiers of Akron belonged to the American Legion, the Veterans of Foreign Wars, the Army and Navy Union, and half a dozen other groups. Politicians ran these veterans' societies, and for years judges and mayors and county sheriffs had used the veterans' organizations to raise Red Scares and carry the county for the Republican Party.

But, with the deepening depression, the veterans' organizations

22

of Akron were swept by restlessness. The politicians could no longer hold the ex-doughboys in line with speeches about the Flag. Most of the members of the veterans' societies were out of work, even on relief. The bonus was a golden dream which the ex-soldiers were determined to make come true. Bewildered officials of the veterans' clubs watched the bonus-army fever sweep their organizations, and finally were reluctantly forced to give lip-service to this pathetic crusade to Washington.

The officials of the Akron veterans' societies were, however, like the newspapers, profoundly disturbed when they saw the hungry and ragged ex-soldiers depart for the country's capital to demand payment for services long since forgotten. The bonus-march seemed vaguely revolutionary to the polite society of Akron—but nobody, not even the editorial writers or the Mayor, dared say so.

And while their official leaders sat home worrying, the Akron bonus-marchers rattled off down the highway relieved to escape, for the moment, from the monotony of unemployment, the dreary hopelessness of life in a family on relief. They meant to get the bonus and come home with money in their pockets. If a bonus-march to Washington was a Communist tactic, so be it. A man couldn't simply sit down and watch his kids starve.

Forging On   *June 7, 1932*

George Dunn, Vice-President of The First-Central Trust Company, Akron's only big bank, made a cheerful speech at the opening session of the Ohio Bankers Convention. The bankers sat around on gilt chairs, very uncomfortable, in the mirrored ballroom of the Mayflower Hotel and nodded approvingly throughout Mr. Dunn's address.

Rotund Mr. Dunn said, among other things, "Each of us here has battled through. We may still feel the strain and fatigue of the struggle, but it is no longer overwhelming. We can forge on now with renewed courage which will carry us through to an undisputed victory."

23

The Governor Speaks
June 9, 1932

The bankers' convention wound up in Akron with a fine big banquet. The rubber-company presidents attended the affair, eating sparingly of the inevitable fruit cocktail and looking guardedly at each other. The Governor of Ohio, George White, appeared wreathed in set smiles.

The Governor made a speech after the waiters cleared away the ice cream dishes. "The epidemic of bank closings is at an end," he said, making the bankers wince. Nobody had mentioned bank closings during the convention, at least in public, although several Ohio cities had seen all their banks fail during the last year.

"The country," Governor White said reassuringly, "was never richer in material resources than it is today." That was more like it, the bankers thought. Several other speakers assured the bankers that the upturn was practically here and things couldn't possibly get any worse. The banquet finally broke up on a sustained note of hearty good cheer.

Wet or Dry
June 13, 1932

The Republican Convention prepared to open at Chicago. Both Akron newspapers filled columns with special stories, editorials, interviews, on the Prohibition issue. Main Street cigar-store gossip centered around the wet or dry question, but Akron remained strangely calm on an issue that had once been violently argued in every man's home.

The Depression was the only thing Akron really cared about in the summer of 1932, but the newspapers as well as the Republican Convention ignored it completely.

Hoover Again
June 16, 1932

Herbert Hoover, best-hated man in Akron, was renominated by the Republican Convention in Chicago. No bells were rung in Akron and even the Republican paper, the _Beacon Journal_, re-

24

strained its cheers. The Republican wet plank proved a disappointment.

The Beginning   *June 24, 1932*

Earl Paternoster woke up feeling sweaty. His wife stirred as he slipped out of bed, and one of the kids in the next room squawked a little as he put on his dirty shirt and a pair of heavy, patched trousers. He listened to the whining baby, but as he hesitated, the child's voice trailed off into sleep.

Paternoster went next door. Pete answered his knock and came out to sit beside him on the porch steps.

"I was here last night, but you were gone."

"You got the notice for sure then?"

Paternoster's big heavy face quivered. "The sheriff is comin' today. I got a letter. The bank says they are sorry but they got to do it, it's out of their hands now, on account of the court or something."

"The bastards." Pete spewed out the words between yellowed stumps of teeth. Paternoster did not answer. He slumped beside his neighbor, his thick arms hanging soft on his muscled thighs. Three years ago, when the Pennsylvania Railroad had passed him the final layoff slip, he had worn the look of a hefty and powerful man, but now the flesh around his mouth quivered like soft rubber. Mist covered his mild blue eyes.

"That ain't no way," Pete said anxiously. "We got to fight, see; we got to stand up for our rights. The bank can't throw you outa that house. Why, you got it almost paid for. Your kids got no place else to go."

Paternoster dragged himself to his feet. "It's awful hot today," he muttered. "I dunno. I can stand the cold, but this heat—it gets me, it makes me feel sort of sick. I didn't used to be that way. It gets plenty hot firin' on an engine. but lately the heat kind of gets me, makes me . . ."

"Ain't you going to do anything?"

Paternoster answered slowly, "Ain't nothin' to do."

Pete hesitated and then began, "Well, I heard a guy talkin' on

25

a street corner the other night, and I went up and told him about the bank takin' your house, and he told me to come down and tell him when it was and maybe he could do somethin'."

"A rich guy?" Paternoster's voice was eager.

"Naw. He's the boss of this here Unemployed Council."

Paternoster shrugged. "Go ahead and tell him, but there ain't nothin' to do now. The law is the law."

"Well . . ." Pete's voice dimmed. "I dunno. Maybe he was just talkin' a lot of crap. You want me to go down and tell him? It's way downtown."

Paternoster moved toward his front steps. He heard the baby yelling in the hot bedroom upstairs. "My wife is feeling sort of sick," he murmured. "I got to take care of the kid."

"Well, should I go?" Pete persisted.

"I don't care," Paternoster said heavily. "It won't do no good anyway."

He left Pete alone on the sidewalk. Pete hesitated, felt in his pocket, discovered a streetcar token, and muttering, "I got nothing else to do anyway," he set off down the street. Paternoster watched him go from the bedroom window and sighed.

Pete was discouraged when he walked into the dark little store-room where the Unemployed Council had "headquarters." He had expected a professional bustle, excitement, crowds of people. In-stead, a deep silence hung over the dusty narrow room. A solitary man was tying up bundles of badly mimeographed leaflets at a rickety wooden table. A hand-painted markedly amateur sign hung crookedly over the back wall. A few old wooden chairs were scattered against the dark floor moldings. The place stank with heat.

Scotty Williamson looked up from his leaflets. "You're the fel-low who spoke to me about the eviction," he remarked. "When is it?" Pete smiled, showing his yellow teeth, to hear the roll of the Scotch burr.

"You remember good," he said.

"That's my business," Scotty answered briskly. "Besides, we ain't had so much to do yet. This outfit's only a month old and I don't mind tellin' you, it ain't hardly caught on yet. The unem-ployed of this town are so goddamned whipped and sort of paralyzed-like they won't even get out on a picket line to yell for more beans."

"Yeah." Pete backed away a little.

"That's all right though," Scotty continued, stacking up some more leaflets. "They'll catch on, and when they do, believe me, this town's goin' to see something. Why, Christ, people's kids are starving on the relief they hand out now."

"Uh-huh."

Scotty looked up from his work. His face and hair and hands and neck and even his pants and shirt were all of a color—a faded tan. Only his eyes stood out from his gaunt face. They were bright shining blue, startling against the weather-beaten skin.

Pete watched the eyes catch fire and burn. "The working people of this town," Scotty said, "have got guts—plenty of guts. When they learn how to stick together, boy, things will be different in this town now and forever."

"Yeah," Pete gulped. "I guess they will."

Scotty's burr died away. "Well, when is the eviction?" He listened carefully while Pete talked, now and then drawing him back from some long bypath, asking questions: "How old is Paternoster? How many kids? Address? Size of house?" He wrote down in a little notebook: "Thirty-five, five kids, wife, 2432 Talbot Avenue, Cuyahoga Falls, six rooms, valuation, $3,890, paid in, $2,900."

When Pete was finished, Scotty said, shortly, "Listen, can you get ten guys who don't want to see a fellow with little kids evicted?"

Pete shook his head. "I don't know any guys who would do anything."

Scotty frowned. "You be there, then, and go back now and tell Paternoster not to worry."

Pete raised his eyebrows, shook hands without much warmth, and walked out into the blazing sun and the hot rubber smell. When he was gone Scotty sat in the dark heat of the storeroom for a moment wondering how to conjure up a hundred or seventy-five or even fifty fighters out of the sullen numbed Akron working class. Then he put on his battered felt hat and, whistling softly, went out into East Akron, an obscure and anxious Paul Revere.

27

He knocked on doors all morning, stopping to see a few men he had met at street-corner arguments.

"For God's sake," he would say to these men while their hungry kids hid shyly behind doors, "let's do something. You'll be next."

"Not me," most of them answered. "It ain't no good. Nothing's no use."

But sometimes the man at the door said, "Why not?" and now and then the woman shouldered her husband aside and said, "I'll get in on this. I ain't got no cookin' worth mentioning to do around here. I got plenty of time."

A little after one o'clock Scotty started from Akron to go up the hill and over the bridge into Cuyahoga Falls leading thirty-eight men and women in a caravan of an old battered truck and a decrepit Ford. Scotty stood on the truck keeping the fellows singing and joking, sometimes yelling up to the gang in the Ford. The heat sizzled the tin sides of the truck, and it was hard to hang on as the old machine rattled and bumped, its springs long since gone, over the rough roads.

But even the ride in the afternoon heat did not dampen the spirits of Scotty's army. The fellows felt good to be out doing something again, and the women sang in shrill voices and kept kidding Scotty about his burr. When the truck finally turned into Talbot Avenue, Scotty led a big cheer, and the Ford drew up in front of Paternoster's house with all its passengers leaning out and yelling, "Here we are, fellows! Hurray for the Unemployed Council."

The cheers fell into a soundless motionless scene. Under the blazing white sun, the stove stood naked on the sidewalk. An old armchair sprawled beside the stove; two wooden kitchen chairs leaned against it. A brightly colored photograph, framed in dark wood, showing a woman in elaborate wedding dress and veil of war-time style, a man in soldier's uniform, lay across a rickety wooden table. A child's toilet chair lay on its side in the burned grass just off the sidewalk.

Mrs. Paternoster sat in a small rocking chair near the curb. The tears ran steadily down her face and were burnt away by the fierce sun. She held the softly complaining baby in her thin arms. Helen,

28

nearly seven, crouched beside her mother, shocked into deep silence. The three smaller kids squatted in a patch of shade near the porch, their round button eyes fixed first on their mother, then on their father, then on the strange beefy men who carried the stove and the beds and all the familiar chairs and old frayed rugs and the picture of mamma when she was married, down the porch steps to dump them in a heap on the sidewalk.

Paternoster sat on the edge of the porch, his heavy legs hanging down near the ground. Sweat poured down his face and neck, but he did not raise a hand to wipe it away. He stared at his weeping wife.

A handful of men and two housewives stood just off the sidewalk watching the eviction. They craned their necks to see the deputy sheriffs struggle out the door toting a heavy dining-room table or part of a bed. The women winced as the movers rolled a chair down the porch steps or kicked a rug into place on the growing heap of household goods on the sidewalk.

The two police officers worked steadily in great discomfort. They felt the soundless protest. They felt the woman's tears and the man's despair. They shrank in their flesh under the wordless hostility of the witnesses.

The cheers cut across this silence like a whip. The bustle of Scotty's little army clambering down from the truck, squirming out of the Ford, brought the deputy sheriffs hurrying through the door of the little frame house to stand, arms akimbo, watchful and tense, at the head of the porch steps. Mrs. Paternoster got to her feet with a sudden stiff motion that bounced the baby and made her whine. The little children scrambled up and silently edged over to their mother's skirts. The handful of witnesses turned to face the invading crew. Paternoster slipped down from his hard seat and stood watching Scotty.

No word of welcome was spoken. The cheers died away in the enveloping quiet. The men and women from Akron took their places on the little patch of front lawn in growing embarrassment, as though they had laughed stridently at a child's funeral. The baby let out a high-pitched squall, piercing and clear in the growing depth of silence. The police officers on the porch moved closer to each other, clenching and unclenching their hands nervously.

Men licked dry lips and women reached up to wipe sweat off their foreheads and push back their straggling hair.

Scotty stood near the truck frowning in the blazing heat, paralyzed by the silence. He felt the gathering appetite for movement. He quivered under the eyes of the whole crowd turned towards him now.

Scotty forced himself to move forward. No one spoke to him. No one reached out to touch him. He climbed the porch stairs in absolute quiet. The deputy sheriffs moved away from him. He turned to face the crowd. The silence infected him. The heat sent a wave of nausea flooding his throat and palate. He drew in a deep breath and, straining all his muscles, clenching his hands, he yelled, "Men and women!"

Instantly, the crowd moved toward him, their faces lifted up to his.

"Are you going to let this man, a good worker all his life, and his wife, and his little kids, be thrown out on the street?" There was no answer. The nausea came back again to Scotty's throat. They would not follow him. He was a lousy Communist. No ripple swept the crowd with his words. They were paralyzed. Dear God, there was no rousing these people. They were too far gone in despair.

"The children," Scotty screamed in the hot quiet. "The children! Where will they sleep tonight?"

He watched the sturdy broad-hipped women look away from his face. They could not bear his words. Maybe the women would do something. Take a chance on action. Nothing else to do now. Words couldn't touch them. But his feet felt like iron. The heat kept him rooted to the porch. He couldn't move. The despair came over him. The pity made him blind. Poor people, poor suffering people, poor children. Dear God, there was no cure for them unless they cured themselves.

The blindness passed. Scotty jumped down from the porch, ran to the pile of furniture, grabbed a kitchen chair and, holding it before him like a sword, he marched up the sidewalk roaring, "Take the furniture back in!"

The crowd fell away before him, surprised, shocked. Scotty bellowed a song to the tune of an old Negro hymn. "They tried to e-vict us!" he shouted in a hoarse, off-key voice, "but we shall not be mo-ved. Just like a tre-e-ee be-side the wa-a-ater, wee-e-e shall *not* be moved!"

Scotty's shrill voice was the only sound in the heat-sodden scene. The deputy sheriffs stood stupidly, like the crowd. The gap between Scotty and the policemen narrowed. The crowd leaned forward aching with the need for motion. Scotty marched to the stairs, still singing desperately, bearing the battered chair proudly. He had stopped thinking. Now he prayed that someone in the crowd, one voice, one man to jump forward, would break the paralysis. The policemen waited for him, but he had no sense of danger.

Scotty sang, "Just like the tre-e-ee be-side the wa-a-ater," and started up the porch stairs.

Then Pete cried out from the crowd, "For God's sake, help him!"

The stillness broke. A dozen hands reached out for the shabby furniture. Four men shouldered the stove. Women swept up the porch stairs carrying rugs, pictures, a heavy brass stand for a potted plant. Men screamed, making noise without words. Women began to chant, "They tri-ed to e-vict us, but we shall not be moved!"

The sheriff's men retreated before the crowd. In a few minutes the furniture was back in the house. The crowd stood around singing. Presently the sheriff returned with more men and the crowd stood, under Scotty's orders, jeering and screaming while the stove was carried out. Then strong men shouldered it and once again trotted merrily back to the kitchen.

The crowd grew. By four o'clock it overflowed into the street. Paternoster stood on his porch, wild with excitement, slapping strangers on the back, shouting curses at the police who returned from time to time. All evening long until after nine the crowd grew.

Scotty made several speeches, leaning from the porch into the soft darkness of the hot night, yelling at the crowd milling around in the little front yard. He always wound up, "Tell everybody you know about this. Tell them if people get together they can stop evictions and get more relief." The crowd answered back, "You said it! You bet!"

Just before ten the sheriff came back again. He made a little speech too. He said that The First-Central Trust Company, in view of Paternoster's needy children, had decided to allow him one more chance to meet his mortgage interest. The crowd screamed and booed and yelled, "Yeah, it took a lot of convincin' them." Scotty finally had to come out and stand beside the sheriff and say, "O.K., boys; our job's done here. I want all of you to turn up tomorrow at the office downtown to get a batch of leaflets. We'll tell the world about this."

Pete and a bunch of the crowd followed Scotty downtown, too excited to be tired. They laughed and slapped their knees on the bus, but Scotty didn't have much to say. When they got inside the oven-hot little storeroom, Scotty headed right for the battered old typewriter.

"What's the matter, Scotty? Ain't you set up?" Pete asked, grinning through his yellow teeth.

"Sure," Scotty answered, burring the r's in his words, "I got to write this here leaflet."

"What're you goin' to say?" Pete inquired, looking over his shoulder.

"Well," Scotty said thoughtfully, staring up at the fly-specked banner on the wall, "I'm going to say that this is the beginning of something big."

Franklin D. Roosevelt   *July 1, 1932*

The Democratic National Convention, in session at Chicago, finally nominated Franklin D. Roosevelt, Governor of New York State, for President of the United States. Nobody was either greatly excited or much pleased in Akron.

The *Beacon Journal* wrote, "With such strong men as Governor Albert C. Ritchie, Al Smith, Melvin Traylor, Governor George White and even Newton D. Baker from whom to make its choice, the convention stampeded to Franklin D. Roosevelt, as neuter [sic] and colorless a standard bearer as any ever chosen to lead its cause."

Washington Massacre   *July 28, 1932*

Men turned dark with rage this night when the details of the Washington bonus-army eviction battle came leaking through in newspaper extras and radio announcements. The original Akron contingent of bonus-marchers had grown rapidly in the past summer weeks. A hundred and more Akron veterans fought in the bloody and tragic battle.

Akron heard the news of the violent attack on the ex-soldiers' camp with fury. The *Beacon Journal,* one of the cagiest newspapers in America, at first adopted an impartial attitude, but the next day, catching the mood of the town, appeared with a stern editorial denouncing the National Administration and calling the bloody eviction an "outrage."

Out of the White House   *August 6, 1932*

The Summit County Veterans Association adopted a new slogan at its meeting today: "Get Hoover out of the White House!"

Ask Loan   *August 18, 1932*

The City of Akron and Summit County jointly asked the Reconstruction Finance Corporation for a $300,000 loan to finance relief in the district.

Refused   *August 19, 1932*

The Reconstruction Finance Corporation announced that no further loans would be made to states or cities for relief purposes until local communities did "more" to help themselves through the Depression. Akron relief and civic authorities were, when they heard the news, frankly appalled.

Some Figures *August 30, 1932*

Forty-six thousand eight hundred and forty persons were on relief, the monthly report of the relief authorities showed. Nine thousand three hundred and sixty-eight family units were cared for by public funds. No attempt was made to estimate the number of unemployed in the city. Charity organization officials believed, however, that at least as many persons as were on relief were unemployed and had not yet applied or been accepted for public support.

Estimates based on this opinion put the number for September, 1932, of unemployed and persons dependent on those unemployed in Akron at 93,680 out of a total county population of 300,000.

Unpaid Bills *August 31, 1932*

Crippled school children, who are usually fitted for new braces and equipped with new crutches at the beginning of the school year, will not receive the usual state aid this season, Judge Oscar Hunsicker of the Juvenile Court announced.

Summit County has been unable to pay its share for the treatment of local crippled children and, Judge Hunsicker explained, the State department has, therefore, withdrawn its usual county subsidy.

Labor Day *September 2, 1932*

The West Virginia Society had a big picnic today. Otherwise Labor Day in Akron was uneventful.

Return of the Native *September 8, 1932*

Harvey Firestone, the only man in Akron who actually owns one of the three big rubber companies, came back from a European trip today. Smiling affably, Mr. Firestone favored New

York ship news reporters with a few political and economic opinions.

Mr. Firestone, the Associated Press wired Akron newspapers, "talked cheerfully of business conditions, deplored any thought of supplanting Hoover with any other candidate, applauded the six-hour day, and flayed unemployment insurance."

"In such unsettled times as these," Mr. Firestone told reporters, "I feel it would be hazardous if Mr. Hoover was not re-elected this fall. I told the people over there [Europe] we were going to re-elect him."

Play Ball   *September 28, 1932*

Business practically suspended today. The World Series opened, with the Chicago Cubs playing the New York Yankees. Rubber executives and prosperous businessmen were out of town watching the Series. The rest of the male population clustered around radios.

Inside the big factories, the tirebuilders laid ten-cent bets on their favorite team and tore out of the factory gates with record speed on the afternoon shift to get the series' score.

Up and down Main Street every cigar store, every little corner confectionery, had its blaring radio, and the sound of distant cheers and excited radio announcers' hoarse cries drowned out the clanging bells of streetcars.

Award   *September 30, 1932*

Harvey Firestone was presented with an honorary certificate for founding polo in Akron.

Begin Firing   *October 1, 1932*

The police prosecutor announced a "war to the finish" today against Akron prostitution. He opened hostilities by arresting half a dozen mournful streetwalkers and two indignant bawdy-house keepers. This was the fifth war-to-the-finish against prostitution of the year.

New Low Levels   *October 3, 1932*

Parts of the Fourth District Federal Reserve Bank Report were published today in the back pages of the Akron newspapers, without benefit of large headlines or editorial comment.

The report, in the laconic language of bankers, stated briefly that the manufacture of rubber products, including tires, had "declined very sharply" during July, August, and September. Crude rubber consumption went to new low levels for the industry. "There was no indication," the report read, "of any reversal of the trend downwards."

The Akron newspapers did not care to write editorially that in a town where eighty-four per cent of the population was dependent directly or indirectly on employment in the rubber industry the new Federal Reserve Bank report was indeed a harbinger of doom. Instead, the report, which predicted by implication a winter more dreadful than the last one, was received in dead silence.

Volunteers Wanted   *October 4, 1932*

Family Service Society, once a compact little group of professional social service workers, let down the last bars today and called desperately for "high type" volunteers.

Faced by a rush of new charity cases as the cold weather approached, operating on a budget so small that each month it was a question whether or not the bills for beans and potatoes could be paid, officials of Family Service Society at last admitted defeat. The old days of scientifically administered charity were over. It was simply a question, now, of handing out grocery baskets and praying the money would stretch far enough to feed the starving.

With the call for volunteers, Family Service Society passed out of the picture as a social service workers' unit. The organization had once functioned to care for the incompetent, the insane, the crippled. In August, 1929, for instance, there had been 257 families on charity in Akron. Each of these families had a complete dossier in Family Service files. Social service workers investigated the intelligence quotients of every member of each family, and the Akron charity case got free psychological treatment along with the weekly basket of groceries.

Social service workers were accustomed to treating charity cases with a professional bedside manner. It was held as an established fact that something was wrong with a family that wound up on charity. Of the 257 cases on relief in August, 1929, nearly every family was listed as "society misfits," or "maladjusted" or "incompetent." Many of the families were dependents of men sent to prison for rape or theft or the like. Some were the unhappy children of parents judged insane. For before the Depression struck Akron, a man temporarily out of a job could depend on his relatives or friends to tide him over until he got work and keep him from the stigma of taking relief.

The city of Akron supported Family Service Society, in part, in pre-Depression days, and the secretary and functioning head of the organization was a minor officer in the Mayor's cabinet. The Community Fund, an annual high pressure charity drive, contributed to Family Service and divided the rest of its funds among the Jewish and Catholic charity agencies, the hospitals, the Girl and Boy Scouts, and the Y.M.C.A. and Y.W.C.A. These agencies were supposed to supply "character building" and other special services, not especially to charity cases but to what in those days were called the "underprivileged."

When the blight of the Depression fell over Akron, Family Service social service workers, women largely, were suddenly faced with an altogether different kind of relief case. Starting from the premise that a charity case family was "incompetent" or "maladjusted to society," the social service worker got into increasingly hot water. The new unemployed stubbornly refused to be classed as "incompetent." The lanky mountaineers who came

37

into the relief office and demanded, not asked for, food resented being termed "maladjusted to society."

The social service workers struggled with a vastly increased work load. Once each worker had supervised a dozen families taking charity, now, overnight, she had a hundred, then two hundred, and finally, during one hectic period, as many as four hundred. It was absolutely impossible for the case workers to make very many calls on the new unemployed in their homes. Besides, the new unemployed were sullen and bitter instead of grateful and pleased to get some attention. If a case worker did turn up at a charity case home, she was more than likely to be greeted with a slammed door and round West Virginia curses.

In the old days charity cases threw themselves on the city and expected, and got, shoes for the kids, rent, coal, food, Christmas trees, bedding, soap, and even sometimes a stick or two of furniture. These "extras" almost immediately disappeared with the Depression. The new unemployed got a basket of food and nothing else.

It was characteristic of the old social service worker's point of view that for many, many months of the Depression, through bitter protests and furious argument, Family Service Society continued to pass out selected baskets of food instead of cash or money orders on a grocery. The social service worker, until at last bitter experience said her nay, honestly believed that an unemployed family was unable to select wisely its own diet. To women who had cooked and cared for their families for years, the social service worker handed out a basket of groceries and a diet sheet with a stern warning not to waste food.

Food basket riots were the order of the day in Family Service headquarters. Italian families got potatoes and put up a fearful squawk. Mountaineers missed salt pork and demanded coffee, which was considered a luxury and so did not appear in the food baskets. Even when these errors were adjusted by a frantic staff, the unemployed continued to be sullen and fierce in the face of the food baskets. They demanded, over and over, through delegations from the Unemployed Council, parades and sudden riots, to be allowed to pick their own food.

38

"What's the matter?" bitter women used to howl at the top of their voices in the Family Service headquarters, "you think I'm a fool? You think I don't know what my man and my kids like to eat? They won't eat this stuff you give me. My man wants coffee; my kids don't like canned tomatoes."

As the city funds for relief grew slimmer and the number of unemployed grew greater, even the hated food baskets diminished in size and cost. From week to week the family allowance for food grew less and less until social service workers admitted, in private, that the unemployed in Akron were starving.

Food, however, was not the only bitter bone of contention in relief administration. Family Service never paid rent, never supplied carfare or electric light or kerosene, and never took care of gas bills. From time to time the Red Cross organized sewing groups and got grants of cotton cloth from the Government. These poorly made garments of thin cloth were then doled out to the unemployed. Otherwise there was no clothing allowance.

As the Depression grew worse, no family was accepted for relief until its last resource was gone. By this time, the desperate housewife had cut up her bedding for coats for her children, sold her furniture for food, and was months behind in rent, electric, and gas. When a family went on relief in Akron it needed, not only food, but also money for all the services that are necessary in a complex city civilization. Family Service from the very beginning never had the funds to supply anything but food to the unemployed, and very little of that.

During the summer of 1932, the city financial crisis sharpened, tax collections fell, the city credit was exhausted. The Mayor and the County Board of Commissioners frantically begged and borrowed and diverted funds from every conceivable source to feed Akron's hungry. As the winter approached, the local government had already used up every possible tax fund and expended for charity nearly every penny it could lay hands on.

Funds for unemployment relief were practically gone. Factory production schedules were falling. Relief cases mounted.

Family Service Society threw up its hands and called for volunteer workers, unpaid, to pass out beans to the starving, providing there were any beans to pass out.

39

In Memoriam

Falling mist, mixed with smudgy flakes of rubber smoke, made the streets damp and slippery Friday. Even at high noon the sky was quite dark and gusts of raw wind bit deeply into thin-covered chests and gloveless hands.

The deputy sheriffs who came to move the furniture out of the little frame house on Moon Street wore thick lumberjackets and warm knit caps with eartabs. Still they flapped their arms across their big chests and shuddered in the clammy cold.

The Miachiaroli kids, all eight of them, followed the deputy sheriffs silently in and out, back and forth, from the front door to the curbstone, watching with eight pairs of round black quiet eyes while the strange men carried out the stove, and the parlor best chair and the two bedsteads, and all the other familiar things of the household.

Just as the deputy sheriffs trundled the last big sofa down the porch steps, Mr. O'Lari, the man from the Unemployed Council, came running down the street. The Miachiaroli kids, huddled around the pile of furniture, shivering in the wet and cold, were glad to see him. He was such a pleasant jolly man. He called the oldest Miachiaroli boy, who was nine, "Old Man."

"Hello, Old Man," he said now. "I see they got a head start on us. Well, keep your chin up, fellow. It ain't all over yet."

The Miachiaroli boy grinned. Mr. O'Lari was funny and nice, and he cheered Pa up too. It was terrible to see Pa cry just like a baby. It made you ashamed. So it was good Mr. O'Lari came, because Pa sort of brightened up and that look on his face that scared you so, went away.

The Miachiarolis built a little bright fire on the curb and put their hands near its warmth and that made the long afternoon easier. Mr. O'Lari kept going away and coming back and every time he said to wait a little longer, everything would be all right in the end.

The sky began to get darker at four o'clock, and the mist turned into a fine rain that was almost sleet. Most of the Miachiaroli kids began to cry. The little bright fire could only warm your hands and feet, and the wind and rain made your back ache with cold.

Then just when Pa began to look all broken in the face again, Mr. O'Lari came back, and this time he brought with him a lot of big cheerful fellows in sort of ragged clothes. Two wheezing old Fords rattled down Moon Street and a lot more men clambered out. The neighbor boys came running and for a few minutes Moon Street was filled with the sound of big men rushing and running and marching down to the Miachiaroli house.

The rain was so cold, but these fellows from the Unemployed Council didn't seem to mind it. They were cheerful, and their voices were loud and sort of happy. Mr. O'Lari and a short little man climbed up on the front porch.

"Here's Scotty," Mr. O'Lari said, and all the big fellows standing around in the yard began to cheer.

Scotty didn't say much. It was getting dark and the rain was growing heavier. He just said, "Is this what we are coming to? Children, poorly clothed, being snatched out of bed and thrown into the streets? Are we goin' to stand it?"

After Scotty's speech, the big fellows picked up the furniture, the bedsteads, and the good chair, and the stove, and all the rest, and carried them back in the house. The crowd hurried, to get out of the rain, but they were careful of the furniture too; they didn't bang it up. The Miachiaroli kids danced around clapping their hands and saying, "Are you goin' to move us back in, mister? Are you?"

Finally their mother called them into the kitchen and told them to stay put; they would all catch colds. One of the big strangers made a nice fire and Mrs. Miachiaroli began to strip the wet coats off her kids and stand them up close to the stove to get warm. The lady next door brought over a kettle of soup, but the Miachiaroli kid Mr. O'Lari called "Old Man" was too excited to eat. He kept running out of the kitchen to watch Pa and the men from the Unemployed Council finish up the moving job.

Now it was nearly pitch-dark outside. Scotty called out to the crowd, "O.K., fellows, let's go. O'Lari, keep a dozen or so to see nothin' happens, and stay around for an hour or so."

Slowly the crowd trickled away. Mr. Miachiaroli stood on the front porch shaking hands. Scotty climbed into a ramshackle Ford and started down the street. A few young boys milled around in the front yard. O'Lari and a gang of workers were shoveling the coal back into the coal bin. In the rainy night a police cruiser turned into Moon Street, passed slowly by the house, disappeared, and then returned.

The rumble of the coal drowned out the first yell. On the second call for help O'Lari raced through the Miachiaroli house, stumbled over one of the smaller kids, burst through the front door to the porch. In the shadows he saw a policeman, night stick raised, aiming a blow at a gangling boy who stood arguing with him. O'Lari caught the night stick, crying, "Hey, what's the idea?"

Patrolman Emery Davis turned sharply. The shouting angry crowd pressed on his heels. He was alone. His cruiser partner had gone to call the station house for reinforcements, leaving him with a final warning. "Don't start no trouble. Just stand by until we get some help."

"What's the idea?" O'Lari repeated. "We ain't doin' nothin'. You can't hit a kid like that."

"You tell him, Alex," somebody in the crowd roared.

"You're under arrest!" Patrolman Davis shouted.

"What for?" O'Lari countered boldly. "Where's your warrant? What are you arresting me for?"

The crowd, muttering, closed in tightly around the cop and O'Lari. In the darkness the faces of the intent weary men seemed frightening to the policeman. He struck out wildly at O'Lari, hit him a glancing blow with the night stick.

"Hey!" O'Lari grunted, surprised. He swung out with his fist at the cop and missed. The policeman struck again with his night stick. O'Lari ducked. The cop, put off balance by his wild lunge, slipped and missed his footing. Kneeling, he drew his gun and fired.

The shot deafened the crowd. In the wild stampede to escape from this cop with the gun, men fell over each other, women screamed. O'Lari crumpled up silently and, spitting blood, fell to the porch.

O'Lari took four days to die. During those days the police and the city authorities made a desperate attempt to cover up the killing. First they said Patrolman Davis was critically injured too, but when Davis went home from the emergency ward next day, that fell through. Then they said O'Lari had attacked the policeman and egged on the crowd to beat him up, but in the end they had no witnesses to prove that.

Finally even the newspapers, which, the first day, carried savage stories blaming the riot on O'Lari, backed down. "Hunger cannot be clubbed down," the *Beacon Journal* wrote three days later; "neither can a destitute family's right to shelter be denied."

Everywhere in Akron men waited to hear whether O'Lari would live. Many people knew this man and many more in the four days he lay dying heard about him. O'Lari was a rubberworker. He had four pretty daughters. His wife ran a boardinghouse to keep the family alive after O'Lari was laid off at the shops two years ago.

O'Lari joined the Unemployed Council in exactly the same fashion that hundreds and thousands of other men in Akron joined it during the summer and fall of 1932. He was desperate for a job, embittered and discouraged by the months he had been out of work. The Unemployed Council gave him a chance to strike back directly at what was hurting him. He became a talented organizer. Men liked him. He was soon president of his local, and he helped organize gas squads to turn the gas back on in people's houses, and electric light squads to string wires around the meter after it was shut off by the company, and delegations to protest food baskets.

O'Lari was the leader of a folk movement in his own neighborhood. He got people relief when the authorities turned them down. He yelled for shoes for the children. He helped move desperate families into empty houses the bank owned.

Now he was dying. He fought very hard to live. He was only thirty-nine years old, and his life had been very hard and bitter. He struggled against death long after the doctors had given him up. Once during the four days, his daughters thought he would win his fight. They were sure he would live. They kept telling him so and begging him to fight a little harder. When finally he died his smallest daughter still wouldn't believe it. Until they led her away and pulled the sheet up over his head, she kept telling him he had to live—he had to.

His body lay in "state" in the new offices of the Unemployed

Council. For two days men tramped up and down the rickety stairs to look in the face of Alex O'Lari, one of their own. Even late at night men came from the night shifts at the rubber factories, looked and went away dark and angry.

On the day of Alex O'Lari's funeral, the police were frankly afraid of the crowd. By noon the courthouse steps and the streets all around the old stone building were packed with silent men and women and children with red arm-bands. They came with flags and placards, crude signs lettered painstakingly at home. Nearly eight thousand men and women stood in the crowd to hear the funeral speeches.

Afterwards sheets of cold rain began to fall but, unmoved, the crowd lined up behind the casket and marched slowly down the street nearly two miles to the cemetery. When, in the pouring rain, the procession stopped beside the muddy open grave, Scotty Williamson stepped up. He looked around at the cemetery filled now with drenched workers standing quietly in the sodden day. Then he said slowly, "This man, Alex O'Lari, gave his life for the working class."

That was all. Men walked home from the cemetery carrying their dripping banners, remembering Alex O'Lari, a rubberworker.

Last Chance   *October 14, 1932*

Sterling B. Cramer, an icy-faced hard-bitten Chicago banker, was elected President of The First-Central Trust Company today. Cramer, who had a reputation of the most conservative variety, was brought in by a desperate board of directors who hoped against hope that somehow, by some sleight of hand, Cramer could save the bank. It was the last chance.

Hail to the Chief   *October 15, 1932*

President Herbert Hoover went through Union Station in Akron today on his special train. He made a brief speech to the small crowd. Nobody booed, which was a great relief to local Re-

44

publican leaders who had been very much afraid of an ugly scene.

The *Beacon Journal*, the day before, published an appeal to the citizens of Akron, asking for tolerance and politeness upon the visit to the city of the President of the United States.

Not a single Republican leader in Summit County really expected that President Hoover could carry the district against Governor Roosevelt in the coming election. They hoped, very much indeed, that they could, in a normally Republican county, manage to get the local ticket through. Although in their campaign speeches they gave a little lip service to the national ticket, they soft-pedaled Herbert Hoover and hoped to elect a Republican sheriff.

Report   *October 18, 1932*

The sheriff's office reported today that deputies had performed 557 forcible evictions in the past eighteen months. The figure did not include men who voluntarily ceded possession of property to the new and lawful owners, nor did it cover renters in the city of Akron who were legally dispossessed from premises they occupied by municipal court writs.

Red Scare   *October 24, 1932*

Mayor C. Nelson Sparks explained the principles of Communism in a speech made tonight at the annual American Legion banquet held in the general offices of The Goodyear Tire and Rubber Company.

Mayor Sparks dwelt rather fulsomely on the Communist tenet of nationalization of women, touched on the question of whether or not Russian Communists were cannibals, and wound up with a strong statement on unemployment. "Communism preys on the unemployed," the bantamweight Mayor shouted.

He pledged himself not to sully the city honor by even meeting with the Unemployed Council delegations.

Mayor Sparks was followed by husky handsome Bill Denton,

a he-man evangelist who charged that the funeral of Alex O'Lari "broke down the dignity" of Akron. All hands were gratified to hear that Bill had just converted two Communist organizers. Reverend Denton did not disclose the names of the new converts.

Share the Work   *November 2, 1932*

Akron's biggest and most important business leaders gathered today in impressive force at a luncheon meeting held in the Akron City Club to launch a brand-new Share-the-Work program. The same business leaders had met at the same place last spring to launch the big gigantic colossal make-jobs campaign to end unemployment.

Record Vote   *November 8, 1932*

Record crowds stood in line outside the polling places election day waiting to vote.

The Results   *November 9, 1932*

Franklin D. Roosevelt was elected President of the United States by a thumping majority.

Republican leaders in Akron woke up with a bitter headache to find that only six Republicans, in the most minor of County offices, had survived the terrible deluge. Famous old Republican leaders like Judge William E. Pardee were wiped out, and for the first time in many years the District elected a Democratic Congressman.

Democrats, about three o'clock in the morning the day after election, literally danced in the streets. In Democratic headquarters, old-time ward leaders staggered wildly up and down the crowded hall drunk and hilarious. Main Street was crowded and lit up long after midnight, and professional politicians celebrated until dawn.

But the rest of the town was buried in gloom or lost in apathy. West Hill was angry and mournful, its candidate soundly defeated. East and South Akron had voted solidly for Roosevelt, but only because the working people despised Hoover. Nobody knew much about the Governor of New York State, and his campaign speeches were little read or understood in Akron.

The new President would be, the rubberworkers hoped, better than Hoover. Beyond that, they expected nothing.

Hope   *November 11, 1932*

John Knight, handsome and very Republican managing editor of his father's *Beacon Journal*, told an admiring audience at the Woman's City Club today, "The fear of radicalism will disappear when Roosevelt assumes the Presidency."

The ladies, whose husbands had all felt that Hoover was the only safe bet for the White House, were very pleased and relieved when Mr. Knight informed them that they could pluck up hope again. Roosevelt, Mr. Knight felt, was no wild-eyed radical and would probably turn out to be a good safe choice for the Presidency.

Romance   *November 15, 1932*

Rev. Evelyn Schumacher, pastor of what she called a Spiritualist Church, married her seventh husband, a photographer for The Goodyear Tire and Rubber Company, today.

"God," Reverend Schumacher said as she posed for a picture entwined with her new husband, "is love. One can only know God through experience."

Silver Jubilee   *November 17, 1932*

More than four hundred men, dressed neatly in dark business suits and fresh clean shirts, crowded the Hotel Mayflower ballroom tonight to eat the usual steak dinner, hear speeches, and celebrate the twenty-fifth anniversary of the founding of the Chamber of Commerce.

The speakers' table, a long thin arrangement of boards covered with white linen, stretched down one whole side of the ballroom. The aristocracy of Akron sat at this table looking, in spite of themselves, melancholy. The three rubber company presidents had, as always, the places of honor, but the only one of them who smiled much or who seemed to enjoy himself was Harvey Firestone.

On the lower floor level the Main Street merchants sat at round tables watching the important men on the dais, gulping the indifferent food, and, when urged, singing in a timid off-key chorus. Afterwards they listened solemnly to the speeches, and some of them even believed what they heard. The speeches were mostly about having faith in Akron. Several referred to the "late Depression," and there were jokes about how bad times were last year.

At the speakers' table, the important men, the bankers and the rubber company presidents, sat stony-faced while one after another of their number rose to speak words of good cheer. Nobody sitting on the raised platform believed one word of what they or their fellows said.

When the speeches were over, the assembly quavered through "Auld Lang Syne" and everybody went home trying to look jolly and feeling very depressed.

One Solution   *November 21, 1932*

Bishop James A. McFadden, of Cleveland, arrived in town today to confirm 285 children. "At a time like this," he said, "men realize as they have not done before that a man cannot live by bread alone, and that the influence of the supernatural must pervade our lives or we are lost."

Cut Again   *December 2, 1932*

The Summit County tax duplicate was cut again today. This time the total tax valuation on property in the county went down

48

ten per cent, making a total cut of thirty per cent from normal.

The cut was ordered by the Republican State Tax Commission, after a hearing at which local Republican politicians pleaded for the reduction. School board authorities and other citizens, including the Mayor, put up a desperate fight against the cut.

Budget experts working on school costs were ordered immediately to slice $67,000 from the annual estimate. The city was notified it could expect $67,000 less annually from tax collections, and the county government $120,000.

This was the final formal cut in the tax duplicate, but during the Depression new valuations were made at the depressed rate, until municipal tax authorities estimated that property valuation for tax purposes in Summit County was about fifty per cent below actual valuation. The real rather than announced tax rate in Akron slid to something under $14 a thousand, one of the lowest tax rates for cities over a hundred thousand in the United States or Canada.

Since property owners, including big real estate dealers and the rubber companies, paid about half what property owners in the ordinary city did, schools and other government functions in Summit County and the city of Akron soon felt the cumulative effect of slow starvation.

Even before the final duplicate cut, police and fire departments in the city government were cut far below the safety margin. County schools were frequently closed altogether for lack of funds, and city schools bumped along on half-pay days for teachers, budget cuts, and the like. When, on top of a thirty per cent cut in the duplicate, tax collections themselves fell far below normal and the city credit was first artificially and then actually exhausted, government slowed down and in many ways stopped functioning.

While the financial crisis in government grew, the community itself faced a staggering new expense which in good times had not even existed—the support of a large section of the population, now dependent upon charity for life itself.

During the month of December, 1932, it became perfectly apparent even to the stupidest and most backward politicians in town that the city and county governments could no longer perform ordinary functions. For years business leaders in Akron had jealously guarded the doctrine of city rights, community rights, against State aggression. After that, the industrialists were for State rights against the National Government.

Now Main Street turned to the State and then to the National Government calling for help in no longer guarded tones. Only the big rubber companies were silent. Their corporate bodies, owned by New York brokerage houses and banks, were not much concerned with the truly frightening condition of the community in which their largest plants operated.

But the small businessmen, the government officials, the newspapers, first helped and indeed forced the duplicate cuts, and then, when local government itself was threatened with complete collapse, they turned to Columbus and Washington and said, in effect, "Save us!"

Happy Landing   *December 7, 1932*

Paul Litchfield, President of The Goodyear Tire and Rubber Company, was reported in today's papers to be vastly enjoying his vacation in Arizona. He had been spending part of his time, the items said, shooting rabbits and pheasant from a Goodyear baby blimp. A man on horseback rode along under the blimp picking up the dead birds and animals. This marked the first time a baby blimp had been used by sportsmen for hunting.

Dividends   *December 15, 1932*

The Firestone Tire and Rubber Company declared its quarterly dividend today, twenty-five cents per share on common stock.

Structurally Sound   *December 20, 1932*

Bruce Barton, famous advertising man and author of *The Man Nobody Knows*, a book about Jesus Christ, came to Akron today. He said the country was structurally sound.

Occupational Disability   *December 23, 1932*

Mayor C. Nelson Sparks tore the ligaments in his left arm out
of place during a speech he made at the Goodyear Heights church.
Mayor Sparks pounded on the pulpit to emphasize his remarks
and during the climax to his speech, he pounded so hard that he
severely injured his arm. He appeared at City Hall wearing a
black sling.

Big Party   *December 28, 1932*

The annual Charity Ball, the biggest social event in Akron, took
place tonight in the East Market Street Gardens, held together by
a grim business-as-usual spirit. Akron's upper classes, worried by
the approaching failure of the bank, dropping dividends, bankruptcy of old established merchant firms, nevertheless turned out
in full force to dance half-heartedly for the benefit of Children's
Hospital.

An Advertisement   *December 31, 1932*

The names of more than two hundred small businessmen in
Akron appeared on a full-page newspaper advertisement today.
Shoe repairmen, small department stores, jewelry store keepers,
undertakers, were listed as signers of a sort of proclamation.

"When the history of 1932 passes in review," the advertisement
said in large type above the many names, "it will be a chronicle
of a year in which our country took blow after blow straight on
the chin and came up smiling.

"The men on this page took it with the rest of us, but their faith
in Akron and their hope in a more promising future have impelled
them to greet you today."

Jinx Year   *December 31, 1932*

"The best cause for merrymaking tonight is that this greatest of jinx years is dead and that the community may turn its face at least hopefully to another. . . ."—*Beacon Journal* editorial.

The Celebration   *January 1, 1933*

The New Year began in Akron with the greatest drunken orgy in the city's history. Even in the heyday of the town's prosperity, the New Year celebration never reached such wild heights.

It was not an expensive celebration. Night-club proprietors did not dare raise their prices much, and even the Mayflower Hotel kept its cover charge fairly low. But the wild celebration spread out of West Hill and away from Main Street, even into the jungles of hunger in East Akron.

Indeed, it was hardly a celebration at all. Akron rose up and cursed the old year out of existence with a kind of superstitious fury. New Year's served as an artificial break in the monotony of despair. The expression, "Drown your sorrows," was a community slogan. Men drank themselves out of their fear into unconsciousness.

The furious excesses of this New Year's Eve lived for months afterwards in the community memory and there was never another night quite like this one in Akron. At the Portage Country Club, a distinguished rubber-company executive, past middle age, played leap frog in public with the wife of one of his subordinates. A respectable lawyer stole a man's car quite by mistake and ran it into a lamppost.

Police rushed frantically from one riot call to another, removing crazed celebrators from night clubs and taking drunks who refused to go home quietly to the city jail.

A little after midnight Mrs. William H. Sullivan's baby was nearly killed when a random shot from some drunk's gun went through the kitchen window of her home at 1033 Chalker Street.

Ray Potts Talking   *January 4, 1933*

Ray Potts, the new Democratic sheriff of Summit County, made his bow in the newspapers today. He announced that he would not arrest motorists who still used 1932 license plates. "You can't arrest poor people, can you?" he said.

Potts, a jaunty little man with slicked-back hair and merry eyes, moved into his official quarters behind the county jail this week.

He had been elected in the big Democratic landslide, the first Democratic sheriff in years. Dark rumors went the rounds of Main Street cigar stores about Ray Potts long before he took office. He was said to have been elected by a combination of bootleggers, whorehouse proprietors, and petty gamblers. If this were true, Potts was only following a long tradition.

Many Summit County sheriffs had their campaign expenses paid by the very lawbreakers they solemnly swore to obliterate when they took office, and nobody except a few naive voters, ministers, and the like, really expected local sheriffs to enforce the Prohibition and gambling laws. They were colorless fellows who collected their protection moneys quietly, tried to keep the peace and stay out of the papers until election time. Potts soon showed he was made of different stuff. He was famous in a month.

His first attempt at publicity made the city police very angry. They were forced to announce that if the sheriff of Summit County would not arrest drivers who used 1932 license plates, they would.

"Oppressors of the poor!" Potts replied via the newspaper headlines. The Republican City Hall administration squirmed.

Coolidge Dies   *January 5, 1933*

Calvin Coolidge, former President of the United States, died today. His death went unremarked in the rubber shops, but Main Street put its flags at half mast.

A symbol of prosperity, Coolidge was publicly mourned by Akron's leading citizens. John Thomas, President of The Firestone Tire and Rubber Company, said solemnly, "Coolidge was one of the greatest men of this age."

"When I think of Calvin Coolidge," William O'Neil, President of The General Tire and Rubber Company, declared, "I think of common sense."

Milk
January 7, 1933

The consumption of milk in Akron dropped from 107,797,000 pints in 1930 to 62,660,437 pints in 1931, with 1932 figures, not yet complete, showing a further and sharper decline, the Department of Health announced today.

Insurance
January 10, 1933

The North Howard Street Merchants Association complained that its members could no longer get burglary insurance from reputable companies because the number of police in Akron had been so reduced. The Mayor replied briefly that Akron still had more police protection than it could afford.

Billy Sunday De Luxe
January 14-22, 1933

Akron's *haut monde* suffered an acute attack of religious hysteria this week. For five exciting days, rich rubber men publicly confessed their sins, and luxurious and famous ladies, in full evening dress, told the world they were "converted."

Ever since the importation of the Southern hill-billy by the rubber shops, Akron had been rich pickings for itinerant evangelists, but until the arrival of Frank Buchman, a society Billy Sunday, the revivalists had pretty much confined their activities East Akron and Kenmore Hill. Now, however, the Mayflower rang with "amens," and bewildered traveling salesmen had prayer meetings at the town's best hotel.

whole affair, which afterwards proved so embarrassing to

many of the town's leading citizens, began on a Monday morning when the newspapers printed advance notices of Buchman's arrival with his troupe of evangelists. Most traveling revivalists were lucky to get two paragraphs on the church page in Akron newspapers, but Dr. Buchman's Thursday night prayer meeting was heralded on page one with big headlines and columns of respectful type.

The headlines, however, were no surprise to Akron. It developed, from the breathless newspaper accounts, that Dr. Buchman's local appearance was sponsored by the Firestone family, including Mr. and Mrs. Harvey Firestone, Senior.

"Akron is to have the opportunity," began the *Beacon Journal's* front-page story, "for the first-hand study of a movement that has claimed world-wide attention and is exerting a vast influence. The Oxford Group—men and women who have found a common spiritual awakening and who are pioneers in their faith—is to come here for five days."

After this awestruck beginning, the story tripped lightly over the information that the powerful Firestone family was sponsoring the Buchmanite invasion of Akron, and stated that Dr. Buchman was a "noted scholar."

On Tuesday the newspapers printed the exciting news that Mr. and Mrs. Harvey Firestone were having a big dinner Thursday night before the prayer meeting to which more than a hundred distinguished guests had been invited to meet Dr. Buchman.

On Wednesday Russell "Bud" Firestone, son of the rubber-company owner, announced, for the *Times-Press* and the *Beacon Journal*, that he had been converted by Dr. Buchman and was a member of the Oxford Group. This stirring front-page story made a sensation in middle-class homes.

"The younger Firestone," the *Beacon Journal* wrote with frank partisanship, "although a busy executive in his father's plant, is admirably fitted for the role he plays in introducing the Oxford Group to Akron. Everywhere, the tolerant frank religion of Dr. Buchman and his colleagues appeals directly to skeptical analytical minds in university and college circles."

The *Beacon Journal* was quick to defend the Oxford Group

against preliminary criticism in town. "It is Buchman's theory," Wednesday's story stated, "that he can best advance the study and adoption of the belief by introducing it first among those who can afford to spread it."

Thrill followed thrill for Akron newspaper readers as the press campaign to convert the town's nicer people to Buchmanism picked up speed. Harvey Firestone himself, on the very eve of the arrival of the traveling evangelist, called in reporters and told them he was for religion.

"In watching my son's and his wife's activities in the group," the foxy old rubber magnate said, "I believe that the Oxford Group has a vital contribution to make to the religious and social life of today."

Thursday morning the Buchmanites finally arrived at Union Station in a blizzard of newspaper headlines. Twenty-nine "disciples," in all, clambered from the New York express and obediently, indeed enthusiastically, posed for pictures with Mrs. Russell Firestone. The disciples were, in the opinion of the porters who carried their expensive English luggage, a queer lot.

There were several pink-cheeked beardless English youths with heavy Oxford accents. There was Baroness Lillian van Heeckeren van Kell de Steeg, a large lady with a prominent nose, in a leopard coat. Sir Walter Windham, a London disciple, gave station hands quite a start with his bright yellow sweater and green hat with Bavarian feather. Several of the gentlemen disciples affected knee-length neck scarfs of bright colors which fluttered in the cold January wind.

The chattering, merry little party of evangelists was led by Dr. Buchman himself, a portly, rather oily-looking character who carried a handsome overcoat with a mink collar and wore a large-brimmed felt hat. Dr. Buchman took his flock of modern apostles to the Mayflower Hotel in a fleet of taxicabs and saw them installed in twenty-nine expensive rooms. He had a commodious ite for himself.

The Firestone dinner started the Akron religious revival with ite bang. The Seiberlings, the Litchfields, the superintendent ools, the president of Akron University, a brace of bank vice- ts, a half dozen corporation lawyers and their wives, as-

56

sorted judges, scores of rubber executives, two fashionable doctors, attended the dinner in full evening dress, to gape politely at the twenty-nine apostles and Dr. Buchman. By the time the distinguished dinner guests were through eating, the advance front-page publicity had already jammed the Mayflower ballroom.

Unfortunately, the crowd packed into the gilt auditorium was not so elegant as the group assembled at dinner. The balcony was filled with persons apparently without a tuxedo to their names. Dr. Buchman and his disciples appeared on the small platform only after the dinner guests had filed into the auditorium to take the reserved front seats. Reverend Walter Tunks, pastor of Harvey Firestone's ultra-fashionable Episcopalian church, appeared beside Dr. Buchman. The unfortunate Akron minister, a High-churchman, looked acutely uncomfortable.

The prayer meeting was a huge success. Bud Firestone furnished the chief thrill of the evening when he rose to testify. "When he got up to speak," the *Beacon Journal* wrote the next day, "an almost painful hush spread over the auditorium. Here was the occasion for which many in the audience had waited, expecting to hear this young man, sheltered and privileged scion of a great name, talk of things that touch upon the intimate."

Bud Firestone's testimony wasn't quite as intimate as the audience expected, although he mentioned that his "mode of life and companionship" had been, before he joined the Group, "colored with discontent." With pleasing modesty, young Mr. Firestone declared that he was only a businessman. "I'm not an idealist," he stated. "I'm practical, but I can see how the principles of this group fit into everyday life."

Besides Mr. Firestone, several other Buchmanite disciples described their conversions. Miss Marie Clarkson of Oxford, England, said she had spent her time drinking cocoa at college veranda parties until she saw the light.

"It was a silly drink!" she cried.

Mrs. Ruth Buchanan of Virginia said she had spent all her life fox hunting until she joined the Group. "A few years ago," she said, "it would have been hard to make me believe that I would desert my horses in Virginia for a trip out here."

57

Jimmie Watt, from Edinburgh, Scotland, confessed he had been a Communist until he was converted.

Halfway through the prayer meeting Akron's upper classes were considerably startled to hear a solitary "amen" from the back of the house. Apparently some East Akron religious enthusiast, accustomed to more ordinary revival meetings, had wandered into the Mayflower by mistake. In spite of Dr. Buchman's tactful requests, the lonely "amens" continued coming, loud and clear, for the duration of the meeting. They made everybody uncomfortable.

Dr. Buchman himself spoke briefly. He said a trade revival could only come through a spiritual awakening. He also said that Prime Minister Stanley Baldwin of England approved the Oxford Group.

"Get right with God," he shouted to the front rows of his audience.

Friday morning all of West Hill was agog with tales of the Buchman meeting. By ten o'clock the lobby of the Mayflower Hotel was crowded with ladies on their way to the women's meetings upstairs. Traveling salesmen gaped as English disciples chattered merrily at late breakfast. When the papers came out at noon, all of Akron was startled to see nearly two full pages of news and pictures about the Buchmanites in both newspapers. Late Friday afternoon a real note of religious hysteria was sounded on West Hill.

The men hung back a little, somewhat shamefaced, but their wives, those ladies who ordinarily played bridge and went to night clubs, packed one meeting after another, knelt in prayer, and said they felt God moving them.

By this time dark rumors of Oxford Group practices had begun to spread among a few West Hill cynics. Magazines which had printed articles describing the origin and customs of the society evangelistic movement were quoted in noisy conversations. It appeared that members of the Oxford Group were asked to confess publicly their sins, no matter what they were. Another Buchmanite custom was the "quiet time." Oxford Group members sat around, saying nothing, with a pencil and paper in their hands. God spoke to them, during the "quiet time," and they wrote down what he said for future guidance.

But cynics were disappearing by Saturday morning. One after another of Akron's leading society matrons were more or less converted to the new cause. Their husbands went sheepishly to prayer meetings, but emerged proudly in the company of Akron's leading lawyers and rubber executives.

Bud Firestone led the Saturday night businessman's meeting. "A man with Christ in his heart," young Mr. Firestone said, "can outsmart all others."

After that statement, everything else was an anticlimax. Churches that were supplied with Oxford Group speakers Sunday were very nearly mobbed. Great crowds heard Dr. Buchman speak at the Episcopalian church, and nearly every middle-class church heard the call to "Get right with God" in Oxford accents.

But on Monday the bubble burst. West Hill had time to sit down and think it over. Dr. Buchman left town with his twenty-nine evangelists. Newspaper editors decided, abruptly, that even the Firestones should be satisfied by this time. Most of the men and a majority of the women who were all but Buchmanites on Saturday and Sunday were coming to by Monday morning. By Tuesday most of West Hill was explaining that it had attended the Mayflower meetings "just out of curiosity."

A handful of rich and fairly rich ladies, mostly past middle age, were left to form the permanent nucleus for the Oxford Group in Akron. The rest of West Hill preferred not to talk about the great five-day religious boom.

Technocracy   *January 24, 1933*

Technocracy bloomed over West Hill just as the bubble of Buchmanism burst. Technocracy swept every polite dinner party, turned up at the Akron City Club luncheons, reverberated at the Rotary Club, echoed in the executive suites of the big rubber shops. Everybody in town except the bulk of the population in the working-class districts was talking, for a fortnight, about Howard Scott and a scientific world.

Howard Scott was a Greenwich Village philosopher and economist with a weird scheme for transforming modern society. Mr. Scott's ideas were never more than darkly understood in Akron, but rubber technicians who populate West Hill thickly, at least got the idea that in Technocracy's utopia, engineers would rule the roost. This seemed, to the rubber engineers, a splendid idea.

Technocracy spread like a gasoline fire through the West Hill streets. Men talked of nothing else. The newspapers reflected the new fad. Peculiar headlines, which would certainly have puzzled Mr. Scott, appeared in the daily press. "Stork Defies Technocracy," one streamer line read, over a column of type announcing that the City Hospital record for twins had been broken, with four sets of twins born in twenty-four hours.

Technocracy faded away, not as suddenly as Buchmanism, but more completely. The bitter realities of unemployment and salary cuts conquered, in the end, any soporific West Hill could imbibe. Men came out of the cloudy vague dream to realize that things were getting much worse, not better, in Akron.

News Note   *January 30, 1933*

Adolf Hitler, an Austrian paper hanger, was appointed Chancellor of the German government today by President Paul Hindenburg. The news created no stir in Akron.

Potts Again   *January 31, 1933*

Sheriff Ray Potts ordered all his deputy sheriffs into spats today. During the rest of his administration, his deputies, who wore turtle-necked sweaters, greasy caps, and dirty shirts, also sported, as a final touch to their costumes, pearl-gray spats. The effect was tremendous.

Mr. Ford Speaks   *February 1, 1933*

"This nation," Henry Ford said in an interview appearing in the Akron newspapers, "is on the threshold of an inconceivably bright future."

Price Cuts   *February 3, 1933*

The three Akron rubber companies, Firestone, Goodrich, and Goodyear, announced another cut in tire prices.

The city was appalled. Everyone on Main Street, in East Akron, even on West Hill, agreed that this last price cut was plain clear suicide. The February, 1933, tire price cut climaxed a long wolfish battle between the tire companies, a battle in which the noncombatants—the rubberworkers—were the casualties.

Tire companies sold directly to the big auto concerns for the original-equipment trade. But, after years of the fiercest kind of competitive bidding, by 1933, little profit remained in selling tires to Chrysler or General Motors or Ford. Some of the rubber companies were in the mail-order business too, but here again competition (often referred to by rubber barons as the life blood of trade) had wiped out profits. The prices quoted by The Goodyear Tire and Rubber Company to Sears, Roebuck, for instance, were practically cost.

The only field left where rubber barons could earn a pretty penny for themselves, then, was the replacement business. By 1933, the overlords of the tire industry had very nearly ruined even the retail tire field through successive and increasingly ruinous price cuts. In a desperate attempt to grab off the small Depression trade in dealer-sold tires, Goodyear, Firestone, then Goodrich, sliced prices. All three blamed the continuous price cuts on secret underbidding by their rivals.

Factory managers were urged on by boards of directors, faced with an increasingly narrow margin of profit, to cut the cost of production. Rubberworkers watched their hourly rate of pay decline and their speed of work increase. But every time the cost of production went down a notch, the rubber barons cut the price of tires again.

The February tire price slash was the last straw. Main Street businessmen turned with fury and exasperation on the rubber companies. The *Beacon Journal*, edited by a bank director and big real estate owner, thundered:

"One of these times a tire industry suicide attempt is going to prove successful. . . . Always the cuts have been at the expense of workers and stockholders, but this time they are in worse shape to stand further punishment than has ever been the case. Share owners with but this one source of income have drawn no dividends for years; factory hands are now sweating for $10 to $12 a week. They can't continue taking it forever. There is a limit to human endurance."

Regretful Robber   *February 4, 1933*

A lean gaunt robber who held up the Sun Oil Company gas station at 845 Copley Road and stole $33, told the attendant, Harold Beck, as he left, "I'm sorry to do this, but I have a wife and three children to support. I hope you are covered with insurance."

About a Third   *February 6, 1933*

Trustees of the Better Akron Federation were told today by E. J. Larrick, secretary of the charitable organization, that relief costs in Akron would probably pass the $2,000,000 mark for 1933.

The number of relief cases, Larrick said somberly, was steadily on the increase. During 1932, relief cases averaged 5,223 a month. During 1933, Larrick reported, the relief cases averaged about 8,500 a month.

During 1932, 13,000 different families, representing about 55,000 persons, went on relief at one time or another. The cost per case averaged $15 a month. This represented total expenditure for a family of five for a month. The cases now cost, Larrick explained, $16 a month.

Larrick added that estimates indicated 5,000 fewer wage earners were employed as of January 1, 1933, than on June 1, 1932.

Mr. Larrick's somber figures showed that about a third of the 300,000 population of Greater Akron was, in early 1933, either actually on relief or living in families where the wage earner was unemployed.

The Weather   *February 9, 1933*

The weather turned bitterly cold. The thermometer at the official airport weather bureau dropped to four below and on the hills around Akron private citizens reported readings of ten and twelve below.

Family Service headquarters were jammed with a rush of unemployed trying to get on relief. They hoped, apparently, to get fuel to keep their families warm.

Election   *February 11, 1933*

A moribund Central Labor Union re-elected president Frank Patino, head of the local Bricklayers' Union. Mr. Patino had no opposition.

The Central Labor Union, which in good times represented nearly a thousand organized building service workers and newspaper printers, was now on its last legs. The various building service unions made no provision for unemployed members; when a carpenter let his dues lapse he was dropped from the membership rolls.

In February, 1933, the C.L.U. had a scattered four hundred members.

Mayor C. Nelson Sparks predicted the complete disintegration of the Akron city government unless funds were raised immediately to carry on government functions. His "appeal" appeared without comment on the front pages of both newspapers.

"With the closing down of the street maintenance repair department completely," Mayor Sparks wrote, "I appeal to the Chamber of Commerce to wake up and find out what the situation really is."

"Policemen and firemen," the appeal continued, "have been fired because of lack of funds to pay them. We have now closed down a department vital to the requirements of every person in Akron. Our streets will crumble into holes. The building department is practically shut down.

"The planning commission is functioning with one man. The engineering division is only a skeleton. The water bureau is losing money every day. The garbage department is operating at such a minimum that in certain areas farmers have been asked to take over the collection, using the garbage for hog feed."

"I want," Mayor Sparks wound up desperately, "to impress on the city of Akron that our government is crumbling."

The Farmer   *February 21, 1933*

Farmers in the country surrounding Akron made headlines today when they rioted at two farm foreclosure sales.

Far-away Drum   *February 21, 1933*

On page twenty-two of the *Beacon Journal* appeared a modest little story of three short paragraphs. Dated Lansing, Michigan, the article began, "Governor William A. Comstock announced this morning that he will issue sometime today a new proclamation permitting Michigan banks to reopen for restricted withdrawals."

News Items   *February 22, 1933*

Mr. and Mrs. Paul Litchfield attended an official White House dinner, one of the last of Herbert Hoover's receptions. Mrs. Litchfield wore a heavily beaded Hattie Carnegie gown.

Another meager story in both newspapers, well back in the classified advertising, described plans to reopen Michigan banks after the official bank holiday.

Dance   *February 23, 1933*

Reservations were reported rushing for an Akron City Club dance, billed as "gay and elaborate."

No further mention appeared in the Akron newspapers of the Michigan bank holiday. Plans to reopen the Detroit banks had failed, but local newspapers did not consider this news fit to print.

Satire   *February 24, 1933*

The Portage Country Club, whose members voted solidly last fall for Herbert Hoover, announced an "Inauguration Ball." The party, which was to have red, white, and blue appointments, was understood to be a clever satire on the Inauguration Ball in Washington to be held the same night.

No further news of bank closings.

Tear Gas   *February 25, 1933*

Shots were fired and tear gas bombs exploded during another eviction riot on Kenmore Hill today. Six persons were arrested.

Both newspapers carried small items on their back pages about the Maryland bank holiday.

Dark Sunday   *February 26, 1933*

Horrible rumors spread through West Hill. Bank officials
didn't show up at church services and weren't home at one o'clock
to eat the usual big Sunday dinner with their families.

Bombshell   *February 27, 1933*

The Akron banks went on a "restricted withdrawal basis" this
Monday morning. The naive section of the population, the bulk
of the 100,000 depositors of The First-Central Trust Company,
was completely flabbergasted.

A stunned city read with touching faith the words of good cheer
that both the *Times-Press* and the *Beacon Journal* printed about
the bank situation. In this crisis, when rumors spread up and down
Main Street, chilling the hearts of the little depositors in the five
small banks and the one big one, Akron turned to its newspapers
to get the "truth."

The *Beacon Journal*, whose owner was also a director in the
bank, said cheerfully, "Akron welcomed the restrictions placed on
withdrawal deposits from commercial and savings banks as an
emergency move to permit a continuance of the normal business
activities of the community."

It appeared, from the hearty newspaper stories, that Mayor
C. Nelson Sparks, with the welfare of the city in mind, had issued
an order restraining Akron banks from paying out more than the
usual withdrawals, or more than ten per cent of accounts, to depositors.

"No bank holiday is necessary," Mayor Sparks declared. "The
'Akron Plan' of restricted withdrawals will forestall such conditions as have resulted from the Michigan bank holiday, which have
been reflected in Cleveland institutions."

George W. Merz, Vice-President of The First-Central Trust
Company, said:

"The public is apparently highly elated over this plan which

66

enables depositors to conduct their business without handicap. Every banker in Akron was bombarded with congratulations over this practical method of handling the present financial situation brought on by the general hysteria existing countrywide."

While the vulgar public pored over such newspaper items, the lobby of The First-Central Trust Company was a madhouse. Bewildered grocery store owners and frantic housewives stood in line with their passbooks shrilly demanding their money. Soft-voiced clerks explained, over and over, that "everything was all right."

On the mezzanine floor of the great bank office, reporters lounged on leather chairs waiting for orders from the bank officials. Now and then, during this hectic day, a vice-president came out with the news, "Litchfield has endorsed the Akron Plan," or "F. A. Seiberling endorses the bank plan."

Tuesday   *February 28, 1933*

The city of Akron was quiet. No crowd rioted in the streets; only a few hysterical women fainted in the lobby of The First-Central Trust Company.

"Akron has every reason to be pleased with its bank plan," the *Beacon Journal* wrote.

It appeared, however, from a careful reading of the local newspapers, that the Michigan banks were still shut, that the Maryland banks hadn't opened, that banks in several Ohio cities were closed down.

Wednesday   *March 1, 1933*

All morning and early afternoon Wednesday the Akron newspapers carried headlines such as, "New Bank Accounts Growing as Akron Situation Clears."

Until three o'clock the local newspapers spread great cheer over the local banking situation. Pay rolls were said to be passing through the bank, taxes were being paid, business places were finding their operations unhampered. Of course a somewhat sinister note appeared in the back pages. Tennessee, Kentucky, West Virginia, Pennsylvania, Indiana banks were closing. Some 200 Ohio banks were on "restricted withdrawal plans." But the newspapers tush-tushed these ugly stories.

While everyone in town who had three cents was rushing out in the streets to buy early editions of the newspapers, the reporters sat stiffly outside the conference room at The First-Central Trust Company, where the frantic men who ran The First-Central Trust Company were facing facts. The bank was failing. Its cash reserve was dropping. Every hour brought nearer the moment when a clerk would say to a depositor, "We can't give you ten per cent of your account. We can't give you anything."

New York banks didn't even answer telegrams from the Akron financial wizards. The Secretary of the Treasury was not answering telephone calls. At intervals the Akron bankers received telegrams heralding new closings of banks. The long-distance operator said, "Cleveland calling." It appeared that the Cleveland banks were gradually folding up.

A little after noon, the Akron bankers were on the telephone to Columbus, arguing. They wanted the State superintendent of banks to send them a telegram ordering them to go on a straight one per cent withdrawal basis. The State superintendent was stubborn, not caring to take the onus of closing the Akron bank. Whose fault was it that the bank was failing?

The Akron bankers insisted. They couldn't just say the "Akron Plan" was a failure. They couldn't come right out in the open and say the bank was busted. The State superintendent of banks was not impressed.

Finally the telegram came. The bankers handed it over to the newspapermen with the order, "Not to appear until after three o'clock." The last editions of the newspapers, appearing an hour after the bank's business day was over, announced the practical closing of the Akron banks.

68

The *Beacon Journal:*

"Akron struggled Thursday to recover from the wrecking of its smoothly operating bank structure, paralyzed by an order of Ira J. Fulton, State banking superintendent."

For the first time in the long hectic days, both bankers and newspapers in the city of Akron began to speak soberly and somberly of the financial situation. Sterling B. Cramer, president of the bank, said, "I cannot predict how long the one per cent order will continue. The man who could predict that could predict the end of the Depression."

Both newspapers reported flatly that business in Akron was paralyzed.

The blight which, from Monday, had been gradually falling over the city wormed its way into every back street, into every eddy and nook of Akron. Life slowed down. The rubber companies alone had money to meet week-end pay rolls. The department stores, the grocery stores, the streetcar company, a hundred other business places had no money to pay their employees. Coal companies, unable to meet C.O.D. freight charges, predicted a fuel shortage.

The city funds were frozen in the bank. Relief funds were frozen in the bank. The county funds were frozen in the bank.

Grocery stores refused credit to old customers. Even speakeasies told favored friends, "Sales for cash only. Nobody may ever get any money again."

Panic spread over West Hill. Housewives who still had cash on hand, rushed out to buy huge hams, sacks of flour, case after case of canned goods. Department stores sold out every candle in Akron. West Hill had read about revolutions. The electric light plant would go first.

As Thursday slowly passed, the rich and well-to-do tasted the bitter fruit of fear. The telephone company reported an increased use of electric power on the West Hill exchange. Women frantically called their friends, retailing rumor after rumor, each wilder, more sinister, than the one before.

West Hill waited, expecting the poor, the unemployed, the mob down in the valley, to do something. The rich shuddered in the long night listening for the sound of riot and revolution.

Friday   *March 3, 1933*

Akron awoke to live with panic for another dreadful day. In the nearly empty streetcars, men told new scare stories. The morning papers headlined, "Thirty States Now on Bank Holiday."

Throughout the unnaturally quiet city streets, the last faith in the old order of things went up in a bright fire of anger. The valley, calm on Thursday, began to seethe on Friday. Hysterical women wept on neighbors' shoulders, "Everything we had is gone. Now we go on relief."

The small merchants who had fought for months against the mounting unemployment in the city and the falling pay rolls, gave way to despair.

George Attalla, a small shoe store owner, said, "This is going to be worse. Everything is crumbling, crumbling, and the common man is left to carry the burden."

His partner, J. Nahmi, added, "Shut up. Why should the little man talk? No one listens to him; no one cares. The big man just takes the money he has worked so hard to save."

Frank Brescani, a chicken shop merchant, said, "Just watch; they'll aggravate the people until there just won't be any banks. Business? Since Monday there hasn't been any. They say this is the richest country in the world. Well, where has all the money gone to? Who took it? Where is it?"

These statements and dozens of others like them were printed in the now badly scared *Beacon Journal*. For a week the Akron newspapers had done their best to cover up for the bank. Frightened at last by the ugly spirit in the town, they suddenly shifted ground to reflect their readers' desperation.

The *Beacon Journal*, for instance, appeared with an eight-column editorial in ten-point boldface type spread all the way across the top of the front page. The editorial called for a Federal guarantee of bank deposits, and represented an amazing shift from its traditional Republican policy of keeping government out of business.

"The fact is," the *Beacon Journal* trumpeted, "the whole American business world is in a desperate situation, and it may be saved only by heroic and instant action. Either take this course [Federal guarantee of bank deposits] or confess that we are whipped, close the doors of our banks, stores and factories, and let chaos and revolution take their course, with all that these imply in the overthrow of American institutions."

"A blight," this editorial in Akron's most conservative newspaper continued, "has fallen over all American industry. A foreign invader making easy conquest of our shores could do no worse. The ransom extracted from a subject people would be no greater than the staggering price we are now paying for our own panic and failure to keep business moving when there are at hand all the resources for prosperity."

"America is fighting to save its institutions," the editorial concluded, "the homes and savings of its people, their jobs, and the right to earnings that will give them a decent living. They are the chief sufferers from the collapse."

The Savior   *March 4, 1933*

On Saturday morning all business came to a complete halt. The rubber shops closed. Streetcars ran on half schedules. Coal companies shut. Thousands and thousands of men, still employed despite the Depression, were sent home from work "temporarily laid off." Money nearly disappeared from circulation. Pay rolls were not met. Checks were not honored.

Early Saturday morning the telegraph editors of the two newspapers turned the power on in the wire ticker rooms. Shortly afterwards they came out with the first strips of early morning copy.

"New York," thay said flatly to the news editors and the business managers and the editors, who were already standing around the city rooms at this early hour in the morning.

"New York," the telegraph editors said, holding up the long strips of wire service copy. "New York and Chicago."

"Oh, my God," the editors said. "Oh, my God."

At nine, The First-Central Trust Company opened for business. The lobby was jammed. Women swung their umbrellas wildly and bank guards rushed from one vice-president to another removing hysterical clients. Clerks paid out the one per cent allowed, under orders not to argue. The bank officials, faces drawn and harried, drank coffee at their mahogany desks and ate cheese sandwiches in full view of the depositors. Decorum disappeared.

"I haven't got a dime to feed my family on myself," clerks yelled at men who demanded, not asked for, ten dollars, anyway, please, from their accounts.

"I didn't get paid this week," men in work clothes shouted. "You got to give me some of my money."

"No!" said the clerks, signaling for the bank guards.

At noon the bank guards hustled the crowd out. "Closing time," they shouted.

The old First-Central Trust Company never opened again.

The newspapers appeared on the streets at the regular hour, just after noon. Their front pages were equally divided between details of the inauguration of the President of the United States and the closing of all of the banks in Chicago and New York City. Forty-six states were on bank holidays. The dollar quotation was dropped from European money markets.

A little after one o'clock, the city of Akron turned on its radios to listen to the new President of the United States, to listen with despair and cynicism. At least in the Middle West, in Akron, nobody expected very much of President Franklin Delano Roosevelt. He was just a politician who beat Herbert Hoover. The world was falling apart, and it wasn't very likely that a politician who beat Herbert Hoover could do much about it.

Still, all of Akron, everyone, rubberworkers and rubber bosses, the Mayor and the ministers, everyone listened this cold March day to the voice of the new President. In a hundred little confectionery stores men huddled around radios. In cheap off-the-arm restaurants waitresses put down their dishes and let the short orders wait while they stood, transfixed, listening. In the spacious drawing rooms on West Hill, perfumed and polished women drew up easy chairs and listened.

72

The whole town was listening, listening, as the scion of a rich and aristocratic Hudson River family, the polished graduate of Groton and Harvard, stood up, in Washington, D. C., a thousand miles away, and began to talk.

His words cured the panic in Akron. After a dreadful winter, coming at the end of the most terrible week in the history of the city, President Roosevelt's first inaugural speech gave the city of Akron hope. "We must drive the money-changers from the temple," the voice from the radio said. "There must be an end to speculation with other people's money," the vibrant voice went on.
· When the radio announcer said, "You have just heard the President of the United States," people clicked off the power and sat sighing, a little breathless from listening so hard. Then all over East Akron, in the little frame houses, in the cheap restaurants, men said, "Jesus, who'd 'a' thought it? Why, that baby'll show those son of a bitching bankers where to get off at. Boy, did he tell 'em!"

Franklin Roosevelt was a hero in the valley at three o'clock, Saturday, March 4, 1933.

Monday   *March 6, 1933*

Signs on the ornate doors of The First-Central Trust Company announced that the bank was closed by presidential proclamation. Monday was a troubled holiday.

The first printings of private scrip were appearing throughout the town. Before the week was out a dozen different kinds of informal moneys solved the immediate question of barter for food and the necessities of life in a big city. The *Times-Press* issued grocery books to their employees, orders on chain stores that advertised in the paper. Young men with no families who ate in restaurants soon learned to trade off their grocery orders to the fathers of five for cash. Speakeasies reluctantly discounted A & P grocery orders.

The *Beacon Journal* put its engraving department to work and produced beautiful *Beacon Journal* scrip, good against advertising bills. The scrip was nobly engraved and each week the artists in the engraving studio improved their design until, when the financial crisis was finally over weeks and weeks afterwards, the *Beacon Journal* scrip was nearly as intricate in design as a United States dollar bill.

The informal scrip, based on barter, spread over the town. Dry goods stores paid clerks with orders on the store, coal companies issued paid coal bills to truck drivers. The expression "United States money" was a by-word. A storekeeper asked, as a man bought a shirt, "You got United States money?"

The city and county governments turned almost immediately to scrip as a way out of their dismal financial condition. City and county scrip was good against taxes. Schoolteachers, university professors, elevator operators, policemen, every employee of the city and county government, soon had a pocketful of the crinkling scrip.

On this Monday, not only business houses, but the bankers themselves were turning to scrip to cure the paralysis in the city. The Akron Clearing House Association evolved an elaborate scrip plan. Millions of the proposed city money were actually printed, but at the last moment, the rubber companies who were supposed to furnish the necessary United States money to guarantee the new scrip, backed out, and the scrip was never issued.

As the day passed in town, the details of the President's bank plan were announced over the radio and in the newspapers. It appeared that all sound banks would be allowed to open soon. Shaky banks would have to prove that they were liquid. Some banks would simply have to fall by the wayside. Akron waited, this time fearfully and cynically, to see what First-Central would do.

Tuesday   *March 7, 1933*

Spring spread over the harassed city. Warm sunshine fell on the streets and kids played with roller skates and marbles.

On Main Street, men came out of their winter cigar-store forums and stood lounging on the corners, talking. The talk was bitter. Akron's average man had, suddenly, a very poor opinion of bankers, businessmen, and all Government officials except President Roosevelt.

"With my right hand tied behind me," rubberworkers drawled in their mountain speech, "I could run a bank better than them dopes at First-Central."

Wednesday   *March 8, 1933*

Food prices rose, reflecting the circulation of informal scrip. The business paralysis deepened.

Thursday   *March 9, 1933*

The Seiberling Rubber Company shut down. The Firestone Tire and Rubber Company closed. Falls Rubber Company suspended production. A half-dozen smaller rubber companies shut down, temporarily, of course. The Goodyear Tire and Rubber Company announced a continuation of the two-day week. Smaller industries all over the city closed their doors. Stores suspended business. . . .

Cold rain fell over a dismal city. Earlier in the week, the hope placed in the new President, even the warmer weather, had lifted the spirits of the city. Now blow after blow fell on the already groggy town. Mothers, who sent their children to school as much for the warm free lunches as for the book-learning, were appalled when they read the flat school board announcement. Schools would probably close at once; all operating funds were frozen in the bank.

Late Thursday afternoon a dreadful hint appeared in the newspapers. The President's message allowing the immediate opening of sound banks appeared side by side with a grim statement by Sterling B. Cramer, president of The First-Central Trust Company.

Mr. Cramer said, "I doubt whether either Akron or Cleveland banks will benefit by the President's message. I do not think they can post the type of adequately secured assets which President Roosevelt indicated."

This was plain talk, but still Akron didn't quite believe it. It couldn't be true; it couldn't be absolutely, finally, completely true that First-Central would never open again. The bank had 100,000 depositors, with $30,000,000 in accounts. It would have to open. "They" couldn't let it fail.

Friday   *March 10, 1933*

The two Akron newspapers admitted, in an off-hand way today, that The First-Central Trust Company had failed. The bank, the newspapers stated without headlines and buried in the financial crisis story, was closed, and would not open under the provisions of the President's message.

Upstairs in the bank lobby mezzanine floor, exhausted bankers, unshaven, bleary-eyed, slept on customers' leather chairs, stretched out on mahogany conference tables, drank cardboard containers of coffee, and listlessly put in long-distance telephone calls.

Since Monday, the officials of The First-Central Trust Company had been huddled in their suite of executive offices desperately trying to find some way of opening the bank, perhaps on a restricted withdrawal basis. They stayed in their ornate offices day and night, afraid to go out in the town to meet questioners, afraid to miss a telephone call that might solve the terrible dilemma. The town's leading businessmen drifted in and out of those offices and were shocked to see bankers who had maintained the usual fishy-faced, icy-eyed bankers' calm through many another crisis, now show every outward evidence of complete panic.

In the confusion that resulted from the closing of every bank in the nation by presidential proclamation, the Secretary of the Treasury had no time to send out individual messages to local bankers. So by Tuesday, Akron bankers, once so haughty with the press, were reduced to begging news from the very reporters who begged news from them.

Each new bulletin from Washington was a fresh blow to the Akron bankers. They alone in the town knew that The First-Central Trust Company had hardly a nickel in securities that would make the grade with the Government.

76

All the First-Central securities worth a thin dime had long since been pledged to the Reconstruction Finance Corporation for a much earlier loan. The only things left to pledge in the vaults of the big marble bank were some odd millions of second mortgages, a lot of worthless South American bonds, and the like. The good bonds, the good mortgages, the Government securities, were the property of the R.F.C. until First-Central could repay its $20,-000,000 loan, floated to bolster up the big merger a year and a half before.

The reporters sat in a big luxurious anteroom at telephones. The bankers came out of their offices, the men who until two weeks ago had carried themselves so proudly in the city, and asked the reporters to call up their offices and see what was new. Then the bankers stood around hesitantly until the reporters hung up their receivers. The young men from the papers would say then, quietly, a little kindly, "A new United Press bulletin is that the President says liquid banks will have no trouble getting operation certificates."

"Ah, yes," the bankers would murmur and go back into their handsome offices and sit staring into space at their great bare desks.

Once the reporters brought in a new wire bulletin describing the securities the National Government would accept for proof that a bank was liquid. The Akron bankers glanced down the list and turned away. "Nothing to say, no comment," one of the group finally managed to murmur in a hoarse voice.

All day and all night Akron bankers were on the long-distance telephone. Ceaselessly, endlessly, one or another of the vice-presidents, the treasurer, the secretary, the president, was on the wire, calling Washington, calling New York, calling Cleveland, calling Columbus. The bankers called up the new Congressman, that Democrat, and demanded action. They tried desperately to get the Undersecretary of the Treasury, they talked to the State superintendent of banks, they talked to men at the great New York banks, so remorselessly liquid.

But nobody wanted to listen to a bunch of desperate provincial bankers. Too many desperate provincial bankers were praying for help on the long-distance telephone. Kansas City and Pittsburgh

77

and Cleveland and South Bend, Indiana, and Atlanta, the whole country was on the long-distance telephone asking questions, demanding to know the meaning of the last press bulletin, wanting help, wanting a loan, or just calling up officials because there seemed to be nothing else to do, and calling up somebody was a relief.

So all the long-distance telephone calls did no good, and all the conferences, and the endless talk on the mezzanine lobby of The First-Central Trust Company. The bank, to put it brutally, was busted, and nothing these harried businessmen and officials could do would save it now. The bank had gone broke long ago, when the bankers took a gamble with other people's money that prosperity would last forever.

So while The First-Central Trust Company came to the end of the trail, the city of Akron awoke gradually to the horrible truth. Friday the rumors were confirmed. The bank was not opening. It was true. Everybody's money was gone.

Life in the city of Akron drew up to nearly a full halt. Marriages dropped to the lowest weekly figure in the recent history of the town. Only fifteen couples in a population of 300,000 were married the week of March sixth. Akron University canceled the Freshman dance and all other social activities. West Hill gave up too. The society columns nearly disappeared from the newspapers. The only items were notices of cancellations of parties and dinners.

The relief funds frozen in the bank were released by executive order of the President of the United States, so the unemployed did not do any more than the usual starving. But the thousands and thousands of wage earners in the city, employed until this week, began now to come to the end of their last week's pay envelope. From all over Akron the cry went up, "We are hungry!" Relief authorities begged the city grocers to carry their regular customers on credit, but even so, the relief offices were flooded with hundreds of new cases.

In the back alleys, a new and sinister racket got a foothold—trade in passbooks. Slippery-looking gentlemen with a pocketful of United States money offered to buy First-Central passbooks, discount seventy or eighty per cent. In the block around the bank there was, all day, a smallish crowd standing around on the cor-

78

ners talking desperately. In front of the doors, women cried and men swore.

Diversion   *March 11, 1933*

The tragic city was mildly diverted today by the christening of the new airship, the *Macon*. A bevy of Georgia beauties arrived for the ceremonies, a rear admiral turned up, the sailors stationed in town marched around in their smart uniforms, and the newspapers turned gratefully from bank failures to front-page pictures of airships.

But the christening, and even the elaborate ball which followed it, was pretty half-hearted. The crowds were comparatively small, and although Akron society women who entertained the Georgia girls and the rear admiral's wife, tried to keep a stiff upper lip, the financial crisis leaked through.

Pioneer Spirit   *March 19, 1933*

Mayor C. Nelson Sparks went on the air this Sunday night with a rip-roaring broadcast in his best campaign style. He apologized for bankers. "This never would have happened if the bankers hadn't been reckless," he roared, stating publicly for the first time what was to be the bankers' official plea, "but everyone was reckless in 1929."

Mayor Sparks lashed out at "rumor mongers," and added that Akron was a city worth "rebuilding." He pleaded for the revival of that "old pioneer spirit that built this town in the first place."

Rumors   *March 20, 1933*

Some of the more sinister rumors floating up and down Main Street leaked into the newspapers today. Headlines hinted, "Bank stock transfers to be traced," and newspaper columnists speculated for the first time on whether or not the double liability bank stock laws would or could be enforced in the case of The First-Central Trust Company.

Late Monday night the energetic Mayor was on the air again, this time in a virtually impromptu speech, attacking "whisperers" before "they literally undermine this city."

Only Fifty Per Cent   *March 21, 1933*

President Cramer came out in the open today with his plan for reopening The First-Central Trust Company. He wanted the R.F.C. to make a fifty per cent loan to the bank to put it "in highly liquid state."

The plan was quite a shock to everybody. If the bank needed a fifty per cent loan to put it in a highly liquid condition, obviously it would never open again.

Saturday   *March 25, 1933*

The third week of business paralysis closed in Akron today. The rubber shops were still either shut down or operating on a two-day week. United States money was, in the speech of the valleys, scarcer than hen's teeth. Relief was struggling desperately with floods of new cases, and Akron's small middle class was gradually waking up to the fact that its savings were wiped out and its resources smashed.

Trade in anything but the barest necessities—bread, milk, oatmeal—sunk to the lowest levels in the history of the town. Department-store clerks stood all day without making a single sale, and the consumption of gasoline, cigarettes, magazines, dropped off to a trickle. Bus and streetcar passengers all but disappeared. Movie houses were empty. The luxury trades, the florists, fancy bakers, high-priced bootleggers, sent up howls of despair as the newspapers headlined mournfully, "Society faces another empty calendar week."

Scrip of all kinds began to circulate widely—some at a terrific discount, some at face value. Prices rose in the face of the informal money.

Strange rumors rocked the city. In spite of the rapid somersault the newspapers made on the bank story, public faith in the local press began to disappear. The newspapers had lied about the bank holiday. Now nobody believed anything they read in either sheet. Instead the Main Street cigar stores, the bookie joints, even the off-the-arm rubberworkers' restaurants were breeding places for the latest "news."

Favorite rumor of the time were stories of bankers' suicides. Main Street reported every vice-president of First-Central dead by his own hand at least once during the week. Dark tales of raids on the cash reserves of the bank circulated in every speakeasy. The city flatly rejected the Mayor's explanation that the town bankers had simply been "reckless." Akron was convinced that the bankers had been more than reckless. There was dirty work, the whole town believed, in the affairs of The First-Central Trust Company.

The city did not recover from its anger. As the days passed the small merchants, the clerks, the middle class, turned more and more sullen until they were one with workers in shaking a clenched fist in the general direction of West Hill.

The workers' districts were quiet enough this past week. The county judges hastily called a moratorium on mortgage fore-closures for the duration of the financial crisis, and there were no sheriff's crews abroad on Kenmore Hill or in the rubberworkers' valleys moving old furniture out of little frame houses.

At the bank itself, exhausted officials still carried on, drawing up new and more and more hopeless plans for getting the stricken bank open again. On this Saturday Mr. Cramer suddenly announced a seventy per cent wage cut, not only for bank officials, but for clerks and tellers and even the bank guards. In addition, five notable Akron bankers were unceremoniously fired. Four of them were old friends or members of the ruling real-estate family in town.

Straw in the Wind   *March 27, 1933*

A handful of rubberworkers in a little Cuyahoga Falls specialty rubber factory walked out on strike today.

Once Again
March 28, 1933

Akron was dismayed when the three rubber companies once again announced a cut in the retail price of tires.

Shot in the Arm
March 31, 1933

The rubber companies, large and small, announced a return to the regular five-day week starting next Monday. Regular shifts were called back to work after nearly a four-week furlough. Men will be paid in cash only.

The news was a shot in the arm to a moribund city. Grocers started giving credit to old customers, the bus and streetcar company called back its temporarily unemployed crews, beauty parlor owners called up their girls and ordered them in to work. The financial crisis was over, although its direct effects would linger on for six months or more.

As Akron slowly struggled out of business paralysis, it was a new city. The old fetishes were pretty largely gone. The man who had saved $2,500 for his old age no longer believed that the rich were fit to rule the country. The little merchant who had fought the Depression for years only, in the end, to see his bank account and his chance of expanding into a big merchant wiped out, no longer believed that any honest energetic man could get ahead in the world.

The city seethed with hatred for bankers, but the word "banker" meant, in the speech of Akron, any rich man, a rubber baron, for instance.

West Hill itself was uncertain and unsure. Even the *Beacon Journal* did not rise to defend the bankers, and the Mayor alone, faithful servant that he was, raised his voice in a half-hearted defense of the rich. The class lines were drawn, for the first time in the history of the city, during the bank panic, and forever afterwards people in Akron would speak of the "little fellow" not with, but against, "the big fellow."

82

Foreign Events   April 1, 1933

The Pope launched Holy Year, and Hitler announced the Jewish boycott.

God's Hand   April 4, 1933

The mournful sound of a newsboy screaming an extra in the foggy morning pulled the city from its uneasy sleep. Men stumbled into shoes and put coats over their pajamas. Half dreaming, they stood on their front porches holding out coins to the boy who came running out of the mist carrying newspapers black with headlines.

When the child was gone, yelling hoarsely in the dawn, people stood shivering at their doors staring dully at the big type, saying gently, "It can't be true."

But it was. The U.S.S. *Akron*, the largest airship in the world, the pride, the beloved of this little rubber city, was down with all its crew but three dead. The ship had crashed in flames off the New Jersey coast, had fallen into an ocean angry with storm, just after midnight.

By seven o'clock, every little boy who had watched the *Akron* building in the great air dock knew she was destroyed. This ship was in the hearts of the people of Akron. They knew every beam in her frame, her weight, and her length, and how many motors she had. They thought she was the most beautiful thing they had ever seen.

Goodyear built the U.S.S. *Akron*, but she really belonged to the people of the city. They cherished her all through the months she was building; they came in hundreds of thousands to watch her first flight; they followed her every movement in the newspapers after she had gone away from home. They were proud of the U.S.S. *Akron* and jealous of her. They said she was better than any old German Zep. They said she could easily fly around the world, non-stop, if she had the chance. They said so often as they watched her in the newsreels, "Ain't she love-ly?"

Now the city of Akron was racked by grief. Teachers didn't try to talk about arithmetic that day or any other geography than that of the Jersey Coast. In the grocery stores on West Hill and in little confectionery stores women in smart town clothes stopping in to place an order, and women in old house dresses out to buy a bottle of milk, said with stricken faces, "I can hardly believe it, yet."

The agonized cry went up over the city, "Why didn't they take care of her?"

Nobody in Akron, whether he was an important official of The Goodyear Tire and Rubber Company or the merest tubepuncher, would ever in his lifetime believe there had been anything wrong with the airship. The Navy, they said, "didn't take care of her." They talked of the great airship as though she were a lovely child whose foster parent had delivered her to death.

And the feeling ran deep through this town of Southern mountain folk that somehow, someway, the destruction of the great airship was a tragic symbol. The rubberworkers said, stumbling with the words, "Everything in this town has gone to hell, and, well, she was named for Akron, wasn't she?"

They said, somberly, these men who were almost universally religious, "God's hand is against this town."

The Jitters   *April 5, 1933*

Mayor C. Nelson Sparks, heading a Citizens Committee that went down to Washington to appeal for a R.F.C. loan to The First-Central Trust Company, told startled Government officials, "The difference between a twenty per cent payoff at the bank and a twenty-five per cent payoff is the difference between satisfaction and civil commotion and riot."

Several other leading citizens backed up the Mayor with delicate hints that a revolution was around the Akron corner unless the bank came through with a decent payment on depositors' accounts. The R.F.C. men listened, decided that the Akron businessmen had the horrors, and announced they would make a loan giving a twenty per cent payoff. The loan would be made only if the city of Akron could put up about six million dollars to organize a new bank.

The Citizens Committee came home empty-handed and badly frightened.

Beer!   *April 7, 1933*

Restaurants started selling legal 3.2 beer at 12:01 this morning. Hilarity was considerably restrained. Akron beer drinkers were accustomed to the needled variety, testing well above 12 and 13 per cent alcohol per volume. Legal beer was immediately termed "hog wash" by a corn-liquor drinking population. Cagey ex-speakeasy owners, newly installed in beer restaurants, began to advertise by word of mouth their "special high-test beer," and lots of "legal" beer in Akron was testing 10 and 12 per cent before the month was out.

All Over   *April 8, 1933*

John R. Eckler, a Pittsburgh banker from the Mellon clique, was appointed conservator of The First-Central Trust Company. He was to liquidate the affairs of the defunct bank. The sponge was thrown in with Eckler's appointment, and the last attempt to reopen the old bank was junked.

The word "conservator" suddenly became Akron small talk, and newspapers made valiant attempts to standardize its pronunciation. It was the first new word of the Roosevelt regime to enter the Akron language.

I Resign   *April 10, 1933*

The entire staff of The First-Central Trust Company, the bank that failed, resigned today.

No Funds
April 11, 1933

Akron city schools will close May 5, six weeks before the end of the term, the school board announced. There were no funds, the announcement said, for the continued operation of the city schools.

Out in the Open
April 12, 1933

For the first time, the local press dragged out into the open the underground talk about criminal prosecution of the officials of The First-Central Trust Company. Six million dollars, the papers wrote, was withdrawn from The First-Central Trust Company between January 1 and February 28. Somebody, apparently, knew that the bank was failing.

The *Beacon Journal* called for a blanket investigation of the affairs of the bank, enforcement of double liability, and prosecution of those who illegally transferred double liability stock just before the crash. It was a popular editorial.

This Democracy
April 17, 1933

Parents of children who attended King School, the West Hill grammar school, oversubscribed a fund to continue classes until June 16. It was the custom among West Hill parents to send their small children to this newly built and scientifically equipped public school until they were of high-school age. Then they were sent to private preparatory schools.

Last year, when the school board closed public school kindergartens, King School kindergarten stayed open, supported by tuition fees. This year, parents extended the idea to the upper grades, so that their children would not be deprived of the regular term of instruction. King School will be the only school in the city open after May 5, the school board said.

Wisecrack   *April 20, 1933*

"Why not a free suite of light housekeeping rooms in the big tower for every depositor in the First-Central?"—Howard Wolf in the *Beacon Journal*.

Appeal   *May 3, 1933*

Senator Carter Glass, chairman of the Senate Banking Commission, received today an official appeal from the Akron Citizens Committee, asking action on the Akron bank situation.
The appeal stated:
  1. That Akron industry was operating at twenty per cent of normal levels.
  2. That the tax collection was 62% delinquent on April 1.
  3. That the city's bonded debt required $5,400,000 payment this year.
  4. That thirty-eight insurance companies held Akron bonds.
  5. That the R.F.C. was feeding and clothing one out of every four Akron citizens and would soon be supporting one out of every three Akron citizens.

Government Falters   *May 16, 1933*

The town woke up with a jolt to discover that Mayor Sparks had not been crying, "Wolf." The city was really, positively, completely bankrupt.
Ninety policemen got final lay-off notices today, leaving a force of 88 cops. Fifteen policemen were assigned to each shift. Most of the cruiser cars were retired. Two will operate in the daytime, five at night.
Private collection of garbage was scheduled for June 1. Householders were ordered to make arrangements with farmers for having garbage hauled away to hogpens. City garbage trucks went into storage. There were no funds to pay their drivers or supply gasoline.

All but three firehouses in town closed. Crews of seven fire stations were laid off and equipment stored. Thirty firemen were left to man each shift, a cut of forty men per shift.

The city of Akron officially closed the airport, but the Chamber of Commerce supplied funds to keep it open at least temporarily.

These final retrenchments came after a series of drastic government economies. The schools were already closed, the city engineering, service, planning and health departments had already been virtually wiped out.

Now the bankrupt city was left with fifteen policemen and thirty firemen to guard its property and lives at any given moment.

Alphabet Begins   *May 27, 1933*

An astonished city watched 420 Akron boys crowd Union Station today as they left for Fort Knox, Kentucky, and the C.C.C.

The Civilian Conservation Corps was at first referred to by its full name in the Mayor's speeches and the newspapers, but even before the Akron boys left for their new adventure, the C.C.C. had become the first of the Roosevelt alphabetical relief agencies.

The May contingent of the Akron C.C.C. boys left with a spirit of high adventure. They were desperately glad to be away from hunger and especially away from the rotting idleness.

Start Again   *June 6, 1933*

The R.F.C. informed Akron businessmen today that all the plans submitted for organizing a new national bank in Akron were useless. "Start all over again," the officials at Washington said.

Heat Wave   *June 7, 1933*

The city sweltered in the first heat wave of the season. The official thermometer stood at 98 degrees, but cigar-store proprietors reported temperatures of 102 and 103 at street levels.

The heat was difficult to bear on West Hill, but in the valleys it was intolerable. The rubber shops, running twenty-four hours a day now, belched smoke even after midnight. A small part of the unemployed had been called back to the factories to work at back-breaking pace. The rank smell of burning rubber hung like a sticky cloud over the bare frame houses. Kids gasped and couldn't sleep.

Inside the vast factories, the overpowering smell of processed rubber clung in the nostrils, got in the throat, burned in the eyes. In the pit, where tires are cured with live steam, the half-naked giants who worked furiously with marvelous precision, stood in pools of their own sweat struggling to keep up the inhuman pace. In the tire departments men with great bunched muscles and vast shoulders keeled right over under the conveyor belt. Girls who punched tubes sickened from the smell and the pall of heat. The swelling noise of the factory beat harder on the nerves. The clank and clatter of the conveyor, the uneven smashing sounds of the great machinery, the roar of motors, drove sweating men to frenzy.

At shift end, the factories emptied of men and women looking gaunt, washed out like old sheets boiled too long. The terrific speed of work, coupled with the stifling heat, made these tall husky girls and the big men shuffle out of factory gates, heads down, broken, silent.

The heat wave lasted for five days. Factory hands who had suffered through the winter, making the increasingly rapid pace without a word of protest, began to grind their teeth in the heat and ask God to witness that they could not stand it. Girls who supported whole families and were afraid of losing their jobs suddenly told the woman punching tubes next to them, "We got to do something. This ain't human."

So while on West Hill Mrs. F. A. Seiberling entertained the ladies of the Garden Club on her estate, and was duly photographed carrying a large parasol against the heat wave, in the factories a storm brewed.

The Wheels Grind Slowly   *June 12, 1933*

What the county prosecutor billed as a "sweeping investigation of every unlicensed bank in Akron, an investigation sparing no one," began before the summer-term Grand Jury.

The N.R.A.   *June 16, 1933*

President Roosevelt signed the National Industrial Recovery Act, Section 7A and all.

BOOK TWO

June 26, 1933, to February 14, 1936

The Union *June 26, 1933*

Just before noon today a heavy-shouldered man with a thatch of bright red hair strolled up to the main factory gates at Goodyear. He waited in the broiling sun until the whistle blew and shift end came.

As the factory hands shuffled in a silent mass past the brick walls, past the iron-spiked fence, through the high gates, the red-haired man stepped forward and held out a flimsy sheet of paper.

"The N.R.A.," a bold headline across the page said, "gives workers the right to organize."

Under the very black type about the N.R.A. was a second line, "Come to the mass meeting at the Armory, June 30."

The first few men out of the gates hesitated, looked curiously at the giant with the red hair. "Take 'em, boys," the man said, and the workers held out their hands and walked slowly away reading, "The speedup is killing you. Your wages have been cut. President Roosevelt has given you the chance to organize a union without interference from the rubber bosses. Take it."

Workers stopped to reach for the leaflets and so held up the stream of tired hot men pouring like a turgid river from the Goodyear plant. The company guards soon came and milled around the tall red-haired man, but they didn't stop him passing out the leaflets. Two months before they would have stopped him, but not now. Goodyear was afraid. Goodyear didn't know what to make of the N.R.A. The Goodyear lawyers were advising caution. God knows, they said, what President Roosevelt will do next.

Hundreds of men packed in the gate entrance waiting to stretch out their hands for the leaflet. The red-haired man sweated in the sun and his hands flew. The waiting factory hands spoke in low quiet voices.

"It's about a union," they said. "It's about the N.R.A. It tells you what Roosevelt will let you do."

Just before one o'clock the red-haired man crossed the street for a beer. He told the saloonkeeper that the rubber boys were going to have a union.

"Yeah?" said the barkeep. "Well, Christ knows they need it."

At five o'clock the man with the leaflets was back at his gate, and again at midnight, and then, rocky with fatigue, he was back just before dawn. Men told him now as they went in to work, "Give us a bunch. We'll put 'em in the toilets." Girls paused and put a dozen of the limp sheets in their cheap white pocketbooks. Now and then a worker threw a leaflet in the gutter. Instantly someone picked it up. Although thousands and thousands of leaflets were passed out at this gate in the twenty-four-hour shift period, the street sweeper had only half a dozen to fork with his stick. At seven o'clock the red-haired man went home to bed, too tired to talk, but feeling excited and good inside.

The red-haired man was Wilmer Tate, president of the Akron local of the Machinists' Union, or at least what there was of it, and secretary of the Central Labor Union, what there was of *that*. He was one of the five men in Akron who, in the last days of May, decided the time had come to organize a rubberworkers' union. These five set the match to the tinder already dried and laid neatly for the firemakers.

The first was Wilmer Tate, forty-eight years old, with remarkable blue eyes and a Roman nose, red eyelashes, a square chin, and a huge square head. He had a booming voice and an Iowa accent. He grew up on a farm in Illinois, the son of stern religious parents. When he was nineteen he followed his father to Iowa, and until he was past thirty, he farmed the wheat lands and worked during the harvest until he was drenched with sweat and aching with fatigue.

In 1916 he suddenly tired of the land. He wanted machinery and the city. At thirty-one, with his wife and four children, he came to Akron. While he hunted for a job the first bitter winter, his oldest girl died of diphtheria.

Tate learned to be a splendid machinist, a fine craftsman. Two years after he came to Akron, a man working on the next bench

94

asked him to join the machinists' union. It was literally the first time in his life he had ever heard of a union. Tate joined instantly. He used to tell his rubberworker friends, "It was the most important thing that ever happened to me."

Tate had gone to high school, but in the years he had farmed there were no books in his father's house. He had never read anything except high school textbooks when he joined the machinists' union in 1918. He began to read feverishly. His kids were growing up; they were at the noisy age. He lived in the ordinary little frame house, and his good-natured wife had a big job just doing the washing. He was thirty-four years old, a man past the schooling age, but still, every night when he came home from work he cleared away a corner of the dining room table, and under the overhead light, while his youngsters played on the floor, he read and read. He read Marx and Engels. He read Lenin. He read pamphlets written years before by Eugene V. Debs.

Tate never held a membership card in any radical party. He knew no Communist in the days when he was reading "The Communist Manifesto." He saved his tobacco money and sent away for his books. He went to union meetings regularly, listened. In 1926 he put down his books and went out to organize the rubberworkers. He failed that time. He tried again and again. He failed and failed, but he was sure that someday the rubberworkers would be organized.

The second man in the five who set the spark was James McCartan, a printer, a man with thick gray hair and a roaring voice. He called himself a Socialist, although he too did not belong to any formal party. He had lived in Akron for twenty-five years, had sent his kids to Akron University, and had tried again and again to tell rubberworkers they needed a union.

W. H. Wilson, an electrician, and A. J. Frecka, a plumber, knew Tate and believed in him and believed in the rubberworkers' union. They were in on that first meeting, when every word a man said seemed wild and reckless. The last man was Alex Eigenmacht, a printer with wonderful stories of the revolution in Hungary, a printer who owned a small, and in those days nearly bankrupt, print shop.

These were the five. In the last days of May they sat down together and considered what was happening in Washington. The N.R.A. was up for debate in Congress. The newspapers seemed to think that Section 7A gave workers the right to organize into unions of their choice. These five believed that President Roosevelt would make the rubber bosses let a union alone. In Akron, Tate said at that first meeting, the time was overripe. The speedup in the mills was heartbreaking, mindbreaking. The cry, "It ain't human!" came every day out of the rubber shops, echoed up and down the city streets.

A new spirit was abroad in the city, the five men told each other. The unemployed were standing up for their rights. The small clerk, the little fellow, was embittered and emboldened. The bank failure had wiped out the old community leaders. Akron was in a state of flux waiting for something to happen.

That something, these five said grimly, would be the union. The chance would never come again with the President of the United States sticking up for the workers. Who was Paul Litchfield or Harvey Firestone to gainsay Franklin D. Roosevelt?

So Tate said, "O.K., we're agreed. We want a union now! How do we go about it?"

The five men looked at each other. Tate was on relief. All machinists were out of work in 1933. McCartan had a job on a newspaper; he was lucky. Wilson couldn't get on relief because his daughter had a job at Firestone. She made $5 a week. It was his stepdaughter at that. Alex's print shop was on its last legs.

The Central Labor Union had a little money left over from the days when it used actually to collect dues from the scattered craft locals. The C.L.U. had, to be precise, $696 saved up for just such a thing as organizing the rubberworkers. Unfortunately, however, the money was tied up in a closed bank. The C.L.U. was broke, frozen out like the Board of Education and the city of Akron and indeed everybody else in town except the rubber companies.

Tate went into the back alleys, hunted up one of the furtive little men who bought passbooks. He sold the C.L.U. bankbook for fifty-two cents on the dollar. The labor movement couldn't wait for the banks to pay off. They had $360, then, these five men. With this little nest egg they hired the armory, got out leaflets,

96

invited a speaker, paid his expenses, wrote letters, bought postage stamps. Alex printed the leaflets. He worked all one night and ran off 50,000 of them. They wanted more, but the ink ran out and even after Alex had begged and borrowed from every printer friend in town there was only enough for the 50,000.

The A. F. of L. sent the speaker. Tate wrote a letter on official C.L.U. stationery, long since yellowed, and in due time got a reply. A man from Detroit would come to speak; the Akron C.L.U. would pay his expenses. The strange man from Detroit was a little disappointing. Rubber is a basic industry. The five men thought the A. F. of L. might have sent somebody famous. But, after all, the speaker didn't really matter. What mattered was bringing a huge crowd to the meeting. If the rubberworkers saw a big crowd, they would take heart and join the union. There is safety in numbers—safety and excitement.

The C.L.U. building was filled during the day with union men long unemployed—plumbers and electricians. They sat idly around in the dark main hall playing tong and poker, gossiping. Tate counted on these men to pass out leaflets, but when the day came, they wouldn't go. They didn't believe a rubber union was possible, and anyway, frankly, they didn't care. Why should they pass out leaflets in the hot sun and get out of bed to make the dawn shift?

The five men were desperate. Fifty thousand leaflets take some passing out. The rubber factories stretch over miles with hundreds of gates where men enter and leave. Tate drafted his son. Wilson got his daughter. Mrs. Tate enlisted her friends. On June 26, the little band sallied forth to the rubber factories carrying the news that a rubber union was on the way.

The Union Continued   *June 30, 1933*

On the last day in June, towards evening, Tate went home to supper. He was too sick with fear and excitement to eat. Suppose nobody came to the meeting? Suppose a bitter handful turned up? Maybe the leaflet wasn't written very well. Maybe it hadn't said the right thing. Still, the workers had taken the sheet. They had read it. They would come. They had to come. This was the time for a rubber union.

"Oh, God," Tate said, and pushed away the food his anxious wife put before him.

He went down to the armory before seven o'clock, although the meeting wasn't scheduled until eight. He looked bitterly at the ugly stone building. The armory, he thought, was in a strategic spot, directly across from City Hall and the police station, next door to the County courthouse and the County jail. Two meager-looking guns stood on the patch of green grass in front of the dark fortress. Tate idled near one, grateful for the evening coolness. He was past caring what happened. For the moment he was simply curious. Then his heart jumped a beat. At a little after seven o'clock, a whole hour early, a band of fifteen men marched rapidly up the concrete sidewalk, marched with their heads up, fast. In fifteen minutes the grass was black with rubberworkers pushing into the armory doors. At seven-thirty Tate went inside. The bare hall with the steel girders was already filled. At fifteen minutes to eight men sat in the aisles shoulder to shoulder. At eight hundreds and hundreds of men were jammed in the back. Tate prayed the fire warden wouldn't show up.

Outside hundreds of workers stood on the grass pushing and shoving to get in. Tate rigged up a hasty loudspeaker outside, and on the platform in the hall the speeches began. Nearly five thousand men listened to those speeches, and that meant another five thousand either working or sleeping for the midnight shift would have come and listened if they could.

The man from Detroit turned out to be quite an orator. He talked about the N.R.A. and President Roosevelt. "Now is the time to organize." The men in the armory listened raptly, breathlessly. They cheered him in broken yells. They whooped and hollered when he said, "Stand up for your rights. End the speedup. Get higher wages. Join the union."

When he was through Tate and McCartan spoke briefly. The men listened hard. The man from Detroit, Paul Smith, an old A. F. of L. organizer, a trained speaker, was the froth, good to listen to, a nice talker. But Tate and McCartan talked business.

98

Sign the cards on the seat. Come to the C.L.U. Spread the word. It cost $2 to join the A. F. of L. Federal Rubber Workers' Union. Anybody who worked in the shops could join. What do you say, boys? Do you want a union?

After the meeting, the men didn't go home. They stood in little clusters talking, and the excitement in their hearts infected their voices. The cry, "It ain't human," spread through the hall, but this time the tone was different. Before, men had said, "It ain't human," and the words had been a mournful cry of despair.

Tonight, June 30, the old phrase sounded like a battle cry.

Tate was surrounded by eager rubberworkers. The janitor turned off the lights, and Tate walked out followed by a gang of men from the Goodrich tire department. He said he would see them tomorrow, but in the end they won out. He took them through the quiet night streets of downtown Akron, up the ten blocks to the C.L.U. hall. He fumbled for the light switch, found his cash box, and there, a little after midnight on the first day of July, he signed up the first members of the rubberworkers' union.

"Tomorrow," one of them said, grinning at his new union card, "is too long to wait to join the union."

Some Figures   *July 4, 1933*

Goodyear and Goodrich jointly reported that since April 1 they had rehired 7,000 men and women shopworkers. A partly seasonal drop in the charity load was reported.

The Union Continued   *July 6, 1933*

Tate's wife told her next-door neighbor, as she hung out the wash, that Dad was certainly going to make himself sick. He hadn't been home to sleep in two days. He couldn't eat. Men kept coming in while he sat at the dinner table talking union, union, union.

During the first weeks of July the C.L.U. building was a mad-

99

house. Every little corner, every cubbyhole was jammed with men laboriously signing their names to union cards. Lights burned all night long. The men from the six to twelve shift held department meetings after midnight. At seven o'clock, while the rest of Akron straggled out of bed, the midnight to six shift sat in organization meetings and counted up initiation fees.

In the great factories, foremen got the jitters and went to their noisy factory offices and sat down, trying to calm themselves. The men had gone crazy. It was like a revolution. It was like a religion. Guys who hadn't opened their mouths to squawk in the memory of the oldest foreman were leaving their machines and yelling, not whispering, to the next guy, "Join up. Join up."

The rubber factories were the town's nerve center. Two days after the union hit rubber, it hit the rest of Akron. Tate sat bleary-eyed and wild with excitement behind his desk at the C.L.U. answering the telephone.

"This is that bakery down on Elm Street," a voice would say. "We got all the fellows signed up in the union. What do we do next?"

"Bakery?" Tate would say. "Well, I guess you guys would belong to the bakers' union, if there is one. I'll look it up. Call me back."

At intervals Tate and McCartan sent desperate telegrams to the A. F. of L. national office in Washington. "Send us an organizer." They wrote letters explaining they didn't exactly know what to do next; they weren't professional organizers; everybody in Akron was joining unions. They asked, in their letters, was there a union for matchworkers? How about men who worked in a fishing tackle factory, what kind of union should they belong to? Their letters were never answered.

Although thousands and thousands of men joined unions the first weeks of July, the C.L.U. literally had no money. Men hanging around the hall chipped in to pay the telephone bill because the $2 initiation fee Tate was collecting like wildfire was shipped on, intact, to the American Federation of Labor.

Finally something had to be done. Tate and his friends simply couldn't run what had overnight turned into a monster labor movement. Tate went to Washintgon and saw William Green, president of the A. F. of L. Green said he was very, very surprised to hear that an organizer hadn't appeared yet. He would see about it. Tate hinted and finally said frankly that they desperately needed money—perhaps some of the $2 they were collecting. Green was gently shocked. The initiation fee belonged to the A. F. of L. However, he could offer Tate $30 apiece for every new charter the C.L.U. turned in. In a town where most of the workers were employed in three rubber shops, with a charter apiece, that seemed scarcely an overpowering offer.

But Tate went back to Akron heralding the coming for sure of an organizer. The $30 per charter allowed Tate and Wilson grocery money. They solemnly turned in their grocery bills for the records.

The union movement in Akron continued without stop, an industrial union movement for the simple reason that nobody had time to divide up the recruits by crafts. Indeed, the new union members would have resented bitterly any division in their own ranks. They were completely innocent of formal trade union experience. They knew the initials A. F. of L. stood for a national federation of unions. Beyond that, they knew nothing of union rules and regulations. The word jurisdiction was simply unheard of.

This July enthusiasm was innocent of other things beside A. F. of L. jurisdictional disputes. Night after night the rubberworkers met by departments at the C.L.U. Always the cry was "Join up." But nobody said what came after you joined. The rubberworkers believed, blindly, passionately, fiercely, that the union would cure all their troubles, end the speedup, make them rich with wages. They had no clear idea, and nobody told them, just how the union would accomplish these aims. Vaguely, they thought President Roosevelt might just order the rubber bosses to raise wages and quit the speedup. Some of them talked strike, but when they spoke about a strike, it was always something gay, like a picnic, a contest that you won right away without any trouble.

Indeed the first weeks of the new rubber union were something like a cross between a big picnic and a religious revival, except that under the surface ran the current of hunger and despair and poverty. The rubber barons themselves were uncertain and nervous. At any other time they would have tried to kill the union with firings and spies. Indeed, Goodyear did try just that, but the company suddenly backed down and the dismissed men were put back to work. The rubber company officials were frankly afraid of the N.R.A. They were afraid of the mood of their workers. Their spies told them that the factories were infested with wild men who talked about the union out loud at their machines. Anything could happen, the rubber officials told each other.

The Fallen Mighty   *July 7, 1933*

The Summit County Grand Jury indicted A. E. Albright, secretary of the Akron Savings and Loan Company, for perjury and forgery in connection with the defacement of school children's passbooks.

Mr. Albright, Sunday School teacher, pillar of the community, was the first of Akron's bankers formally accused by the Grand Jury. His indictment sold out newspaper extra editions and electrified West Hill.

The Akron Savings and Loan Company, like most Ohio saving societies, had months before the crash of First-Central stopped paying out depositors' accounts. The company was quite within the law, of course. But among the depositors of Mr. Albright's bank were hundreds upon hundreds of school children. These youngsters had been urged to buy thrift stamps at school in order to learn the value of a penny, the necessity of frugality, the satisfaction of accumulation. The school children were originally given passbooks that stated they could withdraw their little accounts at any time, with the written consent of their parents.

As the Depression deepened, Mr. Albright's bank woke up suddenly to the fact that hundreds of little boys and girls with $2 and $4 and $1 on deposit could come down and get their money any time they liked, unlike regular customers whose passbooks clearly stated the savings society could refuse to pay out funds when it chose. So, as the youngsters came in every week or so with their ten-cent and twenty-cent deposits, a teller stamped the back of their book with a rubber stamp. He didn't explain to them, because after all, they were too small to understand, that their passbook was being altered in a rather important way. For the stamp said that the bank had the right to withhold deposits.

One day, when a youngster decided to eschew the delights of accumulation for the even greater delight of buying a new pair of shoes, the bank regretfully informed him that it did not choose to pay out his account.

The Akron Savings and Loan Company's business relationships with its horde of small clients developed into quite a scandal. Mayor Sparks, sensing a good thing when he saw it, galloped into battle. He roared, with all the stops out, tremolo, that things had come to a pretty pass when little Johnny Jones, aged eight, who had been taught the value of saving his money, woke up one morning to discover that his $2.34, the fruits of two years of hard saving, had, for the time being, gone blooey. Mayor Sparks said, with some truth, that little Johnny was never going to have much faith in banks again. It would put a mark on his life. He would grow up to distrust bankers and probably wind up as a Communist.

Finally, the state banking department, prodded by Republican politicians, ordered the Akron Savings and Loan Company to pay Johnny Jones his $2.34. The bank replied with an injunction brought by a lady depositor restraining the savings society from dissipating the resources of the institution by paying out the school children's accounts.

Mr. Albright was now indicted for what the Grand Jury stated had been collusion in connection with the injunction. It was a popular indictment, in spite of Mr. Albright's long service as a Sunday School teacher. Akron thought freezing school children's accounts a bit thick.

But the indictment brought a cold shudder all over West Hill. Mr. Albright's bank was well known to be perfectly solvent, even if its accounts were frozen. If a solvent banker was indicted, what came next for the officials of that stupendously insolvent bank, the First-Central?

Workers at Babcox and Wilcox Company, a big Barberton factory, were said by company officials today to have indicated their preference for the brand-new company union over the recently organized A. F. of L. Federal union.

Thus, with a roll of drums and editorial applause from the local press, the company union entered the Akron labor situation. The phrase "company union" was still used by the factory officials, which indicated how new and undeveloped the device still was. Very soon, publicity men for the big factories would tear their hair at the very expression "company union," and the town's newspapers would dutifully term the new system "employee representation."

Akron was the home of the oldest and most elaborate company union in industrial history, the Goodyear Industrial Assembly. For years high-class magazine writers traveled out to Akron to do handsome pieces on Goodyear's "Industrial Republic." The Goodyear company union was the brain child of Paul Litchfield, now the president of the rubber organization.

There was some controversy over the precise reasons for the establishment of the famous Industrial Republic back in 1919. Mr. Litchfield said he set up the Industrial Assembly for the purest humanitarian reasons. Doubtlessly, he always looked upon his Industrial Assembly as a wise and honest system for the mutual benefit of workers and company.

But Goodyear had once, in 1913, been bothered by a brief I.W.W. strike. The strike didn't last long, and its back was broken by William Green, then a member of the Ohio Legislature, who raised a notable red scare. But the memory of that strike lingered in the minds of the Goodyear efficiency experts. From 1913 to 1919 Goodyear took various steps to insure itself against another strike. The company set up a sick fund system, a model of its kind, built a hospital for its workers, published a paper.

Then, in 1919, Mr. Litchfield announced his Industrial Assembly. It was nearly an exact duplicate of the national government. It had two houses, a Senate and a House of Representatives. It had an elaborate balloting system. The Industrial Assembly sat in handsome wood-paneled chambers high up in Goodyear Hall. Goodyear Hall itself was another step in the new approach to workers. Here was housed Goodyear university, here were club-rooms for free sewing lessons, a large theatre, and a big gymnasium.

When Mr. Litchfield announced his new Industrial Assembly in 1919, he spoke largely of the necessity of "Americanizing" foreign-born workers (although most of his workmen had ancestors who fought in the Revolutionary War), of giving workers a voice in industrial management. He also said, "Today, unfortunately, many people in this country are getting together in groups and classes and demanding what they want and deliberately holding up the country to pay tribute to their demands." He added, "If a condition of that sort was allowed to obtain in this country, we would have conditions bordering closely on those existing in Russia today."

Union leaders in Akron always stated that Mr. Litchfield's Industrial Assembly was less a humanitarian program than a device to forestall genuine organization in Goodyear. Both sides in the controversy used the same source book, a history of the Industrial Assembly.

Goodyear said of the Assembly, "It does not set up two hostile groups, at swords' points and at arm's length, demanding, making reluctant concessions—but men working together for the general good."

"That's exactly what we mean," union leaders echoed, and added, "Anybody who thinks that a tirebuilder and Mr. Litchfield have anything in common simply hasn't been a tirebuilder."

The Industrial Assembly's record spread over the years. In 1920 the first assembly got an East Akron branch of the public library, improved the streetcar service, and passed a factory rule that overtime should be on a daily, not weekly, basis. The 1927 Assembly set up a new sick plan, called the Hospital Association, which provided hospitalization for Goodyear workers at considerably reduced rates. Later assemblies saved the Goodyear vacation plan for workers with five years of service from Depression cuts.

Goodyear said proudly, in 1933, that its Industrial Assembly allowed its workers a genuine voice in management and gave them machinery to arbitrate grievances. Union leaders said sourly, "Well, your company union has been working since 1920. The speedup is something awful and wages are a crime. How about that?"

Curiously, while Goodyear spent thousands of dollars on its Goodyear Hall, its university, its Industrial Republic, Firestone and Goodrich followed their competitor's lead in only the most half-hearted way. No Industrial Republic ever blossomed in South Akron and Harvey Firestone made no flowery speeches about allowing factory hands a voice in the government of the factory. Then, suddenly, in July, 1933, the high-priced company lawyers said they didn't see why something like Mr. Litchfield's company union would not satisfy the demands of Section 7A in the N.R.A.

Overnight, Akron sprouted brand new company unions, hastily and pretty crudely set up. The Firestone Employees Conference Plan had none of the Goodyear frills. The factory officials sat boldly in the same room with the committeemen while they "deliberated." There was no limit set on the extra pay committeemen received, while Goodyear had long since worked out a system of extra pay for delegates to the Industrial Assembly that didn't, on the surface, look so frankly like a bribe. The Goodrich company union went the Firestone system one better by openly passing out money to workers on the factory council. Goodrich paid its company union officials at a monthly rate—$15 for a delegate, $20 to the chairman of a committee, and $30 a month to general chairmen. Firestone committeemen were paid by the hour, at their average earning rate plus ten per cent.

The Industrial Republic had flourished in lonely magnificence in Akron for years, but with the birth of the union movement and the passage of clause 7A in the N.R.A., company unions sprang up until every rubber factory, big or small, every little machine shop and store suddenly sported a brand-new system of "employee representation."

The employers of Akron said they wanted their workers to have a voice in the management of their corporations.

Just after eight o'clock this morning, Akron's full force of postmen ceremoniously marched down the new post-office steps carrying the N.R.A. code agreement cards and the N.R.A. Blue Eagle signs. Before the day was out, most of Akron's thousands of small shopkeepers, all the big department stores, the wholesale hardware offices, and the newspapers had been served with their N.R.A. marching orders. The big drive was on.

Hysteria swept over the city. Slumbering in the terrible doldrums of depression and hunger, Akron was prodded into frenzied response to the greatest program of propaganda unleashed since the War.

Precisely like the old draft board, a local N.R.A. Compliance Committee was set up, its members the very "best" people in town. Mr. Litchfield and Hugh A. Galt, Vice-President of the Columbia Chemical Division of the Pittsburgh Plate Glass Company, were appointed on the national N.R.A. board from Akron.

The newspapers "co-operated" at first wholeheartedly with the N.R.A. drive. The *Beacon Journal* turned up with an eagle in blue ink on its masthead, and overworked reporters were dazed when they actually were ordered onto a five-day week. Very little precise understanding of the National Recovery Act existed in Akron. Small shopkeepers were told that until their industry code was drafted they had to put their employees on a five-day forty-hour week and pay at least a $13 minimum wage. In return, they hung a blue eagle sign in their window.

All over town, department store clerks and grocery boys, doctors' assistants and bus drivers went on the five-day week. Blue eagles blossomed in every store front. Every Boy Scout in Akron was drafted for a great consumer campaign, and the youthful patriots, in full regalia, toured every street in the city pushing, "I will co-operate" cards at housewives. Blue eagles thereupon turned up in front windows, reminding people of the "I have given" signs during the War. Details of code signings in Washington filled newspaper columns. General Hugh Johnson, the N.R.A. national head man, became an overnight hero.

"General Johnson, Akron's chief recovery hope, enemy of depression, celebrates 51st birthday," a headline in the *Beacon Journal* ran, during the top of the N.R.A. hysteria.

While small shopkeepers struggled to meet the N.R.A. General Code standards, the rubber companies wrangled endlessly in Washington over the new tire code. Thousands of little merchants in Akron were bullied into paying their clerks a half decent wage while the tire companies deliberated throughout the whole summer.

But in Akron few remarked this surprising contrast during the last days of July and the hysterical month of August. The N.R.A. was a big propaganda success. People believed, for the moment, that it would cure the Depression by lowering working hours and improving wages. The desperate town turned to it, blue eagle and all, with a kind of superstitious frenzy.

And in the rubber shops, the tirebuilders talked endlessly, not of blue eagles, but of Section 7A.

The Union Continued   *August 2, 1933*

Coleman C. Claherty came into town today to take over his job as official A. F. of L. organizer for the rubber industry.

The first thing he did was to rent a neat office in a downtown bank building, install a carpet and a big desk, and hire Wilmer Tate as an assistant organizer. Then he settled down to bring order out of what he considered confusion.

Coleman Claherty was so perfect an example of the usual A. F. of L. field organizer that he was very nearly a caricature. He was a well-fed, rather handsome man in his middle forties, with thick, iron-gray hair. He dressed neatly, as becomes a respectable citizen, in expensive ties and matching socks. He was an expert orator. He addressed a union meeting precisely as a politician addressed an election crowd. He roared like a bull, or let his voice drop away to an impressive whisper. In private, he had a shrewd, rather cynical manner of buttonholing local union leaders.

This A. F. of L. organizer started his labor career in the great steel strike of 1919. He worked for William Z. Foster during that heartbreaking struggle, but when the steel companies broke the strike with guns, Claherty and Foster took different paths. Foster turned to the Communist Party, Claherty threw in his lot with William Green. During the 1920's, Claherty roamed the country settling jurisdictional disputes, collecting dues, watching A. F. of L. membership drop. He was a faithful follower of the Green tradition, deploring the notion of class struggle, mouthing phrases about co-operation between capital and labor.

Claherty came from the doldrums of A. F. of L. interunion squabbles into the heart of a great folk movement. Rubberworkers joined the union in hundreds and thousands, expecting the new organization would end the unbearable speedup and send them home every week with enough to feed their families. The fever of the N.R.A. swept the whole town with hope and a wild determination to change things, to put an end to the fearful years when every other man and his children starved. Claherty said he was sitting on top of a volcano.

Getting down to work, the first thing to do, Claherty said, was to separate the machinists and the carpenters and the electricians, and so on, from the Federal locals. Nobody questioned the great Claherty. The rubber machinists dutifully joined the machinists' union, the electricians obediently paid dues to the electricians' union, the carpenters docilely signed up with the carpenters' local. Curiously, though, the machinists and the electricians kept coming to the Federal local meetings. Claherty could never make them understand they were supposed to stay away, supposed to belong to a separate union. He could never teach them that their interests were different from the common ordinary rubberworker. Stubbornly and stupidly, they clung to the Federal locals. Sometimes the backwardness of rubberworkers who just couldn't seem to understand what a craft union was, infuriated even such a cool and experienced A. F. of L. organizer as Coleman Claherty.

The next thing to remember, Claherty said, after the division of the Federal locals into crafts, was the slogan, "Not so fast," or, as Claherty liked to put it, "Rome wasn't built in a day." In this case, Rome was the conquering of the speedup and the upping of wages. Time and again Claherty spoke at Federal local meetings to packed crowds of wildly cheering rubberworkers. He started off by denouncing the rubber bosses in no uncertain terms. This part of his speech always brought down the house. He certainly could sail into Harvey Firestone. The second half of his speech wasn't quite so popular. He recommended caution. He said, Wait, wait, the National Government is moving fast. We must string along with the President. Rome, Claherty always jovially wound up, wasn't built in a day.

While Claherty talked about Rome, the union movement in Akron swept on around and behind and above him. Claherty and his staff were hardly union organizers. They were clerks. The unions grew practically by themselves and Claherty and his office staff worked night and day just recording the names of new locals and collecting their dues. Before August was out, there were 12,-000 union members in Akron. On June 1 there had been fewer than three hundred.

Roof Over Your Head   *August 11, 1933*

The Home Owners Loan office opened for business. Before seven o'clock the line waiting at the doors of the new office stretched double file down North Main Street for three blocks. When the guard finally unlocked the doors, five hundred anxious homeowners pressed fiercely into the little lobby, frantically eager to sign their applications for Federal relief from mortgage foreclosure.

Akron was a city of homeowners. Forty-eight per cent of the private dwellings in the city were owned at least in part by the occupants. Most of these private dwellings were little five-room frame houses with a sagging front porch. Eleven per cent of the houses privately owned had a resale value of less than $2,000; 25.8 per cent had a resale value of less than $3,000 and more than $2,000; 30.1 per cent were valued between $3,000 and $3,999. In other words, 66.9 per cent of all the houses privately owned in Akron had a resale value of less than $4,000.

So now these little people, the sixty-six per cent whose houses were worth less than $4,000 on the open market, lined up in front of the Federal Home Owners Loan office. The first day many interesting dramas were played right out on the sidewalk in front of the plate-glass windows of the new offices. Newspaper photographers were able to catch authentic pictures of old ladies fainting in the hot sun, of half-starved men crying in public because they thought they had a chance to keep their homes.

Most of those in the endless line which all day long and all the next day and for weeks after that stood patiently in the hot sun waiting their chance to tell their story did not precisely understand the operation of the Home Owners Loan Corporation. They did not understand, for instance, that the bank which held the mortgage on their property had to agree to taking H.O.L.C. bonds for the debt. Lots of the banks were pretty stubborn about that. They preferred to foreclose and hold the little frame houses for a rise in land values. Then the homeowners didn't understand that the Government could be as fierce a creditor as any bank.

But on this first day in August, no doubts touched the minds of Akron's homeowners who stood so hopefully in the broiling sun. Roosevelt was saving their homes. There was still justice somewhere, and life was looking up.

Fly in the Ointment   *August 13, 1933*

The employees of the Babcox and Wilcox Company held a mass meeting today to protest the wage cuts which followed the adoption of the N.R.A. code by the management.

Interesting Figures   *August 17, 1933*

The conservator of The First-Central Trust Company filed with the courts today certain figures which proved very interesting to the city of Akron. Some of the statistics filed as a matter of court record were:

That officers and directors of the First-Central were listed for loans from the defunct bank totaling $3,376,583;

That notes amounting to $2,584,920 had been charged off as complete losses by the First-Central;

That the First-Central wrote down notes to the amount of

111

$1,693,850. Bank officers owed $370,690 of the amount written down;

That unsecured loans totaling $595,908 were made to bank officers.

Socko   *August 22, 1933*

The Grand Jury indicted six bankers, all except one officers of The First-Central Trust Company, charging misapplication of funds. The sixth indicted gentleman was already serving time for an earlier indiscretion.

The news broke late on a hot afternoon. Newsboys appeared on Main Street screaming as they raced to their corners with their still wet extras, "Hey! He-e-e-ey! Six bankers put in jail! Six bankers pinched!"

The newsboys anticipated the story. The thick black headlines only reported indictments. But the screams of the excited youngsters filled Main Street and drowned out the rattling streetcars. Men tore out of cigar stores to grab a paper. Girls clerking in little stocking shops rushed to put their three pennies in the fist of a newsboy and walk slowly away reading.

Akron rejoiced grimly. The big shots, the guys who had ridden so high, wide, and handsome, were about to get theirs. The only place in town where the cry "Bankers Pinched!" didn't bring solid satisfaction was West Hill.

Drastic Action   *August 25, 1933*

Mayor Sparks, over the fearful howls of his own Republican party, and against the vigorous advice of leading businessmen and the Chamber of Commerce, rushed into print today with a demand, not a proposal, that the city of Akron pass a $7,000,000 bond issue in the fall elections for work relief. The Federal Government, he explained, would supply additional funds for work relief projects.

The harassed Mayor, who had been filling the air with Cassandra cries for more than a year, now stepped forward with some blood-chilling figures to give the town pause.

The City of Akron, Mayor Sparks roared, was feeding 6,800 heads of families and their dependents. He added:

"In Summit County, which means Greater Akron, relief authorities are supporting 11,000 heads of families and their children and wives.

"Approximately 25,000 heads of families, or about 100,000 persons out of a population of 300,000, are without employment or dependent on persons without employment, and are being supported either by the public relief authorities or by their friends and families."

These appalling figures, Mayor Sparks said, were computed for a Government report.

The Mayor added that naturally he was against any further bond issues since the City of Akron was already unable to carry its debt load. "But," he said bitterly, "could we visualize two years ago that thousands would walk our streets during the last year and a half and beg for work, with as many begging for work today and none in sight? . . .

"The present humiliating character-breaking method of doling out life's necessities should not be permitted to continue indefinitely in Akron," Mayor Sparks wound up.

Thirteen Thousand   *September 2, 1933*

A total of 13,033 homeowners filed applications for a government homeowner's loan during the period from August 11 to August 31, officials announced today. Applications are still pouring in fast.

The Union Continued   *September 4, 1933*

Labor Day was breathlessly hot. The sun melted the asphalt covering the brick pavements. Men stood on street corners in shirt sleeves, holding seersucker coat jackets and mopping red faces with big handkerchiefs.

William Green, president of the American Federation of Labor, drove into town with his family. Governor White arrived in a big limousine. Mr. Green was, in spite of the heat, in an affable, expansive mood. His wife and daughters and daughters-in-law and sons clustered around him as he talked to reporters at the Portage Hotel. Carefully dressed, his bland, round face shining with sweat, his mild eyes watering a little behind his glasses, Mr. Green looked and talked like a rather prosperous generous-minded businessman.

Mr. Green came out for the local Community Fund drive. He said labor should support it. He came out for the N.R.A. and President Roosevelt. Governor White, a rich politician from downstate Ohio, also came out for President Roosevelt and the Community Fund. Governor White was a Democrat.

Mr. Green was introduced, during the morning, to the Akron labor leaders. He carefully shook the hands of a dozen rubberworkers, greeted Tate pleasantly. Then he sent everybody away and talked for some time to Coleman Claherty. Governor White shook the hands of assorted Democratic leaders.

A little after one o'clock Tate went down to the armory to check over the last-minute arrangements. The hall was already filling up. At two o'clock the place was jammed. The basement was crowded for the loudspeaker overflow meeting. At two-thirty, the grass patches outside the armory were obscured by rubberworkers standing patiently in the blistering hot sun. Nearly six thousand rubberworkers packed the armory and the armory basement and the armory lawn. When William Green arose to speak, the rubberworkers cheered furiously, cheered until a pleasant, slightly self-conscious smile hovered on Mr. Green's face, cheered until he lifted a hand, like a preacher calling for prayer, to stop the frantic noise.

Mr. Green's speech brought a lot more cheers. Mr. Green spoke ecstatically of the N.R.A. He said Section 7A was labor's Bible. He thundered his praise for President Roosevelt. He attacked the current layoffs at the rubber shops. Mr. Green's rather high-pitched voice rose to an angry crescendo when he got around to denouncing the cutthroat competition in the rubber industry. He deplored price cuts and he shouted that ruthless vicious competition hurt stockholders as well as labor.

Mr. Green's speech was slightly disappointing to Tate and other people from the new rubber unions. They had hoped that Mr. Green might say something about what to do next after you have started to organize. But apparently Mr. Green felt it was enough to tell rubberworkers to trust in the N.R.A.

Mr. Green and Governor White attended a banquet after the armory meeting and then all the celebrities left town feeling pleased and satisfied. Next day the *Beacon Journal* ran a nice editorial praising Mr. Green's speech.

Education   *September 9, 1933*

Superintendent Gosling, addressing the assembled Akron teachers the day before schools opened, lectured the instructors on "the spirit of education under the New Deal." He asked the teachers to "adopt their organizations to the spirit and letter of the N.R.A."

The Other Side Talks   *September 11, 1933*

Paul Litchfield, President of Goodyear, sidled into print today with a plaintive statement defending the current crop of rubber company layoffs. The *Beacon Journal*, Congressman Harter, the union officials, the Mayor and other notables had been sniping away at the rubber industry for the past two weeks. Now Mr. Litchfield had his say.

"I deplore," said the President of The Goodyear Tire and Rubber Company, world's largest rubber company, "the growing tendency to place the rubber industry and rubber executives in the 'public enemies' class."

Mr. Litchfield said he was sorry about the layoffs, but he explained that production was slumping from its summer peaks. During the August peak, Mr. Litchfield said, Goodyear employed 15,994, which was 6,000 more than on April 1. The layoffs totaled about 1,200 from the August peak.

Mr. Litchfield was also very indignant, he said, about loose statements made in newspapers on the subject of sweatshop wages at Goodyear. The average earnings of Goodyear employees stood at seventy-five cents per hour, thirteen cents higher than on April 1.

Mr. Litchfield did not comment on charges made by critics about the speedup at Goodyear.

Surprise   *September 13, 1933*

Mayor C. Nelson Sparks had an unpleasant little surprise today. The worthy Mayor had decided not to waste his time and money running in the non-partisan mayoralty primaries. Instead, he planned to collect petition signatures and thus get on the ballot in the easier way.

His petitions were ruled out by political enemies on the local Board of Elections. The Mayor could not run for a second term. The local Republican party was appalled and went off into corners to have a good cry. The Republican scheme to let two Democrats win the primaries, split the party, and then enter Mayor Sparks at the last minute by petition was drastically foiled. Horse laughs were heard all over town, especially from the Democratic party campaign headquarters.

Dismissed   *September 15, 1933*

The indictment charging Sterling B. Cramer, the man from Chicago brought in to save the failing bank, with misapplication of funds was dismissed today by Judge Carl Hoyt. Mr. Cramer, with a new and good job with a Cincinnati bank, wiped the dust of Akron from his feet forever.

To the fury and embarrassment of the rubber moguls, now becoming thoroughly troubled by the steady march of the union into the rubber shops, the United States Bureau of Labor Statistics unleashed a ten-year report today on the rubber industry.

The report, a thick document studded with figures, put into solid type what every tirebuilder knew through his own experience. Laconically, impassively, the Government report rolled out the figures that showed beyond any shadow of doubt that the rubberworker was sweating blood to earn his daily bread.

The bulky document covered the rubber industry from 1922 to 1931. That fact alone startled even the average tirebuilder. Everybody working in a rubber shop knew that from 1931 to 1933 the speedup in Akron was pushed up frantically by factory managers to meet the demand for lower production costs. Many a big husky mountaineer had worked in the rubber shops all through the twenties, well through 1931 before he began to feel the dreadful weight of the rawhiding system on his back and kidneys and in his very soul.

The Government report said that between 1921 and 1931 the poundage output per man in the rubber industry tripled. That figure was the most important one in the big heavy document, for poundage output, not number of tires, is the most exact measure of a man's work in a rubber shop.

The report put the same fact, the fact of the speedup, another way. From 1921 to 1931 there was an actual increase of 21,393,000 tires produced per year. Presumably this vast increase in production should have required the employment of many more workers. Actually, 7,155 fewer workers were employed in the industry which produced 21,000,000 more tires.

The Government estimated that 42,691 workers were eliminated by the rubber industry from 1921 to 1931.

The figures on the weight output per man told the story better, however, than any other comments in words or graphs the Government could make. Starting with an index figure of 100 in 1914, the weight output per man rose to 250.56 in 1922; to 506.25 in 1929.

117

Then came the real push in the rubber shops. Between 1929 and 1930 the index of weight output per man increased to 581.03. Between 1930 and 1931 the index rose more than 100 points, to 681.05. There the report stopped, but the rubberworker knew that from 1931 to 1932, and from 1932 to 1933 the weight output went up, not steadily, but furiously.

Of course, and the Government report gravely noted this, part of the increase in output per man was due to vastly improved machinery. Every rubber company spent millions of dollars on new machinery, employed whole corps of engineers to perfect labor-saving devices. During the twenties, work in the pit, for instance, was changed from back-breaking manual labor to the operation of hydraulic lifts. The rubber companies never stopped saying that the increased output per man was due to improved machinery.

But no one, least of all the rubberworker, believed that any really important part of the fabulously increased poundage production per man was accounted for by the new factory equipment.

Akron called the increased production the speedup. The Government said it in figures. East and South Akron said, "It ain't human."

Defendant Acquitted   *September 30, 1933*

A. E. Albright, first banker in Akron to go on trial, was acquitted today amid the polite cheers of a courtroom filled with West Hill sympathizers. Mr. Albright, the Sunday School teacher secretary of the Akron Savings and Loan Company, was found not guilty of perjury and fraud in connection with the alteration of school children's passbooks.

Mr. Albright's acquittal stunned Main Street and East Akron. Nobody this year could believe a banker innocent of anything. Angry rumors spread over town, and men shook their fists in the general direction of the Summit County common pleas courts and the county prosecutor. Meanwhile, West Hill clapped hands and all but danced in the streets. Mr. Albright's acquittal was taken as a good omen and the First-Central bankers waiting trial heaved sighs of relief.

Halfway

The hysterical campaign to get signatures of 90,000 First-Central Trust Company depositors for the new bank reorganization plan reached the halfway point today.

After months of argument and backbiting and trips to Washington, Akron businessmen had finally worked out a bank opening plan that had the reluctant approval of Federal authorities and the blessing of a promised loan from the R.F.C. to make a twenty per cent payoff on depositors' accounts.

The bank plan, which nobody understood very well, was enthusiastically endorsed by both Akron newspapers. The public was urged in full-page ads and editorials to rush down and sign its consent to the new plan. "Get the Bank Open at Any Cost!" Akron businessmen shouted over the radio, in the newspapers.

Victory Parade

The downtown streets filled slowly, a little after six o'clock, with people dressed in their best, wearing little red, white, and blue N.R.A. buttons, carrying babies. At seven, an hour before the scheduled start of the great N.R.A. "Victory" parade, the sidewalks on Main Street were quite impassable. People stood pressed stomach to backs, shoulder to shoulder, waving little American flags and comforting already tired children. Streetcars and busses had long since stopped running. Police worked frantically. Motorcycle cops worried the thick crowds like dogs herding sheep.

It was a fine October night, and the bunting on the electric light and telephone poles stirred in a slight breeze. A sound truck alternately playing popular records and shouting, "Keep back, please, please. You will be hurt. Keep back there, lady," drove up and down the cleared space on the streetcar tracks. Roars of laughter swept over whole blocks as a little dog would venture out into the street. Girls leaning out of office building windows let torn-up paper flutter to the sidewalks and boys on the street below shouted up greetings and dares to come down.

At last with a great blare of brassy music, with the nervous compelling noises of a band playing "The Stars and Stripes Forever," the parade started. The firemen, the policemen, the Ohio National Guard, the president of the Chamber of Commerce, and Conrad H. Mann of Kansas City, an official of the fraternal order of the Eagles, led the march.

For nearly three hours, Akron's most colorful and surprising parade poured past 150,000 people. Every high school, grammar school, fraternal order, and veterans' band in the city made music of a sort. Every motorcycle and sound truck in town turned up to make more racket. Every business concern was represented by a float followed by dozens and sometimes hundreds of sheepish workers who trotted along on the hard pavement not quite sure why they marched. Most of the more astute corporations in town seized the happy chance to do a little advertising. Bakery companies entered floats with big "Buy So and So doughnuts" signs and rather smaller N.R.A. insignia.

The entire body of Akron schoolteachers marched. No excuse except practically fatal illness was accepted by the determined superintendent of schools and 1,200 young women in high heels trotted dutifully along the city streets, each carrying a small flag. The American Legion in natty brass hats paraded along smartly. Floats went by with dummies labeled "N.R.A. chiseler" lying apparently dead. A slowly rolling beer company float served free beer.

A municipal float pleaded for the passage of the public works bonds, and behind it, in solemn order, marched hundreds of unemployed carrying home-made crudely lettered signs reading, "Give us a chance. We want a job."

The crowd greeted most of the parade with noisy hilarity, and all but mobbed the beer truck. Pimply youths threw spitballs at band drum majors. But near the end of the parade came a group of marchers the sideline watchers greeted with solemn and loud cheers and hoarse cries of encouragement.

For the rubber unions made their first public appearance in the N.R.A. parade and, nearly 5,000 strong, paraded slowly and a little self-consciously before the town. The union men carried no signs and kept no great order. Wearing their best suits, with felt hats and gay neckties, the rubbermen kept close together behind brand-new banners. "Goodyear Federal Local," one said, and Goodrich and Firestone and Mohawk and Seiberling followed. From the sidelines men yelled, "Attaboy, Goodyear. Give it to them, boys!" The marchers nodded grave acknowledgments to the sidewalks.

"Ahm for yew!" people yelled, and sometimes the union men yelled back, the rich mountaineer accents rolling over the crowds, "Jine up. Jine up."

The first appearance of the rubber unions was a bad shock to company officials. While the rest of Akron got splendidly drunk and stayed up half the night celebrating, factory managers went home to West Hill feeling jittery and depressed. Next day everybody agreed the N.R.A. parade had been a colossal success. The *Beacon Journal* story began, "Not since the Armistice." The hilarity and excitement lasted around town for days. Speakeasies did a rushing business. It took nearly a week for the town to wake up and ask, "What was the celebration about?"

All Rise, This Honorable Court   *October 16, 1933*

Four First-Central bankers charged with misapplication of funds went on trial today. The fifth was not brought from his cell in Atlanta to face the new charges.

In These Times   *October 17, 1933*

Selection of a jury to try the four First-Central bankers proceeded with maddening slowness.

Defense attorney Frank Rockwell said, "In these times there is a widespread brooding prejudice against anyone connected with the banks. We are making a lengthy inquiry into the feelings of the prospective jurors because we are seeking a fair and impartial hearing."

The Campaign   *October 18, 1933*

"Honest Ike" Myers, aged 72, and J. Earl Cox, a Sunday School teacher who kept trained skunks, began a hot campaign for the Mayor's office. Mr. Myers, a somewhat enfeebled old man whose chief interest in life for years had been the Izaak Walton Fishing League, posed for pictures with his fishing rod. Mr. Cox told reporters all about his Sunday School record.

War   *October 30, 1933*

Mayor C. Nelson Sparks declared "war" on Akron gangsters today.

The Union Continued   *November 4, 1933*

Wilmer Tate proudly announced that union membership in Summit County had gone to 30,000 on November 1.

All during the month of October workingmen poured into the unions. More than forty Federal charters had been granted in Summit County, although of course the bulk of the new union membership was in the rubber shops. Goodrich local alone had more than 7,000 and Firestone and Goodyear were not far behind.

Every week union meetings, held usually on Sunday, were packed to the rafters. A curious parade of speakers appeared at the rubber locals. Congressmen, vaguely liberal lawyers, editors, thundered over and over again about the New Deal and President Roosevelt.

Coleman Claherty kept his finger in the pie of every important Federal local in Summit County. He gave an interview, carefully stating that there was "nothing radical, and no Communism" in the union movement. He supervised the selection of a slogan for

the Goodrich local banner and eventually the hall sported a great
rectangular flag reading, "Goodrich Federal Local Number 18319,
Where Labor and Capital Meet."

Claherty estimated that about sixty per cent of the workers in
the rubber industry now belonged to Federal or craft locals, and
rubber moguls did not rise in fury to dispute his claim.

"Honest Ike" Wins   *November 8, 1933*

"Honest Ike" Myers was elected Mayor today in one of the
smallest municipal election votes ever cast. He beat Mr. Cox by
7,649 votes. The public work relief bonds carried on the ballot.

Prohibition repeal won in Ohio and nearly every other state.

Justice   *November 10, 1933*

The four First-Central bankers were acquitted today by a Common Pleas court jury. The verdict of not guilty was read to a
wildly cheering courtroom, jammed with bankers' wives and
daughters and their Junior League friends. County Prosecutor
Ray B. Watters joined in congratulating the acquitted bankers.

Insult to Injury   *November 13, 1933*

A corn sugar war broke out on top of the current slot machine
battle. A bomb explosion which by chance killed nobody marked
the opening of hostilities on the corn sugar front. Mayor Sparks
pulled himself together and told newspapermen his war on gangsters was still going strong, but apparently the Mayor's heart
wasn't in his latest manifesto.

White Death   *November 15, 1933*

The heaviest snowfall in the history of the city blanketed Akron
today with soft white misery. Busses and streetcars stopped, auto-

mobiles stalled in the main streets, and all through the city the poor struggled desperately to keep warm. Hundreds of miserable shivering unemployed jammed the relief office begging coal.

C.W.A. *November 16, 1933*

Mayor Sparks announced that 8,834 jobs would be available at once on the new C.W.A. relief projects. Rate of pay was scheduled at forty-seven cents an hour for a thirty-hour week, or $14.10 a week.

The laconic announcement stirred East and South Akron to fury and despair. For weeks the unemployed had anticipated the passage of the public works bonds and the beginning of a large-scale work-relief program.

Since according to the rules only one wage earner in a family could be employed on public works, a family on relief, must, willy-nilly, exist on $14.10 a week. Fuel and food costs were going up and a bitter winter was just setting in. Children needed clothing for school. In the face of all this, a family of five or even six and seven and eight must live on $14.10 a week.

The Unemployed Councils rallied the slum districts of Akron to the battle cry, "Make Home Relief give supplementary donations to C.W.A. families."

Instrument for Fraud *November 27, 1933*

The bank reorganization plan was approved by the Common Pleas bench five to one. Judge Walter B. Wanamaker wrote a sizzling dissent.

The scheme for liquidating First-Central and opening a new national bank came before the court with the signatures of ninety per cent of the depositors of the old bank.

Judge Wanamaker's dissent pointed out that the court hearing on the plan was held after, not before, the campaign to get signatures from depositors. He suggested that if facts brought out in the court hearing had been published during the hysterical cam-

124

paign to get depositors to sign their approval of reorganization, the number of signatures collected might have been different.

The new bank plan, Judge Wanamaker said with cold sarcasm while the reorganization lawyers squirmed, allowed payment of double liability on bank stock to be deferred just past the constitutional limit for prosecution of persons who had fraudulently transferred stock during the weeks when the bank was failing.

Judge Wanamaker also commented that while a small depositor would have to wait for years for the full payoff on his account, a large depositor could offset his account against debts to the bank at one hundred per cent of the account value. Thus if a man owed First-Central $10,000 on a loan, and had a deposit of $8,000, he could offset the loan with his account and wind up owing only $2,000.

Warming up, Judge Wanamaker pointed out that the price of stock in the new bank for sale to stockholders in the old was set at an arbitrary price. The price should be fair, he thundered.

The courtroom listened nervously while Judge Wanamaker read his blistering opinion. The Judge wound up, "This plan has become an instrument for fraud."

The lawyers in the courtroom and the businessmen didn't really need to worry, however. Judge Wanamaker's dissenting opinion was printed in six point type back by the advertisements in the town newspapers. The community, bored by columns of type and unable to read through pages of technical details, was more or less unaware that a judge of the Common Pleas Court had said, in so many words, that the depositors of The First-Central Trust Company were being royally gypped by the same men whose slight errors had shut down the bank and lost everyone's money.

Good News, Maybe   *December 1, 1933*

The Firestone Tire and Rubber Company announced a net profit, for the year ending October 31, of $2,397,059. While a two-million-dollar profit looked like chicken feed to the gentlemen who owned the big yellow-brick rubber fortress in South

125

Akron, the announcement brought an uneasy stir to the rubber valley. The union picked up new members.

Sensation   *December 9, 1933*

Mary Pickford sued Douglas Fairbanks for divorce amid a welter of sighs from the female population of Akron.

The Union Continued   *December 11, 1933*

Goodyear Federal local had the largest meeting of its history. Congressman Dow Harter addressed the overflow crowd of hundreds on "The Meaning of the New Deal." Coleman Claherty also spoke. "Rome wasn't built in a day," he said.

New Prophet   *December 12, 1933*

Father Coughlin, the Roman Catholic radio priest, broke into Akron newspapers for the first time.

For weeks his Sunday afternoon political sermons had been attracting growing attention. Workers listened with increasing eagerness to his "fearless" attacks on Wall Street bankers and approved his extravagant praise of President Roosevelt.

The Akron newspapers printed a feature story about the stout little priest. The *Beacon Journal* asked in big type, "Is the Detroit Radio Priest a New Savonarola?" It was a question which did not interest Akron in the least, since most of the population, Southern mountain-born, had never heard of that fiery Italian martyr.

No one in town except the local branch of the Communist Party raised the question, "Is Father Coughlin a Fascist?" Later on, this problem would be popular street talk, but Father Coughlin was still something new under the sun, a Roman Catholic whose opinions were seriously considered in Akron.

An Opinion   *December 17, 1933*

"I feel that the real harm from capitalism as it affects labor has come from anonymous capital and not from the widely known capitalists. For example, men like my father, John D. Rockefeller, and Henry Ford believe in aiding those who work for them. They live for service and really are altruistic about it."— Russell Firestone, in an interview in the *Beacon Journal.*

No Rejoicing   *December 19, 1933*

A muttering crowd filled the lobby of The First-Central Trust Company. Persons with $40 or less on deposit were being paid $10 on their accounts.

The long lines of quiet dark-faced men and women curled around the marble counters. Clerks worked rapidly, handing out $10 bills and stamping the frayed old passbooks. Nobody said "Thank you" to the tellers. The rows of desks for vice-presidents were empty. The vice-presidents of the new bank were upstairs, and the vice-presidents of the old were resting up from their trials.

Reporters and photographers arrived early and tried to get pictures of happy citizens grinning over their crisp new ten-dollar bills. "Smile," said a little black-haired photographer to a shabby man standing at the teller's window.

"What for?" the man growled.

"I'll bet you're going to buy Christmas presents with that ten bucks," a reporter said with false cheerfulness to a solid old lady on her way out.

"I am NOT," the old lady snapped. "They turned my gas off this morning, and I'm going to try to get it turned back on."

"Oh," said the reporter, and did not write it down on his notepaper.

Part of the crowd had come out of hope rather than understanding. Men with passbooks reading $320 or $162 stood at the tellers' windows begging for a $10 advance. They held up the long sullen lines pleading for a "little something" right now.

127

Their voices cracked with fear. The clerks kept repeating, "Only depositors with $40 or less in their accounts will be paid today."

A man with $41.50 marked on his passbook burst into hysterical tears. He kept shouting, as the harassed bank guards led him away, "I gotta have some dough. Jesus Christ, we're going to have to go on relief if I can't get some dough."

A homely girl with pimples and mild blue eyes stood patiently in line for more than an hour. When her turn came, she pushed a check for $9.23 under the window bars. The clerk shoved it back.

"It was my week's pay, and then the bank closed," the girl said patiently, not moving away, "so maybe now I can get some money on it?"

"No, no," the clerk snapped. "Only depositors today. Later on."

The girl did not move away. She started again slowly. "You see, I work in a grocery store, only now it is closed, but they paid us every Saturday and that Saturday when I went to get the money, I couldn't get it because the bank was closed. So I thought now . . ."

"No," the teller rasped. "No, no, not now. Later maybe."

The girl kept standing close beside the window, but now the next in line shoved his passbook around her shoulder. The clerk reached past her to hand out the $10. The girl kept standing silently by while three more depositors came and went and then she leaned her pimply face in through the bars and said, "You see we got paid on Saturdays . . ."

"No," shouted the clerk, his nerves frayed by the procession of sullen faces passing before him. The bank guard sidled up and took the homely girl by the arm. She went quietly away.

New Era, Maybe   *December 20, 1933*

The N.R.A. code for the rubber industry was finally signed today after nearly six months of bitter wrangling. Both local newspapers said it ushered in a new era.

The code was guaranteed to end the ruinous tire price war. It provided a forty-cent minimum wage for workers in the industry, a thirty-six-hour week, and a $14 weekly minimum, slightly under the C.W.A. wage.

The tire code was blessed in public statements by presidents of the big rubber corporations and denounced, somewhat late to be sure, by Coleman Claherty.

Christmas   *December 25, 1933*

Nobody in Akron pretended, this year, that all the little children in the city were warm and happy Christmas Day. The holiday was celebrated with appropriate hilarity on West Hill.

First Statement   *December 30, 1933*

Mayor "Honest Ike" Myers made his first official statement slightly in advance of taking office.

"Drunks," the aged white-mustached mayor-elect quavered to the press, "should be taken home by the police and not locked up in City Jail. Taking a man to jail ruins his self-respect, and when a man loses that, he loses all."

The Glad New Year   *January 1, 1934*

Not a single great man of Akron made a happy prediction for the year of 1934.

Honest Ike   *January 10, 1934*

Honest Ike Myers, Mayor of Akron, was discovered wandering around City Hall today, lost.

"I can't find my office," he complained plaintively to an elevator boy.

Newspapermen restored the white-haired quavering city executive to his mahogany desk where he lit a big stogie and gave an interview.

"I am a great believer in psychology," Mayor Myers began. "When I was in the clothing business in 1920, I found out that you can use psychology to sell things. Well, I'm going to use psychology to run Akron."

"Yes, yes, Mayor," the reporters chorused, leading the old man on.

"Well," Honest Ike continued, pleased to be the center of attention, "I'm going to use 1920 psychology on the city. I'm going to declare a regular holiday, schools out and everything, to encourage people to pay their taxes."

"Well," a reporter said flatly.

"I think that's a pretty good idea." Mayor Myers was deliberate. He rolled the stogie over his tongue. "Yes, sir, it's all in the psychology of the thing. I'm going to see how much each one of the C.W.A. workers will give out of his salary for taxes."

"They only make 14 bucks a week," the young man from the *Times-Press* remarked.

"Well, it won't be compulsory," Mayor Myers said hastily, "but I think it's good psychology if each one of the C.W.A. workers would give a few pennies out of his pay to help pay taxes. It would encourage other people to give money for taxes."

"Yeah," said a reporter. "What else?"

"Well, I haven't got very much more of my idea worked out," Mayor Myers drawled, "but psychology is the gist of it. Of course some of the things I say probably sound crazy, but using psychology to run a city is a pretty new thing."

"Yeah," the reporters said, from the door.

Trance   *January 12, 1934*

The *Beacon Journal* today, in a vigorous front-page editorial, demanded that the city come out of its "trance" and do something about the city's credit. Akron, its biggest newspaper said, was currently in such a desperate situation financially that nobody would lend it a dime except the Federal Government.

F.D.R. or Ruin   *January 17, 1934*

Father Coughlin, the radio priest from Detroit, raised a new
slogan: "F.D.R. or Ruin." Father Coughlin's rapidly growing
Akron audience thrilled to the latest bombast of the Michigan
orator, and in a few days "F.D.R. or Ruin" was common Akron
talk.

Twenty Per Cent   *January 19, 1934*

Every C.W.A. worker in Summit County was cut to twenty-
four hours a week work, starting today. Wages dropped from
$14 a week to $12 a week.

The cuts, the first in a national work-relief program, brought
an immediate howl of protest from all sides. Even city officials,
afraid the local direct-relief costs would mount, screamed to the
newspapers. The C.W.A. workers themselves, still unorganized,
had impromptu work stoppages. They milled around foremen
and supervisors when told the news, shaking pickaxes and shouting angry questions.

"How do I feed my kids on twelve bucks a week?" men yelled.

No answer to that question came from Washington, and none
from Akron relief officials. The C.W.A. twenty per cent cut affected some 11,425 wage earners in Summit County, every one the
sole support of a family.

The Saloon Comes Back   *January 19, 1934*

Legal liquor by the glass was sold today in Akron for the first
time since the passage of the Prohibition amendment.

The town hailed the great day with deafening apathy. Akron
had celebrated legal-beer day and legal-package-liquor day weeks
before. Night clubs and speakeasies had kept open all during the
months the State Legislature wrangled over the new liquor law.

The city was extremely calm, therefore, while ex-speakeasy
proprietors, with considerable nervousness, set about the task of

pulling enough political strings to get liquor licenses. The new State liquor law had been carefully written by down-State dries to prohibit the return of the "saloon." Criminals, including gentlemen convicted of violating the Eighteenth Amendment, could not be issued liquor licenses. Stand-up bars with brass rails and such were forever banned. Drinks could be sold only in bona fide restaurants and hotels.

For a few uneasy weeks Akron believed all this. Even the excited ex-speakeasy boys mourned their earlier sins and prayed they could get a license some way or other. Then, gradually, the town's favorite night-club owners got State licenses. Crusading newspapers raised a furor when some of the better-known rumsellers of the past proudly hung legal documents over their bars, but people were not much concerned. After all, ran the argument of the man on the street, the ex-speakeasy owners were the professional liquor dealers in town. Why deprive a man of his livelihood?

The fiction about the bona fide restaurant went next. Lots of speakeasies, when they came to the surface and took down their peepholes and barred doors, hired a Greek cook and put up a menu board. But none of the regular customers came for dinner and the Greek cook languished. The menu board grew dusty.

The section of the law about the stand-up bar went down last before the deluge of custom. In the first days, a smart lawyer discovered high stools pulled up before the bar were quite legal, but he cautioned his clients to make the customers actually sit on them. The tony night clubs and bars and hotels in town installed fancy leatherseated bar stools and for weeks anxious bartenders kept reminding annoyed customers kindly to sit down, what's the idea, you want to get us pinched? The humbler fifteen-cents-a-shot bars bought up a lot of rickety wooden high stools and put up signs, "Please sit down. It's the law."

Gradually bartenders got tired of reminding paying customers, and after a few months, the stand-up bar was a fact in custom if not in law.

So the old-time saloon came back, gradually, shorn of nothing but its name. The post-Prohibition saloon was called "Bar and Grill," or "Eats and Liquor," or "Red-Hots—We Serve Liquor."

Since nobody called it a saloon, down-State legislators got re-elected in farm districts on the proud slogan, "We kept the saloon out of Ohio."

Everybody was pleased.

Only Our Machines   *January 26, 1934*

A Goodyear factory worker wrote the following paragraphs. The essay, in pencil on cheap school children's tablet paper, was mailed to Howard Wolf, columnist on the *Beacon Journal*.

The piece was entitled "Factory Hand, 1934 Model" by its anonymous author. The Akron newspapers never published another description, by an actual rubberworker, of life in the shops. Mr. Wolf's column, carrying the worker's essay, created a sensation on Main Street.

"Only our machines," the rubberworker's letter began, "are alive. We must treat them with respect or they turn against us. Last week one of the boys who had been back only a month grew a little careless or maybe the long layoff had made him dull or maybe he had grown so accustomed to the change from sleeping at night to working at night—and his mill swallowed his hand and part of his arm. . . .

"The mills stopped only long enough for us to pull him out, and then they resumed their steady turn. Two of the boys carried him to the hospital and the foreman called for a Squad man to take his place.

"Unbelievably it is 3 A.M., and we hastily gulp tasteless sandwiches, working and eating at once. The soapstone which is flying around everywhere clogs our throats and tongues and nostrils so that they seem dry. If we drink much water, we become fat and bloated, so we chew great handfuls of licorice-flavored tobacco.

"Someone has grown drowsy. 'Ha, ha,' we laugh. 'Old Bill has forgotten to weigh his batch. That's a good one, ha, ha.' Bill doesn't laugh. He knows that to do this once more will cost him his job. The foreman has warned him.

"Somehow the night is passing; quitting time is here. Silently we wash up and change clothes, ring out our time cards and take

133

a bus home for breakfast and a few hours' unsatisfying sleep. We used to work eight hours and feel fine when the quitting whistle blew. Now we work six hours and are dead-tired.

"We can't be cheerful, remembering the hard days of the past three years, and knowing that the work may not last much longer. We've nothing to look forward to. We're factory hands."

Out on Bond   *January 30, 1934*

Gus Regakes, one of the local corn sugar kings, showed some pretty fancy footwork today during a North Howard Street gun battle. Mr. Regakes was attacked by a hidden enemy as he left his favorite Greek coffee shop. Six bullets flew through the air while Mr. Regakes, taking a page out of World War soldiers' technique, flattened himself on the sidewalk.

Then the nervy little dealer in liquor manufacturers' supplies drew his own revolver and returned the fire. Police interrupted his attempt to polish off his business rivals.

Mr. Regakes was out on bond for carrying concealed weapons.

The Union Continued   *January 30, 1934*

Coleman Claherty, addressing the Sunday Goodrich local meeting on the interesting subject of the N.R.A., was rudely interrupted today.

"We want action," a big tirebuilder bawled, bored with the N.R.A.

"Sure you do," Claherty shot back, "and you're going to get it." His handsome, rather heavy face reddened, but he kept his temper well under control.

Claherty never liked the curious atmosphere of Akron union meetings. He tried to prevent the back talk. He deplored the universal notion of rubberworkers that a man had a right to get up and have his say, whenever he felt like it, at his own union meeting.

But the rubberworkers had carried over the technique of Baptist prayer sessions, where anybody was free to "testify" as the spirit moved him, to their union meetings. Tirebuilders rose in the Federal locals to "testify" about "why ain't this union gittin' anywheres," whenever the thought struck them, which was rather often. Pitmen cut through Claherty's trained oratory to ask questions. The questions were enough to unnerve any old-line A. F. of L. organizer.

"We shall demand that the rubber industry recognize our unions," Claherty thundered this Sunday.

"How you goin' to git 'em to dew that?" somebody yelled. It wasn't a sarcastic question meant to confound the speaker. It was the voice of a millroom man, wondering out loud, in a voice trained to carry above clattering machinery.

"He asks a question like that," Claherty shot back, "when everybody in this room knows that President Roosevelt is for the unions."

It was a good answer. A lot of the men clapped and the millroom man in the back of the hall seemed satisfied. The Sunday meeting turned out to be a big success. Men filed out of the bare halls feeling big in the chest and full of hope.

"It won't be long now," some of the men said, clattering down the steps of high school auditoriums. "Roosevelt will fix those bastards pushin' up our rate schedules."

Mr. Claherty, on his way home, reflected somberly on the inexperience of Akron rubberworkers. It made him a little angry.

"Every labor gain," he told his assistant, red-headed Wilmer Tate, "is a gradual one. You can't expect to get everything the first five years. These fellows expect the moon on a platter all in a month."

"Well," Tate said dubiously, "we got a lot of members now, and they're all set to go ahead."

Mr. Claherty snorted.

This is Poverty   *February 9, 1934*

The official weather bureau report put the temperature at fifteen below zero in Akron today. In many windswept places, men read the thermometer and reported that it said eighteen and twenty below.

The fierce cold nearly paralyzed the city. On West Hill women turned up the oil-burner controls in their living rooms and kept the children in from the streets. Chauffeurs struggled to get limousines under way in the morning and lots of men resolved to have heat in the garage next winter.

In the valley, the poor struggled desperately to keep warm. Kids stayed in bed, home from school, and their mothers piled old coats and rugs on their small bodies. Men on relief packed the charity offices begging coal.

On the outskirts of Akron, where many hundreds of rubber-workers lived to escape the summer heat and smell and higher rents of the crowded sections of the city, the wind whistled through the chinks in the cheaply built wooden houses. Children huddled around pot-bellied stoves, their backs freezing.

At Sawyerwood, one of the real-estate developments for rubberworkers, four cottages burned down as desperate mothers over-stoked stoves to keep their children warm. The kids ran screaming with fear into the bitter cold, while their parents watched everything they owned go up in flames.

The fires brought bitter tragedy to these four families, sending them back to the shadow of evictions. Next day, twenty-three more fires broke out, all but one in working-class districts.

"They're either too cold," a relief official said, not smiling at his bitter joke, "or too hot."

Hallelujah! *February 12, 1934*

The Goodyear Tire and Rubber Company announced that its board of directors had decided to double the dividend rate on common stock. Net profits, the statement said with restrained joy, were well over six million dollars.

Last Stand   *February 13, 1934*

Akron newspapers, ordinarily printing little foreign news, used black headlines and long columns of type to describe the tragic last stand of Viennese Socialists against Fascism.

Workers died, the newspaper accounts said, on the roofs of the great municipal apartment houses they had built, in a last attempt to prevent a dictatorship in Austria. Women and children were mercilessly bombed by Fascist airplanes.

It was, newspaper correspondents wrote, the first fight to the death against Fascism.

Slight Mistake   *February 24, 1934*

Mayor Myers, a man who kept his mind on psychology and fishing leagues and above worldly cares, attended the wrong luncheon today and didn't discover his mistake until the ice cream course.

The honest Mayor, scheduled to address a meeting at the Y.M.C.A. banquet hall, shuffled into the Y.W.C.A. by mistake, and ate through most of the weekly session of the Metropolitan Life Insurance salesmen before he was discovered.

"Aren't you the Mayor?" a puzzled guest finally asked the kindly white-thatched gentleman at his right.

"Uh-hum," said lonesome Mayor Myers, brightening up.

"What are you doing here?" asked the blunt life insurance salesman.

"I'm the honor guest," the Mayor sighed, spooning his ice cream.

The Mayor's excited secretary finally retrieved His Honor, after desperately combing every cigar store on Main Street.

Again, the Mayor   *February 26, 1934*

Mayor Ike Myers summoned the Civil Service Commission, and then admitted he had forgotten why he called the meeting.

Problem   *March 1, 1934*

Charles Stephen, an unemployed rubberworker, broke into newspaper headlines with his question, "How can a C.W.A. worker care for himself, his wife, and his eight children on the C.W.A. wage of $12 a week?"

Stephen first addressed this question to local, state, and national relief officials. He received, he explained, a whole batch of mimeographed form letters. He summarized them: "Dear Friend; communication received; being referred; utmost regret; hope for a brighter outlook; sincerely yours."

This C.W.A. worker described his family as follows: himself, 39; his wife Margaret, 40; children, Rolland, 20; Edison, 17; Rosalie, 15; Louzetta, 14; James, 12; Jack, 9; Avis, 8; and Patrick, 6. Mrs. Stephen expected another baby soon.

The Stephen family was not accustomed to luxury. Mr. Stephen had worked in the rubber mills continuously for sixteen years, but had been laid off in 1930 and never rehired. Forced by foreclosure from their half-paid-for five-room frame house, the Stephenses lived in a one-story shack without heat, water, gas, or electric lights. Cooking was done on a kerosene stove, washing in a neighbor's house. The children all slept in two very cold small back rooms under a sloping roof that leaked. The rent had not been paid for a long time because the family used the money for food.

The Stephen weekly budget:

Coal	$1.00
Kerosene	1.00
Transportation	.50
Milk, two quarts daily	1.40
House rent	2.50
Life insurance	2.45
Newspaper	.18
	$9.03

That left $2.97 a week for all other living expenses, including shoes and clothing for the children, food, medicine, doctor bills, entertainment.

Charles Stephen wound up his letter to the local newspapers, "I have tried and tried. No supplementary relief is allowed. There is nothing left for me to do but to give up my C.W.A. job and go back to direct relief."

Public Enemy   *March 3, 1934*

John Dillinger, famed Indiana bad man, escaped from the Crown Point, Indiana, jail. Small boys were terribly excited by this daring venture, executed with the help of a wooden pistol.

We'll Move Out   *March 3, 1934*

"We'll move out of Akron, lock, stock, and barrel," Goodyear Tire and Rubber Company engineers thundered at city council. They demanded a bigger and better water system to be built with city funds, plus a sharp cut in the current water rate.

Water, necessary for cooling purposes in the big rubber plants, had long been a bitter bone of contention in city politics. The B. F. Goodrich Company, fortunately well supplied with water from a near-by chain of lakes, turned up at the city council meeting and screamed at their trade rivals across the table, "Not one drop of Goodrich water does Goodyear get."

The Goodyear engineers laid out plans for an elaborate new water supply system and threatened again and again to move Goodyear away from Akron unless the city fathers paid for the new dams and pumps.

"We need more water and a cheaper water rate," Goodyear men told city councilmen, "and if we don't get it, we're leaving Akron."

Council adjourned with the question still undecided.

Please Don't Move Out   *March 7, 1934*

City council cut the industrial water rate from eight cents per thousand gallons to two cents today. Council still considered Goodyear plans for a new water supply system.

Scattered opponents of the new water rate pointed out that the city was bankrupt, the schools in danger of closing, and the relief problem pressing. The Goodyear Tire and Rubber Company, on the other hand, speakers shouted, recently declared a double dividend.

These arguments got no reply. Council voted by a large majority to lower the water rate.

Dreams   *March 7, 1934*

Police reported today that newsstand dealers were selling a vastly increased number of dream books. Stenographers, rubber-workers, and even the unemployed used dream books to guide them in the choice of a number to play in the lottery games.

The Teachers   *March 7, 1934*

A Teachers Association survey showed that Akron schoolteachers, despite a thirty per cent reduction in salary, had already contributed $10,000 during the year from their small incomes toward funds for feeding hungry pupils.

Rumble in the Background   *March 13, 1934*

The General Tire and Rubber Company Federal local electrified the city with its plan to take a strike vote.

"We're tired of bellyaching around," men at the union hall explained. "We're serving notice on Green that we're going to take a strike vote, and we mean it. We want action."

Coleman Claherty had nothing to say for publication. But he called several of the noisiest militants down to his office in the bank building and talked to them long and earnestly. The rubber companies remained undisturbed. They knew the policy and philosophy of the A. F. of L. They expected Claherty to hold his unions in line.

For God So Loved . . .   *March 16, 1934*

Howard K. Gross, once a prosperous hardware merchant, threw his three-year-old son, an only child, into his basement furnace today. The child died of burns and shock.

Gross mumbled to police who took him away, "God told me to sacrifice my only-begotten son to save the world, as He had done."

Mrs. Gross, wild with hysteria and sorrow, told detectives her husband's mind began to wander when his business failed during the Depression. She was in the house and heard the dying screams of her child.

Brother Workers   *March 18, 1934*

A stir, like the waves in a quiet lake made by a passing motor boat went through the rubber factories today. A whisper, and it gathered strength. A word, and the word passed from tire machine to tire machine, from a man in a washroom to a friend, who told it over a bar after shift end.

"They're goin' on strike, in Auto."

Men in the Main Street cigar shops picked up the whisper and turned it over, examined it carefully, and shuddered. But in the rubber shops there was grim exaltation.

Auto was very close to Akron. The rubber factories got their biggest orders from Detroit. Men in the rubber shops knew their tires would go to Ford or General Motors or Chrysler.

But Auto was closer than mere orders to Akron. Detroit was a town like Akron, only bigger. The hill-billies in Akron all had cousins who worked in Detroit. Thousands of men in Akron rubber shops had stood at the conveyor belts in Michigan. In the early twenties men used to float from Detroit to Akron and back. There was a tie, like a twisted hemp rope, between the men in Rubber and the men in Auto.

So, this day, word went from one rubber shop to another, and everywhere it was received with slow excitement: "They're goin' out in Detroit. They're goin' to show the dirty bastards."

But the newspapers reflected the opinions on Main Street. "Fear Big Walkout in Auto Industry," the *Beacon Journal* headline read.

No Dice   *March 19, 1934*

"The auto bosses say, No dice. They ain't recognizing the union, so now it looks sure," said the man on the tire machine.

What's Wrong?   *March 23, 1934*

"What's wrong?" the man on the tire machine grumbled, "with this auto thing? The boys are all set to go out. I got a letter from my brother; he works in Detroit. But the papers say Green is talking to Roosevelt or something."

I Say It's a Sellout   *March 24, 1934*

"So the papers say a lot of crap about a labor grievance board or some such bilge, but I don't make that out. They didn't get nothing. They didn't get any more dough or anything about the speedup. I say it's a sellout. These sons of bitching union leaders, they ain't no better than the bosses."

The man on the tire machine spat tobacco juice and turned away with a sigh from his partner. All over Akron the angry sigh went through the rubber shops. William Green, President of the American Federation of Labor planted the seeds of the C.I.O. early but securely in Akron.

Strike! Strike!   *March 24, 1934*

A thick-necked, heavy-set man stood on the platform. He was sweating from excitement. He had a broad flat face and bright blue eyes. He looked honest, the kind of man scrupulous about pennies and slow to get angry.

He was angry now. "Listen, you guys," he roared. "You been working at the Diamond Match factory how long? Plenty of you ten years and more. It ain't easy work, is it? Sulphur in your lungs, and they work you until you drop—the good old speedup."

"You tell 'em, boy," somebody shouted from the thick-packed hall.

"Atta boy, Gerhardt," another yelled.

Francis Gerhardt paused and took a long noisy breath. It was almost his first speech. He was a matchworker, and speeches were new to him.

"I say strike," he yelled suddenly, after he got his wind. "I say, if we're men, we got to have guts. How much longer are we going to take it? You say, maybe, nobody's been on a big strike here in Barberton or in Akron, nobody's done it yet. Well then, we'll be the first. We ain't afraid. I say strike."

At eleven-thirty a group of cheering snake-dancing men, roaring slogans, appeared at the tall iron gates of the Diamond Match Company.

"This factory," they yelled, "is hereby called out on strike."

The midnight shift turned back and joined the picket line. The lights burned inside the factory for a while and then the management shut them off. The Diamond Match factory was on strike. It was the first strike of any importance in the Akron area since the I.W.W. called out the rubberworkers in 1913.

The Fever Grows   *March 30, 1934*

The dingy streets of Barberton, Akron's industrial suburb, seethed with strike talk. Square, squat women in old house dresses, and tall big-boned women in sweaters and cheap heavy jackets stood in the March wind talking across front yards.

In three union halls, men debated strike. The Diamond Match Company strikers booed down the management's offer. The men asked five cents an hour increase, and the company offered two.

"Two lousy cents they want to give us," speakers shouted from

the platform. "Let's take the argument back to the picket line."
"You said it," the strikers yelled.

The workers from the Ohio Match Company and the boys who built sewer pipe at the Babcox and Wilcox Company also met this night, heard speeches, and voted quickly—to strike.

When, a little after ten, men began to come home, street corners of the little working-class suburb rang with excited talk. Inside the dirty frame houses men in work shirts sat at kitchen tables telling their wives, "You ain't to worry. We'll win, I tell you. We got to strike. Things can't go on the way they are."

For many years, nearly as many as the town was old, people who lived in Barberton under the shadow of the great factories had held their peace. When the Depression came, factories laid off whole shifts until half the wage earners in the little city were out of work and their families starving on what relief passed out.

Barberton despaired those first years of the crisis. Schoolteachers stopped classes to cook breakfast for youngsters too hungry to learn how to read. Men sat endlessly on narrow front porches staring at smoke-blackened houses across the street, apathetic, too stricken even to visit the corner cigar store and talk baseball.

The union came to Barberton in the summer of 1933. The word "organize" spread through the dingy streets and filled the hearts of silent men.

Now Barberton marched proudly into battle. The plain people laid down a challenge with these three strikes. No rich people or even very well-off people lived in Barberton. The poor had the city to themselves and from that night on, they planned to make it their own.

Black Day   *March 31, 1934*

Thousands of silent men filled the armory, overflowed its steel-raftered hall, spread out over the dry winter-frozen grass of the armory lawn, and curled, in a slump-shouldered line, along the street.

The Government relief program, which began with 12,000 enrolled C.W.A. workers, suffered cuts to 7,500, had now been permanently disbanded.

These men, pushed together in a grim quiet mass, waited for their last pay checks. Tomorrow they would be back on grocery orders, back to waiting in line for charity, back to the endless idleness of the unemployed.

It rained a little while the men waited for the last C.W.A. pay check. Most of the crowd did not bother to turn up coat collars. They were too miserable to care about rain.

Solution   *March 31, 1934*

Mayor Myers announced to the newspapers that he planned to ballyhoo Akron out of the Depression, "the way we did in '96."

The Union Continued   *March 31, 1934*

Coleman Claherty, wily master of union strategy, invaded union halls this Easter Day and carried his message right into the enemy's camp.

"I plan a monster mass meeting at the armory soon," he roared in the teeth of lanky hill-billy critics. "The meeting will demand union recognition from the rubber industry. It will stir up enthusiasm for recognition."

He paused for applause and effect. The union audiences applauded dutifully enough, and only once did a fresh sniper from the back of the hall yell, "What's the matter? We're enthusiastic, all right. It's the bosses who ain't enthusiastic about it. Why don't you have a mass meeting for them? Quit stalling."

"So I'm stalling, am I?" Claherty yelled back. "Well, let me tell you, I'm inviting President William Green himself here for this mass meeting."

There was more dutiful applause, but each union meeting, this Sunday, heard a tirebuilder yell, "Ain't that the man who sold out the autoworkers?"

"Who said that?" Claherty invariably shouted back in a voice loud enough to shake down a rubberworker's house. "Stand up and let's see who calls the President of the American Federation of Labor a traitor."

Nobody stood up, of course. Akron's mountaineers were too new at public speaking and too shy to battle it out in public with Coleman Claherty.

The mass meeting announcement appeared in the papers, with the suggestion that maybe William Green himself would turn up to speak.

"Another mass meeting," they said in the shops and sighed.

Snowed Under   *April 4, 1934*

Local relief officials threw up their hands in panic today, literally snowed under with relief applications from the discharged C.W.A. workers. In three days 11,500 men applied for grocery orders.

Lines of pushing furious men curled around the old relief headquarters in the post-office building. Police kept order, knocking relief applicants into orderly lines and shouting, "No disturbances now. Keep quiet. Wait your turn."

Social service workers could not stop to argue with the new relief clients. They passed out grocery slips and said nothing.

In their upstairs offices, head relief officials pored over charts and argued endlessly, trying to solve one difficult question: "How shall we feed these people when we have no money?"

Mass Meeting   *April 15, 1934*

President Green couldn't come to the rally at the armory after all. Thousands and thousands of rubberworkers attended the mass meeting dressed in their best Sunday clothes to hear John P. Frey, a famous old A. F. of L. official, speak.

The rubberworkers stood patiently on the sidewalks around the armory, after the hall was filled, and cheered frantically every time anybody said "recognition" or "Roosevelt." Since nobody explained exactly what recognition of the union meant, the rubberworkers decided it meant the end of the speedup and higher wages. They were grimly and fiercely for it.

It was quite a fine mass meeting. Coleman Claherty made a red-hot speech. For the sixty-first, or perhaps it was the sixty-second, time he denounced the rubber bosses in a thundering voice, to everyone's satisfaction. Mr. Frey also denounced the rubber bosses. He spoke of discipline and organized strength and faith in President Roosevelt.

Several speakers attacked the speedup and that brought the loudest yells from the audience. When the meeting was all over most of the thousands from the rubber mills were sure that within a month they would have recognition, the end of the speedup, and higher wages.

A New Thing   *April 20-21, 1934*

A little after ten o'clock, in the warm spring night, running men appeared on the narrow streets of Barberton and loud voices awoke children sleeping in narrow bedrooms. Impatient couriers made frame houses tremble with the hurried weight of their feet.

"Hey, Joe!" they yelled, and their voices reached down whole blocks. "Hey! There's trouble over at Chemical! Shake a leg; get goin'."

Men stumbled down porch stairs, slipping into coats, sometimes fastening trouser belts and tucking in pajama tops for makeshift shirts. They piled in the back seats of ancient Fords, stood on running boards of 1926 Buicks, and were carried away leaving a tense-throated silence behind them.

"What's up?" they asked, and the men driving the old cars answered briefly: "Well, you know the boys are out over at Columbia Chemical because they canned eight union guys and started a company union."

"Yeah," the new men said impatiently.

"Well, they got a railroad spur going into the plant out at Chemical. The strikers figure the company will try to bring in

147

scabs on box cars, so they build a lot of fences on the tracks and sit down to wait."

"Yeah."

"Pretty soon along come some railroad dicks and fire a lot of blanks and even try to get the engineer to run over a bunch of pickets, but it doesn't work and the railroad dicks beat it like hell."

Men chuckled in the darkness.

"Yeah, but you know what them bastards at the plant are up to now? They got themselves a whole private army, no less, from Cleveland. These guys turn up when the pickets ain't looking, drive an engine right through the fences, hop out and start a free-for-all fight, and our guys get beat up pretty bad, and the thugs get through the line."

"Jesus."

"Yeah, but they only get a handful in. They figure to bring in a lot more; they think they got us scared. So we decide now is the time to go out and get the boys everywhere in town. You game?"

"Yeah."

When in the dark shadows of the soft night the old trembly cars began to arrive, men greeted each other gently, almost tenderly.

"They got guns inside there, those bastards," a man said quietly in the dark.

Some of the newcomers turned their faces toward the square brick factory and stared into its floodlighted grounds. They looked with deep and dreamlike intensity, filling their minds and eyes and hearts with the square brick building and the men they could see far away moving about in the lights.

The strikers had a few campfires, not so much for warmth in the spring as for light. The new men gathered around these campfires, standing in deeper and deeper circles and listening.

"They got Pete a nasty one," a man crouched near a fire said. The man wore a bandage on his head, and his right eye was swollen. "They took him to the hospital."

"How many did they get bad?" a voice asked quietly.

"Six."

The picket-captain appeared. His jaw was bruised and his suit

148

jacket was torn and spotted with blood. He breathed like a man after a hard race, but he had not been running. His eyes looked as though he were eaten by excitement and the exhaustion of excitement, but his words and his voice were perfectly calm.

"O.K., boys," he said, beginning in a conversational voice. Hands lifted him to an old packing box, and someone turned a flashlight on him so the men in the shadows could see the face of the strike leader.

"Now listen, boys," he began quietly, in the same flat, almost dead tone. "We ain't to start anything. They ain't got anybody inside yet who can work the factory. All they got in there is some thugs. All we got to do is to see they don't use them there thugs to take any workers inside that factory. Also we see that none of them thugs get away. We figure maybe when the sheriff sees how Barberton feels about those babies, maybe he will arrest a couple of them, see?"

As he talked this man did not once raise his voice. Still the many hundreds of men in the darkness heard him perfectly. The flashlight picked out the bruised jaw and showed the rips and the blood on his jacket.

"Them bastards," somebody said pretty loud from the shadows. "Them dirty rats."

"Sooner or later," said the man on the packing box in a perfectly matter-of-fact voice, "we'll get them babies and the guys who hired them to come in here and beat us up. But not now. Maybe not this year. Right now we got to win this strike." His voice faded a little.

"Louder," the men in the outer layers of the circle cried.

"I said," the leader shouted, and his voice began to flicker with the excitement in his eyes, "that now we got to win this strike. Maybe I ought to thank you guys for coming down here on our picket line, but why should I thank you? This is your fight. If they lay a hand on one union man in Barberton, they lay a hand on us all. If they bust this strike, they'll bust every strike. We're fighting, you guys and us, for the whole union movement in Barberton, and that means for our kids and our wives and the chance to hold our heads up like men."

149

"You said it," a man screamed from the shadows. A thin small striker near the packing box pulled at the dirty bloody jacket of the speaker.

"Take it easy," he whispered. He was afraid the picket-captain would explode, all at once, with the rage and excitement set forth so exactly in the man's blazing eyes. The strike leader was a proud man, and he had been beaten and mauled and dragged in dirt and kicked by half a dozen gangsters. The little thin striker had helped the picket-captain to his feet after the attack, and he had seen the man go off in the darkness and be sick to his stomach, not so much from pain as from rage and disgust.

So now the strike leader felt the soft tug on his torn suit coat, but from a great distance. The flicker in his voice mounted and mounted, and he cried out in trembling anger, "Listen, them bastards think they can kick us around like dirt. Well, they can't! We're Americans! We're men! They can't do it to us, see? They can't."

The excitement passed from his throat to the throats of his listeners. Men licked dry lips and swallowed in gulps to loosen the tightness at their Adam's apples.

"Take it easy," the little man whispered again, and pulled at the torn jacket. It ripped a little under his anxious hand. The small noise of the tearing sounded in the speaker's ears. He paused. When he spoke again, his voice was quiet and the tone was dry and hard.

"Here's what we got to do," he said.

When he was through men had to help him down from the packing box. His kicked and beaten legs were already too stiff to move very well. Nobody suggested that he should go home and go to bed. He was needed for this night, and the men around him felt his stiff legs as an inconvenience. Later on they would be sorry and later on he would savor his pain. Now he had no time.

Nearly a thousand men of Barberton arranged themselves in good order around the gates of the plant. Carrying clubs and pieces of paving brick, their only weapons, they advanced steadily on the plant until they came blinking within the range of the lights. They acted with quiet and deep concentration. Sometimes a man roared an insult into the plant, but his friends felt the shouted epithet to be a peculiar kind of social error, something gauche.

When the lines were formed the strike leader limped around them to survey the defenses. Every gate was covered by hundreds of men. They stood and sat and squatted in a thick solid mass, a human barricade. The railroad gate itself was crowded twenty deep with rows of men. In front of this solid mass a gang worked swiftly, under the direction of a foreman, building a series of pyramids made of old ties and wood and stones on the railroad tracks. No engine would pass this way tonight.

The picket-captain said to his men, "Just keep waiting. Just wait. Stick it out until we tell you to go. Don't leave until we're safe."

Then began the vigil of the night. It was a little before midnight when the strike leader had at last arranged the defenses to his liking. He also sat down to wait.

The sheriff appeared, followed by ten beefy deputies in sweaters and carrying sub machine-guns. They carried the guns rather self-consciously.

Sheriff Ray Potts liked to think he was smart. When he saw the masses of men in front of the gates he decided instantly to be a hero. True, he had already made agreements with the management at the plant to "protect" the property, but these quiet men had votes, and Ray Potts was no sucker.

So he sought out the strike leader. The silence of the thousand men ready to use their bodies as a barricade frightened Ray Potts. He had no understanding or experience of men who were ready to die for each other, and this new thing made him feel insecure and afraid.

"You sure got all of Barberton out here," Potts began uneasily. The picket-captain and the men arranged around the campfire stared at the sheriff.

"Yeah," the strike leader replied, very dry.

"This kind of picketing is sure against the law," Potts said, as an experiment. He did not say it emphatically.

151

"Yeah?" the picket-captain replied, like a man asking a polite question in which he really has little interest.

"The Governor ordered that them railroad cars is supposed to go through," Potts ventured again. His voice was mild.

"The Governor." The strike leader said the word dispassionately, reflectively.

"He's a dirty bastard," the little thin man burst out. "We're striking to keep our union from being bust up, and the Governor horns in with a lot of crap about property rights. We got rights too."

The leader hushed the thin man, for he did not want to argue with the sheriff. He knew the sheriff. The sheriff was not a man who understood talk. The sheriff did not even care about property rights, like the bosses did. The only thing the sheriff understood was power or votes.

The picket-captain regarded Potts with contempt but some curiosity. In the firelight, the sheriff's ratty face wore its conventional grin. He was a vain man, and he wanted people to like him. So he smiled constantly, hoping that the smile would make people think him a jolly fellow. Now, surrounded by a thousand men and more who stood in the night ready to die for each other, he still grinned.

"The boys," the strike leader said, "think you ought to do something about them guys in there. Them babies got guns and it's against the law. They come from Cleveland. Out-of-town rats. Barberton don't like it."

"Well," Potts said softly, "maybe the company's got a right to protect its property. The Governor said the trains should go through."

The thin man started to speak again, but the leader broke through his voice. "Maybe they have, and maybe the Governor did say that," the leader replied, "but Barberton don't agree so well with that kind of talk. Barberton is pretty mad about them guys inside there. Maybe when it gets to be light they'll feel so sore about it they'll go in there and get those babies. That would make a lot of trouble."

"Well," Potts murmured. His mind had been made up from

the moment he faced the thousand quiet men. He knew votes when he saw them.

The strike leader understood Potts. He was sure of Potts before the sheriff came to him. He looked at him and wondered why the sheriff hesitated and for what he waited.

"Could I sort of talk to the boys?" Potts asked. The picket-captain grinned. The sheriff wanted to make sure he was going to be a hero.

"Sure," said the strike leader. "Talk away, but be sure and tell them you're going to take those babies out of the plant. Otherwise they might be sore at you." It was a good touch. Potts's grin faded.

Presently his voice came through the darkness. "I say to you," Potts roared, breaking the silence, "no gang of thugs can come in here from out of town and break the law by carrying guns and attacking peaceful innocent men."

The men around the campfire spit tobacco juice.

Potts took his time rounding up the Cleveland strikebreakers. He was surprised when they went with him so gratefully. They had seen the quiet shadows.

Just at dawn the leader went around to the gates. Some of the men lay sleeping on the ground, but many still sat bolt upright, a club across their knees, staring into the coming light of the sky.

"It's all right now, boys," the leader said.

The Victory   *April 22, 1934*

The Columbia Chemical Company reluctantly settled the Barberton strike. The union won its main point, re-employment of the discharged organization men, and beside that collective bargaining.

Jubilant men rushed to the streets when they heard the news and put their arms around strangers. "They can't do it to us," the men of Barberton yelled hoarsely. "By God, we licked 'em."

The story of the Columbia Chemical strike was printed in the newspapers and went by word of mouth from man to man in the rubber shops. It was never forgotten. The old mold was breaking.

More Victories   *April 24, 1934*

The match strikers, out for a month and three days, won a complete victory. They went back to work singing.

Three other smaller strikes were won this same day. The men got raises and shorter hours. They sang.

Plentiful   *April 27, 1934*

The National Re-employment Bureau announced that jobs for women were plentiful in Akron.

"Domestic situations," the statement read, "are available in large numbers. Wages vary between $3 a week and $7 a week, with the average offered wage slightly below $4 a week."

The Union Continued   *April 29, 1934*

Rubberworkers filed into the bare drafty union halls this Sunday with stately pride, dressed in their best. The men wore neat sack suits, not fitting them very well, and loud striped ties and clean shirts and shined yellow-tan shoes. The girls wore chiffon dresses and black silk hats.

Every local in Akron—the three big ones and the many smaller ones—voted this Sunday to ratify the proposed agreement for the rubber industry. Claherty appeared at the big locals to read the carefully prepared document the rubber barons were to be asked to sign. He read slowly, impressively, savoring each word, letting each phrase build dreams among his listeners.

The rubberworkers ratified the agreement with passionate cheers. Already in their mind's eye, they saw a new world—the speedup ended, increased wages, the blessed security against gnawing fear. The intoxication swept them past all doubts. They felt strong and proud. They had made the union, and now the union would put an end to fear.

Claherty said at the end of the day that 20,000 rubberworkers had ratified the agreement. He broadcast the terms of the proposed contract, to serve notice, he said, on the rubber industry. The newspaper stories of the agreement impressed the men in the rubber shops.

They did not impress the gentlemen of the rubber companies.

An Ex-Mayor Speaks   *May 1, 1934*

"The administration must either furnish jobs to the unemployed through a vast public works program or kill them in the revolts sure to come," former Mayor C. Nelson Sparks told the Senate Labor Committee in Washington today.

The headline-hunting ex-Mayor, preparing for his future political career, made a dramatic appearance before a group of fascinated Senators.

"There were Communist uprisings in Akron," Mr. Sparks declared roundly. "There were riots and killings. To stop that I had to take money from the city treasury illegally and give them jobs."

Mr. Sparks testified that there were 28,849 registered unemployed who were heads of families in Akron. With their dependents, these persons numbered about 140,000, or about forty-six per cent of the population. These figures startled the Senators and also startled local relief officials, paralyzed with fear when they regarded their own estimates which hovered around the thirty to thirty-five per cent mark. Mr. Sparks's gruesome opinions about the number of unemployed in Akron made relief officials tremble. It was just possible that he was right.

"Feed the unemployed; give them jobs," Mr. Sparks wound up, "or slaughter them." He made quite an impression in Washington.

Scandal   *May 4, 1934*

Akron was treated to a really rare scandal today. The dapper sheriff, Akron's Beau Brummell, the affable basso profundo, Mr.

Ray Potts, was hauled before the Grand Jury charged tentatively with malfeasance in office.

The garbled story that leaked out of the Grand Jury rooms to electrify the Main Street circuit of cigar stores centered around a midnight raid on a country still. It seemed that an honest but dumb deputy had gone out into the night armed with a warrant and prepared to do his duty.

He found his still, and he found the guilty operator busy at work manufacturing manifestly illegal corn liquor. The honest deputy announced his plans—he meant to arrest the industrious still operator and confiscate the expensive machine. The guilty manufacturer howled. He was filled with surprise and indignation.

"You can't do that," he screamed. "I pay my money every week. What's the idea?"

The honest deputy fell back in confusion. At that very moment a second deputy arrived with a few friends. He said, too, that the manufacturer couldn't be arrested. In the excitement the still operator fled into the darkness just to make sure nobody could arrest him.

The Grand Jury investigation that began with such promising fireworks fizzled out, however. Mr. Potts was observed wandering around the county jail shouting, "Arrest somebody for that still job!" but there seemed to be no other confirmation for the honest deputy's no doubt honest tale. Everybody denied everything, everybody contradicted himself and everybody else, the sheriff denied everything and accused political enemies of dragging his name and family honor in the mud.

In the end the Grand Jury threw up its hands and called it a day. The sheriff was safe for the time being.

The Bakers   *May 9, 1934*

Every bakery in Akron was closed today by a general bakers' strike. The union men asked a closed shop and increased wages. The *Beacon Journal* appeared with a front-page editorial denouncing the union for asking a closed shop. A closed shop is not, the editorial said, a democratic American institution.

The bakers paid no attention to the editorial. They sent squads to cover the incoming motor highways. Out-of-town bakers' trucks were met with barricades. The drivers turned back to Cleveland with their bread still stacked neatly in the trucks.

Again, the Bakers   *May 10, 1934*

The *Beacon Journal* appeared today with a front-page recipe for home-baked bread and an indignant reply from the union to its anti-closed shop blast.

"A closed shop," said the infuriated president of the bakers' union, "is really a union shop. It's the only way we can protect our overtime agreements. If we don't get that, we get nothing really, because the bosses can break up our union in a minute by bribing men not to belong. A union shop is insurance against long hours and low wages."

Restaurants, hotels, and grocery stores began to run out of bread. Some chain stores had bread shipped in by railroad from Cleveland. The bakery truck drivers joined the bakers' strike. The Salvation Army called on the women of Akron to bake bread for them. The county jail steward said he was "plenty worried."

Overnight the bakers' strike made the women of the city labor conscious. Everybody gossiped in grocery stores about the strikers' demands, and men ate muffins for breakfast for the first time in years.

The Prelude   *May 11, 1934*

In a paid advertisement in both papers the Bakery Owners Association trumpeted that the bakers' demand for a closed shop preluded the demand for a closed shop in rubber.

Mr. Claherty replied that he knew for a fact that one rubber company in town was spending $50,000 a week to prevent union organization in Akron.

The Bakers Win   *May 14, 1934*

Jubilant bakers went back to work today with a wage rise, preferential shop, and seniority under their union's belt.

Chamber of Commerce circles did a good deal of serious head-shaking over the bakers' victory. Forward-looking men deplored these retreats in early union skirmishes. Too many easy gains through strikes might give rubberworkers the wrong idea.

The bakers' strike did give ideas to lots of rubberworkers. The strike made headlines for days. After it was over, both rich and poor remembered it.

Extremely Awkward   *May 22, 1934*

Sheriff Ray Potts found himself today in an extremely awkward, not to say downright embarrassing, position.

Two of the armed guards he arrested at the late Columbia Chemical strike turned out to be Pinkerton detectives from Cleveland. When they came up for trial on charges of carrying illegal weapons, they both swore on the witness stand that Mr. Potts had agreed to deputize any number of guards, armed or otherwise, which the company might bring from Cleveland.

"Mr. Potts," stated the company's smooth-faced lawyer, "was in perfect agreement with the company that the plant needed protection. He agreed to provide any guards the company might employ with papers deputizing them as officers of the law in this county."

"What," continued the lawyer, "could have changed Mr. Potts's mind? Not any sudden belief that armed guards were not needed at the plant, for Mr. Potts accepted and presumably used a large sum of money to employ special deputy sheriffs for the protection of the company's property. Many of them were on duty in the plant at the very moment when Mr. Potts was arresting these Cleveland gentlemen.

"No," thundered the enraged attorney, "no, what changed Mr. Potts's mind was the opinion of the lawless mob gathered at the gates of the company's plant. Mr. Potts wanted to make political capital from the distress of this company."

The lawyer added that Mr. Potts was "a schemer, a liar, and a he-butterfly."

During the trial it was charged that Mr. Potts took $10 a head from Columbia Chemical Company for special deputy sheriffs he employed and paid out only $5 to the men he drafted for the jobs. Several relatives of Mr. Potts's also appeared on official lists as special deputy sheriffs.

The jury found one of the Pinkerton detectives guilty and acquitted the other. The trial annoyed Mr. Potts, but it did not surprise the Barberton strikers. Howls of laughter were heard up and down Main Street, most unfortunately at the expense of the Columbia Chemical Company. In this case, the company not only lost the strike, but got the doublecross from a two-bit local sheriff.

Campaign   *May 24, 1934*

The clergy of Akron girded its loins and went into battle to make the city a better place in which to live. The big anti-Sunday dancing campaign got under way with the personal visit to several night clubs by two embattled pastors and their wives.

The religious leaders, who wanted to make night clubs close Saturday midnight so that no one would be tripping the light fantastic at 12:01 on the Lord's Day, expressed dismay and surprise at what they saw in the various dine and dance spots they visited.

They posed for pictures at a ringside seat in the Merry-Go-Round night club, and several scantily clad chorus girls stood in the background while the pastors roundly denounced their lack of proper covering. The campaign, political wiseacres said, would probably not come to much. Akron was a Saturday night town and the citizenry would be enraged if council actually did close up night clubs at the first minute of the Sabbath.

Death in Toledo   *May 28, 1934*

Two men lay dead in Toledo. They were the victims of the Ohio National Guard, shot during a battle on the Electric Auto-Lite Company picket lines.

Toledo, a city of nearly the same size as Akron, was wild with fear and excitement. Soldiers paraded the streets. Dozens of victims of gas bombs jammed emergency wards. Whole blocks of crowded dirty houses near the plant were deserted by their occupants because the gas fumes still lay low on the streets and curled in through living-room windows to choke housewives and small children.

But, as black headlines in every Ohio paper trumpeted the tragic story of the Auto-Lite strike, public opinion rose to confound the Auto-Lite Company and the National Guard, rose up to ruin the political career of Governor George White, who took time off from a fishing trip to order the soldiers into Toledo.

Akron seethed with fury. Men in rubber shops swore and narrowed their eyes and stood at the factory gates saying, "Jesus, they shot them down like dogs because they were on strike. Jesus, it makes a man's blood run cold." The Central Labor Union called a special meeting and wrote a resolution packed with rage and sorrow.

The *Beacon Journal*, which not so long before called the bakers' strike "unjustified," came out with a front-page editorial roaring, "The Governor is enjoying a pleasant little holiday hipping the trout streams of Michigan while death stalks the streets of Toledo." The *Time-Press*, with other Scripps-Howard papers in the state, called for the withdrawal of the troops at once.

The Governor emerged from the trout regions of Michigan to find that even regular Democratic party machine politicians were calling him "murderer." The troops left hastily.

"Well, I'll be a son of—"   *May 29, 1934*

Something very extraordinary happened today, something pleasant that made the people of Akron feel all warm and soft and sentimental. People talked about it on the busses, and men left off arguing about strikes and city deficits and suchlike, to discuss this curious event.

For the Akron newspapers printed the first news of the birth of quintuplets to a farm woman in the Canadian north woods.

"Quintuplets!" people said, hesitating over the word, and not pronouncing it correctly. "Five at a time! Jesus Christ, think of it! Five kids all at once."

Men in the rubber shops roared with laughter when they heard about it, but the laughter was jovial and rather pleased. "Well, I'll be a son of a sea cook!" tirebuilders howled. "Did you git that, Pete? Five babies at a time."

Later editions carried Papa Dionne's famous reply to the news that an excited midwife brought him. "Five?" the newspapers quoted the distracted father as saying. "Five? I'm the kind of a man they ought to put in jail."

Naturally the infant Dionnes produced a lot of dirty jokes. Wits along the Main Street cigar store row made obscene comments about the birth of the five little girls, but the jokes weren't very successful. Akron was, a little shamefacedly it is true, genuinely and warmly interested in the fate of the tiny Canadian children.

At first it looked as though the small Dionnes would not survive. Born in terrible poverty, their parents had no money to provide milk and incubators and medicine to preserve their flickering lives. The first pictures of the miniature babies, spread out, one after another beside their exhausted mother, brought a deluge of telephone calls to Akron newspaper offices. Women sent little sweaters and piles of neatly laundered diapers to bewildered city editors. "Please see that these get to the Dionnes," said accompanying notes. "I hear the babies do not have sufficient clothing."

Ministers in Akron prayed for the lives of the quintuplets, and hard-boiled businessmen mailed checks to Canada for incubators and medicine. Ladies' bridge clubs collected small purses and schoolteachers explained to excited grammar school kids what "quintuplets" meant.

After the first flurry passed, Akron did not lose interest in the five little sisters. Something about the faces of the children, soon

161

appearing on billboards and covering whole pages of newspapers, caught the attention and won the hearts of the people of this Ohio industrial town. Everybody followed the daily diet of the Canadian children; everybody knew when one of the sisters had a cold; everybody discussed Mr. Dionne's relations with Dr. Dafoe. The quints—for the awkward word was soon shortened for American use—became gradually part of the everyday life of Akron.

The Union Continued   *June 3, 1934*

Early Sunday morning the workers' streets began to stir. Women on back porches said to their neighbors across hardened dirt back yards: "It's awful hot. I don't know as how I kin git to church this morning and then to the parade. I got to git the kids ready too."

Women answered, "Boy, you sure said it. I put off ironing the boys' shirts till today. I hoped it would let up a little, but it sure don't look as though it will."

All over the valleys women worked in the blazing heat to get their families ready for the parade. They stood over irons pressing pants, and in damp muggy basements doing last-minute washes so that their menfolks could march in clean white duck pants. At noon they called the kids in to a hasty lunch, just pick-me-ups, and stacked the dishes.

A little after one, Kenmore Hill and Barberton and East Akron and South Akron began to empty. Knots of people walked along the streets waving to neighbors and yelling greetings to families still loitering in their front yards waiting for Ma to finish dressing. Sometimes the men walked alone or with other men, but mostly the whole family turned out, the women and kids to stand lining the street and cheer, the father to march.

By one-thirty, Perkins Square in front of the schoolhouse was black with thousands and thousands of men. The official thermometer said 98. In the sun on the square it was hotter than that. But the men stood cheerfully in the molten heat, smiling while perspiration poured over their faces and dripped down the small of their backs and ran in rivers down their legs.

162

The square was a carnival place. Ice cream men ran about with little boxes of wrapped frozen suckers and did a great business. Ice-cold Coca-Cola, men yelled from every corner, and the popcorn and peanut salesmen operated, even in the blazing heat. Balloon venders smashed in and out of the crowds, bumping people, holding their bright burden over the heads of the closely packed crowd.

The girls who were going to march stood together, and men from the columns next to them whistled and cheered and yelled, "Oh, boy, Susie, haven't I met you somewhere before?" The girls yelled back, "Sure, at your wedding." The big strong girls who worked in the rubber shops wore their best summer dresses, fluttery ones, and new high-heeled white shoes. A few of the older women turned up in work dresses and low flat shoes, but most of the girls were as carefully dressed as though they were going to a dance. They were proud to march in a union parade.

By two o'clock the marshals began to arrive. They brought bales of white caps stamped with red legends: "Goodyear Federal local; in union there is strength," and "Goodrich Federal rubberworkers' local, labor omnia vincit; affiliated with the American Federation of Labor." They brought big American flags and a few blue-and-gold union banners. They worried the bands into line. They trumpeted orders through megaphones, and gradually the parade took shape.

At 2:30, in the broiling, fierce heat, a band struck up, and while the rest of the dense crowd in the square cheered, the first division, the men of the Goodrich local, marched proudly down Exchange Street. For more than an hour, the streets of Akron were filled with marching rubberworkers.

Every foot of the way to the armory was packed with spectators, women and kids who stood in the still-mounting heat waiting for Pa to come by, union bakers and union bus drivers and union printers who yelled themselves hoarse and went in for a quick beer and came back and yelled some more.

In the heat, on the slippery asphalt pavements, over brick cooked oven-hot by the merciless sun, the rubberworkers marched in profound good humor shouting to the crowds and smiling and laughing and getting a laugh and a smile back from the audience.

"How do you like us?" big tall mountaineers whooped to the sidelines, and men from the curbs yelled back, "That's showin' 'em, boy; that's showin' 'em."

There was no menace and no threat in this cheerful parade, except the very fact of the parade itself and the brave 40,000 who dared a thermometer of 100 and more to march for the union. Here were men confident and happy and proud expecting a victory over the rubber bosses tomorrow or the next day, afraid of nothing and ready for anything.

The parade panted its perspiring way up the hill to the armory. The first divisions marched inside the hall for the speeches, and the rest of the crowd stood on the armory front lawn and afterwards jammed the streets for blocks.

The parade celebrated the opening of the first convention of the United Rubber Council. The men who sat inside the hall in the stifling heat and the men who stood outside in the direct glare of the fierce sun heard some fine upstanding speeches about the opening of the Council. The Council, they were told, was about to draw up an agreement with the rubber bosses. The speedup and the low wages and the insecurity in the shops were all but ended. The Council was about to sit down around a conference table and straighten things out.

About five o'clock the speeches were over and the workers went home. Lots of them drank too much beer and got drunk and were very happy, celebrating.

The Union Continued   *June 4, 1934*

The United Rubber Council, chief governing body of the unions in the industry, went into secret session at the Portage Hotel.

Although the bulk of the membership of the Federal locals had been paying dues to the A. F. of L. for nine months, the United Rubber Council was a complete mystery to most rubberworkers. Coleman Claherty, chairman and boss of the Council, furnished no very lucid explanations to either the press or union members.

Tirebuilders and pitmen had been given no chance to vote for delegates to the United Rubber Council, but Claherty said the

164

new governing body was perfectly democratic all the same. Each local, represented by its president or business agent, had two votes —Goodrich Federal union with its 9,000 members in June had a perfectly equal voice in the Council with the electricians, 300 strong. Of course it was mere happenstance that craft locals outnumbered Federal unions ten to one.

The United Rubber Council plunged briskly into business at its opening session. The unhappy presidents of the Federal locals, with six votes, sat silently by while greedy business agents from Indianapolis and New York sliced up the Federal union pie—in theory. Claherty presided over the battles of doughty warriors defending the honor of the electricians and brave chieftains fighting the good fight for the carpenters.

Complaints from organizers on the Akron field injected a harsh note of reality into the proceedings. Assigned members of craft locals in the rubber shops often refused point-blank to pay initiation fees and join up with the machinists or carpenters. The Federal union presidents pricked up their ears, only to slump back into their conference chairs. Claherty promised his personal attention to the complaints.

Jurisdictional quarrels over, the United Rubber Council turned its attention to the draft of the proposed industry-wide agreement. The humble Federal union presidents listened for hours to wrangles between business agents. Machinists wanted to ask more than electricians; and vice versa. At last the rubberworkers' delegates suggested timidly that since tirebuilding and tirecuring were the most highly skilled jobs in a rubber factory, craft minimums should be set no higher than rates for rubberworkers.

Business agents pooh-poohed such an ignorant idea. Federal locals were for the unskilled, the left-overs, the unfortunates, who couldn't be fitted into one or another of the ancient honorable craft unions. Several of the officers of the Federal locals were pitworkers or tirebuilders themselves. They flinched at this insult to their skill and regarded the foreigners from Indianapolis and New York with sour indignation.

Just before Claherty closed the first convention of the United Rubber Council, the Federal union presidents made a last attempt to break the united front of the business agents. They asked that the Council set aside a fund from the dues and initiation fees collected, to organize rubber factories in the south, east, and west. Unorganized rubber shops threatened the union in Akron, they explained. The craft union representatives looked shocked at this suggestion, but Claherty smoothed down the awkward situation. All in good time, he said. Rome wasn't built in a day.

When the United Rubber Council finished its business, Claherty took the first plane to Washington where he planned to confront the Rubber Manufacturers' Association with the now final draft of The Agreement. All that now remained between the rubberworker and his goal of ending intolerable working conditions through union organization were the signatures of the rubber barons to this imposing document, The Agreement.

The Union Continued   *June 19-20, 1934*

Shortly after seven-thirty, without any kind of formal meeting, without Mr. Claherty's knowledge or sanction, without announcement or consultation, without advice from William Green and other experienced trade union leaders, the rubberworkers at General Tire and Rubber Company struck.

Going on strike is rather a formal way of putting what really happened. Tirebuilders simply stopped work and began yelling, "The hell with the speedup! We're through."

Management of the General Tire and Rubber Company, a small plant in East Akron employing about 1,500 factory hands, had decided, early in June, to replace its own wage-rate system with the famous Bedeaux or group speedup plan. Time-study engineers appeared in the factory. Tirebuilders, to whom the very word "Bee-do" was a threat, grew restless. They muttered at the first piece-work rate cuts.

The six to midnight shift came in feeling sore this warm evening in June. Things were bad, and now they were going to get worse. A little after seven the foreman announced some "rate adjustments." Two or three of the tirebuilders told him to take his goddamned rate-cards and do something with them. Tirebuilders were not soft talkers, and the foreman was burned up. He said they couldn't talk to him like that.

The revolt spread up and down the tire machines. "The god-damned speedup is working the guts out of me," men growled, and suddenly, without any warning, a tirebuilder yelled, "I ain't going to stand for it. Let's quit, boys!"

They backed away from their machines. A frantic foreman shouted threats. The grapevine telegraph flashed the news instantly to other departments. The tirebuilders were quitting. They were washed up with the "Bee-do" system. The plant emptied. Men straggled away from half-finished jobs and milled around in the courtyard near the gates yelling.

The plant manager appeared in the yard, his face red and outraged. "Go back to work," he bellowed from the steps of the office building.

"Boo-o-o-o!" yelled the tirebuilders and after them the pitmen and the moldworkers.

"Listen," the plant superintendent said earnestly, his voice betraying panic. "Listen, we'll raise your wages. I absolutely guarantee that any injustices in pay will be adjusted. I guarantee it."

"Boo-o-o-o-o!" replied the crowd jovially. Some of the men laughed. It was rather funny, seeing the plant manager so red in the face, promising pay raises, begging.

Now a man leaped up on a truck-engine hood. "Let's have a meeting tomorrow and take a strike vote. What do you say, boys?"

The plant manager broke in, "You can't talk like that on company property. You get out of this yard. You're fired, whoever you are."

"Fired?" said the speaker. "Fired? Hell, I'm on strike. How about it, boys?"

"You said it!" screamed the crowd. "You said it."

That was the way it began. A man in the truck tire department said he wouldn't stand for it any more, and out of that came the strike. The crowd marched out of the gates singing and booing the plant manager and laughing. The rubberworkers went home confident and easy in their minds.

The President of General Tire and Rubber Company, a jovial Irishman named William O'Neil, was away in the East watching his son being graduated from college. Mr. Claherty was in Washington. Both men took the first train home to see what could be done to save the situation.

They came too late. Next morning the strikers packed East High School auditorium to the doors. They sang and cheered. They voted to strike until their wages went up and Mr. O'Neil abolished the company union and recognized the General Tire Federal rubberworkers' local.

The vote came after several high-spirited fist fights. Mr. Claherty watched the executive committee of the local recommend that the men accept the company's hasty wage proposals and go back to work. The harassed union leaders were booed off the platform. They looked reproachfully at Mr. Claherty as they filed out. Several earnest strikers started scraps with executive committee supporters on the floor. Mr. Claherty observed these fights carefully. One of the officers of the local shouted that the strike wasn't legal. It couldn't be legal because the United Rubber Council executive board had to give permission to strike. The tirebuilders hissed him off the rostrum.

"Who said they had to O.K. what we do?" a man yelled from the floor. "We ain't never heard anything about that before."

Mr. Claherty regarded the man who asked the question with some interest from his vantage point on the platform. Tirebuilders had, it seemed, a remarkable way of ignoring things like the United Rubber Council. They had never heard of it; ergo, it didn't exist.

Mr. Claherty tried once himself. He began to speak about the company's wage proposals which seemed to him rather fair. He suggested negotiations while the men went back to work. "You're trying to stall us," a tirebuilder howled from the floor.

"Throw that man out," Mr. Claherty roared back. The striker was duly thrown out. When the noise died down, Mr. Claherty did not return to his first arguments. He attacked Mr. O'Neil. He said Mr. O'Neil built tennis courts and airports with the tirebuilders' money. Then he sat down, thoughtfully.

The strikers marched from their meeting to the picket lines. By noon, strike organization got under way. Squads of pickets

168

raced down to the railroad yards to prevent tires from moving out of town. In a dingy little shack across from the plant, pit workers sweated in the heavy heat, to set up food committees and appoint picket-line captains. Out of the noisy crowd of the night before, the drawling-voiced mountaineers forged their own strike machine.

The Union Continued   *June 23-24, 1934*

The hot sun held the threat of another molten day, but the morning was fresh and cool. The strikers, in rare good humor, crowded around the gates of the General Tire and Rubber Company a few minutes after a faraway whistle blew seven o'clock. The soft drawl, the rich and racy metaphor of mountain speech floated from the hum of general talk. Belly laughs punctuated the sound of strikers' speech; lanky men bent over to slap big knees, applauding some rich joke.

A man with a megaphone appeared. He shouted orders in a familiar easy style and the crowd, with that deplorable habit Mr. Claherty mourned so much, shouted back suggestions and questions. Presently the thousand and more strikers shuffled about in the street, arranging themselves in loose military formation. Row after row of tall husky men in blue denim pants and shirts with the sleeves ripped out at the armholes spread out over the pavement. Marshals yelled blistering curses, and strikers answered back jovially. By seven-thirty, the General rubberworkers' local was ready for the day's work.

The strike captain yelled "Let's go!" through his megaphone, and the little army marched briskly down the street, leaving the main plant gate to the careful attention of six pickets. The pickets yelled, "Be careful, boys!" and the marchers howled back, "Don't take any wooden nickels."

The march was short, not quite two blocks. "O.K.," the marshal yelled and the straggly parade halted. Most of the strikers promptly sat down on the curb. They didn't have long to wait. At exactly seven forty-five, right on time, the first big yellow streetcar, marked "General Tire—Main Street," carrying office workers, swung around the corner, and, its bell clanging frantically, rocked down the street.

The parade re-formed instantly, only now men stood close together, shoulder to big shoulder, packed tightly, toe on the next man's heel, covering the streetcar tracks with a solid mass of men.

"Hold that line," somebody yelled, and a roar of laughter went through the human barricade.

The streetcar crawled slowly closer and closer. It came near enough so that the strikers could see the surprised face of the motorman. His hand was lifted to clang his bell. The strikers stood perfectly still. The streetcar came to a final shuddering stop. In a split second, twelve strikers stood at the side exit, twelve more ganged the front entrance. The strikers' ranks moved up, so that the motorman could not go forward an inch without knocking down a row of human beings.

The clanging bell stopped. Girls leaned out of the open streetcar windows and yelled, "What's the idea?" A few men inside the car banged on the exit doors. The strikers cheered. The motorman stepped down and began to parley.

"Won't you let me through?" he said with absolutely no conviction.

"No, sir," one of the strikers replied very cheerfully. "You take your old streetcar and trundle it right back to town. These boys and girls ain't going to work today."

"You let us through yesterday," a girl shrilled from an open window.

"That was yesterday," a striker called back. "Lady, this ain't no picnic. This is a strike. Office workers ain't getting through no picket line today. Go on home and take a vacation."

"Sure," a young fellow howled to a pretty stenographer in one of the windows. "It's a nice day. Go on home and get your boy friend to take you swimming."

"Who's got a boy friend?" shrieked the pretty girl.

"Maybe I'll do?" the young fellow shouted. "You just wait for me, baby, and when I get through picketing I'll be around."

Everybody laughed and the pretty girl screamed, "Ain't you fresh though. I suppose you seen me somewheres before?"

"I sure did," the young fellow began, but the motorman interrupted this early-morning idyl.

"Well," he said with enthusiastic resignation, "I suppose if you won't let me through, you won't let me through."

"That's right, captain," the strikers yelled. "Take the old boat away."

"I'm a union man myself," the motorman said in a low tone, and clambered back up his folding stairs.

"He's a union man himself," one of the strikers shouted. The rubberworkers were delighted. They felt it a piece of lovely good fortune that the motorman was a union man himself. They felt warm in their hearts, and pleased. Here was a brother where there might have been an enemy.

"Yay-ay-ay," the strikers howled. "Yay-ay-ay for the motorman, whee!" Blistering sky rocketing whistles deafened the blushing motorman. He turned on his power and backed his lumbering streetcar away, his smiling face gradually fading away from the strikers.

"Good-by, baby," the young fellow howled. The pretty girl's answer was lost on the breeze.

Not all the cars were as easy as the first. Only the merest clerks and the real underdogs came to work on the seven-forty-five. When the big shots, the office managers and the private secretaries to the big bosses started arriving on the eight-fifteen, there was some pretty rough talk.

But the motormen settled the question. While trembling-lipped men shouted out the window, "You can't keep us from going to work," the streetcar men said, "You win, boys. I ain't running anybody over, and I don't look for no trouble." One by one the big yellow cars backed away.

The police came too, and looked and went away thoughtfully.

At nine o'clock the strikers marched back to the gates and broke up the parade. They spread out over the big plant, covering even the little out-of-the-way gates with a dozen and twenty men. At the main gate a hundred strikers hung around talking.

Promptly at nine-fifteen a large limousine pulled into the street and stopped before the picket line. William O'Neil, president of the company, wanted to go in to work.

171

"Sorry," somebody yelled. "Nobody gets in."

"Now you listen," O'Neil said furiously. "You're being misled by a lot of agitators."

"No, sir, I don't think we are," one of the strikers said pleasantly. "We want better wages, and we want this company union to be bust up."

"You get paid good wages," O'Neil growled. "Plenty good, but we promised to adjust wages. Why don't you call off the strike?"

"Why don't you settle it?" a striker said, not impudently, but as one reasonable man talking to another.

O'Neil retreated, muttering.

Presently the works superintendent arrived and was sent away with the word, "Nobody gets in."

"Listen," he yelled as he left, "you're all fired."

The crowd roared with laughter. "You can't fire us, mister," they yelled. "We're firing ourselves until you guys talk turkey."

That was the kind of strike it was. The president of the company came down on the picket line and bawled out the strikers. The superintendent turned up not once but half a dozen times and got red in the face yelling at his ex-workers. He kept thinking that the next time he yelled at them they'd surely stop all this nonsense and go back to work. On the surface it looked like a friendly, good-natured strike. The police hung around the picket line and ate the strikers' sandwiches. The strikers cracked jokes with the maintenance engineers allowed in and out of the plant.

Akron's first rubber strike passed almost unnoticed after the first few days. People on West Hill slept easy. Hadn't Claherty himself said, the first day, "There will absolutely be no other rubber strikes. No sympathy strikes will be allowed. Anyone talking up such a strike will be expelled from the union."

The big three, then, Firestone, Goodrich and Goodyear, were safe. Their workers might grumble and might go down to General and help the boys out picketing, but Claherty himself had guaranteed there would be no trouble. "Big" rubber was safe.

Of course, West Hill sympathized with Billy O'Neil in his hour of need. But the rubber industry suffered from fierce competition, to put it mildly. Rubber executives might tut-tut at polite

172

dinner parties about the General strike, but the next morning they went down to work and sent batches of telegrams ordering their salesmen to call on General dealers. An honest penny is an honest penny and if a man is so dumb as to get caught with a strike on his hands, he must take the consequences.

East Akron, the valley, slept easy too. The rubberworkers expected to win. It was their first strike, and nothing could stop them —nothing. The union was on its way. No shadow of doubt arose in the valley. No fear clutched at hearts in the night. In these dingy working-class streets, there were no old women who still mourned husbands shot down on half-forgotten picket lines. These were mountain people, only ten or twelve years away from scraggly farms on the sides of lonely hills. They had no group memory of bullets cracking into fleeing crowds, of men smashed by clubs, of women kicked in the stomach as they crawled screaming from police attacks.

These were young people. For years men had worked out their strength and energy in the rank-smelling factories. Years women had suffered hopeless insecurity. Years they had worried over where the next pair of shoes would come from, and when Hank would be laid off. Now at long last they were striking back. They felt good about the strike. They were proud and happy.

The union men faced the strike with a kind of naive courage, a blinding faith. They had never heard of union spies. They didn't have the faintest notion that among them, in their very ranks, stood men who sold their secrets for money. They had no idea that the cards were all marked in this game. These mountaineers with their first union cards in their pockets never dreamed that the American Federation of Labor officials looked upon their strike with considerable, not to say vast, suspicion and annoyance. They walked among pitfalls and beartraps like proud blind men.

The Union Continued   *June 26, 1934*

Four "loyal workers" appeared at the General plant gates today and began to distribute company-union literature to the pickets. They went away with bloody noses.

Mr. Claherty met Mr. O'Neil at the Mayflower Hotel for the third consecutive day of dickering over a strike settlement. The conference broke up without results.

The Union Continued *June 28, 1934*

Coleman Claherty left Akron today. He had business, he said, in Albany, N. Y.

The picket line was slightly bewildered by Mr. Claherty's business trip. The strikers' feelings were hurt. They thought their strike, the first rubber strike of any size, was so important that the A. F. of L. general organizer in rubber should stay home and take care of it.

Mr. Claherty did not share their opinion.

The Union Continued *June 29, 1934*

The temperature went to 105 on the streets of Akron today. Official recording was 99. The rubber stink settled down over the valleys. Inside the big factories men stood beside tire machines and were sick with heat, men worked in the pits with live steam and staggered as they worked, blinded and tortured by heat.

At the gates of the General plant, stubborn strikers sat crouched in blank silence on the sizzling bricks of the street, holding the picket line under a blazing sun. The stench of burning rubber from the near-by Goodyear plant gouged at throats and nostrils.

The picket line held all day. Men stood immobile, but their presence told the world the union held the General plant.

The Union Continued *July 3, 1934*

The scene shifted on the General strike today. Ralph Lind, the government negotiator, flew to Washington to powwow with his Washington superiors.

The picket line buzzed with talk. Nobody understood what Lind was doing. The strikers were nervous. They wished Claherty would come back home and see what was up. This waiting got on a man's nerves.

The Union Continued   *July 9, 1934*

The General strikers were all excited this morning. Men stood around on the picket line brandishing sheets of paper. Lanky mountaineers spit out blue curses and strikers threatened dark vengeance to a man they called variously "Broose," and "Browse," and "Br-r-owe-se."

Edwin Brouse, respected, nay, distinguished, Akron attorney, was the author of a letter which each and every striker had found in his morning's mail. The letter stated that he, Edwin Brouse, a disinterested Akron citizen, wished to assist the cause of industrial peace in his native city. Since, he wrote, many statements had been made, apparently in good faith, that most of the General employees were not on strike and wished to return to work, he proposed that all the strikers and employees of the company attend a meeting under his auspices and vote yes or no on whether they wished to continue the strike. He offered his services, he said, in determining the truth of the situation at General Tire.

The picket line considered tearing Mr. Brouse limb from limb. Some hotheads were all for marching downtown to Mr. Brouse's office and telling him a few things. Reason prevailed, however.

The newspapers published Mr. Brouse's letter and they also published Mr. O'Neil's statement that he had sent copies of the letter to his employees. Mr. Brouse saw nothing strange in the letter of a disinterested person being mailed to strikers by their employer. He said he considered his position on the strike that of a just and honorable man. Mr. Brouse was a Latin scholar, a gentleman of culture, a skillful and successful corporation lawyer, an old resident in Akron, where nearly everyone is a new settler. Mr. Brouse held the opinion that wicked outside agitators had misled a few General Tire employees. The rest, he believed, were ready and anxious to go back to work. They were prevented from taking this step by violent and lawless men on the picket line.

The day of Mr. Brouse's disinterested General employees' meeting dawned hot and bright. This summer, everybody said, was certainly turning out to be a scorcher. Everybody always said that in Akron, as though each year the intolerable heat surprised them.

Mr. Brouse arrived at the East High School auditorium neatly dressed in well-fitting clothes, carrying a polished leather briefcase. A well-built man, not too large, not too small, his shoulders were broad enough for a lawyer but not vulgarly large like a workman's. His face had regular features. He had a noble forehead, and he wore plain eyeglasses. Nothing about Mr. Brouse was gaudy or flamboyant or in bad taste. Nor was Mr. Brouse's manner nervous or excited. His face was perfectly impassive as he sat in the wings of the East High School auditorium waiting for the loyal employees of the General Tire and Rubber Company to arrive. Presently a few men straggled into the auditorium. They walked in diffidently, rather embarrassed, like people who come too early to an afternoon tea. They craned their necks, staring into the empty balconies, and talked in low voices. Men wandered around the platform. They were, it developed, members of the county election board here to count the vote. Presently ushers began to distribute little red ballots, putting them on empty seats.

The quiet in the auditorium, the empty seats, were an insult. Mr. Brouse appeared on the platform and suggested hearing from a few of the men in the audience while they waited for the crowd to assemble.

Then a cheer sounded faintly inside the auditorium. Mr. Brouse stiffened as the noise of marching men filled the empty hall. Ushers glanced nervously at the doors. The scattered men in first row seats shifted uneasily. The song of triumphant workers, the tread of marching feet, grew louder. The doors of the auditorium burst open. Hundreds of men rushed down the aisles shouting.

Mr. Brouse stood perfectly still. His face did not lose its cold composure as he stared at his new audience, more than a thousand strong. No muscle moved when he saw the marchers pounce on the red ballots and throw them in the air like a shower of big confetti. He heard, but he did not answer, the cries, "Here's the Red Apple boys! Look at 'em!"

"Red Apples!" the newcomers roared. "Take an apple to teacher! Ya-a-a-h! Lousy scabs! Dirty Red Apples!"

Mr. Brouse took up his polished real leather briefcase and walked out, leaving the stage to the canaille.

In a Far Place   *July 16, 1934*

In San Francisco, organized labor began a general strike to protest the attacks on the maritime union's picket lines.

Akron newspapers screamed the story in huge headlines. A thrill went through the city, and so rapidly was the old mold breaking in this Ohio town, that in one part of town it was a thrill of horror and in another part a thrill of pride.

In the old days, you could say that people in Akron thought so and so about a happening. But by July 16, 1934, you could only say, "Rich people think so and so about this; poor people on the other hand think exactly opposite."

In the valleys of Akron men read about the general strike and said, "Well, Jesus, that's showing 'em, boy. That's something."

And they remembered.

On the hills, on West Hill, men read and said, "It's revolution. You give 'em an inch and they start a revolution."

And they remembered.

"We Won! We Won!"   *July 19, 1934*

Old cars roared through the streets of East Akron long after midnight. Young fellows hung on the running boards screaming, "We won! Boy, we won! The strike's over! We won!"

Saloons kept open until dawn. Men danced in the streets and sang on street corners. It was like Armistice Day, it was like the day Lindbergh landed in France. The kids stayed up and hopped around first on one foot then on another shrieking, "Daddy, let me blow the horn now."

177

The men on the night shift at Goodyear just quit work and came on out into the happy night to help celebrate. East Akron was wild with joy. The strike was over. The strike was won. Now things would be better. From this day forward things would be new and different.

Next day, in the heat, the valley was quiet while exhausted men slept off the celebration. In the new stillness a few men carefully reread the strike settlement. In the light of day it seemed very different from the document Claherty had declaimed so dramatically at the union meeting the night before. In the new day, the settlement lost its glamor.

The union had not won recognition. The settlement said that the company would deal with those persons represented by the following: and they named the officers of the General local. Mr. O'Neil hadn't backed down from his stubborn insistence he would never talk to "outsiders" about his business affairs.

The company agreed not to support the company union financially. That was something.

The company agreed not to reduce wage rates. That also was something.

Finally, the company agreed not to discriminate against strikers.

Not bad, the careful men said to themselves, not good. A beginning, but only a beginning. With O'Neil on the run, with the big rubber companies stealing his distributors, forcing him to settle, it might have been more.

Nevertheless, the strike ended in a wave of good feeling. The valley people were satisfied for the moment. The newspapers said proudly that no head had been broken, no arrests had been made. In Akron, both employers and employees knew how to conduct themselves in a labor dispute.

That's what the papers said.

The prelude was over.

They Got Him   *July 23, 1934*

Federal detectives shot and killed John Dillinger, the outlaw. His death brought editorials about "Crime never pays" and

178

sermons along the same line. People in Akron discussed the details of the shooting with morbid excitement and the newspapers published a gruesome picture of the dead man showing the bullet holes.

Carnival   *August 8, 1934*

John Dillinger, Senior, father of the late famed gangster, was a sideshow attraction at the American Legion fair held on the airport grounds. He did not, contrary to advance billing, display the bloody bullet-torn shirt in which his son died. Church groups protested so loudly against this proposed feature of the fair that Legion officials at the last moment canceled the bloody garment part of Mr. Dillinger's act.

Rattlesnake Man   *August 25, 1934*

The Rev. Albert Teester arrived in Akron ready to take up his work as an assistant to the well-known evangelist, and local Billy Sunday, Bill Denton. Reverend Denton ran a mission on Furnace Street, but was famed throughout the city for his sledgehammer attacks on slot machines during the last *Beacon Journal* campaign against petty gambling. Reverend Denton swung, it was reported, a mean sledgehammer.

Reverend Teester had also won fame, although not for swinging sledgehammers. He made newspaper headlines from coast to coast on a hot dull day when he allowed a rattlesnake to bite him. Then, while his congregation alternately prayed and watched, Reverend Teester called on God to overcome the power of the snake bite and put the Devil in his place. Reverend Teester's arm swelled, his face turned blue and his congregation feared that the Devil was winning. Just as his audience had given up hope, Reverend Teester showed signs of recovery. Three days later he looked as good as new.

Reverend Denton, with a quick eye for news, immediately telegraphed an offer to the West Virginia "snake-bite preacher," and the holy man of the mountains turned down a World's Fair contract to come to Akron to do the Lord's work.

Reverend Teester, a tall lanky minister with a deep voice and a heavy mountain accent, had been a preacher for four months. After Reverend Teester's wife died, in March, leaving him the care of his five children, the sorrowing farmer felt the call of the Lord. He took to preaching at his neighbors', and soon God told him to let the snake bite his arm.

A curious crowd surrounded the bewildered mountain preacher when he climbed down from the bus at Union Station. "How does it feel to be bitten by a rattlesnake?" somebody called out to him.

"Lak ah bee sting," he replied in his deep voice. He explained that he scorned the World's Fair offer because it was too "worldly."

Reverend Denton, a squarish man with a bland face and a smooth voice, met his protégé and hurried him away from newspaper reporters. Reverend Teester, Reverend Denton explained, would tell the story of his experience with the snake exclusively at regular Sunday night meetings in the Furnace Street mission.

The Union Continued   *September 1, 1934*

Akron's "little boom" collapsed on the first day of September. Since spring, employment in the rubber shops had been steadily rising. During some hot summer weeks the big factories ran close to capacity.

But now foremen walked through the shops, stopping at first one tire machine and then another, passing out the dreaded layoff slips. Freshly wrapped tires filled warehouses, and the rubber companies prepared to sweep their factories clean of unneeded workmen.

Now that the "little boom" had ended, and the rubber shops laid off instead of hiring, Akron began to understand the implications of speedup, or as they said in factory managements, "increased production efficiency."

"Why, even when the shops were working good," women said slowly, meeting their friends in little groceries at the corner, "they didn't take back on a lot of the fellows."

"Yeah," angular big-boned girls answered, shifting a bag of potatoes from one sharp hip to another, "it seems as though they don't take on so many any more, even when they're hiring good. It's funny."

"Don't be so dumb," men said heavily, over the supper table. "I been telling you about the speedup in the shops, and you never catch on. Sure, they ain't hiring so many. They just work the ones left harder."

Men and women in the valleys began to see, the fall of 1934, that the speedup was not only a question of working harder, of working so hard your back ached and you couldn't sleep nights. It was also a question of never working again.

The Government figures, published some time before, might have furnished a statistical explanation to millhands of the meaning of speedup in the Akron factories. But the figures were never blared in newspaper headlines and even if they had been widely broadcast, they wouldn't have meant much to rubberworkers and their wives. Properly so, too. A rubberworker's wife was not concerned with how many pounds of rubber her husband produced in a year. She was only interested in how tired he was when he came home at shift end. She only cared whether he could get a job at all to feed the kids.

In the fall of 1934 proletarian Akron watched the shadow of permanent unemployment fall over the city. Now, too, men who had held out so far against the union, men who still cherished some vestiges of the old "American dream," realized that even when what the newspapers called the "Depression" was over, even when prosperity came back for sure, even then, thousands of rubberworkers would never again have a job.

Akron turned to the rubber union. Local meetings picked up attendance. Speeches from the floor grew fiercer. Sunday after Sunday, in one local after another, men demanded action.

"Do something," big pit builders shouted while the chairman pounded for order. "I ain't smart enough to tell you what to do, but do it, quick, for God's sake, before they lay everybody off in the whole damned shop. There won't be a job left for anybody in two years, if we don't do something."

Mr. Claherty teetered on his straight wooden chair, listening to the talk, and marking out the men who did too much of it.

Then he answered. Mr. Claherty called for National Labor Relations Board elections in the rubber shops. The rubber union, he said, could win any election in any Akron rubber shop. With the rubber union certified for collective bargaining, workers could end the speedup by peaceful, legal methods through a signed union contract with the rubber bosses.

The rubberworkers were pleased. The law said you could have an election, and if you won an election your employer had to bargain with you. It seemed very simple, in fact so oversimple a few of the tirebuilders made objections.

"Them bastards ain't going to give in that easy," men yelled from the floor at Claherty.

"They can't fight President Roosevelt" Claherty yelled back, and his audience cheered.

The Union Continued   *September 26, 1934*

The United States Government, in the person of mild-voiced Ralph Lind, called The B. F. Goodrich Company and The Firestone Tire and Rubber Company to Cleveland and asked them to show cause why a National Labor Relations Board union election should not be held in their factories.

The hearings took place in a tense strained atmosphere. The Goodrich company lawyers buzzed around Mr. Lind like angry bees. In fifteen minutes these gentlemen had denounced the legality of the whole proceeding and objected specifically to nearly every question Mr. Lind put to the officers of the rubber company.

The lawyers objected again when Mr. Lind questioned the union men. "You're coaching the union witnesses," the lawyers barked.

Over their objections, Sherman Dalrymple, president of the Goodrich local, told Mr. Lind that the Goodrich rubber local had 7,654 members, and wanted an N.L.R.B. election badly.

Bland Vice-President Graham of The B. F. Goodrich Company

followed Mr. Dalrymple to the stand. "In view of the conditions in our plant, which are excellent, there is no justification to hold this election," Mr. Graham stated under the watchful eyes of his lawyers.

The Firestone case proved a mild duplicate of the Goodrich affair. Firestone lawyers denounced the National Labor Relations Board. Firestone lawyers denounced Mr. Lind and his questions. Firestone officials declared conditions in the plant did not warrant an election. Firestone union men claimed as members a majority of the workers at the plant.

Mr. Lind took the matter under advisement and adjourned the hearings. Cynics stated plainly that even in the event Mr. Lind ordered the elections, they would not be held. Obviously the Firestone and Goodrich lawyers would take the case to court.

But rubberworkers were not men-of-the-world. They waited for Mr. Lind to order the elections. They cheered when they read Claherty's statement, "Goodrich will take a strike vote if the N.L.R.B. does not order the election."

Rubberworkers were not familiar with the expression "testing a law in the courts." They imagined that when Congress passed a law citizens of the United States were thereupon forced to obey it.

The Supreme Court meant very little to Akron factory hands.

When Winter Comes   *October 1, 1934*

George Missig, Summit County relief director, announced that Akron faced the hardest winter of its history.

"Fifty-five thousand men, women, and children will be supported by relief this winter," Mr. Missig said. "Last year it was only 44,000." He added that there simply were no funds in sight to provide for such a large number of charity cases.

Birthday Party   *October 6, 1934*

Three hundred of Akron's top businessmen, rubber barons, leading lawyers, and best-paid clergymen turned out for F. A. Seiberling's seventy-fifth birthday party, held in the ballroom of the Mayflower Hotel.

Mr. Seiberling, a stocky little man with a round chubby face and an air of great good nature, whom all of Main Street called "F.A.," was Akron's best-liked business mogul. A natural gambler, he was a shrewd and daring rubber baron.

Like most of America's millionaires, he did not really start from scratch—his father owned grain mills, and "F.A." grew up in a prosperous home. But "F.A." was just a minor Akron businessman at the turn of the century. He owned an electric railway connecting Akron with Cleveland and assorted other small enterprises. Then he struck rubber, as other men strike gold. He jumped fearlessly into the industry with the roughest competition in American business. Year after year he gambled with competitors. He sunk all his money in automobile tires when automobiles were still a fad. He was there first, and he cleaned up.

Year after year he gathered every dime he had, and every dime his brother and his friends and relatives had, and put it into a new process, a new rubber idea. He won time after time. The Goodyear Tire and Rubber Company, his baby, grew enormously. While dozens of other rubber companies that started with more capital fell by the wayside, "F.A.'s" Goodyear marched forward.

In 1920, "F.A." took one long shot too many. Or perhaps he shot dice with the wrong people. For Wall Street bankers closed in on Mr. Seiberling and took away the company he had nursed from its birth, closing an era in Akron. In the honeymoon days of rubber, every smelly little factory in town was the personal property of some local businessman. When the Seiberlings were thrown out of Goodyear, only Harvey Firestone remained, like Henry Ford in the automobile business, to go it alone.

But F. A. Seiberling, past sixty when he lost Goodyear to Wall Street, was made of stern stuff. Broke and with the howling of outraged stockholders in his ears, "F.A." surveyed the rubber industry. Obviously there was no room for another Goodyear. But, he thought, there was plenty of room for a small specialty tire company.

At seventy-five, old "F.A." was the boss of a thriving rubber mill. Even more spectacular, he had organized the small rubber companies and spent his time as the spokesman for "small" rubber, baiting the big boys with government .edicts, investigations, and codes. The rubber industry still trembled when "F.A." opened his mouth to roar.

Now, on his seventy-fifth birthday, the power and wealth of Akron gathered rather self-consciously at the town's leading hotel to do the old lion honor. It was an enormously sentimental occasion. Harvey Firestone, the pale, hook-nosed little friend of Henry Ford's, turned up and somewhat reluctantly posed for a picture with his arm draped around "F.A.'s" neck. The two men had been business rivals for thirty years and regarded each other with about as much trust as two tigers.

All the rubber barons sat solemnly at the speakers' table. One by one they rose and spoke sweetly of "F.A." The rotund little hero of the event stared at the silverware while one bitter rival after another rose to say that in spite of certain business differences he really loved dear old "F.A."

"F.A.'s" own speech was a declaration of faith. He cut through the sentimental hypocrisy of the evening to defend his own life, and indeed, the lives of the men to whom he spoke. Gathered before him, on this evening, were all the men in Akron who amounted to anything in the old-fashioned sense of the word. Here were the newspaper publishers, the expensive corporation lawyers, the town's leading capitalists, celebrating the birthday of the most talented businessman the community had ever produced.

F. A. Seiberling felt, and his listeners felt too, although they lacked the courage to put it into words, that on this evening their small close world was threatened.

"The country cannot be happy," Mr. Seiberling said earnestly, repeating the classic apologia of American capitalists, "if this class idea is promoted." After a lifetime of belonging to it, "F.A." denied the existence of an owning class.

"Money is not important," said the little Napoleon of the rubber industry. "Business is fun. That's why I gave my life to business, because it was fun, not because of the money."

He ended his speech by looking over the listening crowd. He

noted the marks of care and worry. These 300 were not so assured or so smug as they had been five years ago. So he sounded a call to arms. Courage, the old man said.

"I am an optimist," Mr. Seiberling declared firmly, and sat down.

Figures   *October 11, 1934*

The United States Department of Justice, announcing its latest figures on crime, revealed that among eight major cities in Ohio, Akron stood first in manslaughter, first in cutting and shooting to kill, first in rape.

The Department added that Akron had the smallest police force, per capita population, in the nation. The city had 172 policemen, whereas the average municipality of its size had 250.

Haw!   *October 19, 1934*

All of Akron laughed today when the *Times-Press* published the calling cards of a bevy of flashing-eyed local prostitutes. "I am working my way through Akron University," said the cards. "I live in a hotel protected by the city for twenty-five years."

The *Times-Press* solemnly denounced the city police for allowing ladies of the evening to go around advertising they were co-eds at the city institution of learning. Akron University officials solemnly denied that any prostitutes were working their way through *their* college, and Akron police denied that they had been protecting any "hotels" for twenty-five years or any other period of time, indeed, and forsooth!

Mayor Honest Ike Myers added the final fillip to the town's best joke in months when, asked if he knew about women "soliciting" on the streets, saying they were Akron University co-eds, he replied, "Girls at Akron University begging dimes to get through college?"

"No, no, Mayor," chorused the reporters, and told the old man the facts of life.

A Matter of the Budget   *October 25, 1934*

The bankrupt city postponed flushing the town's sewers until indignant citizens sent a delegation to the Mayor. "The smell," said the spokesman of the delegation, "is unbearable." The Mayor explained that there wasn't any money to flush the sewers, but the outraged citizens demanded action.

Finally the sewage disposal department was ordered to flush the sewers, money or no money.

Wolf!   *October 31, 1934*

The Goodyear Tire and Rubber Company again threatened city council with moving its plant out of Akron. Goodyear engineers said the company could not pay 1½ cents a thousand gallons of water and demanded a further reduction in the industrial water rate.

By-Election   *November 7, 1934*

Republicans, locally licked to a frazzle in the 1932 Roosevelt landslide, started a comeback in yesterday's elections.

A Democratic New Deal Congressman, Dow Harter, won hands down and colors flying, but sixteen minor county offices went Republican. Sheriff Ray Potts, swashbuckling county police officer, was decisively defeated by Jim Flowers, a big handsome exhorseman and military man pledged to enforce the law.

Organized labor counted for nothing in the elections. One of the ablest of the town's labor leaders, James McCartan, ran for Congress on an Independent Labor ticket and received only 1,489

187

votes. The new unions in Akron gave the elections no official consideration whatsoever. A normally Republican county returned Republican county officials to office, but voters crossed party lines to elect a New Deal Congressman.

The Union Continued
November 16-December 5, 1934

Rubberworkers spent three passionate weeks hoping that the Government would cure the speedup and low wages in Akron —and then the N.R.A. and its National Labor Relations Board went blooey as far as the man on the tire machine was concerned.

The big rubber companies touched off the debacle by refusing, first collectively through their association, then singly, one by one, to bargain with the A. F. of L. Federal unions or even to consider the famous proposed agreement Claherty had so carefully drafted. The companies said they found "collective bargaining" satisfactory with their "employee unions."

Next the N.L.R.B. leaped into the battle. In sizzling statements, the Government denounced the company unions as "corrupting" and breeders of "strife and violence." Elections in the Goodrich and Firestone plants were ordered immediately.

The rubberworkers prepared for the elections, full of hope and wild excitement. William Green came to Akron for a madly enthusiastic pre-election rally. The Government set up polling places and had ballots printed. Men in the factories thought peaceful victory was all but in their hands.

Two days before the elections were scheduled, Firestone and Goodrich lawyers asked an injunction against the N.L.R.B. order from the Federal court in Cincinnati.

As simply as that, rubberworkers stopped believing the Government could step into factories and make life bearable. The N.L.R.B. cases were in court. It would be months, maybe a year, before the Supreme Court would get around to them.

Bitterly disappointed, shocked, the rubberworkers turned back to the union and the A. F. of L. with the cry, "Now what?"

Sheriff Ray Potts and four of his deputies faced Federal prosecution for protecting bootleggers, accepting bribes, and shaking down rumrunners and distillers, Akron newspapers headlined.

Government agents appeared in Akron to complete their investigation of what they called "the biggest graft probe in America."

The Tax   *February 17, 1935*

First returns, published today on Ohio's new three per cent sales tax for school and unemployment relief allowed the gentlemen of the Manufacturers' Lobby in the Legislature to indulge in a bit of sober rejoicing.

For it appeared that the new levy, for which they had fought so gallantly, gave the poor of the Buckeye state the Democratic privilege of paying to feed the poor.

In the beginning the Manufacturers' Lobby had battled for its favorite money-raising bill against what had seemed long odds. Many politicians, especially those from industrial cities like Akron and Cleveland and Youngstown, had entertained un-American notions about taxing the rich to feed the unemployed. The halls of the Legislature rang with speeches about passing State income taxes, raising the corporation taxes of rubber, steel, and auto companies.

The astute and never-say-die gentlemen of the Manufacturers' Lobby had countered this wild sort of talk with sober arguments about spreading Democracy by spreading the tax base. At the last, representatives of Ohio's leading industrialists in the State capital had reluctantly been forced to bring up their big guns. They pointed out that Recovery was hardly a possibility as long as politicians talked about raising corporation taxes or played with "Communistic" plans for levying a State income tax on the already troubled captains of finance.

The opposition pretty much folded up before such logical and impressive arguments. Organized labor, unorganized politically, didn't amount to anything in the minds of the State legislators. Politicians, who had been troubled at first by the thought that the voters could hardly forget a tax that meant the payment of a dozen pennies or so a day, found comfort and safety in numbers. After all, a man's constituents could hardly hold the sales tax against a good honest Republican (or Democrat) when nearly the whole legislature had voted the same way.

The sales tax went into effect February 1. Preliminary returns showed that purchasers of food, very cheap clothing, and fuel contributed the great bulk of the first collection of moneys. And the tax turned out even better than the Manufacturers' Lobby had hoped. Through the levying of a whole penny for any fraction owed, the three per cent tax actually amounted to a 3.4% average.

The politicians made the only serious miscalculation on the sales tax. To their surprise and distress, voters in great hordes registered fury and even a certain amount of vindictiveness about the payment of a few little pennies on every purchase of a loaf of bread or pair of cotton stockings.

"They'll be takin' the food out of our mouths tomorrow," housewives said sourly as they plunked down three cents for a dollar's worth of groceries.

"Tomorrow?" other customers answered. "They're takin' it now."

Politicians, with nervous ears to the ground, were horrified to discover that not a single housewife in Akron rejoiced, during the first month of the sales tax, that Democracy had come closer to her life.

Worse, it saddened jittery legislators to learn that large sections of the voting population regarded as so much horse feathers the heart-rending plea of the Manufacturers' Lobby that industrial leaders could not promote Recovery until relieved of the fear of unjust and un-American taxation.

Anxious wardheelers reported unanimously that Akron seemed to regard the sales tax as a piece of deliberately oppressive legislation foisted upon an already suffering population by the rubber barons and their friends from the Cleveland auto shops and the Youngstown steel mills.

First returns on the sales tax gladdened the hearts of the gentlemen of the Manufacturers' Lobby, but they cast a deep gloom over the Ohio State Legislature.

The Union Continued   *March 22-April 14, 1935*

As the heavy winter came slowly to an end in this city of factories and smoke, as the first winds of spring swept the dirty back streets, strike talk began in dead earnest.

This last winter had been too hard. The misery in the streets near the great factories had corroded men's hearts. The relief funds were so low. So many children turned pale and listless for want of decent food. In the factories, men struggled in sour sweat to keep pace with the conveyor belt, and after a week of the backbreaking speedup, stood in line to draw wages not sufficient to keep the kids in shoes or the wife in groceries.

So in every factory washroom, up and down the rows of tire machines, whispers spread. Strike, men repeated grimly, now or never. How much longer can we go on like this? How much longer?

Early in March, Claherty called his organizing staff together. He felt the union movement in Akron slipping from under his feet. Dues were way off. Conditions in the factory were terrible. The Labor Relations Board case would take years to get to the Supreme Court.

Claherty's advisers were bitter. "The men think we're bastards too," big red-headed Wilmer Tate growled savagely. "I tell you, I ain't going to sit through another meeting like the one last Sunday at Goodyear, with guys yelling for a strike all over the place and booing the very name of the A. F. of L. We got to do something. Conditions are terrible in the factories."

"Yeah," Claherty nodded thoughtfully.

On March 11, the three big rubber locals adopted a resolution, drafted in Claherty's office, empowering the officers of the union to take "whatever action necessary, even the use of economic power" to force the rubber companies into collective bargaining.

On March 26, all three rubber companies for the tenth or eleventh time formally refused to consider bargaining collectively with the A. F. of L. rubber union. Claherty told the newspapers, "It looks as though the inevitable is here. Labor must take its affairs into its own hands."

On March 27, at a great mass meeting, Claherty announced that a strike vote would be taken during the next week in Firestone, Goodrich and Goodyear locals.

A thrill swept the city like a grass fire on a brittle hot night. Newspaper editions were sold out on the streets. In the dirty smoke-blackened houses in South and East Akron, in the great gabled brick houses on West Hill, people anxiously, feverishly, talked about the strike.

Sinister rumors, sinister knowledge, filled the town. The *Times-Press* described the strike preparations of the rubber companies. Food supplies, great vans of canned milk and meat, and barrels of flour for bread, were trundled into the courtyards of the shops and stowed away in basement hiding places. In the raw spring wind, men worked on the great fences and brick walls that surrounded the factories, strengthening weak links, adding spiked borders at the top. Railroad shipments of heavy boxes, marked nails and filled with shining new machine-guns and bullets, arrived at the rubber factories. Electricians climbed factory roofs to install great searchlights. Sometimes, just before dawn, when nobody was about on the streets, the electricians had little dress rehearsals, flooding the area around the factories for blocks. Yes, they said, you can see with these lights to operate your machine-guns at night.

On March 28, the three big rubber companies announced that the company unions in each plant would themselves take a strike vote.

On March 29, Goodyear announced that its company union poll showed 11,516 against a strike and 891 for a strike. Officials added that as a result of this poll, they had decided to continue to operate the plant in the unhappy event of a strike. "We cannot deny our loyal workers the right to their jobs," the statement said.

The Goodrich poll officially stood at 6,019 against a strike, 2,015 for a strike.

The union immediately denounced the polls, pointing out that the votes had been taken on company property under the supervision of company foremen. It was a miracle, the union said, that even 891 men at Goodyear had the foolish courage to declare for a strike in a company-conducted election. The rubber companies replied that company union balloting was secret.

Great signs reading "Goodyear workers vote not to strike" fluttered on the Goodyear gates. Crowds gathered around the signs, hands shot out, hands no guard could identify for the pressing crowd, and the signs fell crumpled to the ground. Fresh signs appeared five minutes later.

In Goodyear Hall, that auditorium so generously dedicated by the company to the use and cultural profit of Goodyear workers, 200 men drilled all day, drilled at machine-gun practice, marched and countermarched, like soldiers. The tread of their marching feet turned union men cold with rage.

But machine guns can be less impressive than "public opinion." West Hill, always vocal in this Ohio community, grew shrill as the days passed. From a dozen sources, whispered from wholesaler to grocer to rubberworker, came the news that "decent people" were against the strike. And just as the tension began to tauten the nerves of the town, came the first public announcement of an organization called the Akron Civic Justice Association. Formally set up three weeks before, the fledgling association stepped forward on March 30 to busy itself with the strike. With a gilt-edged membership of service clubs, big merchants, lawyers, the Association packed a wallop in the "public opinion" battle.

On the day that the Akron Civic Justice Association made its public bow, Claherty got around to wiring William Green for permission to take a strike vote in the rubber unions.

Next day, March 31, the Civic Justice Association bought full-page ads in the two Akron newspapers. "We must give every man the right to strike," the advertisement said severely, "if that is his wish, but we must also insist that every man has the right to work." The Akron Civic Justice Association added, rather frankly, that it believed most Akron rubberworkers wanted to stay on the job. The company union polls proved it.

In the general fever, the two newspapers felt impelled to lift their voices. The Akron Civic Justice Association and the company union polls convinced the editors that the rubberworkers wanted to stay on the job. The *Times-Press* and the *Beacon Journal,* reluctantly they said, concluded that the A. F. of L. union was wrong.

On April 1, the union began taking a William Green sanctioned strike vote at Goodyear. Six craft unions and the Federal local balloted. The union meetings preceding the strike votes were so jammed that more men stood outside listening to loudspeakers than could cram inside the school auditoriums. Claherty spoke, and now he yelled for a strike vote as in the old days he had yelled against it.

The balloting at Goodyear was scheduled to last three days to give every shift a chance to cast its votes. On the first day Sheriff Flower swore in 1,000 deputies, nominated by the rubber companies. Each plant had some 330 newly appointed officers of the law assigned to its property. Sheriff Flower also announced, along with the news of the appointment of extra deputies, that he was "neutral." He added that every man in Summit County who wanted to work was "going to get the chance to work." He wound up his statement with the remark, "All chain or mass picketing in this strike is out. I will bust up any mass picket line that tries to get started."

On April 2, Ralph Lind, the Federal mediator, said, "The position of the companies is inconsistent. They insist only a minority want to strike, but they refuse to allow a Government-supervised National Labor Relations Board union election." Mr. Lind asked the rubber companies in the interests of industrial peace to withdraw their court proceedings against the ordered elections and allow the Government poll to proceed.

On April 3, Firestone announced the results of its company union poll: 7,162 against a strike and 1,659 to walk out. This balloting, Firestone said, was a mandate for the company to keep operating despite "trouble."

Claherty rushed into print denouncing the Firestone poll, taken on company property under company supervision. "We refuse to accept the responsibility for trouble," Claherty said. "The rubber companies are breaking the law of the land. Why don't they allow National Labor Relations Board elections?"

The Rotary and Lions clubs, meeting for luncheons at the Mayflower Hotel, unanimously adopted resolutions approving the Akron Civic Justice Association.

"Flower is instigating a riot," William Carney, a Goodyear union man, shouted during a pep rally at Goodyear local headquarters. "He's trying to start something with his 1,000 deputies. I don't think they can stop us from mass picketing. They won't stop me except over my dead body. I have as much right to picket as the sky pilots have to stop this strike."

On April 4, Goodyear flatly refused to bargain collectively with the A. F. of L. union and refused to sanction a Labor Board election. Ralph Lind, Government mediator, said this ended the possibilities of averting the strike and effecting a compromise. He left Akron for Washington.

On Sunday, April 7, Goodrich and Firestone locals began their strike polls. Written on a blackboard near the Goodrich ballot box, in uneven script, were the words, "Our children's future depends on us now."

Monday morning, the eighth of April, broke on a jumpy and nervous city. The *Beacon Journal* reported that William Green would go before President Roosevelt to discuss the rubber strike. "There is no hope of averting the strike," Mr. Green told reporters, "but I want the President to have the facts."

In Akron, Mr. Claherty said, "It is a question now who is the stronger—these rubber companies or the United States Government?"

Railroad freight hands began working on a twenty-four-hour schedule this Monday. Tires left Akron faster than at any other time since the World War. Firestone installed shatter-proof glass in employment office windows.

Tuesday, April 9, the papers carried headline stories of the National Government heading off the strike. Madame Perkins, Secretary of Labor, planned to confer with the rubber officials in New York, and Green summoned Claherty to Washington with the words, "There is always hope a strike can be prevented."

Late in the evening of Wednesday, April 10, Claherty left for Washington flanked by the three presidents of the rubber locals, solemn, tall men, only a few months from the tire machines. "Boys," Claherty said from the train steps, "I'm going to Washington because Green sent for me. But the rubberworkers will settle their own fate in Akron." The crowd seeing him off cheered.

He went on, "Whatever the labor leaders do at Washington will be satisfactory to the rubberworkers in Akron. You must be satisfied. We won't make a settlement without consulting you."

The last part of this train-step speech troubled a few of those standing around. But not much. They were too busy to think much about speeches. The strike had been tentatively set for the following Monday. Food committees worked twenty-four hours a day. Strike headquarters had to be furnished with loudspeakers and cooking equipment for hot lunches had to go in the basement of the union halls.

Union meetings would be held Sunday and the delegation would be back to make final pre-strike speeches. The picket lines would go into action Sunday at 11:30 P.M. to stop the first Monday shift.

On Thursday, April 11, officials of all the rubber companies left for Washington, summoned by President Roosevelt and Madame Perkins.

On Friday, April 12, Akron sickened with anxiety. Rumors spread over the town. The companies had given in; the companies had not given in. The President said they would be forced to give in; the President said the union must back down.

On Saturday, April 13, stories of a Washington settlement started to spread as early as three o'clock in the afternoon. They weren't true, though, for in Washington two groups of men sat in two separate offices, near Madame Perkins's headquarters, arguing. The rubber barons wouldn't meet the union men face to face, so Madame Perkins had to walk back and forth carrying proposals and counter-proposals. The union made the proposals and the rubber barons said no.

The valley met these rumors with violent fury. Men stood in bars and said, "Green can't doublecross us like he doublecrossed the boys in Auto," and "Claherty had better watch his step, there ain't no way to stop this strike unless the rubber bosses give in, and they won't do that, and any settlement is a sellout unless it's got the rubber bosses backing all the way down."

In Washington, the last plane left for Akron and the union men fidgeted, sorely pressed. They had to be back for the union meetings Sunday morning. The last train was leaving. Madame Perkins telephoned and the Baltimore and Ohio held the train. Then a paper was signed, and the union men ran for the station.

News of the settlement broke in Akron before Claherty was well on the train. Nobody knew the details, but Claherty and Green had signed something. Fury broke over workers' Akron. What did they sign? What could they sign, anyway? The strike had to come. The strike remained the one way out for rubber-workers. What did Claherty do in Washington?

Nobody knew in the valley. The terrible suspense made men wild. Their fate hung in a balance, and indeed had already been settled, but they couldn't read the scale figures. They didn't know yet whether they had won or lost. This was the last time, men thought, win or lose, that we let somebody else decide our lives.

But on West Hill men all but danced in the streets. They didn't know the details themselves, but they knew that the rubber companies would never have signed away what they were ready to fight for. West Hill trusted its leaders.

The Washington train arrived at nine o'clock on the raw, cold Sunday morning. A few union men at the smoke-blackened old station met Claherty, but nobody cheered as he got off the train followed by the three pale miserable-looking presidents. The delegation drove off in an old Ford directly to the Goodrich meeting.

The rubberworkers in the high school auditorium waited in almost dead silence. No hum of excited conversation rose from the rows and rows of big pitmen and heavy-shouldered tirebuilders. Men looked at the floor, avoiding the eyes of their friends. The Ford drew up at the auditorium steps in the misty fog.

"Your President," Claherty began heavily, to the somber audience before him, "William Green, wrote this agreement. I shall read it to you."

The document started off with a promise by the management to meet with chosen representatives of employees to settle grievances and to negotiate wages and hours. Every rubberworker in the union hall knew instantly what Claherty denied, that since the union was not specifically mentioned, the rubber companies would go on "negotiating," as they put it, with the company unions.

The second point in the agreement was a promise by the companies to post on the bulletin board notices of any agreements they had come to concerning wages and hours with the above-mentioned representatives of their employees. Some laughed as Claherty read that paragraph.

Third. Labor Board Elections were postponed until after the court hearings on the cases. This was the meat of the agreement. The rubber unions had decided to strike because the Labor Board elections would be held up for a year or two years in the courts. Now the rubber unions agreed to postpone the elections indefinitely.

Fourth: The rubber unions agreed not to strike pending the final decision on the Labor Board cases. However, should grievances not be settled satisfactorily, a Government fact-finding board of three would hear the case and recommend a solution. If the companies failed to live up to the decisions of the fact-finding board, the union was relieved of the no-strike section of the agreement.

When Claherty had finished reading, workers turned to their neighbors and with pain in their voices sighed, "But we don't get nothin' this way, absolutely nothin'."

Claherty broke through the subdued murmurs. He spoke skillfully. He called the agreement a victory. He said the rubber unions had made the bosses back down. He promised negotiations would end the speedup now.

Somebody yelled, "It's a goddamned lie."

"Throw that damned Communist out!" Claherty thundered instantly.

Nobody protested. The fight seeped out of these men. Defeat lay heavy and sore on their minds. Already their shoulders slumped. What was the use now? The agreement was signed. If they voted to strike now, every man's hand was against them.

Claherty said the agreement was good. Maybe it was. Who knew, and who, really, cared?

They voted quickly. They wanted to get out of that meeting and go home and never hear of a union again. They were ashamed. They wanted to get away from the sound of Claherty's voice, and the look of the man who sat next to them, the look of a rubber-worker at shift end, drunk with fatigue.

It was all over in a few hours. After Goodrich local voted to accept the settlement, Firestone and Goodyear were forced to agree. The solid front broken, Claherty pushed that fact for all it was worth. "You can't strike when one local has already said this settlement looks good to them," he shouted.

Men cried on the streets of Akron. Gangling tirebuilders, men with blue eyes and big ears, shuffled along the dirty smoky streets and gouged tears out of their eyes with the backs of their big hands.

Men cried. But more stood on street corners and tore up their union cards, sending the pieces fluttering in the raw wind, fluttering into the gutters.

"Why didn't you vote no?" women asked their husbands.

"What good would that have done?" they answered heavily. "You can't do nothin' about that. They run the union, and they run it for the bosses, not for us. I'm through. I'd see myself in hell before I ever belonged to another dirty stinking union."

"What'll we do now?" the women asked. "Aren't things ever going to be any better? Can't you strike anyway for more money?"

"Naw," the men replied. "Naw, we're washed up. We just got to take what comes now. We're through."

The anguish changed to a slow rhythm of despair. Men went to the shops Monday morning very quietly. They walked with heads down. In the factory washrooms they changed into work pants silently. No man had anything to say to his friend. The foremen stalked through the mills jauntily, whistling and yelling above the racket, "Come on, come on. Get a move on there. This ain't no slow-motion movie."

The ministers and the newspapers and the rubber-company officials applauded the bloodless and eminently fair settlement of a strike that might have been a tragedy.

199

Headline
April 25, 1935

"Happy Days Are Here Again for Akron Society."—Headline on the *Times-Press* Society Page.

Lockout
April 26, 1935

The India Tire and Rubber Company, the only rubber company in town which had recognized the rubber union, locked out its 200 union employees.

Signposts
May 5, 1935

Akron business, the newspapers announced proudly, continued its 1935 forward march well into the spring. Building was up sixty per cent over April, 1934. Connected water-meter figures climbed. Gas consumption had increased. The Ohio Edison Company reported a gain of 10,000 clients over last year.

The rubber companies, of course, had made money, lots of it, all through the worst years of the Depression, but now, business writers for the newspapers said, smaller manufacturers in town, merchants and the like, reported a slow climb out of the red.

Unemployment, however, did not drop.

The Union Continued
May 15, 1935

A handful of men straggled into the Goodrich local meeting, the first since the agreement. Nobody had expected a very big meeting, but it was pretty sickening to see the rows of empty wooden chairs.

The tirebuilders and pitmen who sat solemnly in the front rows waiting for the meeting to begin, looked weary. Outside it was warm. Sometimes the wind blew the rubber smell away from the valleys for a moment, and then soft, restless spring swept down the dirty streets and filled the hearts of these mountain people, so far away from their homes.

These May nights men sat on their front porches, and up and down a workers' street you could hear the melancholy twang of a guitar and the nasal but somehow moving chant of "The Arrow," or the ballad of the outlaw who shot his judge, or "The Wreck of the Old Ninety-Nine."

Spring was like a heartache to the valleys of Akron. Young people walked sadly in the streets, for who could get married now, with things so bad and never to get better? Women pressed their lips into a hard line as they put away a week's groceries from the relief, and sometimes they stood out on the back stoop and felt the spring air and remembered the days of their youth when they went barefooted in the new mountain grass.

Nostalgia filled the streets. The dirty smelly town with its hopeless backbreaking labor, its prison-like mills, weighed like stone on the hearts of its people. But there was no way out, no escape to the mountains. A man had children and a wife, and there was no way to make a living on those barren beautiful hills of the south. The kin folks were down from the hills working in the cotton mills. A man had to stay in Akron. A man had to work in the rubber shops.

So the valley people sat on their front porches and chanted softly over their guitars.

And only a few went to the union meeting. But those sitting solidly on the rickety wooden chairs and staring grimly at the platform were strong, hard, stubborn men. A handful at Goodrich, at Firestone, and Goodyear had resolved to hold the union together. Some of these men were Communists.

For when men had stood in the March wind tearing up their union cards, when men had walked in the streets gulping back tears, the Communists had called a meeting in a weather-beaten little frame house out past the Goodyear plant. The men from the rubber shops who belonged to the Communist Party attended —only a dozen or so.

A tall dark pitworker from West Virginia called the meeting to order. The workers sitting around the narrow living room were, like the chairman, nearly all from the Southern mountains. The debate, like the debate in a union hall, was in the rich soft speech of Kentucky and Tennessee.

It was not a happy meeting. These men, like the others, were heartbroken, embittered. First, they discussed the agreement, cursed it, and cursed Claherty and William Green. The meeting had little formal order. Men testified as the spirit moved them, and this night the spirit was sad.

But at last the chairman said, "And now where do we go, boys?"

He called first on one, then another, and after three hours, these rubberworkers who were also Communists evolved a simple plan. The Communists would press at once for an international union, insist that William Green grant an industrial charter. While they prepared for a charter convention, they would organize to prevent the appointment of Claherty to the presidency of the new union.

"The whole idea of this plan," the chairman drawled, "is to let the rubberworkers run their own union. Once they get a democratic union, one they can control themselves, they'll run it all right. These boys are the greatest natural unionists in the country, they got guts and brains. All they need is to have a union they can run themselves."

"An industrial union," somebody else broke in. "A union where everybody belongs."

"They all know that," the chairman said. "We don't have to sell them anything. They're all for an international industrial union. But now they feel licked and hopeless. We got to hold the union together until we can get a charter and elect officers right out of the rubber shops, then they'll come back in, the majority of them."

And these dozen Communists went out into the rubber shops and talked. They talked endlessly to every man of good will they met. They discovered a handful of hardbitten workers, not Communists by any means, who had anticipated their ideas, men willing to grit their teeth and last it out until they could build a real union to be run by rubberworkers themselves.

The little band of men who still believed in the union called themselves "Progressives." They never had a formal organization, but sometimes they met in one of the rickety frame houses and

202

talked over what to do next and cheered each other up. Even the best union men needed cheering up these days. Nobody to speak of belonged to the A. F. of L. anymore. The speedup got worse all the time. The company spies were thick as flies on honey. The foremen were arrogant and suspicious.

In these dark sad days the Progressives were the core and heart of the union movement. They believed in the union. They had hope.

This evening at the Goodrich local meeting, a man in a work-shirt, a big tall gangling pitworker, moved that the local go on record demanding an industrial charter from William Green. After him a half dozen men spoke, saying, "Give the union back to the rubberworkers."

The motion carried.

Fun   *May 18, 1935*

The Junior League dance this evening was a huge success. Chief feature of the party which everybody agreed was very "original" was a "Raw Deal Gambling Club." Guests played roulette with paper money.

The Court Says No   *May 27, 1935*

The newspapers appeared on the streets late this afternoon with bombshell news: the Supreme Court had thrown out the N.R.A.

"It ain't constitutional," men in the shops grunted, and made jokes. "The old Blue Eagle, she was pretty sick before, but she croaked today."

The N.R.A. died just at the right time for West Hill. When it came along in 1933, it had been a lifesaver, for even though it temporarily reduced working hours in department stores and the like, it let manufacturers cut wages.

The rubber barons, too, had liked the N.R.A. at first. They had a code which allowed them to forget the Anti-Trust laws and price-fix tires at a time when the industry was about to commit suicide with price-cutting. The code set minimum wages in the factories lower than the C.W.A.

True, the N.R.A. gave the first impetus to union organization in Akron, and that was bad. The rubber barons hadn't expected Section 7A to stir up a revolt in the factories. But union organization can be wiped out with a little effort, and in 1935 West Hill could sit back comfortably and agree that only unimportant remnants were left.

The death of the N.R.A. really came at a very opportune time. With the rubber-company suits against a Labor Board election in the courts, the unions could always hang on to a last wisp of hope. But the Supreme Court had killed Section 7A along with the rest of the act. The suits were as dead as the Blue Eagle.

West Hill clapped hands and said the Supreme Court could be trusted to interpret properly the Constitution. In the valleys men shrugged. They might have known the N.R.A. would die before it did them any good.

But the few union men still in the shops said, out of the corner of their mouths as the foreman passed, "The reason the N.R.A. is out is because the unions weren't strong enough to make it last. We got to really organize and get the unions into politics and then the Supreme Court won't dare to go around throwing things like the N.R.A. out."

"Uh-huh," tirebuilders said absently, not too interested. A few asked questions:

"How about these elections now?"

"How about them?" and the union men spat tobacco juice. "Well, what did you think? You think the rich guys in this country are going to knuckle under to some law they don't like without a fight? You must be crazy. No rubberworker is ever going to get anything without fighting for it."

"Yeah, and no goddamned union is going to do any fighting for us either."

"You're crazy. The union is what is going to save you," men answered earnestly, "once we get rid of Green and get an industrial union."

"Bull," said the tirebuilder. "Don't talk union to me."

Layoffs

Seasonal layoffs in the rubber plants started this week. The rubber union made no protest, and relief rolls jumped as men went home from the factories to wait for charity.

The Union Continued *August 3-September 17, 1935*

A handful of rubberworkers gathered with solemn elation the first week in August to make plans for the first convention of the United Rubber Workers of America.

Claherty, and on his advice, Green, had decided to send out the call for the fateful meeting. True, the membership in the Federal rubber locals had fallen so low Claherty hated to look in his books at the fearful facts. In the A. F. of L. office where two years, and even a year, ago crowds of men had rushed in and out, where there had been the sound of marching men, there was, these hot summer days of 1935, absolutely no sound at all. Even the telephone didn't ring very often.

The union movement in Akron was shot to hell. When the rubber unions fell apart everything else went with them. Only a year ago there had been 40,000 organized workers in Summit County. Now there probably weren't 5,000 who paid dues even every other month. Membership in the Federal rubber locals totaled about 4,000, and many of these were only paper members.

But when Sunday after Sunday the handful of men who still came to union meetings kept demanding an international convention, Claherty finally agreed. He phrased the formal call in fancy language, and some items on the scheduled agenda the union men regarded with less than pleasure but, on August 3, the date of the convention summons, the union men still left in Akron celebrated an impressive victory.

Then they sat down and made plans. The plans centered around two general ideas: First, to get rid of Green and Claherty and everything that smelled of the old leadership. Second, to form a democratic industrial union.

Claherty's newspaper announcement of the coming convention

sounded the call to arms in clear language. "The details of the coming convention are being worked out by Mr. Green," the gray-haired organizer told reporters. "Mr. Green will come to Akron to supervise personally the work of the convention."

This was greeted with snorts and even less polite sounds in the nearly empty union halls. Mountaineers drawled loudly that Mr. Green had better keep his nose out of Akron or he wouldn't like it. Progressive caucuses met. Men sat on front porches in the half darkness or teetered back on chairs in barren halls and discussed endlessly how to beat Claherty and Green at their own game.

Green opened the hostilities. He appeared in Akron once again on Labor Day. He turned up at a widely advertised picnic to which all union men in both Akron and Canton were invited. Goodrich local stubbornly held its own picnic the day before. When Green rose on the hot sunny platform at Myers Lake Park, Canton, he addressed a scattered audience generously estimated at 5,000 persons.

The speech was cut on the usual Labor Day pattern, dull stuff. But an interview Green gave after the picnic was read with absorbed interest by the union men. The *Times-Press* said:

"The new International Rubber Workers' Union will have the firm hand of the A. F. of L. in control during its formative period after a charter is issued in September.

"This was disclosed by William Green, A. F. of L. President. Mr. Green said that the A. F. of L. had a precedent for this, set recently in the auto industry when Francis Dillon, A. F. of L. organizer, was named president of the union.

" 'I may name officers for a period until the rubber international is placed on an enduring basis,' Mr. Green said. 'It will need a firm financial standing for one thing.' He said he had no particular officers in mind."

This was no bombshell to the Progressives, but it called for harder work. Three days before the convention assembled, men from both sides of the fence began trickling into town. The rubberworkers, fresh from the shops in Massachusetts and Los Angeles, arrived worn out from days on busses or in day coaches. They went straight to little frame houses in East and South Akron. Their first conversations were bitter. They compared notes on the speedup and found it was nation-wide. You got rawhided in Akron and rawhided in Los Angeles.

Soon they settled down to talk business. Tate turned up for the first Progressive caucus with shaggy powerful McCartan from the printers' local. These two men, for years the guts of the old A. F. of L. in Akron, both presidents of A. F. of L. craft locals, offered advice, coached the delegates on procedure, and warned against parliamentary traps. For the rubberworkers gathered in serious solemn conference were slow-talking men, not accustomed to making formal speeches, although quick enough to answer arguments from scabs. Trade union democracy came naturally to these men who thought that every delegate should have his say, and that it was their solemn obligation to represent faithfully the will of the membership.

They lacked equipment, therefore, to battle in the convention against such wily old parliamentarians as William Green and Coleman Claherty. Nor were Green and Claherty fighting alone. They had called in Francis Dillon, tsar of the auto union; Michael J. Lyden, veteran President of the solidly craft-organized Ohio State Federation of Labor, and Eric Peterson, trouble-shooter for the International Association of Machinists. Mr. Peterson was present to see that the rubberworkers didn't go haywire and rob him of his potential members in the shops.

The A. F. of L. contingent held all the cards. They had convention experience and authority on their side. The Progressives had passionate faith in the union.

The first session of the United Rubber Workers of America's first convention, September 13, 1935, was, as Mr. Green himself said so fulsomely, an historic occasion.

However, this particular historic occasion started off very badly for Mr. Green. Just before the session was called to order, Thomas Burns, stocky handsome rubberworker from the boot and shoe factories of the East, handed a signed petition to the President of the American Federation of Labor. The petition prayed Mr. Green to observe democratic procedure in the selection of officers for the new International. Mr. Green's stodgy worried-businessman's face flushed dull red when he glanced at the first words on the paper.

"Who signed this?" he snapped, taken off guard.

"Forty delegates," Burns answered. There were forty-seven delegates attending the convention. Mr. Green's hand shook as he turned the pages of the document. He looked like a very angry man.

The convention opened tamely enough. Old Mayor Myers fumbled onto the stage and gave a fuzzy frightened speech. Organized labor always terrified him, and the sight of a lot of rubberworkers in a convention seemed very depressing indeed. In the good old days the rubberworkers never even dreamed of a union; now here they sat, big as life, and, as he would tell his wife later, twice as sassy. It was enough to make an old man of seventy-two years break right down and bawl.

"I feel sure," quavered Mayor Myers, reading rather uncertainly from his secretary's notes, "we have had less trouble than any other industrial city in the United States. I attribute that to the good sense of the employers and the good judgment of our employees, and to the co-operation of our labor element under the leadership of Mr. Patino and other men at the head of labor here. Through their help I know we will come back, and it is my hope and belief that Akron, Ohio, will be one of the first cities to come back, and when we come back, all of us, we can again all be happy."

When Mayor Myers ambled sadly from the platform, Michael Lyden, the astute President of the Ohio Federation of Labor, got up and talked about nothing for some minutes. He threw in a few words about "that great leader, Ohio's favorite son, William Green," but nobody clapped, so he went on pledging co-operation and finally sat down. He was followed by Thomas Donnelly, secretary of the state A. F. of L. organization. Mr. Donnelly spoke at some length and even contributed a poem to the occasion. Mr. Donnelly declared that the "brothers" of the Ohio labor movement had been waiting for the rubberworkers to join the A. F. of L. for many, many years. In fact, he added somewhat elegantly,

> We have waited for you day by day,
> You are as welcome as the flowers in May.

208

Mr. Donnelly also felt that the rubberworkers should not be "impatient."

The Akron delegates sat impassive under the oratory. Next came their favorite "sky pilot," Rev. Charles MacLennan, a Presbyterian minister from a little industrial town some forty miles away.

"I am not telling you anything you don't know from your own experience," Reverend MacLennan said quietly, "when I say that the factory system is achieved by grinding into dust the lives of millions and millions of men, women, and children. For the great mass it has only meant poverty and cruelty through the years." Reverend MacLennan's listeners were painfully still. "The only hope of the laboring class is through organized labor and through organizations, need I say, of course, under independent leadership."

The applause was thunderous. The gentlemen from the Ohio State Federation of Labor regarded Reverend MacLennan sourly as the delegates passed a motion of thanks for his speech.

The Progressives held a hasty caucus just after lunch. The main thing at the moment, they agreed, was to prevent Green handing them a ready-made charter before they could vote to accept it. They read the early editions of the Akron newspapers with grim faces. Green, it appeared, had been talking to newspapermen again about appointing officers. Asked by reporters if he planned to appoint Claherty president of the new rubber union, Green had replied, "I hadn't thought of it. However, he has done good and constructive work here."

"He hadn't thought of it!" the rubberworkers growled, gulping down coffee in a one-arm lunch stand around the corner from the Portage Hotel.

"All of these new internationals pass through these probationary periods," Green's interview had continued. "The delegates left Detroit perfectly satisfied after Dillon was appointed to be their president."

"You don't say," delegates snapped, slicing into store-made pie with angry cuts. "So they was perfectly satisfied, was they? They sure had a funny way of showing it, raising all the hell they did about it. Well, we ain't getting any of the same they got in Detroit."

The afternoon session opened with every delegate sitting on the edge of his ballroom chair. Claherty, the chairman, sniffed the excitement from the platform. An old hand at this kind of thing, he stood calmly waiting for silence. When the whispers quieted down, he said, "At this time I would like to appoint a committee to go to Room 426 and escort William Green to this hall to present the charter of the United Rubber Workers." The committee was shrewdly chosen. It included the ringleaders of the Green opposition. They would be out of the convention hall in the interval between the announcement and Green's arrival. They couldn't start anything.

The chosen men hesitated, rose slowly from their seats, looked around in confusion.

A big lanky fellow from Firestone called out, "Why the presentation of the charter?"

"I believe Mr. Green will be able to speak for himself," Claherty replied smoothly.

"Would it be out of place," the delegate continued desperately, while the escort committee still hesitated at the door, "for the delegates to elect a chairman and a secretary at this time?"

Claherty's face did not move a muscle despite bombshell number one from the insurgents. The bombshell was a dud. He took it apart slowly, with quiet pleasure. Claherty replied that Mr. Green would have to explain the convention call before any business might be transacted in the new union. Claherty spoke at length of committee appointments, and said he hoped that everyone was represented on some committee. All this had nothing to do with Thompson's question, but Claherty simply kept talking. The escort committee left. What else, they said afterwards, could they have done?

Green appeared, looking very sure of himself. Claherty gave him a royal send-off, introducing the President of the American Federation of Labor with all the fanfare possible. "President Green has devoted his entire life for the welfare and uplifting of mankind, and he is here to help the rubberworkers take their place under the sun."

Green's speech was a masterpiece of its kind. He had been making platform orations for years and years and now he did not spare the horses or scorn the hearts and flowers. With a throb in his voice he recalled the men who had died to make the American Federation of Labor great. He welcomed the rubberworkers into the fold of the organized workers of America.

"Now, my friends," Green went on, with all the stops out, "at this solemn moment, solemn to you and those you represent, significant beyond your comprehension and your appreciation, because in the days to come when you and I have passed into the great beyond, your children and your children's children will refer to this historic event when the International Union, of which they will be proud, and the obligation rests upon us to protect it, to safeguard it and to preserve it at any cost and to transmit it unimpaired as a common heritage to those who will follow."

The remainder of the speech was cut on the same incoherent pattern, except for a few odd sentences here and there. Now and then Green talked business, but he talked fast and not too clearly. It appeared that the A. F. of L. was conferring this charter on the rubberworkers from the kindness of its heart and in accordance with the San Francisco convention resolution. Green read that famous resolution to the delegates:

". . . It is realized that in many of the industries in which thousands of workers are employed a new condition exists requiring organization upon a different basis [not along craft lines] to be most effective. To meet this new condition, the Executive Council is directed to issue charters for National and International unions in the Automotive, Cement, Aluminum and such other mass-production industries as in the judgment of the Executive Council may be necessary to meet the situation."

The resolution sounded good to the rubberworkers, just as it had sounded good to the Progressives at the 1934 A. F. of L. Convention. Indeed, it read as though the executive council had been directed to issue industrial-union charters in mass industries.

After reading the resolution, Green quoted—talking fast—from the charter of the new rubber union. The charter covered all those in the industry engaged in the mass production of rubber products, "same not to include or cover such workers who construct

211

buildings, manufacturing or installing of machinery, or engage in maintenance work or in work outside of the plant or factories."

The rubberworkers blinked. It was rather worse than they had expected. Under that charter the electricians would probably try to horn in as well as the carpenters. The machinists were especially provided for, and heaven only knew what they would decide "manufacturing or installing machinery" really meant. "Maintenance work" could imply almost anything to scattered and venal craft locals hungry for dues. The last phrase capped the whole. "Or in work outside . . ." That included truckdrivers, freight-loaders, switchmen in the company railroad yards, the really strategic men in a strike. Shades of the San Francisco convention resolution! The executive council apparently had decided that the 1934 convention had no right to make decisions about industrial unions. The charter was a joke, a charter to cripple rather than encourage the rubber union.

"That charter to me," Green continued, not unaware of the surprise and horror in his audience, "represents a very broad scope of jurisdiction. You must respect the rights of all other International unions."

The deadest kind of silence accompanied the rest of the speech. The enraged delegates saw that they had been tricked and despoiled by a bunch of old men sitting around on their fat hams in Washington hotels. They listened in sullen quiet while Green wound up, "This new International which I have launched will ever be close to my heart and as long as I live and breathe I will give my life and service to protect it from its enemies within or without."

Green stopped. Instantly Salvatore Camelio, a dark little man from the East, was on his feet.

"I would like to ask if we, the delegates assembled, accept this charter, does this give the President the right to appoint its officers?"

Down went Claherty's gavel with a mighty smash. He roared something, but he was drowned out in a burst of applause and loud cries, "You tell him," and "Don't let him get away with it." Claherty banged again and again. Finally, Green lifted his hand. White around the lips, furious that his hearts-and-flowers speech

212

should be answered so abruptly, he snorted, "It is not for you to accept the charter. That has been decided by the Executive Council. It cannot be amended and it cannot be accepted and it cannot be rejected. The parent body is creating a new International and it cannot barter with the Union it is creating."

He paused. Angry men, some still standing in their excitement, stared at him. Green continued coldly, "This confers upon me the right to designate or appoint your officers for a probationary period providing I think and in my judgment it seems necessary to do that to protect your International union, but before I do that I am going to consider the situation and then arrive at a conclusion, but in anything I do, please be assured that it will be inspired by a sincere desire to protect the officers and members of this United Rubber Workers' Union of the American Federation of Labor."

He sat down. Claherty rose and with his powerful voice forced the delegates back into the familiar position of sitting and listening to speeches. Claherty spoke fulsomely. "You don't know, President Green, how much the rubberworkers appreciate the time and effort you have put in to bring this meeting here and to bring it about."

The moment Claherty paused to catch his breath, Thompson shouted, "Will you please read again from the charter about the jurisdictional rights of this union."

Green read the paragraph slowly. The delegates listened and felt sick. Little Salvatore cut in with a shrewd query. He wanted to know whether machinists and steamfitters and the like who were already members of the Federal locals could be snatched away from the International by craft unions.

Green's face darkened. The question hit home hard. Green hesitated and then found an answer, "That is easy to settle at the conference table. I think we can all trust each other. We will settle these things later."

Before anyone else could ask something else disastrous, Claherty adjourned the meeting. He left with Green, but the rubberworkers stood around talking wildly. No doubt about it, they had lost round one. It remained to be seen whether the determination of men who wanted to be free was enough to defeat Green.

213

The evening papers looked bad too. Green was reported to be determined on Claherty's appointment. He had done it in Detroit; he would do it again.

Next morning, Friday, Francis Dillon himself turned up, rushed into the breach by the now worried Claherty. Another smooth-talking, smooth-looking A. F. of L. veteran, Dillon gave an extended account of hardships of his childhood and the love he bore for organized labor. He spoke of the famous Toledo strike. Most rubberworkers in the audience believed they knew the lowdown on that auto strike. Now Dillon explained everything. The explanation, however, failed to convince the delegates. Nothing could convince them now. They hardly listened to the speeches. Let Claherty bring on his Dillons, let him bring on St. Peter himself. The rubberworkers would show them!

Dillon wound up on Green's theme of the day before, "In the years to come your children and your children's children will remember with reverence the decisions and actions you have taken here."

Immediately after lunch Claherty asked for committee reports. A member of the resolutions committee called out, "Mr. Chairman and delegates!"

So far as the rest of the convention delegates and the other members of the resolutions committee were concerned, the out-of-town delegate then proceeded to make a perfectly amazing resolution, asking Green to appoint Coleman Claherty president of the United Rubber Workers. He read rapidly, but he didn't sit down after the Claherty section of the resolution.

He continued. "And be it further resolved that we respectfully request President Green and the American Federation of Labor to establish and finance an International Union headquarters and staff capable of handling all detail work." The next "resolve" was a request to pay the officers' salaries.

The rubberworkers were painfully stunned. Here was a resolution which, if they defeated it, would mean they would vote down financial assistance from the A. F. of L. They had to have money, every delegate in the place knew it. And how strange that this resolution appeared just now, when the resolutions committee had been working on another separate resolution, with the finance question clearly separated from the Claherty problem. How strange that the resolution came before the convention as a minority report of the committee, with five out of seven members of the committee reported as voting against it. Obviously, there was dirty work at the crossroads.

"It is moved and seconded," Claherty said smoothly, "to accept the minority report of the resolutions committee. Any remarks?"

Before anyone could object, Claherty made a little speech of his own. He said he was embarrassed to sit in the chair while he was the center of discussion. Therefore, he murmured pleasantly, he would turn the chair over to William Green. With an amiable if nervous smile Green walked to the platform, only too happy, he said, to be a good soldier and help out. Then he briskly recited the parliamentary question up for debate. The decks cleared for action, Green stood facing the rubberworkers, deliberately present to abash them.

A pause. Short, stocky, blue-eyed Callahan from Goodrich: "I move for a roll-call vote!"

A delegate asked to have the resolution read again. Green read it impressively.

Another pause. Green stepped forward. He tried to cut through the fury he felt in his audience. "I want to speak to you," he began, "in the most friendly way and in all sincerity." Men stared at him.

Inflamed by the hostility he saw in the faces of the delegates, Green lost his temper. He said he could, if he chose, appoint the officers of the union even if the convention voted down the "request" now up for its consideration. He went on, furiously, "You will have to have some money to start this union with, won't you?" His voice rising, he asked, "Now, if you take it all over today you will have to have funds to finance yourself, and where are they? You will have to find headquarters. You will have to print your constitution."

He continued talking about money, making it very clear: No Claherty, no money. "The American Federation of Labor," he concluded, "wants to help you, financially and otherwise. All it

215

asks is that it might give to you all it can in tiding you over a crucial critical period."

Green had hardly finished before Salvatore Camelio, the shrewd little Italian, was up and talking loud. "You just said that as a child we must appeal to our Daddy for funds to establish this International union. It makes no difference in the man who represents this International, because you will have to help him whether it be Burns, myself, or anyone else. You must help him and all this convention asks for is the democratic right to vote for that man whom they feel confident will lead the rubberworkers to conquer."

Green, stung, snapped back, "If you were called upon to employ someone, wouldn't you want to have the say about a selection?"

Camelio shouted, "We forty-eight delegates feel just as confident as the American Federation of Labor that we can pick a man to best represent the rubberworkers."

"That might be a matter of a difference of opinion," Green replied furiously.

Sherman Dalrymple rose. Never a very fluent speaker, in this crisis he chose his words deliberately, his strong big face creased with the effort. He was known as a good middle-of-the-roader, an honest, devoted union man out of the pit. He had gone to Washington with Claherty as president of the Goodrich local. He had worked with Claherty for more than a year. The delegates leaned forward to catch every word.

Dalrymple, it appeared, was mad clean through. "Far be it from me to censure the integrity of the American Federation of Labor," he began, and his drawl betrayed his West Virginia homeland. "But I do say that we had been advised that our organization was to be formed on a pure democratic principle."

He concluded with painful and impressive deliberation, "I want you to give this matter all due deliberation before you vote your democratic principles of organization away."

It was a telling speech. Others followed. Few defended Green. Finally the delegates shouted for the roll call. In tense excitement, the clerk read off the names. Men cast their votes as though they were deciding their fate.

216

The vote stood 45⅝ to 9⅙ against Claherty—a landslide for trade-union democracy.

Green had a few moments to pull himself together after the shock. The roll call had to be heard twice, once to vote "no" on concurrence with the minority report, once to vote "yes" on non-concurrence. Amid cheers, men got up to shake hands with friends, clap delegates on the back.

Green signaled for silence. He spoke to triumphant men, who all but dared him, with the set of their shoulders, the angle of their chins, to undo what they had just voted—their freedom.

He could not take the dare. It was too risky. The papers were full of the issue. Everybody would know the proportions of the vote. He could not damage his own prestige any further. Too many people like John L. Lewis would be anxious to capitalize on any appointment he might make over the heads of angry men.

He withdrew—but not gracefully. His final speech was furious, bitter, petty. "You have decided," he lashed out, "to refuse to request me to establish and finance your International headquarters. I accept that word as final. You may elect your officers now from top to bottom and you may arrange to finance this convention and your organization work and to carry on."

He concluded with a few words about unity, standing together, and the like, old phrases from old speeches, but they were gall in his mouth. Then he left Akron. The rubberworkers were alone—captains of their souls and an empty treasury.

The rest of the convention went smoothly. Delegates finally chose for president Sherman Dalrymple, and stormy Tommy Burns was elected vice-president. The executive board was solidly anti-Green with one exception.

Claherty sat in the chair until the closing session, when he sang his swan-song, in a speech so acid that it was finally stricken from the record. "It is not that I care. The newspapers say I have been repudiated by these delegates, and they have not stood up for me. They have not denied it," he said, while the rubberworkers stared at their feet in embarrassment. "I did not ask to have my name put up. The Executive Council selected me to guide this union for a short time. The rubberworkers cannot make or break me. I have been in this movement too long."

He paused, and then went on, his voice breaking with anger. "Enough about me; now about Green. He has rendered more service to the laboring classes in America than any other man living on the American continent. He has put millions of dollars into the pocket of the poor through his legislation. He is always giving his advice to the rubberworkers, and he came to this city twice when business was pressing. When he came here he expected to meet, to mix, to have a good time and talk with the delegates.

"But," and this was in the voice of an outraged man, "they avoided him. They wouldn't confer with him. They kept away from him. The only ones who would confer with him were those who wanted money. There will never go down in history a man who has done more for mankind than Mr. Green. Yet when he comes to Akron he is rebuffed and ignored by the people he has fought for for fifty years."

Claherty drew in breath and went on, "I told Mr. Green he was highly respected by the rubberworkers, and then you ignored him when he came in the same hotel with you. That hurt me more than anything in my entire life."

It was the lament of a defeated A. F. of L. politician. It was also the lament of a truly blind man. He could not understand, although he had been in Akron for nearly two years, what these rubberworkers really wanted. He had lived in this dirty, fierce industrial town month after month and yet he could not feel the yearning for freedom, for an end to pain. He could not see the old A. F. of L., with its craft-union jurisdiction, its policy of compromise, its admiration of industrial barons, was a chain forged on the spirit of these rubberworkers. He could not understand. He could not feel. He was part and parcel of an organization that, however unwittingly, had served the big capitalists of America for generations in preventing the organization of the nation's factory workers. His farewell was the sorry speech of a puzzled and angry man.

With the end of the convention, the rubber-union delegates faced a new thing. They had, at long last, a union of their own which they could run to suit themselves. There remained the problem of getting rubberworks to join it.

Far-away Drums   *October 19, 1935*

John L. Lewis swung out a ham-like fist and knocked down
Willy Hutcheson, Carpenters' Union president, at the A. F. of L.
convention in Atlantic City.

Mr. Lewis was stung to physical combat by Mr. Hutcheson's
injudicious use of an Anglo-Saxon word, minus the smile, but the
real fight between the two men centered around the Executive
Council's scrapping of the San Francisco industrial union resolution.

The burly miners' union president took the floor to champion
delegates from the new rubber union. Mr. Hutcheson interrupted
with a point of order. Infuriated, Lewis yelled, "That's pretty
small potatoes!"

Green pounded his gavel helplessly while Mr. Hutcheson
and Mr. Lewis exchanged words. As huge Mr. Hutcheson, the
champion of craft unions and status quo in the A. F. of L., scrambled up from the floor with a bloody nose, Green announced that
the point of order was well taken and Mr. Lewis should sit down.

The fight, and the story behind it, made a deep impression on
the handful of union men in Akron. John L. Lewis's name, for
the first time, passed around the rubber shops, spilled over from
the narrow ranks of actual union members to the big crowds of
still unorganized men.

The Union Continued   *October 20, 1935*

All of Akron jumped like a housewife getting a shock from a
loose electric wire on her washing machine. The whole city gulped
at the newspaper headlines. After the first surprise, fear swept the
valleys and was even reflected on West Hill.

For Cliff Slusser, the stocky arrogant factory manager at Goodyear, speaking for President Paul Litchfield, confirmed the dread
rumors around town. Yes, he said flatly, Goodyear will go off the
six-hour day.

The Goodyear Tire and Rubber Company had worked the six-hour day for five years. Forcing the other companies to follow its example, the biggest rubber corporation in the world had cushioned, to some extent, the full effects of Depression unemployment in Akron.

True, the speedup had been accelerated with the shortening of the work week. Men were thrown out of jobs by the implacable drive for increased "efficiency" in factory operations. But the six-hour day spread the work and saved many from going on the relief rolls.

The same board of directors which had ordered the lowering of production costs (another way of saying, Cut wages and increase the speedup) decided to end the six-hour day. Deepest secrecy cloaked the deliberations of this august body. Still, the town felt fairly certain that President Litchfield must have opposed, unsuccessfully, this move to wipe out the shorter work week. The six-hour day was his personal baby. Once he had argued for it before the United States Chamber of Commerce, even served as chairman of a six-hour-day committee.

But Mr. Litchfield was a salaried employee—a very large salaried employee, to be sure—and it appeared that on epoch-making policy decisions he was no match for the board of directors.

Nobody in Akron knew who belonged to the board of directors, with the exception of one or two names. The men who sat at a table changing the lives of Akron workers were considerably more remote from the dirty little Ohio industial city than any English absentee landlord had ever been from his Irish peasants. These men represented the stockholders. But lots of Akron people held stock in Goodyear. Were they represented by these mysterious overlords? Not at all.

In the great 1920-1921 blowup, when Frank Seiberling was booted out of the company he had built, Wall Street stepped into the affairs of the greatest rubber company in the world and emerged with a peculiar form of control. The control worked this way: the company had to be refinanced. A New York brokerage house managed the gigantic financial operation. Common stockholders were deprived of their vote until such time as the company had more or less paid back the huge loan. Control of the company's policies went to Clarence Dillon of Dillon, Read, and Company who, in return for refinancing (at eight per cent), issued new shares of "management voting stock" to himself and his company.

This peculiar deal, with the common stockholders disenfranchised by a Wall Street brokerage house, caused plenty of repercussions. Stockholders went into court charging "wrongfully made" profits of $15,000,000. Mr. Dillon denied everything. The suit was settled out of court.

Later, Mr. Dillon retired from control of Goodyear and in his place came Cyrus Eaton, a Middle-Western daring-young-man-on-the-financial-flying-trapeze. At one point in his spectacular career, Mr. Eaton owned twenty-five per cent of Goodyear stock.

After gyrations whose details leave even financial historians dizzy, Goodyear ended up in the arms of New York and Cleveland banks. Nobody knew, after it was all over, just how this Akron rubber company came under bankers' thumbs. It was all very strange and peculiar to the innocent Akron holders of small blocks of Goodyear common stock. The banks did not by any means hold the majority of Goodyear securities. But apparently they owned enough, under the set-up that emerged from the Dillon-Eaton regimes, actually to control the fate of Goodyear rubberworkers.

When the gentlemen from the New York and Cleveland banks decided to end the six-hour day as a means of cutting wages and thus lowering factory production costs, they did not consider that the end of the shorter work day spelled unemployment and devastating misery both to Goodyear workers and to Akron. Since they were so remote from the small Ohio city, and so remote in understanding and knowledge of a factory worker's life, their hearts could not be wrung by the thought of hungry men. Shielded from seeing the ugly consequences of their policies by physical and intellectual distance, they could not dream of the human havoc they planned to create.

Goodyear workers learned their fate, not from the lips of a group of bankers in Cleveland and New York, but from tough little Slusser. Slusser didn't mince words.

221

"We've been on the six-hour day for five years," he said, "and we're tired of it."

He didn't say much more, but every word was a knife in the heart of those who sweated in the curing room and who worked at the dizzying pace on the tire machines.

"Rates will be equalized for the eight-hour day." That meant, to the factory workers, that Goodyear would see to it that a man on an eight-hour shift worked at the same fantastic rate of speed as he had on the six-hour day—but piece-work rates would be adjusted so that he made almost nothing more for the extra two hours.

"We'll work our guts out for another two hours," men on tire machines growled, "and these bastards will fix it up so that we don't get no more to amount to anything in the old pay envelope."

Without blinking an eye, Slusser admitted that approximately 1,200 men would be permanently laid off as the result of the new eight-hour policy.

"Other companies," he added blandly, "will probably follow suit."

The workers knew it was true. If Goodyear could cut wages and thus reduce production costs by returning to the eight-hour day, the murderous competition in the industry would force every other rubber plant off the shorter work week.

Akron faced a future so black that even West Hill lawyers and merchants, always loyal to the rubber companies, gulped with dismay. Thousands and thousands would be added to relief rolls. The extra two hours in the shops would put such physical burden upon the remaining men that heaven only knew how the workers would be able to stand it. After all, five years before, when men had worked the eight-hour day, the speedup hadn't been refined to man-breaking proportions.

A few hours after Slusser's announcement, the union broke into print with the news that it would fight the eight-hour day to the bitter end. This threat made little impression, even on the rubberworkers. Goodyear obviously wasn't afraid of the union. Evidently Goodyear had waited until its spies reported that the rubber union existed mostly on paper or in the dreams of a handful of brave men.

222

The baldness of Slusser's arrogant statement indicated that Goodyear was not interested in public opinion any more than it was afraid of employee opposition to the new eight-hour policy. The bankers had made up their minds.

Two Days Later   *October 22, 1935*

"Gentlemen," Mr. Paul Litchfield said to the members of his company union, assembled in solemn conclave, "The Goodyear Tire and Rubber Company can yield to no opposition in its plan to return all its employees to the eight-hour day by January 1."

The Industrial Assembly listened without comment. But after the white-haired, big-shouldered, hook-nosed old man strode from the meeting hall, the company-union delegates heard other less famous speakers describe the rage of factory workers and remind them that the eight-hour day meant a general reduction in hourly and piece-work pay rates.

Shaking in its boots at its own temerity, the Goodyear Industrial Assembly voted down the eight-hour day. For the first time a company union bit the hand that fed it.

The Union Continued   *October 26, 1935*

Men paraded slowly before the Goodyear gates carrying great placards: "Resist the eight-hour day; join the United Rubber Workers of America."

At intervals a few faces appeared in the windows of the barren hall where the Goodyear local of the U.R.W.A. had its headquarters. They stared at their slowly moving pickets across the street and went back with a sigh to a little group around a typewriter.

The union men were drawing up their complaint to the United States Government. Under the old agreement signed last March, and so long forgotten, the union had the right to call for a fact-finding body to come to Akron. Now the union prayed Madame

Perkins to determine whether the eight-hour day was just and necessary.

Full of energy, the union struck at the eight-hour day from every front, inside and outside the factory. Yet the membership of the union hardly grew at all. Men waited to see how the company union would come out in its fight with Litchfield. They waited to see what the outside union could do. Factory workers weren't joining unions, these days, unless they were damned sure it would do some good. The rubber union would have to show them.

Election Day   *November 5, 1935*

Lee Schroy, a mild-mannered Republican politician, was elected Mayor of Akron after a singularly apathetic campaign in which union labor took no part. Poor old Honest Ike Myers had lost in his own Democratic primary, and Mr. Schroy defeated the victor.

No Mourners   *November 14, 1935*

The Goodyear Industrial Republic, oldest and best-known company union in America, was done to death today at the hand of its founder, President Paul Litchfield.

Mr. Litchfield swept the veil rudely away from the operations of the Industrial Assembly. He announced curtly that the passage of the anti-eight-hour-day bill over his veto, in the regularly called meeting of the regularly elected representatives of his employees, cut no ice with the company. The eight-hour day was a fact and the Goodyear Industrial Assembly, veto or no veto, could do nothing about it.

The Goodyear Industrial Republic lingered on, a pathetic ghost, for some time after its sudden demise, but Mr. Litchfield had obligingly proved to the world, and, more important, to his employees that when the company union came face to face with a fundamental company policy, it was ludicrously impotent.

A roar of agonized protest swept the Goodyear plants today. The management, swooping down on the weakest, most defenseless departments, began installing the eight-hour day. Foremen went through the great factory rooms, passing up the pitmen and the tirebuilders—those sturdy troublemakers—to distribute layoff slips and mark up new eight-hour-day base pay rates for girls on the looms, scattered mechanics, outside workers.

The eight-hour day was, Mr. Litchfield said, beginning to be a fact. Week after week more workers would be shifted to the new schedule. By January 1, "regardless of the union or the Industrial Assembly, all of Goodyear goes to the eight-hour day."

But while the management issued statements, proud and undiplomatic, the still largely unorganized restlessness in the Goodyear plants infected the whole valley. For while West Hill, recovered from its first shock over the eight-hour-day policy, comforted by the assurance and arrogance of the company, was calm, all of East and South Akron and Kenmore Hill seethed. Up and down the dirty streets, men shouted at their wives over supper tables, "So now after all the speedup, they're going to fire half the damned factory and cut our wages. It ain't human."

Men trembled with anger in the valleys. The Firestone and Goodrich men did not feel safe merely because their companies had not yet announced an eight-hour-day policy. They knew their bosses were only waiting to see whether Goodyear could get away with it. They would follow on the heels of the biggest corporation in town.

But while Firestone and Goodrich waited to install the eight-hour day, they started a new "efficiency" drive. Wages in all rubber plants were paid on a complicated and somewhat varying system of piece-work compensation. Most of the systems in use were variations on the Bedeaux system, a group plan for wage payment. The pure Bedeaux plan, only used by Goodrich, set the base pay at the average achievement rate of a group of workers on a given operation. Thus, if a man wanted to make more than the base rate, he had to work harder than the other factory hands on the operation. Since everybody was in desperate need of money, all the workers tried to go faster than the next man, and the group achievement standard rose steadily. After the hardest kind of work, a tirebuilder found that he had only been able to keep up with the rest of the group. At the end of the fortnight, during which he had produced more than the period before, he found his wages had not increased.

The Firestone wage system was a variation on the Bedeaux plan. A new base rate, established by the company time-study engineers, was set up every time a slightly different tire model was produced. The engineers, to guide their decisions, sent a "pacemaker" into a department where a new rate was to be set.

The pacemaker operated at the new schedule for three days. If he was able during the three days to make the regular base rate at the piece-work scale proposed by the time-study man, the new rate was declared feasible and imposed on everyone in the department. In the language of his fellow workers, a pacemaker was trying to "make time."

In these restless winter days, the mere appearance of a pacemaker at Firestone enraged whole departments. The sight of a workman—invariably a company union representative—setting a standard of speed that would later on break the backs of men who must maintain it, not for three days, but for weeks and months, made big slow-talking tirebuilders desperate.

All over the valley grievances mounted. Surrounded by people half starving on the fearfully low relief standards, afraid momentarily of permanent dismissal from jobs, tortured by the increasingly difficult speedup, faced with wage cuts, and infuriated by the cool arrogance of rubber barons too proud to even waste time on diplomacy, Akron's working people dreamed once again of protecting themselves against injustice.

Signs of the Times   *November 15, 1935*

The Central Labor Union refused to support the Community Chest campaign. Members of the C.L.U. were called upon to withhold their contributions from the annual city-wide charity funds collection.

This step followed a long struggle by the C.L.U. committee to get representation on the board of directors of the Community Chest. For years every worker in the rubber shops had been forced by his foreman to contribute to the Fund. Donations were taken from his wage envelope. Smaller concerns followed suit. The C.L.U. demanded a voice in spending the money collected, in large part, from the working people of the city. However, the Community Chest, dominated by big businessmen, refused point-blank.

The resolution stated that the Community Chest's printed material did not carry a union label; that wives and daughters of Community Chest officials were given jobs in the organization; that "forced contributions" were "undemocratic and an infringement on our rights"; that finally the Community Chest itself "is a device whereby the poor are made to support the poor, thus allowing the wealthy to escape just taxation."

For years the C.L.U. had been the poor creature of the somnolent building-trades unions. At last a fresh wind swept through the old organization. The belligerent resolution on the Community Chest showed a new spirit. The C.L.U. had stopped toadying.

The Union Continued   *November 16, 1935*

Madame Perkins, Secretary of Labor, appointed a fact-finding board for the Goodyear eight-hour-day controversy, naming Major Jesse L. Miller of Washington; Attorney Fred C. Croxton of Columbus; and Hugh S. Hanna of Washington, editor of the United States Bureau of Statistics.

Goodyear officials said they would be only too pleased to cooperate with the committee. The rubber union also approved. Both sides warmed up their complaints and prepared for a wordy battle.

Dress Rehearsal   *November 20-26, 1935*

Little groups of men assembled around the front gates of the Ohio Insulator plant in Barberton, just after four o'clock in the

227

early morning of a cold, raw, winter's day. They wore thick hunters' caps with ear tabs, and heavy old jackets, and woolen scarfs wrapped tightly around their necks, but still they suffered from the penetrating chill.

They stamped up and down before the gates, swinging their arms with a quick flapping motion, talking in the still heavy darkness. For nine weeks they had been picketing the gates of this small factory, three hundred strong, a hundred per cent organized. Every one of these men who fought a wage cut was hungry from living on next to nothing for weeks in houses where there was no coal to keep the children warm.

They had left their beds, this raw morning, to gather at the company gates because there had been a persistent and troubling rumor that the sheriff would try to open the plant. The strikers told each other as they stumbled along in the slippery mud that they didn't really believe the rumor, but they couldn't be too careful. They had to win this strike.

The gradual dawn silhouetted the plant, set back from the street in a yard of mud, protected by high fences and gates of steel. Little frame houses crowded the narrow streets that led away from the factory on every side.

The neighborhood slept as the pickets marched wearily before the factory gates, but, as the men watched, lights went on here and there in the small houses and the strikers heard the faint sounds of angry alarm clocks ringing in the distance. A little past five blankets of gray fog rolled in from the horizon and gradually blotted out the sights and sounds of the awakening neighborhood. The strikers were alone in the heavy fog.

The sheriff's six heavily loaded cruisers almost ran into the picket line before the men made out the dim outlines of the automobiles or heard the muffled sound of the brakes. They lined up quickly, arm linked in arm, before the main gates. In this silent dawn, the strikers clasped hands. They had no weapons. They had nothing but the physical weight of their bodies to use against the danger that awaited them in the fog. But they planned to use their flesh, their bones, as a barricade.

"Hold the line, boys, no matter what happens." A muttered answer went up and down the rows of pickets, "O.K. O.K."

228

Sheriff Jim Flower walked briskly out of the rolling mist. His hearty voice had the sound of a man who has been around horses and stables much of his life.

"Fellows!" he said, squinting into the heavy fog to get an estimate of how many shadowy figures stood before the gates.

A voice answered, "Yeah, what do you want?"

"Now listen, fellows!" The sheriff's voice brimmed over with honesty. "I got something to say to you. I ain't against you. The company wants to open this plant. Well, I want to hear your side of it. How about having a little meeting? Nothin's going to happen until I give the word, so you fellows can leave the gates for a moment."

The strikers, surprised, murmured in the shadows. Finally a picket said, "Well, I guess there's no harm in that, boys. What do you say?"

Sheriff Flower led the way over to his cruiser and slowly the pickets grouped themselves around him, their faces patches of white in the gray fog.

"Now, fellows," the sheriff began. With these words, as though at a signal, the other five cars in the sheriff's cavalcade leaped for ward with a grind of gears. In the first second of the advance, the strikers stood immobile, too shocked by this act of treachery to move. Then they scrambled for the gates.

It was too late. The first three of the cruisers were already through. With murderous anger, blinded by the fog, the strikers crowded on the fenders and radiators of the two cars remaining outside the gates.

"I order you to obey the law," the sheriff yelled. A brick crashing through a cruiser window made a splintering sound. Shadowy men groped in the heavy cold mud fumbling for bricks or stones.

A blinding glare of light suddenly burst from the factory roof —the floodlights. The confused milling bands of strikers near the gates became splendid targets in the brilliant illumination. Out of the fog emerged a group of smartly uniformed and helmeted men wearing gas masks.

A voice rang out, crisp and sharp: "Fire!"

The gas-masked men lifted their arms and swung, as men

swing hand grenades, the bulky objects they had unfastened from their smart military belts. The gas bombs landed at the feet of the strikers, stung their shoulders, hit them on the head and, exploding, spread gas over the whole factory yard.

The scene turned to slow motion. Some of the strikers with bricks in their hands stopped the swinging arc of their arms in mid-air, breathing in the deadly gas. Others, bending over for a bit of stone to throw, stayed crouched, feeling the first fumes burn their eyes and nose and throat.

Then the strikers turned. Their flight was pathetic, like the hopping of a wounded bird. Feet were leaden; men stopped to vomit, to stand clutching their heaving, retching bellies. Some still groveled in the mud, clawing at burning throats. "Oh, my God," men cried from the slowly curling gas and fog. "Oh, oh, oh, God."

"Very good!" the military voice snapped. "Fall back."

In a moment, the scene was blank. Only the floodlights continued to reach their steady glaring fingers into the fog. The strikers had retreated. Men with handkerchiefs over their mouths, tears running down their cheeks, dragged off the fallen comrades from the mud near the gate. The strikers disappeared beyond the lights into the fog. It was six o'clock.

Inside the Ohio Insulator factory, brisk activity followed the battle. The sheriff bustled about, ordering boxes of gas bombs unpacked. His little army of sixty uniformed men lined up in smart military formation to get replacements of ammunition. Standing beside the sheriff, sometimes countermanding his orders, was the real general of this successful battalion, Colonel Joe Johnston.

Colonel Johnston was a man of parts. In the first place, he was the leading Ohio salesman for the Lake Erie Chemical Company, one of the nation's largest gas-bomb manufacturers. Moreover, he had been hired last spring by the rubber companies during the strike scare to train an efficient machine-gun and gas-bomb crew for the worthy sheriff. Also, conveniently enough, his colonel's commission in the Ohio National Guard Reserve cloaked him with authority.

On the narrow brick-paved streets outside the plant, the fog lifted and the gas blew away. The strikers were gone. A few men cautiously stood near the gates, hands stuck deep in their pockets against the raw day, staring into the plant, taking note of the members of Sheriff Flower's private army.

"I guess we learned 'em," Colonel Johnston said, peering into the empty gray morning.

"Hope so." Sheriff Flower felt nervous. Some deep instinct, born, no doubt, of a politician's cunning, told him that he couldn't throw gas bombs at people and have them like it. Even radicals and Communists and long-whiskered vermin like these strikers could vote. It was a sad distressing thought.

Colonel Johnston, on the other hand, was not distressed. He was running for no office and, from a gas-bomb salesman's point of view, everything was going very well. As he gazed out of the window he noted a moving band of men coming closer.

"Aha," he said cheerfully. "Looks like they're asking for more."

Sheriff Flower groaned. Colonel Johnston gave sharp crisp orders and presently his smart little army paraded in full sight of the approaching crowd, to take up its position finally by the gates.

Beyond the fence some three hundred men milled about, armed with stones and bricks and clubs, yelling, waiting. The strikers, on their way home for rest, had left the word at the Barberton C.L.U. This was an advance guard of the rescue crew.

A big hefty man in the crowd pointed to a helmeted soldier at the factory entrance. "See that son-of-a-bitch," he yelled, and his voice carried for blocks. "That sneaking rat is my second cousin, and he lives in Barberton. Why, you dirty skunk, wait until this is over. Just wait. We'll get you."

The soldier trembled, his recent military training evaporating quickly.

"Throwing gas bombs at strikers," the big man continued, his husky voice billowing over the whole neighborhood. "Ain't that a swell way for a grown man to spend his time. You dirty lousy rat, we'll break every bone in your sneaking body."

The special deputy sheriff gulped, broke ranks, and fled. He hid inside the factory the rest of the day. Colonel Johnston was severe. For two cents he'd make a quick raiding sally and arrest that big-mouthed Communist out there. But just as he gave serious thought to this pleasant idea, a runner brought him a telephone message. He read it and barked orders. The "army" detached its gas bombs and stood ready for action.

Presently a squad of heavy limousines screamed around the corner. The crowd howled. Bricks crashed. Men threw themselves in front of the big cars. Women heaved rocks.

"Fire," said Colonel Johnston.

This time the crowd ran in time. The gas billowed about the limousines. Their choking chauffeurs drove into the factory. A block away, the crowd stopped. A man jumped up on a little frame front porch and started yelling orders through an improvised megaphone. Everyone in the group sprang to action. Women, bundled in heavy sweaters, wearing men's frayed gloves, ran into their houses and appeared a moment later dragging old washtubs and ash barrels. Hair flying in the wind, mouths tight with fury, they pushed and carried their household goods to the site of the rapidly rising barricade.

Men, sweating even in the cold damp, brought in enormous beams from near-by dumps. The whole neighborhood helped. In fifteen minutes every side street that opened on the factory was blocked by a strange barrier made of broken armchairs, discarded and rusty old stoves, ash barrels, old Ford fenders, beams, and fallen telephone poles. Colonel Joe Johnston watched these building operations through a pair of field glasses.

"I guess we'd better give it to them," he said finally. "We won't be able to get any cars through those streets now."

"No," Sheriff Flower replied, showing a little authority. "If we start throwing gas bombs two blocks from the factory, there'll be hell to pay, no kidding. We ain't got no right to do that. The city police are responsible for keeping the streets clear."

"Well, what's the use of occupying this factory if the company can't bring any workers in through the streets?" Colonel Johnston asked with sweet reasonableness.

"I don't care," Sheriff Flower repeated stubbornly. He felt scared to death, really, when he thought of all those voters out there building barricades. No good was going to come of all this; he felt it in his bones.

A shout went up, a terrific yell, compounded of the screams of little boys and the piercing howls of infuriated women, and the deep, almost anguished cries of enraged men. Colonel Johnston watched a procession of cars draw up in front of the barricades. He winced, hearing even from this distance the splintering sound of glass breaking. The crowd lined up behind the barricades, heaving stones and bricks in orderly fashion while some improvised general shouted, "Now!" and then, after a pause, "O.K. Now."

"The cars are going back," Colonel Johnston groaned. "They can't get through. I tell you, we got to bust up those barricades."

"No," Sheriff Flower muttered.

A little after ten o'clock in the morning, the crowd thinned out. The barricades were manned by a handful of men, with instructions to yell for help if needed. The women went home to make beds and get lunch for the kids. Colonel Johnston busied himself with giving instructions to some of the new recruits inside the factory. He was bothered because there weren't nearly enough gas masks to go around.

At the factory gates newspaper reporters approached and, after prolonged dickering with the helmeted guards, were let in to talk to Colonel Johnston. Nobody paid much attention to the worried sheriff.

The Colonel, in fine fettle, was only too eager to be interviewed. He said he had 100 specialists trained for gas-bomb warfare, most of them on duty now, and the names of 1,000 more he could use if necessary.

"I've been active in labor disturbances in Ohio for twenty-five years," he said largely. "I know how to handle these babies."

Reporters also hunted up William Marr, plant superintendent. Mr. Marr said that anyone who wished to apply for his old job could do so today, but not afterwards. The company, he said, would never bargain with the union.

"We have 75 men working now, and expect to have our full strength of 300 tomorrow," Mr. Marr said coldly.

The reporters saw considerably more than a hundred men inside the plant, but they didn't seem to be working. Indeed, they

233

were sprawling on the machines and playing poker on work tables.

"This violence must stop," Mr. Marr added. "Law and order must prevail against the activities of this mob outside."

The hours ticked off the chill gray morning. Noon came and the kids ran home from school, goggling at the barricades, excited and curious. Little boys threw spitballs at the guards and scattered like monkeys. The early afternoon passed. Men sat stolidly at the barricades. Most of the strikers were at the Barberton C.L.U. headquarters laying plans. The street was nearly empty of men when a little after three o'clock Sheriff Flower came out of the gates with a paper in his hand.

Immediately the people of the neighborhood turned out to jeer. Women raced from small houses, tying scarfs around their heads. The advance guard of youngsters just out of school hurried down the street to see what was up. Such an exciting day they hadn't had for weeks. They could hardly sit still in class, wanting to go home and see if the barricades were still there.

The crowd collected around Sheriff Flower. Hardly half a dozen men were in sight. The few strikers still on the scene were a block away at the barricades. The rest of organized Barberton labor was either at the C.L.U. headquarters, making plans for organized protests, or in Akron, collecting reinforcements of money and men for increased picket lines the next day. So Sheriff Flower made his little speech to a crowd of a hundred women and kids.

"I hereby," the worthy sheriff said, "order you to disperse." He went on, reading the sonorous phrases of the Ohio Riot Act. He wound up, "I give you two minutes to leave this neighborhood."

The crowd laughed. This neighborhood was where they lived. These houses were their homes. Many of them stood on the little patch of mud they called their front yards. So they laughed.

But the forces of law and order had evolved a crafty scheme to get rid of the barricades. If the deputy sheriffs were forced to disperse an unruly rob, under the lawful provisions of the Riot Act, they could with perfect legality sally out of the factory to pursue the lawless members of the crowd. In the course of this action, they would naturally be able to demolish the barricades which the Barberton police force had no idea, apparently, of razing. Then the company could bring in their workmen over the cleared streets.

So Sheriff Flower repeated, "I give you two minutes to leave this scene."

The women yelled, "You and who else, Mr. Smarty? I live here, I got a right to be here." The kids screamed, encouraged by their mothers, "Ya-a-ah, old brass buttons, we live here!" Their shrill voices nearly drowned out the crisp order, "Advance and fire!"

The Johnston-trained gas-bomb crew marched out of the gates in close order and threw their first volley of gas bombs square into the shouting screaming crowd. The screams died away. For a moment there was no sound at all. People didn't even run.

The gas-bomb crew fired the second volley. Billowing gas swept over the streets near the factory, rising white and menacing all around these strong squat women and their thin little kids. The liquid fire poured down the throats of the babies many of the mothers carried in their arms. The women staggered away, trying to run, holding out a fist to their children, covering the faces of their babies with a corner of a shawl or with the flat of their big work-worn hands. The youngsters leaned against gray frame houses to vomit, crying pitifully.

The gas-bomb crew advanced smartly. Before them the crowd melted. Above every other sound, the wailing cry of "Mamma, mamma, MAMMA" tortured the ears of women who had lost their kids in the rout. No sound rises so sharp and sad as the frightened scream of a six-year-old child who has been teargassed, a cry for help suddenly shut off by nauseated gagging.

Colonel Johnston and his men marched toward the barricades, firing another volley of gas bombs with expert precision. The street was nearly empty. A child on crutches moved her crippled legs and her small wooden sticks as fast as her frail shoulders would let her, but not fast enough. A gas bomb fell squarely at her feet. She toppled over and lay in the gas fumes, gagging and weeping, breathing deeply of the liquid fire. A striker, with hand-kerchief-covered mouth, darted out from behind a house to pick her up. A gas bomb hit his legs, but he staggered to safety.

The deputy sheriffs began to pull down the barricade, firing more and more volleys of gas bombs. Four men, appearing from around the corner where the fainting, weeping sickened crowd of women and kids had retreated, ran down the street. The deputy sheriffs let them have it, but they ran faster than the gas. They burst into a house at the end of the street, and in a second appeared at the back door, three of them carrying very small children. A neighbor had remembered that her friend had gone to the grocery store, leaving her little children, one four years, one three years, one two months old.

The children whom the strikers carried to safety had been badly gassed. They slept together in a bedroom on the first floor, near an open window. The fumes had rolled in from the street and the baby was unconscious when the strikers found her. The rescue squad climbed over a back fence, handing the children over to each other. Once safe from the gas, they carried the children tenderly and said, as the oldest one cried "Mamma, mamma" softly. "Never mind, kid. We'll get your mamma O.K."

They had hardly disappeared over the back fences when the mother came racing down the street. She paid no attention to the deputy sheriffs who yelled at her and then shrugged and let her go. She hardly saw the empty street. She didn't understand. She didn't answer the cries of her neighbors who saw her passing. All she saw was a curl, a white wisp, coming from her door. She saw it far away, and she thought it was smoke. She thought her house was on fire and her children burning.

So she ran furiously, swiftly. She had dropped her bundles of food. Her battered old hat fell off. Her coat was open, flying behind her. Her loose breasts beat a tattoo, a painful drumming, on her chest. Her strong, not handsome face was contorted and her eyes were bulging with terror. She was sobbing. She raced up the little porch stairs, crossed her threshold and saw in one glance, one movement of frightened eyes, that her children's beds were empty. They were gone, safe.

She fainted. She fell with her legs sprawled apart, knocking her forehead a bad blow so that the blood came. She lay in the curling gas fumes until another striker, racing over back fences to elude the soldiers, reached her, partly revived her, and led her off to her children.

In the meantime, the deputies worked busily at the barricades. They were nearly demolished, the old chairs pulled away, the ash barrels rolled off, when, from far away, there came a deep peculiar sound, like waves that beat in an ocean sea shell. It came closer, and the deputies cocked their heads to hear. Colonel Johnston said hastily, "Rear, march!"

But not quite soon enough. The crowd, led by the strikers, turned the corner. This time the men of Barberton were on the march. They carried clubs and paving stones and bricks. They wore handkerchiefs across their mouths, which they dipped in puddles from time to time to keep wet. The deputies hastily retired, throwing gas bombs. Men snatched up the bombs before they exploded and heaved them back. Two deputies wailed, "I'm hit." They had no gas masks.

Colonel Johnston got his men back behind the gates in some semblance of order, but much shaken. It was four o'clock. Now the sheriff looked out the windows and said, "My God, the whole town's here."

The news of the gas attack on the women and children of Barberton had spread through Akron like wildfire. A hundred and then a thousand Paul Reveres carried the word into the workers' districts in Akron proper. Already the city had been preparing an offensive against the broken picket lines. Now every rubberworker in the district was stung to action.

In a hundred dirty streets in East Akron, in whole blocks on Kenmore Hill, the word spread, "They gassed the kids over at Ohio Insulator. Come on!" It was a call to arms.

By five o'clock, as dusk fell on this winter's day, the crowds massed deep around the plant. The fog rolled up again, sometimes blotting out the moving, weaving groups of men. The plant searchlights went on, and Colonel Johnston, apparently undaunted, ordered out his army.

They fired gas bombs into a solid mass of infuriated men, by this time veterans of a gas barrage. The bombs flew back almost as fast as the deputies could throw them. Just after seven o'clock the wind shifted. Clouds of gas blew back into the factory and, choking and groaning, Colonel Johnston's army retreated, blinded

237

by its own fumes. The crowd, organized in almost military fashion, followed up its advantage and pursued the fleeing deputies with showers of paving rock. Colonel Johnston himself went down under a brick. He was interviewed a little later in the hastily improvised infirmary. His wounded leg was being carefully bandaged.

"I'd like to get out there with clubs," said the doughty Colonel, "and let 'em have it."

The offensive had passed to the strikers and their friends. In the murky night, lit by the powerful floodlights, they moved briskly about, tearing up the paved streets with crowbars, to get more ammunition. Gangs worked under the leadership of hastily chosen captains. All through the early night, flurries of bricks burst over the plant, breaking every window in the factory, bruising the deputies who stood too near the doors.

From time to time the besieged forces of the law ventured into the open and heaved gas bombs. But the wind perversely favored the strikers. Again and again the gas fumes swept back into the windowless factory. Dozens of gassed deputies began to vomit and moan.

The crowd worked efficiently and rapidly. Every new recruit was put to work. Hundreds of hands rebuilt the broken barricades, hundreds more roamed the neighborhood looking for additional weapons. The sounds that floated into the factory and to the terrified sheriff were not loud, but they were menacing, a hum of men at work against a steady background of yells and shouts of rage.

"Come out, you rats," voices from the darkness bellowed. "Come out, you yellow-bellied bastards. Fight a few guys your own size, or are you too scared to take on anybody but kids and women?"

While the crowd besieged the sheriff and his army, the Barberton Central Labor Union held a hastily called special meeting. It was a very solemn meeting. Many of the delegates came in wearing patches over their foreheads, or dark glasses to shield eyes injured by gas. The vague smell of tear gas hung over the meeting, an odor coming from the mud-stained clothes of many of the men now sitting tensely in the front rows.

238

The meeting was short. "We called this meeting," the chairman said, "to talk about a general strike. It's been proposed that unless this gas stuff and the rest of the stuff they're pulling out there stops right away, we go out tomorrow. Who wants to talk?"

The first man who spoke was a visitor, a man from the Goodyear rubberworkers' local.

"Listen, fellows," he said earnestly, in the drawl of a mountain tirebuilder, "if you don't stop this attack on the picket line, it's all over but the shouting for us. If you fellows lose out, God pity us in Akron." He started to say something more, hesitated, shrugged and wound up, "That's all I got to say. You know what I mean. I ain't no talker."

The rest of the speeches were simple. Most of the delegates with something to say talked about ways and means to carry on the general strike. Patiently the chairman said, "First, we got to talk about whether we want one. You're really sort of out of order, talking about flying squadrons to shut up places that stay open. That comes later."

"Hell," the speakers would answer. "Is there a rat in here that's going to vote against a general strike?"

A committee left to inform Sheriff Flower that unless he agreed to an immediate forty-eight-hour truce, effective at once, the whole town would be on strike at 6 A.M. Another committee sat down and started making lists of unions, appointing general strike police, figuring out ways to feed hospital patients and keep the lights on for the traffic signals. The rest of the delegates stood around waiting for word from the sheriff.

When the committee approached the neighborhood of the Ohio Insulator plant, they stopped their car and walked toward the gates, blinking in the fierce light. For overhead a parachute floated, carrying a torch, lighting the whole of downtown Barberton with ghostly radiance. It was a military flare, the kind used during the World War to facilitate night attacks. Under this flare, thousands of men milled in the streets, packed tightly together, yelling and howling defiance to the trembling deputies inside the plant. At intervals there was the hiss of another gas bomb. Sheriff Flower was running low on ammunition.

239

The C.L.U. committee approached under a regulation white flag. The pickets yelled for silence. Still holding bricks, the crowd quieted. The sheriff came out to the gates. A howl went up.

"There comes the stinker," men screamed, and "There's the dirty yellow bastard. Killing's too good for him."

The sheriff winced. His square face was very troubled. The gas-bomb supply was very low and God alone knew what would happen next, with all those machine-guns inside. Already, at ten o'clock, the sheriff was heartily sick of the whole war.

The parley was brief. The forty-eight-hour truce was to allow mass picketing in front of the gates. Otherwise, the truce was all off and, by God, Akron men could fight too. If the truce didn't go into effect the general strike started at 6 A.M. tomorrow. The sheriff could take his choice—a truce allowing mass picketing, or open war with a general strike in the morning.

The sheriff said he would have to think it over. The committee said he couldn't stall. They had to have word to start preparing the general strike. The sheriff gulped. He said the truce was all right, but the picketing wasn't. The committee laughed.

"We should let them bring in scabs?" one of the union men growled. "What do you think we are, a bunch of crazy people?"

"O.K.," the sheriff said, and passed a weary hand over his forehead. He ordered the guards at the gates to come into the factory. As they retreated, the crowd screamed, and some of the deputies half turned to heave another bomb.

"Lay off," the sheriff said, not so military this time. Inside Colonel Johnston was quite beside himself. A truce, indeed! And what was law and order coming to, please? The sheriff sadly shook his head.

Next morning the sheriff and his army woke from an uneasy sleep on their new cots inside the factory to stare out at an orderly marching picket line in front of the gates. They were effectively besieged at every hand. The sheriff sighed deeply.

Meantime, in Barberton, ministers and respectable public officials formed a Citizens Committee, not to smash the strike, but to stop the gas attacks. Federal conciliators came into town and hunted desperately for responsible company authorities, to start negotiating.

Eventually reporters hunted up a company spokesman who said, "We will operate if law enforcement makes it possible." Asked if they planned to continue using gas, the spokesman replied, "That is Sheriff Flower's business. It is his place to open the plant."

All through the first day of the truce, orderly crowds gathered at the plant gates, marching in picket-line formation, singing, sometimes shouting. And all day long the deputies watched them narrowly from the plant windows. Their fingers itched.

On the second day of the truce, C. K. King of Mansfield, president of the parent corporation, finally turned up to talk for the company. He stated firmly that the company would refuse to negotiate or arbitrate. He added that he planned to call for the National Guard if Sheriff Flower consented to any more truces.

Sheriff Flower, informed of this statement, was stung to the quick. After all he had done, and the company talked about the National Guard. The telephone inside the plant rang pretty regularly, and all the messages were for the sheriff. Every Republican politician in Summit County was ringing him up to point out that he was an idiot.

"You'd better get out of there, quick," voices informed the jittery sheriff, "before you ruin yourself for good. Boy, this whole town is fighting-mad at you."

On the evening of the second day the respectable Citizens Committee called a mass meeting of Barberton people to pass a resolution calling for the extension of the truce. But the meeting ran away with them. Speaker after speaker shouted, "Why continue the truce? They got to get out of that plant, lock, stock, and barrel. We won't stand for an army of rats coming in there and gassing our kids. As long as they are there, they are a menace to peace."

Francis Gerhardt, stocky beloved leader of the matchworkers, spoke. He was against another truce. Get them out of there. Other speakers said it was legal for the sheriff to close the plant—the county prosecutor had so ruled. Eventually a committee of six was picked to call on the sheriff and tell him to get out of the plant, or else. The else was the threat of a general strike.

241

Next morning the sheriff began moving out his men and ammunition. To keep the peace, the plant was closed until further notice, by proclamation. The deputies, considerably bewildered, marched out of the gates to the picket line, where they relieved the worn-out strikers. In full fighting regalia the confused deputies took up the long vigil the strikers had maintained for nine weeks. But they had guns and gas bombs to keep scabs and even company officials from entering the plant.

"Nobody," the sheriff said, trying to regain some of his lost bluster, "goes in or out."

The company officials replied with a burst of fury, and the C.L.U. said somberly, "The general strike call is out. Our men will respond at a moment's notice. We plan to strike at once if some means of settling the strike is not agreed upon very soon."

The following day, all of Barberton and thousands from Akron turned out for a great C.L.U. parade. Barberton police in a cruiser led the parade, smiling and calling notice to the watchers that they attacked no picket lines. Thousands of union men marched, singing. The favorite song was, "We'll hang Jim Flower to a sour apple tree."

Floats went by, with men in false faces representing the sheriff. Men cheered frantically when the Ohio Insulator strikers, many still in bandages, tramped rapidly past, carrying their union banner high and their heads up.

The parade lasted nearly two hours, and many of the marchers carried hastily printed signs, "We support the General Strike."

This demonstration had a final sobering effect on the Ohio Insulator Company and on every other business in Barberton, and indeed, in Akron. Shortly after the parade, the strikers, certain now that they could keep the plant closed until hell froze over, appealed their case to the new Wagner Labor Relations Board.

Barberton hitched up its trousers and settled down grimly to wait. The people had driven the gas bombers out of town. The people had closed down the Ohio Insulator Company. Let anyone who thought he could attack picket lines with gas bombs take notice.

The union men had won the dress rehearsal.

242

The Union Continued   *December 3, 1935*

John L. Lewis sent his personal missionary, Adolph Germer, into Akron today.

Weather Report   *December 26, 1935*

Katie Riley, fifty years old, Negro, froze to death. The temperature stood at four below, a record for the date.

The Music Goes 'Round   *January 1, 1936*

Such of Akron's citizens who had a little money danced and sang the New Year in, today, to the tune of a merry nonsense ballad titled, "The Music Goes 'Round and 'Round."
The song started as a hit dance-band tune and by New Year's Eve was already a folk melody in Akron. The New Year's Eve drunks warbled a dozen parodies of the lilting song, and even in cheerless bars in East Akron, rubberworkers, gay on locally distilled corn, chanted "Oh-ah-oha," and forgot a few of their troubles.

Another One   *January 2, 1936*

John C. Fox, aged 78, froze to death at 33 N. Bates Street, where he lived. The old man was on relief. He had no fuel for his stove.

Discredited Interests   *January 3, 1936*

All of Akron crowded around radios tonight to listen to President Roosevelt address a night session of Congress. With the agitation of the American Liberty League at its height, both rich and poor awaited the President's speech with tense anticipation.
Already West Hill, recovered from the 1933 horrors, hated the

243

President. Most of the people who lived in the pleasant brick houses considered Mr. Roosevelt a dangerous if not demented radical, probably a Communist. With their attack of the jitters nicely smoothed out by rubber-company profits and what they felt was the permanent defeat of the union movement, the citizens of West Hill wanted nothing better than to get rid of the man who, they now hated to admit, had saved them, back in March, 1933, from what they had felt sure was revolution and anarchy.

In the valley President Roosevelt was still a great hero. True, his N.R.A., his schemes for helping workers to build unions, had hardly worked. But that, the rubberworkers felt, was not his fault. On the contrary, the tirebuilders told each other, the only reason the New Deal had not spelled a new world, a better life for Akron, was the bitter and unfair opposition of the rubber barons who dragged everything worth while in the whole program off to the courts.

"And you know the goddamned courts—they're about as much for the workingman as Harvey Firestone," they added.

Akron huddled around the radio to listen to the President's dramatic speech. Mr. Roosevelt, in cultured Harvard accents, heaped scorn and fury on the heads of the "big boys." The President denounced big business "that steals the livery of great national constitutional ideals to serve discredited social interests." The President called on the Republicans to come out and fight.

Next day the papers printed columns of comments on the speech—mostly unfavorable. Cliff Slusser, for instance, the hard-talking factory superintendent at Goodyear, said, quite frankly, "I thought it was terrible."

The *Times-Press* was obliged to add that although businessmen and other community leaders did not seem to have cared for the speech, it was "well received" by other citizens of the town.

The Fuse is Lit   *January 6, 1936*

Madame Perkins's Fact-Finding Board made public its final report on the Goodyear eight-hour-day policy this afternoon. The news broke with a dull thud. The Akron press, headlining the coming trial of the ex-sheriff and the Supreme Court veto of the A.A.A., found little space and not much black type to herald the Government Goodyear report. Few people in Akron were even aware that the Department of Labor had administered a stinging slap to The Goodyear Tire and Rubber Company.

The report came out squarely for the six-hour day, and, in addition, accused The Goodyear Tire and Rubber Company of discrimination and bad faith in dealing with its employees.

In quiet, pedestrian, but sometimes bitterly sarcastic, language, the lawyer from Columbus, the major from Washington, and the statistical expert from the Department of Labor stripped the eight-hour-day controversy to its bones.

"The Fact-Finding Board," the report started off, "can find no justification for the proposed lengthening of hours per day by The Goodyear Tire and Rubber Company."

"The Board is of the opinion," the report went on, "that the adoption of the proposed change in hours per day must result in a material reduction in the number of workers."

The report quoted the estimates of both the Rubber union and the Industrial Assembly on the percentage of layoffs under the eight-hour-day policy. These organizations, they said, thought between fifteen and twenty-five per cent of the employees would be permanently dismissed. They quoted President Litchfield himself to substantiate this.

"We went to the six-hour day," Mr. Litchfield had written years before, "and since that time, in our Akron factories alone, we have been able to give employment to 3,000 workers who otherwise would have been entirely without income. The advantage of having 100 per cent of the workers working 80 per cent of the time, over having 80 per cent of the workers working full time, is apparent to all."

The Board, staying on the conservative side, estimated that Goodyear, under the most favorable circumstances, would have to lay off twelve per cent of its workers to carry through the eight-hour-day policy. The Board further stated that it was the general opinion that other Akron factories would follow the lead of Goodyear.

"With several thousand now on relief in Akron this presents a very serious problem for that locality," the report stated, or rather, understated.

The Board considered the Goodyear plea that the eight-hour-day program allowed greater operating efficiency—considered and rejected it because an expert on rubber-factory management had stated, in a half dozen widely printed articles over a number of years, that this was not the case. This expert, who had argued many times that management efficiency was, if not increased, then certainly not decreased under the six-hour day, was Mr. Litchfield himself.

The report, with devastating exactness, quoted all the words that Mr. Litchfield must at the moment have wanted very badly to eat. Mr. Litchfield had appeared in a variety of national magazines, always singing the same song—the six-hour day was good for plant management, as well as good for the employees and good for the country.

Next, Madame Perkins's fact-finders passed to the union argument that the eight-hour day meant wide wage cuts for the workers still left in the factory. The gentlemen from the Department of Labor were forced to agree with this, especially since, in the departments already put back on the longer hours, increase of the length of the working day had uniformly accompanied hourly wage cuts.

Indeed, once again, the fact-finders turned to the writings of the Goodyear management, with an innocent but deadly air. "There may be," the *Wingfoot Clan,* house organ, had stated, "some readjustments in certain hourly rates."

The Goodyear Tire and Rubber Company, in appearing before the Board, stated blandly that about twenty per cent of the piece rates would be cut with the inception of the eight-hour day. The union stated that this figure would actually be much higher.

The Board did not say in so many words that The Goodyear Tire and Rubber Company planned to go on the eight-hour day in order to reduce wage costs, but the implication was very clear. The fact-finders wound up this section of the report, "The proposed changes in wages in the plant would be a negligible item in the total cost to the ultimate consumer, as wages constituted but twenty per cent of the value of products in manufacture of tires and tubes in Ohio in 1933. Twenty per cent of the manufacturer's value, of course, represents a much less percentage of the consumer cost."

The Board concluded the material on the facts of the controversy by coming out clearly against the eight-hour day and wage reductions.

The fact-finders also considered Goodyear employee relations and found the giant rubber company sadly wanting. In fact, the Board accused The Goodyear Tire and Rubber Company of being mean to its own company union as well as blithely and completely ignoring the rubber union. The Board stated, "In the present controversy, Goodyear management did not fairly enter into negotiations with employees or with any of their representatives, but rather promulgated a policy and then sought endorsement by representatives of employees, or, in effect, merely gave notice of such a policy."

The Board stated flatly that Goodyear had violated the 1935 spring agreement with the A. F. of L. unions, and more, "the procedure was not in accord with the usual method of dealing with the Goodyear Industrial Assembly."

The company union had been refused the right to hold a factory-wide vote on the eight-hour-day policy, the Board found, "the identical procedure which management has encouraged them to use since 1919." The fact-finders could see "no justification" for not allowing the vote. They considered the management excuses for forbidding the balloting on the new policy lame, not to say halt.

The management had told the company union that a factory-wide referendum was impossible, but that votes by departments might be a different matter. When the "assembly" pressed for even that type of balloting, the management replied flatly, "If a vote would be taken in some departments or divisions that it might be impossible to abide by that vote as it might conflict with the economic policies of the management for that department or division."

As for the rubber union, the management didn't even bother to excuse itself to the outside organization. The Fact-Finding

247

Board said, "We are of the opinion that the management has discriminated between the Industrial Assembly and the rubber union."

Attached to the report was a mass of figures which, when studied, provided all the data to prove the rubberworkers' constant cry: "The speedup ain't human."

The Board touched on this question lightly when it agreed with the union and industrial assembly leaders that the eight-hour day might prove too heavy a physical strain for the "older worker."

The report, rebuking The Goodyear Tire and Rubber Company, fell into an ocean of silence. The newspapers beat no drums to call the public's attention to it, and The Goodyear Tire and Rubber Company greeted its publication at first with icy silence.

Concession   *January 9, 1936*

The Tire Department in Goodyear Plant Two, one of the first sections in the factory to go to the eight-hour day, was shifted back to six hours this morning. The management coldly denied that the step was a concession to the union. The "flow of business," Mr. Slusser said, caused the change.

But rubber-union men exulted openly and dozens of tirebuilders, finally convinced that the U.R.W.A. meant business, signed union cards.

John L. Lewis   *January 19, 1936*

The swirling snow of a winter blizzard swept Akron. The wind screamed on the armory front lawn as thousands of rubberworkers, their scanty coats pulled tight around their lean tall frames, filed into the big drafty hall to hear John L. Lewis, President of the United Mine Workers of America, make a speech.

Lewis, the chunky, powerful, heavy-faced miners' leader, came to Akron at the precise moment when rubberworkers were ready and eager, once again, to hear union talk. The Goodyear eight-hour-day policy threatened every fourth man with starvation.

248

Everybody knew, for the company had taken pains to demonstrate it, that the Industrial Assembly wasn't worth a pinch of salt. In desperation, the men in the Akron valleys cocked a receptive ear once more to the idea of a union.

They turned up this Sunday, dubious, doubtful, ready to be shown. Some of them knew Lewis from the days when they worked in West Virginia mines. Others remembered his fight in the A. F. of L. convention. More came because the U.R.W.A. workers in the shops had talked day and night for a week of this meeting, this great man.

Lewis faced the mountaineer workers of Akron calmly. He had taken the trouble to prepare himself with exact information about the rubber industry and The Goodyear Tire and Rubber Company. He made no vague, general speech, the kind the rubberworkers were used to hearing from Green. Lewis named names and quoted figures. His audience was startled and pleased when he called Cliff Slusser by name, described him, and finally denounced him. The A. F. of L. leaders who used to come into Akron in the old days were generally doing well if they remembered who Paul Litchfield was.

The Lewis speech was a battle cry, a challenge. He started off by recalling the vast profits the rubber companies had always made, even during the deepest days of the Depression. He mentioned the Goodyear labor policy, and quoted Mr. Litchfield's pious opinions about the partnership of labor and capital.

"What," he said in his deep, passionate voice, "have Goodyear workers gotten out of the growth of the company?" His audience squirmed in its seats, listening with almost painful fervor.

"Partnership!" he sneered. "Well, labor and capital may be partners in theory, but they are enemies in fact."

He paused, looking out at his audience, and caught the tenseness, the eagerness, the unfolding hope. He raised his voice, "That is what is basically wrong with American economic life and American industry. Here is the record of one great corporation in the rubber industry that has made untold millions throughout the years and yet it has been a constant struggle for its workers to live at all."

249

"The only way out," he said with slow emphasis, "is to organize the workers into unions that can raise articulate voices."

The rubberworkers listened to this with surprise and great excitement. William Green used to tell them about the partnership of labor and capital nearly as eloquently as Paul Litchfield. Here was a man who put into words—what eloquent and educated and even elegant words—facts they knew to be true from their own experience. Here was a man who said things that made real sense to a guy who worked on a tire machine at Goodyear.

"Organize!" Lewis shouted, and his voice echoed from the beams of the armory. "Organize!" he said, pounding the speaking pulpit until it jumped. "Organize! Go to Goodyear and tell them you want some of those stock dividends. Say, So we're supposed to be partners, are we? Well, we're not. We're enemies."

He said these words to an increasingly excited audience. He evoked a dream in the minds of men, a dream of security, and a dream of freedom.

Suddenly he stopped speaking. There was a long pause. Then he said quietly, and very earnestly, "I hope you will do something for yourselves."

The crowd cheered Lewis for minutes. The men walked out into the blizzard so excited that they hardly noticed the bitter winds. They walked home through swirling snow talking fast and hard. Boy, here was a guy who knew something! Jesus, this guy could certainly put a finger on the truth! And, boy, did he give it to old Green? What a talker!

The Akron rubberworkers admired, and found deeply moving, Lewis's rather florid style of speech. Simple men of simple speech themselves, they liked hearing their dreams, their problems, their suffering, cloaked in Biblical phrases. They felt proud that a workers' leader could use so many educated words with such obvious fluency, and they were pleased and a little flattered by hearing their own fate discussed in such rolling periods and such dramatic phrases.

The Lewis speech made a profound impression in Akron. His audience went out of that chilly hall to make John L. the most talked of man in town. A hero to his listeners, he was next morning a hero to every second man in the rubber shops.

But it was not John L. Lewis's gift for oratory that won him overnight top place among Akron rubberworkers. His speech and his appearance was remembered in the valleys because he said what the people already knew.

Long Live the King   *January 20, 1936*

Most of Akron took only a mild interest in the news that King George V of England was dead, and his son, Edward, the new King. The town was much too tense to care very much about who was ruling the British Empire, although the newspapers printed columns of type on the subject and carried dozens of pictures of the dead King and the new Emperor.

The Cold Wave   *January 23, 1936*

Akron was paralyzed this morning, gripped by the annual cold wave that always brought fearful suffering to half the population. The temperature fell to fourteen below on official thermometers and to twenty on the windswept city streets. Fourteen persons were treated for frozen feet or hands in the City Hospital free clinic and hard-pressed firemen as usual fought dozens of blazes caused by overheated stoves.

The First Sitdown   *January 29-31, 1936*

The mountaineer workers of Akron were fond of Alex Eigenmacht, the bullet-headed, blue-eyed Hungarian who ran the union print shop out near the Firestone plant. They liked him because he was the best story-teller in town. Even the gaudy movies hadn't spoiled the taste of the sons of the Southern hills for a good tale deftly spun. And Alex—rubberworkers had difficulty pronouncing his last name, so he went simply by his first—had a real talent for reciting the stories of his improbably adventurous life.

Union rubberworkers used to turn up an hour or so early at

Alex's little office, and while they waited for the last of their leaflets to come off the little press out in the composing room, they listened solemnly, with just the ghost of pleased grins on their broad mouths, to tall tales of Alex fighting in the Austrian mountains; Alex in the Hungarian Red Army; Alex eluding—by the merest hairbreadth—German spies; Alex escaping the White Terror by the very skin of his teeth.

One day four truck-tire builders from Firestone ambled into the print-shop office to pick up some union notices. Alex was in an expansive mood and he began, in his poetic, slightly accented English, to tell them the story of the beginning of the World War.

Like some adventurous men, Alex had a talent for being in the right place at precisely the right moment. He had been a union printer in Serajevo the day the Austrian Crown Prince was blown to bits by the fatal bomb. A passionate Serbian nationalist, along with other members of his union, he had fought to prevent Serbia capitulating to the Austrian ultimatum.

"The men who threw that bomb," Alex told the listening rubberworkers, "were men fighting for freedom. My union decided to protest against the government's arresting them and trying them for murder." This was a new slant on old history and the Firestone union men leaned forward and said, "Yeah, go on."

The printers couldn't actually walk out on strike, Alex said, because they had heard that their boss had a whole crew of scabs lined up ready to take their places at a moment's notice. Besides, if they actually struck, they were quite likely to be arrested and thrown in jail. The times were tense and the Serbian government was trying to do everything to prevent the inevitable war.

"So we had an inside strike," Alex said casually. "We just sat around by our machines, and, by God, nobody could come in and take our jobs, and they couldn't arrest us either. We were on the job."

Alex went on, telling about engineers who struck and finally the mobilization. The pressman brought in the notices and the tirebuilders shook hands and said they liked the story.

Nearly three months later, on the cold winter day of January 28, 1936, Alex was startled to hear the door of his office banging in the wind. He went out to greet his old friends from the Firestone truck-tire department. Their faces were cracked with the wind, and they wore heavy scarfs and thick mittens and lumberjackets.

"Sit down, sit down," Alex said pleasantly. "Pull up next to the radiator and warm yourselves up."

"Nope," one of them replied. "No time. Look, Alex, will you do us a favor?"

Alex had courtly continental manners. He said he would be delighted, it was an honor, what could he do?

"Tell us about that time in that town where the World War started when you guys struck but didn't walk out."

Alex hesitated, trying to recall the story. Then he nodded. "Sure," he said, "but what's up?"

"Just tell us," a big tirebuilder said.

So Alex, considerably bewildered by the air of mystery and excitement written all over the faces of these big tirebuilders, told them the story again, this time in great detail. They stopped him to ask questions.

"Well, didn't the boss try to throw you out?"

"He couldn't," Alex replied. "He was afraid of hurting his expensive machinery if there was any fighting inside."

"Uhmm," men in the little group said, and added, "Go on." When he was through, the tirebuilders pulled their scarfs tight around their ears, jerked their woolen caps down to their eyes. "Thank you," they said briskly and without another word, slammed out the door.

Left alone, Alex drummed on his desk with a pencil, put a thoughtful finger to his nose. Finally, he called up the Firestone local headquarters and asked, in the course of a casual conversation, if there was any trouble in the truck-tire department.

"Boy," said the man from union headquarters, "is there! Trouble and plenty of it!"

"What's it all about?" Alex asked pleasantly.

"Well, you know about how they tried to cut the base rate up there forty per cent to speed the boys up some more?" the union man said.

"Yeah," Alex replied, "so I heard. I was surprised at that.

253

They usually don't trifle much with those babies in the truck-tire department. They're tough."

"You said it," the union man agreed. "Well, anyway, the boys raised holy hell about it, and finally we got Murphy—the factory super—to agree to only an eleven per cent cut."

"Yeah," Alex said. "So?"

"So the boys was still sore," the union man explained. "Sorer than hell. They've been speedin' them up for months now something terrible. My God, it's worth your life to work up there. Nobody but them big husky babies could take it. There isn't one of them in there under six feet two, and they all weigh better than two hundred and, believe me, they ain't fat, not the way they work."

"Yeah, yeah," Alex agreed.

"Well, so this eleven per cent cut didn't go so good. The boys figure if they don't stop this speedup now, they'll all be in the ashcan by the time they're thirty-five. The pace is something awful. Anyway, you know all the boys are scared now of this eight-hour-day thing, and they figure if they let the company get away with this cut, why, they'll start to think they can do anything and end up putting in the eight-hour day."

"Yeah. So?" Alex said.

"O.K., so the boys got together and decided to stall on the rate. You know, they got that group payment stuff up there, so when all the boys slow down, why, they can't cut their wages, see?"

"Yeah, sure."

"So last week Murphy sends a rat in to make the time," the union man went on. "You know the system. If a guy comes in and works like hell and even does sloppy work, the company don't care, and if he makes the base rate on the new schedule, why, then the whole outfit has to make it."

"Yeah, yeah," Alex said impatiently.

"O.K.," the union man went on. "So this skunk comes in and starts making time on the boys. Well, the second night he's in there, it's on the night shift, why, the boys begin to get pretty sore. Things begin to look as though this rat is going to get popped by some of the guys with bad tempers. So Clay Dicks

254

comes over. He's the union committeeman in that department. Clay figures there's going to be trouble, and he wants to quiet the boys down, because he thinks it's not so good having union men slugging rats right in the shop. The company would probably use it as an excuse to fire them."

"Sure," Alex agreed.

"So Dicks tries to smooth the boys down. But obviously this skunk has been tipped off by the management, because he starts to pick on Dicks. Calls Clay a son-of-a-bitch and a lot more— plenty more."

"So?" Alex said, interested. Mountain men, he knew, did not take kindly to insults.

"Yeah. So Clay holds himself in pretty good. He gets the fellows back on their machines, and he says to this rat, 'I'll see you outside after the shift.' That don't suit the skunk so good, he wants to fight right then, which is just what Clay figures. This guy is out to get him canned, because he's the union committee-man."

"So?" Alex said again, getting excited.

"O.K. When the shift is over, Clay rings out at the timehouse. You know how that is. There's a little courtyard there just before the gates. Clay was figuring on meeting the rat right outside the fence and giving it to him. But all of a sudden, as he was walking toward the gate, this rat turns up and slugs Clay a dirty one, from the back."

"Uhmm."

"Yeah, so Clay takes a fall and then he gets up and gives it to this guy. Boy, the fellows said he just knocked the living day-lights out of him, bounced him six feet across the ground."

"Good," Alex said, pleased.

"Not so good," his friend replied, "because, Jesus, Clay hardly had time to lay a hand on this dirty dog when suddenly from nowhere at all, mind you, just by coincidence, who should happen to be strolling around in the middle of the night but a big bunch of factory guards."

"My," said Alex.

"Yeah, so they pounce on Clay, and of course let the other guy go, and Murphy suspends Clay for a whole week, no pay, for fighting on company grounds, which is mighty convenient for Murphy, because here is the truck-tire department without their union committeeman just when they were trying to negotiate about this wage cut."

"Bad business."

"So the fellows is sore. Boy, they're boiling mad," the union man went on. "They're holding meetings here all the time, and Murphy says absolutely he won't take Dicks back, and the boys said he's got to, or else."

"Else what?" Alex inquired.

"I don't know," the union man replied, his voice suddenly blank.

"Yeah," Alex answered. "Well, thanks a lot." After he hung up he sat at his desk, drumming with his fingers, and staring out into the swirling snow. It was four o'clock. Alex bundled himself up in his heavy coat and went home.

The snow fell in patches all afternoon, and toward dusk, the winds grew fiercer. The six to twelve shift at Firestone came stamping into the factory, their ears wrapped in home-knit scarfs. The lights flashed on all over the great factory, and at six-fifteen the steady clatter and crash and whir of the early evening shift blotted out every human sound in the rubber shop.

Outside, in the gathering darkness, automobiles went carefully past the Firestone plant, poking their way along on the slippery windswept streets. People who lived in Akron were used to seeing the big rubber plants of southernmost Main Street, so only a few, as they rode by, even glanced at the great pile of yellow brick buildings. But passing strangers stared, and were filled with unrest. For the Firestone rubber shops, on the dusk of a winter's evening, were a commanding and beautiful sight. Arising black against a pale sky, they were illuminated by a thousand lights twinkling from their windows, making a soft glow on the snow-covered yards around them.

On this bitter night in January, the drafty hall of the union headquarters across the street from the Firestone plant was partly filled with restless tirebuilders. They were huddled, most of them still wearing their heavy lumberjackets, around a fat stove at one end of the big room. A naked electric light bulb hung on a long

256

cord from the ceiling, making a pool of yellow light near the stove. No pictures, no bulletins, no notices hung on the walls, except a badly lettered, homemade sign off in one corner, stating, "Buy union-made goods."

The men were talking quietly but with fierce excitement. They had just decided to give Murphy one more chance: Reinstate Dicks and give him back pay for his time lost, or else.

"He'll say 'or else what' and that would be bad," one of the men objected. He was, like his friends, tall above the average, with tremendous shoulders, but very thin and gaunt, with deep hollows in his young weatherbeaten face and at his big neck bones.

"Yeah, that's right," someone answered from the outer circle around the stove. "We don't want to give him no hint. This has got to come off quick and easy. It's got to be a big surprise. That's what was the matter last year. We was all the time talkin' and didn't do nothin'."

"Yeah," a tirebuilder whose heavy boots were sizzling against the very belly of the stove replied, "yeah, and we let a lot of guys do the talkin' for us. This time we run it ourselves, and we don't tell nobody, and we don't ask nobody if it suits them either."

"Yep," the men in the circle murmured. They sat quietly in their wooden chairs, close to the smelly stove, thinking. They seemed tired. Mostly blond men, freckled on the high cheekbones, with blue eyes, big red ears covered with soft blond fuzz, big heavy noses and wide mouths, they had still, after years away from their mountains, the look of outdoor men. Awkward in repose, their big feet reached out in a dozen queer angles. But even as they lounged silently, their lanky bodies revealed swiftness of action, power in motion.

And indeed these men who sat now, brooding, were said by expert industrial engineers to be the most highly skilled workmen in American mass industry. They built truck tires, partly by machine, partly by hand. They worked at a speed unequaled even in the auto shops. Their tires shoed the busses and heavy motor vans of the world.

In the quiet, the faces of these men were profoundly unhappy. They had been pushed into making plans for desperate action, a final resistance against the way of their lives. Most of them were

257

married, and had three or four young children. During the past years many of them had been off and on relief as they were taken on and laid off again at the factory. Since they were the aristocrats of the rubber shops, they made about $25 a week when they worked—if they worked. They could not feed their growing families on this average annual wage of a thousand dollars or less. With the eight-hour day in the offing, every fourth man would lose his job forever.

Just before midnight the men in the union hall buttoned their jackets and crossed the street to ring in. Murphy had said "No" again to a hasty telephone call. Their minds were made up. The signals were arranged. Everything was ready. Some of the men had trouble slipping their timecards into the punch. They were nervous and their throats felt dry. This was really a hell of a thing they were going to do. Nobody had ever done such a thing before—at least not in this country. It made a man sort of upset.

Promptly at midnight the truck-tire department started work. Under pools of light, the big men stood at their machines. A wheel slowly revolved, as they wound on strips of heavy rubber and fabric. Their hands flashed. Helpers came in quietly and laid piles of carefully folded material beside their machines. Just over their heads, a conveyor belt clattered slowly by. Suspended from the belt were huge thick hooks. Every few minutes, one of the darting hands ripped the finished tire from the machine, slammed it on a hook, and went back to the revolving wheel. Foremen walked slowly up and down the long lines of tirebuilders, checking material, glancing at the finished tires, sending machine repairmen to a faltering wheel.

No human sound came from this vast room. The clatter and shriek and roar of the conveyor belt and the revolving wheels, the drone of motors, the broken rush and squeaking halt of electric factory trucks, drowned out even a brief salute of one worker to another.

But as a flashing hand reached up to slam a tire on the hook, the worker had half a second when his body came near to the tirebuilder on the next machine.

"Two o'clock," a man muttered as he swung up his tire. The tirebuilder next to him did not look up from the revolving wheel.

His hands never stopped their expert, rapid motions. He hardly nodded. But when his tire went up to the conveyor belt he said, his face a blank, with such a tight mouth that he might merely have been shifting his wad of chewing tobacco, "Two o'clock."

The man at the next machine never even looked his way. But, a moment later, and this was strange, for he was such an expert workman, he dropped his heavy tire tool. It clattered to the floor quite near the fourth machine. The foreman looked up, his ears trained to pick out of the constant uproar a different, unexpected noise. But he only saw a tirebuilder picking up his tool, brushing against a friend.

"Two o'clock," the clumsy tirebuilder murmured.

After the first hour, the foremen on the truck-tire floor were considerably annoyed when it appeared that two of their best workmen were apparently suffering from kidney trouble. At least they left the floor to go to the washroom; this was nearly unheard of the first hour. A tirebuilder could hardly afford to go to the washroom so early on the shift, because if he went more than once, his pay for the night would take a bad cut.

When they came back, one of them nodded, the barest kind of jerk of the head. Downstairs, in the auto tires, a man on the top machine was saying, as he reached over to grab material, "Two o'clock." And next to him, an auto tirebuilder was dropping his tool and picking it up, saying, through hardly moving lips, "Two o'clock."

A little after one-thirty, a foreman on the truck-tire floor went downstairs to talk to the super on the auto floor. "Everything O.K.?" he asked, shouting in his friend's ear, to be heard.

"I guess so," the foreman from auto tires replied. The two men stood together watching the rows of flashing hands, the rhythmically moving backs. The noise sounded in their ears as familiar music. They knew every variation and could separate the proper drone of the motors from a sudden brief whine of a machine gone sour. Tonight the noise sounded all right.

"I got the jitters, I guess," the super from upstairs said, shaking his big shocky head like a puzzled hunting dog.

"Me, too," the head from the auto tires answered. "I keep feeling there's something phony going on here. But I don't know.

259

The fellows ain't talking any. They're making fast time tonight."

"It's goddamned funny they ain't talking," the upstairs foreman growled. "The last two nights they've been howling about this Dicks guy. Tonight they're as quiet as a bunch of ghosts."

"Yeah," the auto super replied. "I got a feeling somethin's wrong. Them guys is watching us right now."

The two foremen stared at the tirebuilders. Their hands wove the usual quick pattern. Their heads were bent over their plies. To a stranger's eye, they were lost in their work, each man a picture of useful concentration. But to the two foremen, there was something wrong. They felt the side-glances of these men. They felt the impact of a quick flash of eyes. They sensed hostility.

"Listen," the foreman from upstairs said, "if anything goes wrong, I'll close up the fire doors right away. You do the same."

"What's going to go wrong?" the auto super said.

"Nothing," the truck head growled, "but if it should, we don't want nothing to spread."

"Yeah." The auto foreman stood unhappily in the doorway as the upstairs super left. His eyes wandered from one hefty tirebuilder to another. Nothing wrong, he could see. But he felt queer. In his bones, he knew something was coming off. Jesus, it gave a man the creeps watching those guys at their machines and knowing they were watching you back, and hating you, and planning some goddamned trick to upset the shift and maybe lose you your job. He walked down the line, brushing past a dozen tirebuilders. They didn't even look up, but he could feel their backs stiffen as he passed. The sons-of-bitches, they were up to something. But what? What?

It was 1:45 A.M. on January 29, 1936.

Upstairs the foreman passed down the lines, his ears cocked for a murmur, for the barest whisper. He was determined to hustle the first guy he caught even muttering right off the floor and out the gate. Something was mighty wrong tonight; everybody on this whole line was sort of holding his breath. Zero hour. He smiled grimly. Zero hour for what? He was sure getting the jitters lately. But, my God, the company didn't realize how sore these boys were at the rate cut, and you couldn't tell them thick-headed guys in the front office. No, all they'd say was "We hold

260

you accountable for unbroken production in your department."
Jesus, was that the way to treat a good loyal company man,
threaten to can him if anything went wrong?

The foreman paced slowly past his workmen, his eyes darting
in and out of the machines, eager for any betraying gesture. He
heard no word, and he saw no gesture. The hands flashed, the
backs bent, the arms reached out in monotonous perfection. The
foreman went back to his little desk and sat squirming on the
smooth-seated swivel chair. He felt profoundly disturbed. Something, he knew, was coming off. But what? For God's sake, what?

It was 1:57 A.M. January 29, 1936.

The tirebuilders worked in smooth frenzy, sweat around their
necks, under their arms. The belt clattered, the insufferable racket
and din and monotonous clash and uproar went on in steady
rhythm. The clock on the south wall, a big plain clock, hesitated,
its minute hand jumped to two. A tirebuilder at the end of the
line looked up, saw the hand jump. The foreman was sitting
quietly staring at the lines of men working under the vast pools
of light. Outside, in the winter night, the streets were empty, and
the whir of the factory sounded faintly on the snow-swept yard.

The tirebuilder at the end of the line gulped. His hands
stopped their quick weaving motions. Every man on the line
stiffened. All over the vast room, hands hesitated. The foreman
saw the falter, felt it instantly. He jumped up, but he stood beside
his desk, his eyes darting quickly from one line to another.

This was it, then. But what was happening? Where was it
starting? He stood perfectly still, his heart beating furiously, his
throat feeling dry, watching the hesitating hands, watching the
broken rhythm.

Then the tirebuilder at the end of the line walked three steps
to the master safety switch and, drawing a deep breath, he pulled
up the heavy wooden handle. With this signal, in perfect syn-
chronization, with the rhythm they had learned in a great mass-
production industry, the tirebuilders stepped back from their machines.

Instantly, the noise stopped. The whole room lay in perfect
silence. The tirebuilders stood in long lines, touching each other,
perfectly motionless, deafened by the silence. A moment ago

261

there had been the weaving hands, the revolving wheels, the clanking belt, the moving hooks, the flashing tire tools. Now there was absolute stillness, no motion anywhere, no sound.

Out of the terrifying quiet came the wondering voice of a big tirebuilder near the windows: "Jesus Christ, it's like the end of the world."

He broke the spell, the magic moment of stillness. For now his awed words said the same thing to every man, "We done it! We stopped the belt! By God, we done it!" And men began to cheer hysterically, to shout and howl in the fresh silence. Men wrapped long sinewy arms around their neighbors' shoulders, screaming, "We done it! We done it!"

For the first time in history, American mass-production workers had stopped a conveyor belt and halted the inexorable movement of factory machinery.

"John Brown's body," somebody chanted above the cries. The others took it up. "But his soul," they sang, and some of them were nearly weeping, racked with sudden and deep emotion, "but his soul goes marchin' on."

Downstairs, the echo of the song burst on the first quiet. Men heard the faint music and picked up the familiar words. They leaned out the windows into the cold winter's night air. "He is trampling out the vintage where the grapes of wrath are stored," they sang.

Across the street, in the union hall, men ran to the door and heard the faint faraway song, and said, full of wonder and a deep pride, "Jesus Christ! They done it! Listen to 'em! They're singing! They're singing!"

Over the snow-swept yard, in the winds of January, the song floated out to the whole valley, a song that promised never to die away, a song that promised to live on, fresh and unafraid, in the hearts of workingmen, a song that promised to spread from Akron to Detroit, to New York, and across the whole land of America.

"Glory, Glory, Hallelujah!" the tirebuilders sang. "And his soul goes marchin' on."

The foremen heard the song and retreated. They locked the fire doors and, five minutes later, opened them on demand. They were amazed by the organization of these revolting workmen. After the first hysteria had died down, the confusion disappeared at once. The ringleader, the man who switched the current off, climbed on the foreman's desk and shouted, "O.K., fellows. Now any of you guys here who ain't with us can get the hell out right now. Go home and stay home and don't let's see your yellow-livered face around here again. Anybody want to leave?"

Nobody did. "O.K.," the speaker went on. "Now we got a lot of things to do. First, we got to have a committee to visit other departments, and let's have some volunteers who ain't chicken-livered." The whole truck-tire department wanted to go. The leader picked half a dozen. "You go downstairs and combine with the auto boys' committee and, listen, it's up to you guys to shut this whole goddamned plant down, see?"

"O.K.," the speaker continued quickly. "Now we got to have a committee to police the floor. We don't want no machinery broken we can get blamed for, and we got to keep the place clean. No gamblin' for money either, and absolutely no drinking. We frisk everybody who comes in, for bottles. We don't take no-body's word for it. A couple of drunks would make this sitdown strike look punk."

"Sitdown strike," the crowd repeated. It was a good phrase. The tirebuilders had never heard it before. They liked it.

"That's what I call it," the speaker said, "because we're sittin' down, ain't we, instead of working?"

"Yeah," the men answered and grinned.

"Now," the leader went on. "We're going to elect a committee to talk to Murphy. We figure we got to stay shut down until Murphy takes back Dicks and fixes the base rate."

There were murmurs of approval. The speaker added, "One more thing, and it's the biggest thing. Most of you fellows don't belong to the union. I ain't blamin' you. Some learns fast, some learns slow. But this strike was started by union fellows. The union ain't the same one that sold out the boys last year. We threw Green out on his ear, in case you haven't heard. The union belongs to us now. The only way we can get anywhere is to have an industrial union, and everybody in it. We got application cards, lots of 'em right here. Nobody has to join, but I should think it

263

would be a pretty dumb cluck who couldn't see now, in the middle of this strike, that the union means business. O.K., that's all."

It was enough. By three o'clock, the tirebuilders on the late shift belonged to the U.R.W.A. in a body. Downstairs the union delegate was sitting at the foreman's desk issuing brand-new union cards to a long line of laughing excited men. The foreman himself was gone, and with him his two assistants. They were sitting in the factory superintendent's office, floors away, twisting their fingers and saying, "Yeah, it's easy to say we should 'a' stopped them, but, my God, it's like a revolution. What can you do? There's hundreds of them and a half a dozen of us."

The factory superintendent's office was a glum place. Every few minutes a new foreman came in, his eyes blazing, his mouth twitching with rage. "I don't know how they found out," the new ones would say. "My God, I had the fire door locked, but all of a sudden, one of them was up there pulling the switch and right away they open the door and this goddamned roving committee comes in and starts to appoint a police committee and pass out union cards, and get them to elect somebody to this here negotiation committee."

Firestone Plant One gradually shut down completely. The departments that didn't actually sitdown and strike were paralyzed by lack of work or materials. The delicate mechanism of mass production was dealt a brutal fatal blow. Engineers had worked for years to synchronize every labor process in the great factory. The most remote departments were dependent on the flow of materials from some other faraway corner of the great plant. But once the line was broken, factory operations came to an uneven jerking halt.

As dawn came, the day-shift workers lined up at the timehouse, punching in their cards. Still dazed with sleep, they stumbled off streetcars, not knowing what had happened inside the walls of the great yellow brick factory. Yet they found out instantly. Murphy could never understand this grapevine telegraph. How did tirebuilders standing patiently in line instantly learn that everything had gone blooey up there in the factory? But they did. And they straightened up, joking and laughing and strutting as they walked. Murphy didn't know whether to let them in or not, and being confused, he did nothing. So the new shift came on, and joined the old sitdowners, the veterans, and listened jealously to their bragging tales of how *they* started it, *they* turned off the current. By noon the men who had come to work at dawn were also veterans, able to lord it over the newcomers.

Murphy was at his wit's end. Once he thought of turning off the steam. But when the tirebuilders heard the hissing sound stop, and felt the pipes grow cold, they began to beat such an inferno of noisy rapping on the pipes that Murphy was afraid. Suppose they got sore and busted up the machinery? He turned the steam back on.

The elevators kept running too. Murphy burned up, but what could he do? The tirebuilders rode downstairs in lordly fashion to the factory cafeteria, and ate good breakfasts, and rode back upstairs picking their teeth and talking in loud pleased voices. Maybe he should starve them out? Murphy thought. But, my God, there were 1,200 tirebuilders actually on strike and, as a matter of fact, most of the workers in the other departments were really striking too, only their departments had just closed down for lack of material. But Murphy knew 'em—they, too, were really strikers at heart. Well, that's a lot of men roaming around inside a factory. Suppose he closed the cafeteria. Could he close it? Maybe they'd fight to keep it open. They probably would. Even if he could close it, could he really starve them out? Wouldn't that make them even sorer and wouldn't the guys outside who sympathized—and there were plenty of them—wouldn't they rush the factory with food?

My God, Murphy thought, what does a factory superintendent do on a spot like this? He simply didn't know, this sad pioneer, this superintendent faced with America's first industrial sitdown strike.

The strikers themselves were surprised and jubilant when they found so little resistance. They owned the factory. Nobody dared say them nay. So they used power carefully. Clean-up squads kept the factory floors shining. The police committee looked darkly at a man who so much as swore. A tirebuilder, leaning on his machine to watch a tong game was warned by every other man on strike, "Watch out. Don't bust nothin'." Abashed sitdowners apologized to the union committee for suggesting poker at a penny limit.

By a little after noon, the tire floors were so crowded a man could hardly find a place to sit down. Three shifts were on sitdown duty and men from the fourth shift illicitly sneaked past the gates and came up to get in on the excitement. Runners carried news between the sitdowners and the union hall. So-and-so's wife had called up to say more power to you, stick it out.

About one o'clock the next morning, the end of the first day, the strike committee decided that some of the sitdowners should leave to get a little sleep. Apparently the management would continue to let strikers in and out of the big plant. The committee divided the men into shifts: about half the sitdowners marched out the factory to go into South Akron and Kenmore and get a clean shirt, some sleep, and a chance to tell the world what was happening at Firestone.

Next day they returned, looking fresh, to relieve their comrades standing guard over their machines. All during the second day the strikers sat around at machines singing, playing cards, listening to speeches, and signing union cards. They ate in the factory cafeteria, and some of them caught cat-naps on newspapers stretched out on cement floors.

While they ate and slept and played cards, the news of the sitdown strike spread through Akron. The newspapers carried awestruck and rather incomplete accounts of the amazing strike, but few feature writers penetrated to the sitdown area, no pictures were printed of wives kissing their husbands through fences. The newspapers stuck to baffled and sketchy reports of an incident that they did not understand very well but feared very much.

East Akron, South Akron, Kenmore Hill, and Barberton did not depend on the newspaper stories of the great sitdown strike. The sitdowners themselves came home for shaves and clean underwear, and they spread the story with feverish excitement. Goodyear tirebuilders sat patiently downstairs in little frame houses for hours waiting for a Firestone sitdowner to wake up and tell them all about it. The Firestone local hall was jammed day and night, and men worked twenty hours of twenty-four signing up new members and explaining how the sitdown worked.

The valleys seethed with the story. Women ran, bundled up in old coats, across their front yards, to call on their neighbors and tell them what was going on at Firestone. Little boys boasted in school recess that their Pops were sitting down in the truck-tire department, and other small boys all but burst with envy and rushed home screaming, "Pa, why can't you sitdown?"

The management of the rubber shops were stunned by the news. Here was something they had never heard of before, something frightening and queer. How did you deal with it? How did you break it up? One thing they were sure of: Firestone must be very firm. Not by any chance should the sitdowners be allowed to think they had won their peculiar strike. That would be fatal. That would give the new idea just the proper halo of success to make it spread, and then heaven only knew what would happen next.

The Firestone management agreed at first. For twenty-four hours Murphy refused even to discuss settlement with the negotiation committee. He said the plant would have to be cleared before he would talk about the Dicks case or the base rate either. The second twenty-four hours Murphy began to change his mind. It was all very well for Goodrich and Goodyear to beef about being firm and holding out and standing together. They were making tires, and he wasn't. Their factories were running smoothly and his was a bedlam.

Still Murphy hesitated. But at the beginning of the third full day of the sitdown, after fifty-three hours, his foremen brought terrible news. All of Plant Two was ready to sitdown in sympathy unless there was an immediate settlement. The Plant Two pitworkers had already voted to stand by their curing boxes and cut off the steam. Murphy shuddered, and in his mind's eye, he could see the beginning of a real strike, a strike for union recognition or something of the kind. His spies told him there was plenty of talk about spreading the strike and increasing the demands. Now this terrible news about the men in Plant Two!

Murphy sent for the negotiating committee and consigned to

267

hell the opinions of his fellow factory superintendents at Goodrich and Goodyear. It was all very well to talk about a solid employer front, but in the face of something like this, a man had to act quickly or the whole situation would simply blow up in his face.

The settlement allowed Dicks' immediate reinstatement and three hours' pay for every day lost. It promised immediate negotiation on the base rate. It offered three hours' pay per day to all workers who had lost time during the sitdown.

When the committee, breathless and excited, brought the news to the men up in the truck-tire department for a vote, they could hardly talk, they were so jubilant. And the strikers were quite beside themselves. They were getting paid, paid, mind you, for sittingdown! And Dicks was back, with pay. And the rate would be negotiated. Glory Hallelujah!

The sitdowners marched out singing, and the sound of their voices went everywhere in the valley. The Firestone sitdowners had won! They won! They won! This sitdown business worked.

Two Days Later   *February 1, 1936*

One hundred men in the Goodyear pit satdown today, protesting a ten per cent pay cut which they said was a preliminary to installing the eight-hour day in the department.

None of the men belonged to the U.R.W.A., and the company union, the Industrial Assembly, offered to open negotiations for the strikers. The company-union committee drafted a truce, and persuaded the sitdowners to leave the plant. The pitmen went out, grumbling, on a Saturday night.

The Same Sitdown   *February 3, 1936*

In the howling wind of early dawn, the Saturday sitdowners stood at the gates greeting the first Monday shift and begging them to sitdown to protest the pay cut.

A few minutes after the shift began, the entire pit crew satdown.

Company-union men persuaded them to choose a committee to see the management and go back to work.

The noon pit-shift also satdown as soon as the whistle blew to begin work. Again, they were talked back to work by roving Industrial Assembly delegates.

And Again   *February 4, 1936*

The two night-shifts at Goodyear quit work at their machines and milled around the curing rooms tonight. Forced back to work by foremen who told them that the entire Goodyear Flying Squadron would be rushed in to take their jobs, the pitmen, as they left the factory, went straight to the U.R.W.A. local hall to discuss the situation.

The union officials, faced with a bunch of husky pitmen who carried no union cards, finally agreed to act as a negotiating committee for the outraged curing department.

The Controversy Develops   *February 5, 1936*

Paul Litchfield himself told the union negotiating committee that the pit pay cut of ten per cent was perfectly "fair." He stated flatly that the company would not rescind the cut, nor would it tolerate any nonsense like the Firestone sitdown.

And Another One   *February 8-9, 1936*

The Goodrich tire department went down today, protesting a base rate cut. The sitdown, unexpected and apparently perfectly organized, threw the huge factory into the wildest uproar. The factory superintendent, T. G. Graham, was hastily summoned from a Y.M.C.A. round-table on labor relations to the scene of the strike.

L. L. Callahan, the stocky, determined little president of the U.R.W.A. Goodrich local, told reporters that the speedup at

Goodrich forced the sitdown. The average work load, he said, had been increased 562 pounds per man per six-hour shift in one department, the mill room.

The tirebuilders, faced with a cut in base rate, which meant an additional speeding up, announced they were determined to sitdown until hell froze over or the rate went back to the old standard. The company lunchwagons went through the struck departments as usual, the sitdowners played cards, and the cafeteria was crowded day and night. The rest of the plant soon slowed to a stop and, within a six-hour shift, all the machinery in the vast plant was dead.

Sherman Dalrymple, president of the U.R.W.A., rushed in to negotiate for the strikers, who were rapidly being signed up in the union. Graham, frightened by this determined strike, at first tried to maintain the icy and arrogant policy of Goodyear. But his "advisers" warned him that he was dealing with desperate men, and that anything could happen and probably would if he didn't settle fast.

Goodrich didn't want a major strike any more than Firestone. Both managements felt in their bones that real trouble was more than a possibility in Akron. If Goodyear wanted to fight the good fight for employers' rights, hurray for Goodyear. But Goodrich, like Firestone, preferred to back down in the face of strike threats and sitdowns.

The Goodyear management made it clear that they feared one more sitdown victory in Akron would unleash the hounds of union trouble for fair. They counseled a firm front and no settlement.

Mr. Graham considered the appeals for a flat rejection of strikers' demands. He also considered his quiet factory and the dangerous mood of his tirebuilders. Then he made what he called a compromise settlement: a return to the old base rate, and three hours' pay per day for all but the original shift that sat down.

South Akron hardly considered that a compromise. The strikers had turned off the electric conveyor belt current to force the return of the old rate and the rescinding of the pay cut. Well, they got that, didn't they? And pay for all but one of the shifts besides. The workers danced in the windy cold streets. Victory! Another big victory! That showed that if you stuck it out with the sitdown and let the U.R.W.A., not some lousy company union negotiate for you, you could win.

This sitdown did not go unremarked in the respectable circles of Akron. West Hill was thoroughly alarmed, indeed. The newspapers castigated the sitdown. The "liberal" *Times-Press* ran an editorial titled, "The Sitdowns Must End." They added the pious hope that "responsible" labor leaders would soon censure the sitdowners and put an end to this lawless method of protesting supposed factory injustices.

Good-by Forever   *February 13, 1936*

Everybody who amounted to anything in Akron braved the snow and sleet of the winter's worst blizzard to attend a gigantic birthday party for J. Edward Good and C. W. Seiberling.

The joint celebration was held in the armory, and sponsored by nearly fifty civic organizations of all kinds, including the Chamber of Commerce, the Rotary Club, the Kiwanis Club. The Girl Scouts attended in a body to present bunches of roses to Mr. Good and Mr. Seiberling. A crew of singers in uniform represented the Salvation Army. The rubber-company presidents appeared in full evening dress.

Akron's upper classes, flanked by all the "respectable" people in town—the lawyers, the ministers of the society churches, the heads of the welfare agencies—turned out in one last community splurge to do honor to the two best-liked men of their era.

J. Edward Good was a hardware dealer, Boy Scout backer, and donor of the municipal golf course. Charley Seiberling, the younger and milder brother of the famous "F. A.," was a patron of the Girl and Boy Scouts and nearly every other "civic-spirited" charity that came along. Both men had served on half a hundred community uplifting committees in their time. They had, indeed, as one speaker at the party after another said, given generously of their time and fortunes to benefit the city of Akron.

The celebration went off pleasantly enough on the surface, in a perfect orgy of sentimental speeches. Ministers recalled the old days and Girl Scouts made grateful little thank-you orations. But the lawyers and the rubber-company presidents sat uneasily at the long tables, and in between speeches ministers whispered to famous merchants about the "unrest" abroad in the city.

When Mr. Good rose to reply to the speeches, he was on the defensive. Trembling with earnestness, the old man said, "I can remember the time in Akron when every workingman had the ambition to own property, particularly a home, when employer and employee worked for a common end and settled their mutual problems without outside interference."

He could remember. So could his listeners.

Outside the big hall, the fierce winter storm howled.

The Same Night   *February 13, 1936*

While J. Edward Good talked about the good old days, rubber-workers and their union friends swept out of the Central Labor Union, the last vestige of the good old days in local labor affairs.

Frank Patino, six times president of the C.L.U., friend of mayors and businessmen, he who once boasted that "there never has been a strike when I was in on negotiations," was up for re-election.

He was supported by the building-trades unions. Against him ran Wilmer Tate, the fiery red-headed machinist who had helped organize the first rubber union, served as an A. F. of L. organizer, and offered his friends advice on how to resist Green. He was supported by the rubber unions and the printers.

The debate started at 7:30 and wound up at 1:30 A.M. Patino fought hard. He accused Tate of disloyalty to Green. Tate replied that he stood for trade-union democracy and militant action, and if that meant disloyalty to Green—make the most of it. Cheers.

Patino's friends cited his long record and argued that he had never antagonized employers. That's just it, the rubber union delegates shouted, while the chairman pounded for order.

Finally the vote was taken. Tate won—sixty-five to forty-nine. The Central Labor Union adjourned its meeting early on the morning of February 14, 1936, with Tate and the rubber unions officially in control of the Akron labor movement.

Two Hours Later   *February 14, 1936*

At exactly 3:10 A.M. the tirebuilders in Goodyear Plant Two, department 251-A, shut off the power on their machines.

The Goodyear tirebuilders sat down to protest the layoff of seventy men, dismissed, they believed, in preparation for installing the eight-hour day.

BOOK THREE

February 14, 1936, to March 21, 1936

The Prelude

"Tong!" said a big tirebuilder in Goodyear Plant Two.

"I'll be a son-of-a-bitch," his friend Pete growled. "What's the score now?"

"He gets 117 matches," the scorekeeper said briskly. "Your deal, Pete."

Pete sat crosslegged on a pile of neatly arranged newspapers to keep the cold of the concrete floor from his bones. He wore his heavy lumberjacket and his woolen cap, for the tire room was chilly. His face was covered with a whole day's beard, and his eyes were tired. It was eight o'clock in the evening—the tirebuilders had been sitting down since three o'clock the morning before.

Sprawled on newspapers up and down the big shadowy room, 140 men ate sandwiches, or played tong, or talked in huddled groups. The light fell on idle tire machines.

One of the fire doors opened and three tirebuilders marched in. The men in the big room scrambled to their feet. "Well, what's the good word?" they yelled. "They goin' to settle?"

The strikers on the negotiating committee shook their heads. One of them climbed to the foreman's desk.

"Here's what happened, boys," the speaker began heavily. "Them bastards up there ain't giving an inch. I told them we was going to hold out until they took back the seventy guys they fired Monday. I told them we knew that the seventy guys is being fired to put the eight-hour day into this department, and I told them we wasn't going to stand for it."

"Atta boy, Joe, old boy," somebody yelled from the crowd.

"Yeah," Joe replied, "yeah. But it didn't do no good. They said no. Furthermore they're locking the doors of this department and we don't get no food nor nothing. They won't even talk to us again either."

The strikers growled deep in their throats.

"Yeah," Joe said. "That's the way I felt about it. I said, We won't stand for it, see? We won't stand for the eight-hour day. So they hand us some crap about how these is just seasonal layoffs. It ain't the eight-hour day. Well, I said, if that's so, why don't you lay off according to seniority? Why do you lay off tirebuilders that have been here for years, huh?"

"What'd they say?" one of the strikers called out.

"They said nuts to you," Joe growled. "Only real polite, of course. Such fancy language. You should hear them guys talk. You'd think they was doing us a favor even having a factory so's they can give us jobs."

"So what?" a tirebuilder said.

"Well," Joe answered. "I tell you. We got to stick it out until the union decides what we should do. This is a lot bigger thing than just our department. The union boys will be in here later on tonight, and we'll have a meeting. But we ain't licked, see? This is only the beginning."

"You said it, Joe," the tirebuilders answered loud and clear.

The strikers straggled back to their tong games. The fire doors opened again. Fred Climer, the Goodyear personnel director, walked in casually, followed by a whole crew of company guards in neat uniforms, their revolver holsters swollen with guns. Nine department foremen and supervisors brought up the rear.

"He brought the army," a tirebuilder yelled, and the strikers sprawled out on the floor roared with heavy laughter.

Climer's face reddened, but he spoke gently and persuasively. "Now, fellows, some of you may have been a little hasty. I explained that to Mr. Litchfield. I told him that Goodyear men might misunderstand a company policy, but that in the end they would realize that the company only acts for the long-run good of its employees. I told him that I am sure that you fellows cannot really have forgotten the loyalty you owe the Goodyear Company and Mr. Litchfield."

"Bull!"

Climer's voice sharpened: "The Goodyear Company and Mr. Litchfield will consider the causes of this controversy and you may be sure that they will act fairly and justly to right any wrong, if

278

wrong there has been. But the company cannot act on the causes of this misunderstanding until you fellows show your good faith and go back to work."

His words fell into a deep silence. Climer glanced around at his escort of company guards. "I will give you men," he said, "one-half hour to man these machines. After that, you will all consider yourselves dismissed, and the supervisors here will immediately hand you your passout checks." He glanced at his watch. "From 9:20 P.M. on, you will no longer be Goodyear employees. You may be sure that the company will not care to rehire at any time men who have proved their disloyalty to Goodyear."

Again the pause, and again the deep solid silence. "It's eight-fifty," Climer said loudly. "The foreman will now throw the switch. I will give you one-half hour to begin building tires."

After his words, there was the roar of the conveyor belt, the sound suddenly deafening to men who had lived twenty-one hours in dead quiet. The room came into bright relief under the work lights. The men scrambled to their feet.

Climer, with the guards and foremen around him, waited at one end of the room, watching the belt clank by overhead, its empty hooks a challenge. Three men sidled out of the ranks of the strikers. They didn't look back. Trembling, feeling the burning eyes of their comrades upon them, they stepped to their machines, and one by one, with shaking hands, they picked up the rubber fabric, snapped on the current, and began winding the plies on the revolving drums.

A striker stepped forward, his whole gesture a menace, his eyes flashing, his face contorted. In the racket of the belt, the words that he shouted were lost. A guard reached for his revolver holster. Climer, in this soundless pantomime, put out a restraining arm, and the strikers, too, pulled back the tirebuilder.

They stood there, these two groups of men, divided by the length of the tire room. Between them, in the gulf separating the workers from the management, three nervous miserable tirebuilders tended their machines under the bright lights. They weren't working very well. It took them an interminable length of time to hang their first tires on the hooks.

The strikers conferred among themselves, screaming in each

279

other's ears. Climer watched them, hopeful. But at a signal from Joe, they about-faced with military snap. Climer could only see the stubborn backs. Under his steady gaze, the strikers found their cards, and squatting on the bare concrete floor, began to play tong.

The half hour passed. The noise stopped. In the quiet, Climer heard a man say, "Tong!" and another answer, "I got a jinx on me tonight. I ain't won a hand."

"Thank you." Climer spoke loudly to the three tirebuilders. "Report for work tomorrow." They walked out, glancing back at the groups of strikers, gulping nervously, afraid.

"The 137 men in this room," Climer snapped, "are no longer employees of the Goodyear Company. The foremen will pass out your dismissal slips among you." He turned sharply on his heel and marched out. Silently, the foremen approached the strikers, shuffling slips of paper to find the right names. A few of the men automatically put out hands to receive the fatal notices. Most of them stood stiffly drawn up, letting the flimsy slips flutter to the floor. Finally, the foremen finished. The strikers heard the bolts on the fire doors swing shut. They were locked in.

Across the narrow brick-paved street lights burned in the union hall. Crowds of rubberworkers milled around the bare room and overflowed into the narrow offices of the union president. They talked in deep gruff voices, and the burden of their speech was: "They can't get away with it. We got to stop them now or never. The eight-hour day is right on our necks. Right now."

Some of the men fingered a mimeographed leaflet addressed, "To all Rubberworkers—Union and Non-Union, Organized and Unorganized."

"Our security is being threatened by a ruthless campaign of wage cutting and layoffs," it read. "The rubber companies are cutting rates in one department after another. The bosses intend to wring still more profits out of the hides of the employees. Already it is necessary to work at a hellish pace in order to 'make out.' The companies are also trying to smash the Union, hoping in this way to make the rubberworkers helpless to defend their rights. . . . What can we rubberworkers do? There is but one solution. Organize on the economic field by joining and building the United Rubber Workers of America. Organize on the political field by forming a Labor party."

The letter was signed, "Members of the Communist Party in the U.R.W.A., the Firestone, Goodrich, and Goodyear plants."

It was Friday, the fourteenth of February, St. Valentine's Day. Prosperous burghers swathed in heavy overcoats took their wives downtown to see Bing Crosby, a blond Hollywood baritone, in a musical comedy film called "Anything Goes." Men sat in comfortable armchairs in West Hill living rooms and examined, somewhat sourly, the *Times-Press's* special "Industrial" edition.

The Scripps-Howard paper had chosen this day to issue an elaborate rotogravure section entitled, "Marching Forward in the Second 100 years of Great Industrial ACHIEVEMENT." On the first page, under a huge drawing of a brawny half-naked workman, appeared the words, "The Future of Greater Akron is Safe in the Hands of Our Industrial Leaders." A long list of affirmatory signatures was affixed to this happy proclamation, including those of The Goodyear Tire and Rubber Company, The B. F. Goodrich Company, The Firestone Tire and Rubber Company, The East Ohio Gas Company, and The Ohio Edison Company.

Chief feature of this "industrial edition" was a huge picture of a group of elaborately smiling workmen. The caption said, "It is not the exception but the rule to see such a group of cheerful Akron workers."

This touching exhibit moved even the West Hill readers to sarcastic growls of laughter. With the front page of the paper filled with stories of sitdowns and smaller strikes, it was certainly whistling in the wind to inform the world that Akron workers felt cheerful these days. Indeed, the waves of restlessness and anger that swept the valleys touched even the homes of the rich, leaving West Hill tense, afraid, fighting-mad. The city lay waiting for some unknown dam to burst, for the fuse to be lit on some secret bomb.

Very early the next morning, at two o'clock on the fifteenth of February, the union brought the Goodyear sitdowners out of the

281

plant. Weary, their faces covered with stubble, the tirebuilders marched proudly from the cold tire room, finally convinced by union officials that their battle could be better fought on the outside.

"You got to spread the idea of fightin' the eight-hour day," the union men said. "One department fightin' it ain't enough. They got you locked up in here. Come on out and tell the boys what you think. We can always start more sitdowns."

The tirebuilders left the Goodyear plant determined to fight until hell froze over. While they slept, union officials besieged the Goodyear management with demands for their reinstatement. By the time the lanky tirebuilders turned up at the union hall Saturday afternoon, the company had backed down and agreed to void their dismissals.

The tirebuilders paid little attention to this concession. In the bare union hall they stood talking, talking endlessly, repeating, "We got to fight the eight-hour day. It's our only chance. We got to fight. Maybe we got to strike."

All day Saturday one meeting after another packed the union hall. As the shifts finished work, they crossed the street to hold department meetings. Union officials talked until they were hoarse. Most of the rubberworkers crowding into the hall for one of the three or four meetings going on all the time had no union cards. Gradually the distinction between union and non-union men faded away as Saturday passed. Men signed up as fast as they could, but in the rush on application blanks many a prospective member postponed the actual clerical business of joining the U.R.W.A. until tomorrow or the next day. What the hell, they said, we all are really union men anyway, ain't we?

The rising tide of excitement at Goodyear was duplicated at Firestone and Goodrich. The Goodrich union hall was a bedlam. Tirebuilders and pitworkers and mill-room men packed in tight. Men stood on chairs and yelled, "Everybody from the mill room, everybody from department 211, over here. The meeting is just starting!" or "Everybody from the main plant pit, this way, over in this corner. All pitworkers present now from all shifts, ALL SHIFTS OF PITWORKERS, this way."

The department meetings overflowed the union halls, spread

into near-by confectionery stores and empty storerooms. The union bulletin boards were covered with hastily scrawled signs, "Shift Two, mill-room workers, meet at empty storeroom next to Don's Hamburg Place, signed, J. Ross, shift department chairman." Weary union officials ran out of union cards and ink and dues stamps. The newly connected telephones in the halls rang constantly and above the uproar, men bellowed, "Hey, you. Your wife wants you. When you coming home?" and "Shift Three, tirebuilders, somebody's on the phone. Says to look on the bulletin board for a notice of where to meet. Hey, everybody from Shift Three, man on phone says to hurry up and come on over to the meeting."

Running like a river under all this surface noise was a burning anger. In every crowded union hall, grim-faced, towering rubber-workers talked furiously of the same thing; base rate cuts, layoffs, speedup, the eight-hour day. They recalled ancient grievances. Every orator addressing his little shift department meeting hashed over the old cry: speedup, and the new complaint: still more speedup. But now the speeches were full of confidence, for these workers had discovered a way out: the sitdown.

Darkness came early. The sky was overcast with rubber smoke and snow clouds. Lights went on in luxurious offices of the rubber companies. Apprehensive men sat around smooth-polished tables throwing cigar butts into polished spittoons and saying with anger in their voices, "I'd like to know just what's eating them, anyway. I never saw such a business. Every goddamned department in the plant is on its ear." Now and then some cold-voiced man would suggest, "It's these damned union agitators, this guy Lewis, that's stirring them up."

But his words would be drowned out in his listeners' growls. "Save that stuff for the papers. Half the men in the plant never heard of John L. Lewis, and I hope to God they don't. This isn't any outside agitator stuff. Why, some of the best tirebuilders in the plant were in on that last sitdown, and this report shows pretty clearly that most of the trouble is coming from guys who don't even belong to the union."

The rubber-factory executives spent an unhappy afternoon studying dismal reports from industrial spies. The situation, they

283

agreed as dusk turned to black darkness, certainly looked touchy. The gentlemen at Firestone and Goodrich came to the conclusion, after a long afternoon's sad debate, that they couldn't be too careful. The word went out that this was not the time to "adjust" base rates, and foremen were urged to be a little lenient in settling wage disputes. In the unhappy event of a sitdown, the foremen might be able to settle things within fifteen minutes, before anything so unfortunate spread, by "adjusting" the cause of the dispute, providing, of course, that the demands of the workers were not clearly outrageous. Nobody put this policy into words, but the personnel departments at Goodrich and Firestone began operating on the theory that he who runs away may indeed have another crack at the situation. There were more ways than one of killing a union, and wise men knew when to wait it out.

What the gentlemen who considered the situation at Goodyear thought, nobody knew. Afterwards, all of Main Street, the cynical gentry above and beyond the struggle, would say that Paul Litchfield had been "badly advised." Big merchants on West Hill would mutter sorrowfully that Mr. Litchfield never learned the truth, that his underlings suppressed the information that disaster was just around the corner.

But these theories seemed somewhat romantic even to the apologists making them. Goodyear had declared an eight-hour-day policy months ago. The company had been openly rebuked by the Government for its stand, yet its policy had remained unchanged. Mr. Litchfield, once a crusader for the shorter work week, had sacrificed his own baby, the famous Goodyear Industrial Assembly, to the drive for the eight-hour day.

Goodyear officials could not turn back now. The banking fraternity who owned the world's largest rubber company had decided months ago on the eight-hour day. Their paid employees could only attempt to enforce the edict. Mr. Litchfield hoped that his workers would stay "loyal." He counted on it, despite reports from the personnel department.

The lights in the executive offices went out early Saturday evening. The Junior League was holding a big St. Valentine's Day party at the Mayflower. Weary, and a little restless, the rubber men finally forgot their troubles at the dance. It was, the news-

284

papers agreed, a very gay affair. The hall was decorated with seven-foot-high valentines, the music was loud, and the liquor plentiful. The ladies dressed in either red or white evening gowns, and a number sported orchids in their hair. On the surface, God appeared to be in his familiar West Hill heaven.

On Sunday, the sixteenth of February, Wilmer Tate, the new president of the Akron C.L.U., appeared at the Goodyear union hall and addressed a meeting of tirebuilders, all shifts, all plants. Mr. Tate made a notable speech, and the tirebuilders, nearly 1,000 strong, cheered furiously. He said that the eight-hour day was intolerable, and urged rubberworkers to fight for the right to live like human beings.

On Monday morning the union announced that its negotiating committee, representing the 137 sitdown veterans, would once again present the question of layoffs to the Goodyear management.

Later Monday, both newspapers in town carried a brief item on their front pages announcing the annual statement to Goodyear stockholders by President Paul Litchfield.

"Net profits for 1935," the *Beacon Journal* reported, "totaled $5,452,240.07, compared to $4,553,964 in 1934."

As the union hall began to fill Monday night, February 17, with tirebuilders and Goodyear union men anxious to hear the report of the negotiating committee, nobody talked of anything else except the Goodyear profit statement.

"Five and a half million bucks they made last year," tirebuilders said furiously. "Five and a half million bucks. It ain't enough, so they got to squeeze some more out of us by this goddamned eight-hour day."

The figure stung these men to frenzy. "Five and a half million," men growled, as they sat in the chilly hall. "Boy, what I could do with a hundred bucks of that. Jesus, I could buy the wife a winter coat and the kids some shoes and put another ton of coal in and pay off the grocery bill."

"Ain't it a shame," a big pitworker drawled in his down-State Alabama speech. "The poor old Goodyear company is sure limping along these days with only five and a half millions to show for

285

a whole year's work. Fellows, we oughtn't to be so hard on the company, now that we know how they just pulled through last year by the skin of their teeth. No, sir, we ought to understand now why they got to have the eight-hour day and cut the rates."

"You said it," men roared back, tickled by the irony. "Boy, I lay awake nights feeling sorry for poor old Paulie Litchfield with his five and a half millions only. Yes, sir, we're a bunch of lousy ingrates, not wanting to have our pay cut, with the company just starving along on five and a half million bucks. Ain't it a shame, boys?"

Now and then some new man cut through the savage jests and said, "Whose five million bucks is it? Whose hide did they sweat it out of? And it ain't enough. They got to have more—more millions. They got to cut our wages and lay off half the damn factory so they can have more. Five million bucks. It ain't enough for them, and we're starving. Starving. I tell you, I was laid off last week, and my kids are hungry. Right now they're hungry."

The hall was packed by the time the meeting finally began. Men sat and stood huddled close together, still wearing their heavy boots and warm woolen caps, for the great bare room was chilly. John House, the black-haired, gaunt-cheeked young president of the local, only lately a millworker, was on the platform, and beside him were the members of the negotiating committee.

House, confused and excited, found it terribly hard to keep straight just what was happening these wild days. Formally, this was supposed to be a meeting of the 137 tirebuilders of Plant Two who had sat down to protest the layoff of seventy men last Monday. The negotiating committee representing these 137 men was supposed to make a report on what the Goodyear officials had replied to the demands to reinstate the seventy tirebuilders fired a week ago.

But out of the thousand and more men packed into the hall, House recognized hundreds of faces of men from Plant One, and not only Plant Two tirebuilders, but mill-room workers and specialty department men as well. This meeting was only supposed to consider what to do next about the seventy layoffs, but men were demanding action on all layoffs, all base rate cuts, the whole problem of the eight-hour day.

286

House could hear the talk all over the room—strike talk. But this was no way to call a strike. Men should vote, and the union serve final notice on the company, and the Government offer mediation, and, well, this wasn't a proper strike meeting at all.

As the first speakers began, more and more men crowded into the barren smoke-filled hall. Nearly 1,500 men stamped and cheered and howled. The negotiating committee spoke—one husky tirebuilder after another. None of the negotiators were orators. Most of them had never made a speech before. They shouted from the platform. "The company is stalling. They say, sure they'll take us guys back, they'll be nice and kind and won't fire us for sitting down, but they can't say for sure just what they're going to do about them seventy boys laid off a week ago. They say they'll postpone firing them until they study over the situation. Well, that means until we forget about it. Are you guys going to forget?"

The answer came back, a tremendous fierce roar, "No!" Another tirebuilder shouted from the raised dais, "Stalling, stalling, and we know goddamn well what their stalls mean. The eight-hour day! Boys, are we going to stand for the eight-hour day?"

Again the rubberworkers stood up howling, "No! No!"

The men grew more and more excited with each speaker. Some of the 137 men from the famous Plant Two tirebuilders' department struggled up to the front.

"Boys," they cried, "I been working at Goodyear for six years. I worked hard. You boys know how it is on auto tires. By God, they've pushed up the schedule so I can hardly make out my rate any more. And what have I got to show for it? My wife says she can't feed the kids and pay the rent on what I make any more, and now they're going to cut the rate again and lay a bunch of us off, and I'll probably be the next. Then what'll become of my kids? What'll become of us all, if we don't fight now? What chance we got, ever, if we don't stand up like men now! now!"

Men pulled off heavy jackets, loosened buttoned old woolen sweaters. They sweated around the collars and felt dry in the throat.

"I'm a pitworker," a man cried from the platform, shouldering aside another, "and I say we've put up with enough. Why, by

God, you're hardly a man any more in that damned factory. Just a number—a number they can kick in the face when they feel like it, while they make their five million bucks every year."

Again and again, workers yelled from the platform, "Are we MEN?" Talk passed from details to the cry, "How much longer are we going to stand for it? Are we men, MEN, or are we just a bunch of numbers?"

The first speaker from the negotiating committee fought his way back to the dais. "How many of the tirebuilders in Plant Two is against going to work until the company agrees absolutely to take back the guys laid off?"

The roar of reply was quick, and the announcement that the impromptu resolution had carried was drowned in a flood of cheers.

Men rose all over the room and in a confused din shouted, "Let's strike! Strike! Strike!"

House, bewildered, tried to remember that this was not the way the constitution said a strike should be called. It wasn't legal. Probably half the men in the room didn't have union cards yet. But House recalled last year's formal strike ballot and what had happened to it. This time the rubberworkers were doing the talking. This time it was their union, their meeting.

The cries grew louder. "Strike! Strike! Are we a bunch of yellow-bellied cowards? Let's back them up! STRIKE!"

House gulped. He pounded for order, leaning over the rickety speaker's table. The meeting fell into painful silence. House thought, for a long moment, that he ought to explain about strikes, and how they were called, and everything. He hardly knew that he said, his black eyes burning deep in his white face, "As many as are willing to help these men say Aye."

He heard the answer, rolling back to him, a solemn roar, from 1,500 men, "AYE."

He paused. A stocky little fellow named OHarrah jumped up beside him.

"Fellows," he shouted, and his voice shook the wooden bare walls. "We're starting to picket right away. We're closing Plant Two down tonight, keeping out the midnight shift."

A cheer drowned out his words. He yelled, "We need a picket

288

line for the Martha Avenue gate right away. About two hundred. Line up over in the corner. We need a picket crew for the front gates, about two hundred, up here in front."

The meeting broke up with the tramp of heavy-booted feet racing down the wooden stairs to the street.

The dam had burst. The bomb had exploded.

The strike was on.

It was eleven o'clock, February seventeenth, 1936.

The First Day   *February 17-18, 1936*

Martha Avenue, the street next to the Goodyear Plant Two gatehouse, was empty. A terrible wind swept the sidewalks. Inside the two-story brick guardhouse, a company policeman in a neat belted uniform, revolver holster bulging, pressed his nose to the windowpane, and seeing nothing, hearing nothing above the fierce wind, said, "I bet all that talk about them trying to start something is a lot of bull. Anyway, it's too damn cold."

A company detective in wrinkled street clothes, and with a dirty felt hat pushed back on his head, looked up from a copy of *Liberty*. "It's never too cold for them damned Communists," he remarked pleasantly. "Keep watchin'. We got orders to phone the instant we see something funny."

"Yeah," the guard replied, flattening his nose again on the cold glass.

Gus Riker, the night counterman at Joe's Hamburg Stand, wiped a neat hole in the steam-covered windowpane and also pressed his nose on chilly glass.

"I don't see nothing," he announced. "Ain't nobody in front of the gates now. It musta been just a gag."

"I don't think so," replied a big pitworker from one of the stools. "This time it's coming off. Keep lookin'."

"Sure," Gus said. "Boy, I hope you're right, but it's awful cold."

"Cold don't make no difference." The pitworker talked between munches on his hamburg. "Yell if you see somethin'. I want to get there first."

The lights from the plant picked out a vast pattern of windows, and the dark outlines of the factory rose solid and square, like a prison, above the empty street where the wind howled and picked up a paper in the gutter, sweeping it furiously down the block.

Behind the windows of a dozen little restaurants and bars facing the street a hundred men stared into the darkness, men in white dirty aprons and workers in old sweaters unbuttoned against steamy warmth.

The watchers stiffened. "Hey," the company policeman said, and instantly the detective was at the window.

"Jesus," Gus yelled. "They're here!" The pitworker buttoned his old overcoat as he went out the door.

Eleven men crawled out of two old Fords into the biting wind. The shock of the cold bent them over. They tied scarfs around their ears and pulled felt hats or old woolen caps down hard over their eyes. Fighting the wind, they struggled to the great steel gates, and, very close to each other, began walking in a small oval, around and around, in front of Plant Two entrance.

Inside the warm gatehouse the detective telephoned. "Yeah, yeah, but the cops won't be able to get here until the six o'clock shift. Not enough of them anyway."

Presently he went back to the window. "Jesus, there's a lot of them now. They're coming fast."

"Yeah," the policeman answered. "My God, in that wind, it ain't possible."

One steaming old car after another stopped at the gates to let out pickets. Men came running around the corner bending from the wind. Out of the darkness, through the cold, rubberworkers kept coming.

"Boy," Gus said to the coffee man. "There must be two hundred of them."

The picket line walked in a kind of lockstep, so close together that one man could feel the frosty breath of the marcher behind him on his neck. The howling wind drowned out their cheers. Pickets learned to keep time, so that one man's legs could touch another's and still not stumble.

"There's about four hundred of them now," the detective said into the phone. "We got no chance of bringing in the midnight shift, we got to concentrate on the 6 a.m."

The wind burned through heavy lumberjackets made of blanket cloth; burned through solid heavy flesh; burned to the bones beneath.

"The picket line goes 'round and 'round," a man screamed above the blizzard. The marchers laughed a little through stiffened lips, and took it up. In a hundred keys, hoarse cracked voices screamed above the wind, "Oh-ah-oh-ah, and it comes out here!"

"My God," the company policeman said, wondering. "They're singing."

The detective shook his head. "On a night like this, how the hell do they stand it?"

"It's twelve o'clock," Gus told the coffee man. "Looks like the company ain't trying anything for this shift anyway. The twelve to six guys are all going on the picket line anyway."

The door banged open. A gust of wind swept into the steamy, smelly hamburg joint. Six red-faced pickets tramped in. They walked like men whose feet are stumps.

"Coffee," one of them yelled, "and hurry it up, Gus, old boy. We got to get back on the line."

"Yes, sir," Gus grinned. The door banged again. The narrow lunchroom grew crowded. Gus worked furiously, and still listened to the talk.

"Got every Plant Two gate covered now, and the Plant One boys decided to go inside and start sitdowns, and then bring them out, if the company don't settle."

"My God, it's cold."

"Got to have everybody out for the six o'clock. They'll try to open then."

"My feet are goners. My old lady will raise hell with me."

The detective in the guardhouse watched the crowd on the street set up big ash barrels. Presently the dark street was illuminated with the glow of flames. The pickets crowded six and seven deep around the flickering coal fires. Cars drove up and women struggled with great pails of coffee. A man standing on an old Ford radiator passed out thick sandwiches.

291

"Well, they're sure making themselves comfortable," the policeman snorted.

The detective shrugged. "What time is it?"

"Three o'clock."

The pickets took turns away from the briskly burning fires to march in a long oval before the gates. Men came out of the steamy lunchrooms and said to their friends, "O.K., I'll spell you. Go on in and warm up."

Gus donated four clean dishtowels. His friends wrapped them around their ears and went back into the night. As dawn approached, the thermometer dropped from nine above to four above. It was still pitch-black at four-thirty.

The door banged at Joe's Hamburg Stand. A big tirebuilder hollered into the warm steamy hubbub, "O.K., fellows. Everybody out now. The cops are starting to come." The customers left in a great clatter, emptying the narrow lunchroom. Gus went back to the window. "My God! There must be six hundred of them there, and they said all the other gates were covered too. Jesus, that's a lot of men to be out at this time of the night and in this cold."

The detective turned to the Akron police lieutenant, "You only got forty men for this gate? You must be crazy."

"Listen," the lieutenant replied. "We got 170 men on the force. All right, all but ten of them are on strike duty. My God, men who haven't been in a uniform for years—dicks, everybody—are out there. We got the men distributed like you said. There're picket lines around every gate."

"Well, forty men ain't anything."

The lieutenant snapped, "You got more men on your force than we got on ours. What's the matter with using them?"

"You know." The detective was bitter. "So it ain't legal for our guys to carry their guns over the company property line."

"No? I got orders too. No guns or nothing. We're just supposed to clear a path for the guys that want to work, that's all. No rough stuff."

The detective laughed. "You got a Chinaman's chance in that mob."

"You mean YOU got a Chinaman's chance. It ain't no business of mine." The lieutenant looked bland.

"Christ. I could open up them gates, but not with your sissy cops. Half of them's probably for them damned strikers anyway."

"Yeah?"

"Yeah."

The pickets marched in two ovals, very close together, a moving wall of human beings. They tramped steadily, bent a little in the terrible wind. The cold numbed their hands, the cold made their eyes feel like frozen balls, the cold ate into their chests and made them cough in short aching barks, the cold paralyzed their spines and made their feet burning stumps.

At 5:15 o'clock a bus rounded the corner. The picket line hesitated and then went around in its ovals faster and closer together. The bus stopped. In the lighted, crowded interior, the pickets could see workers waiting patiently in sheeplike order. The first man put a foot down on the ground, and then drew back, looking into the picket line with surprise.

The cops appeared, shouting, "Let 'em through; let 'em through," forming a flying wedge, twenty men on a side. The pickets stood still in their tracks, arms locked in arms.

"Hold fast!" the picket-captain yelled. "Don't give an inch." The pickets cheered. The cops used their heads as battering rams. Above the wind and the cheers, there was the sound of policemen grunting.

The first worker still stood on the bus step. Behind him a crowd of men peered out the windows. The bus riders yelled out, "What's up? What's goin' on?" Their voices were lost in the din.

The police lieutenant shouted, "You got to let anybody in that wants to work."

"How many," the picket-captain yelled back, addressing the men on the bus, "of you guys wants to work? We're on strike! Say yes or no."

"No," screamed the bus riders. The pickets cheered. The picket-captain howled, "Ride down to the next corner and then get off and come on back and picket."

"O.K.," a voice sounded above the shouts. The bus driver

grinned, slammed his door shut, and started with a grind of gears. He waved.

The pickets cheered again. The police lieutenant shrugged; the cops straightened into a long line to wait for the next bus. "Ya-a-ah," a picket yelled, "all that nose-diving and none of them wanted to work anyway. Ya-a-ah." The cops looked sheepish and one called back, "Jesus, it's sure cold. Why don't you have your strikes in the summer?" The marchers laughed.

At 6:30 the picket-captain surveyed the line of marching men. They weren't singing or talking or cheering. They walked doggedly in the terrible cold. The thermometer had dropped to one below zero.

"All right, boys," the picket-captain said gently. "Some of you guys can get warmed up now. The six o'clock shift ain't coming in today."

The door at Joe's Hamburg Stand banged open. "Oh, Christ," gasped one of the half dozen men who stamped in. Gus put a thick mug of coffee before him, and he wrapped his hands around the hot pewter. "Oh, Christ," he said again, in agony as the heat seeped into his half-frozen hands.

"God," Gus murmured.

"Yeah," one of the pickets replied. "But we stopped them. By God, we got a strike now—a real strike."

The man with aching hands looked up, and his stiffened face bent into a grin. "What's a little cold," he asked hoarsely, "to a bunch of guys that's got their minds made up?"

Everyone in the hamburg joint laughed proudly.

The strike was an electric shock to Akron. All of West Hill was awakened early by frantic telephone calls. The first guns had been fired; the hostilities had actually started. Even the most frivolous of the bridge-playing wives understood that this was class against class. For days before the strike, rival rubbermen had been shaking their heads over the obstinate Goodyear labor policy. Now criticism ended abruptly, and all of West Hill banded together to fight to the last ditch for their common interests.

When Charles A. Stillman, Goodyear vice-president, turned up at Mayor Schroy's office early in the morning to demand enforcement of "law and order," he was flanked by Stacy Carkhuff, thin-lipped Firestone secretary, and S. M. Jett, secretary of Goodrich. The Mayor met the rubbermen blandly. Law enforcement, naturally, was his first thought. But, the Mayor added, "Peaceful picketing will be permitted." The gentlemen from the town's biggest industry retreated, grim-eyed and grim-lipped. Peaceful picketing indeed!

The sheriff, meanwhile, sat in his office at the county jail nervous and excited. His telephone rang pretty constantly. Most of the calls were from political advisers. They told him to lie low and keep his shirt on and, for God's sake, to remember that the Barberton business hadn't done him any good. Akron's politicians waited to see which way the wind blew. The first editions of the Akron newspapers didn't give these worried gentlemen much comfort. The cagey editors, slightly dazed from shock, also waited to get their bearings. Only Plant Two was down; workers were still inside Plant One. Perhaps Goodyear would settle the famous sitdown of the 137 tirebuilders and get the men back to work before the thing developed into a major labor battle.

All Akron grabbed the fresh editions and read the first of a great series of statements from union and company.

John House issued the union statement. After rehearsing the story of the tirebuilders' sitdown, he added, significantly, "This thing started as a department matter entirely outside union activity." He stated that the management refused to settle the question of the department layoffs, and wound up, "The management refuses to meet until the men return to work. How can the strike be settled unless men and management get together?"

The Goodyear Tire and Rubber Company's official statement began, "We do not know what the men are striking for. . . . As matters now stand, we are able to operate only at a very sharply reduced rate. Plant Two is virtually completely down, while Plant One is severely hampered. . . . From what we can learn, it would appear that about six hundred men have agreed to keep the remainder of our working force of 14,000 out of the plants and to keep a substantial Akron factory from operating."

The statement added: "Our desire is to operate, and we believe the desire of a vast majority of our employees is to work. Whether

295

we are able to accomplish this must depend upon the support that is afforded us by the forces of an orderly government. We are not recommending violence in any form. But we are calling upon the Mayor, the sheriff, the Governor, and every right-thinking person of this community to support us in our efforts to preserve our right to do business and the right of those who wish to work. . . ."

The company had won the first skirmish in the great battle of statements. The union's appeal to the public reflected the confusion among the union officials, while the company, with its cold remark, "We do not know what the men are striking for," sounded the call to arms on West Hill.

Goodyear, rejecting any argument on policy, the eight-hour day, or broad issues, narrowed the controversy to two ideas: police protection; most of the employees desired to return to work.

The U.R.W.A., with the Government report to back its position, had all the arguments, but the officials of the new union were not yet sure that this was indeed the great, long-anticipated strike. Uncertain, they did not bring up their big guns until days later. Their initial statements outlined no broad list of demands, put forward no basis for settlement except the narrow one of adjusting layoffs in one department, sounded no appeal for funds or for support from the general public.

Jim Keller, section organizer of the Communist Party in Akron, stood up to shake hands with three weary rubberworkers who crowded his office.

He glanced at their red frostbitten faces, noticed the slump to their broad shoulders. "You guys must be plenty tired," he said. "Twelve hours on a picket line in this weather is no joke."

The three Goodyear strikers grinned. "You should 'a' seen it, though," Bill replied. "Boy, I bet none of the strikes you ever seen in your life is like this one."

"If it is a strike," Lister said, sitting down heavily on one of the old wooden kitchen chairs.

"I guess it's a strike all right." Keller drew up the battered swivel chair as the rubberworkers peeled off woolen caps and heavy blanket-cloth jackets. "I've been waiting for you guys."

296

Bill teetered his chair back. "You're sure getting a hot welcome to Akron. In town three months and a strike on your hands."

Keller smiled. "I've seen strikes before."

"Not like this one," Lister broke in anxiously. "You never seen such a mess. House is running around like a chicken with his head cut off. He don't know whether all this picketing is legal or something. And nobody knows exactly what they're striking for, and most of the guys ain't even got union cards yet, and . . ."

"What are *you* striking for?" Keller asked, looking directly at Lister.

The big rubberworker rubbed his reddened face. "Well," he started slowly, "first of all against this eight-hour day, and then for union recognition, I guess. We got to have that, and . . ."

"You know what you're striking for." Keller was brisk. "What makes you think the rest of the guys on the picket line don't know what they're doing?"

"Well, I guess they do. Only House comes out in the paper with this stuff about all we want is to get the seventy guys laid off reinstated."

"Yeah, and I hear he ain't even sure this is a legal U.R.W.A. strike," Bill began. Pete, who had sat silently so far, interrupted, "There wasn't any strike vote—a regular one, see—and House and the rest of the guys from the union is all bawled up about what this is, and what we should try to get from the company and all that."

"Well, you mustn't forget this is a new union. These guys don't have much experience yet." Keller settled back in the squeaking swivel chair. The three rubberworkers talked. Bill said, "Along in the middle of the night somebody says we should close down Plant One, and somebody else says no, this is a Plant Two business, so finally we didn't and . . ."

Keller made notes on an old piece of yellow paper. Now and then, he asked a question, "When the new shift came to the gates, were most of them sympathetic with the strike? How many tried to get through?"

Finally, the rubberworkers' voices died away. They stared at Keller who sat hunched over the desk, fingers beating a tattoo on a crumpled copy of the *Daily Worker*.

297

"Don't you think the first thing the union ought to do is to get the strikers to agree on a full program for a settlement with the company?" he said at last.

The strikers glanced uneasily at each other. "Yeah," Lister nodded slowly, "but that's easy to say."

"Well," Keller began, "wouldn't you say the picket line leaders, or captains as you call them, are the leaders of the strikers? They were chosen by the men themselves."

"You mean we should get a meeting of these picket-captains?" Bill spoke slowly.

"Look," Keller said. "The Communist Party wants the workers to win this strike. But remember, this isn't a revolution. This is a movement to keep the six-hour day and stop wage cuts. We aren't planning on controlling the union. We want to give a little help, that's all. God knows the union needs it."

"You mean we just get the guys together and talk over what the union program ought to be, and then try to convince 'em to carry it out?"

"I think it will work," Keller replied. "In the meantime we get out a leaflet, right now, something for the strikers to think about, see?"

"We better put the six-hour day thing in the leaflet," Lister suggested. Keller turned back to his notes. The men worked steadily. Keller said, once, "They should plan on putting the union's case before the public. Also the signed agreement idea must go in here."

After an hour, a pretty blond girl came in and started making a stencil copy of the statement the four men still worked over.

The leaflet rehearsed the immediate cause for the strike—the sitdown. "It would be the sensible thing for the company, for Mayor Schroy and the city government, not to attempt terror against the strikers. If they do—they will bear the responsibility for a general strike which is sure to develop—if the methods of Sheriff Flower are used."

The leaflet went on to discuss the broader issues of the strike, the eight-hour day, wage cuts. The brochure cited the Government Fact-Finding Commission, and the report on profits by President Litchfield.

298

"So we must be prepared to stand solid for our just and reasonable demands," read the leaflet. "The best way to do this is to Build the Union. Fortify yourself by joining the United Rubber Workers of America. Stand solid for the following demands:

1. Continuation of the six-hour day.
2. No layoffs.
3. No wage cuts.
4. Ten per cent over base rate and no more (end of speedup).
5. Signed agreement."

At a little after five o'clock, heavily bundled women and men left the office of the Communist Party carrying thick piles of the leaflets. They went, some of them, directly to the picket line. Others walked out to the Goodrich and Firestone plants. An hour later workers all over town were reading the first ordered statement on the strike, the first logical suggestion to end the confusion and to turn the deep-running enthusiasm, the fierce determination of the rubberworkers into solid achievement.

The first picket-captains' meeting, held at eight o'clock, adopted the demands listed in the leaflet as a basis for a strike settlement.

The mercury read eleven below zero at ten-thirty Tuesday night. The wind burned men's faces, the cold cut through the warmest clothing.

The gates of the great Goodyear Plant One, the main factory of the world's largest rubber company, were shut. Lights showed from the windows all over the vast pile of brick and steel, but the steady familiar hum of production, the clatter and roar of tire-building that usually seeped through into the city street, were missing.

Inside the plant hundreds of men and girls sat and sprawled on newspapers all over the factory, talking, eating, sleeping, playing cards. Mostly they talked about how hungry they were. None of them had eaten since the midnight before. The company had closed the cafeteria doors, and armed guards prevented lunchwagons from touring the struck departments.

Just before eleven o'clock, a union delegate went quickly from the tirebuilders' room to the fabric department, to the pit, to the

299

millroom. He carried the word, "This is a regular strike now. Come out on the picket line."

At eleven-thirty squads of men arrived at the gates of the Goodyear plant on East Market Street. Bundled in layer on layer of sweaters and vests and trousers, wearing pieces of old linoleum tied around their faces, the advance guard of pickets paced in close formation before the towering iron-barred doors.

At midnight the sitdowners marched, singing, out of the factory to the picket lines.

That was the first day.

The Second Day   *February 19, 1936*

In the furious dawn, with the thermometer reading ten below zero, Paul Litchfield arrived at the gates of the great company of which he was president.

The street lights showed the thickly packed picket lines, hundreds of men and girls moving slowly before the entrance. Shapeless in blankets strapped over their coats, faces obscured by handkerchiefs tied up to their eyes, the pickets shuffled on and on, not looking up, not speaking. Many of them had been walking before the gates since midnight with only half an hour or so off for a cup of coffee.

The wind howled, and the faintest light appeared in the sky. Paul Litchfield surveyed the picket lines with fury. A tall hawk-nosed man with white hair, he cut a handsome figure in his warm overcoat. He walked right into the picket line with contemptuous courage, brushing aside restraining hands. Trembling with anger, he demanded to be admitted to his own factory.

Paul Litchfield was perfectly certain, even as he stood among the half-frozen pickets, that most of "his" men were "loyal." He could not conceive of "his" factory hands revolting, not really. He had, he believed, treated them too well. Was it for no purpose then that he had begun his health insurance program? What was that big building across the street, Goodyear Hall, with its gymnasiums and sewing clubs and theatre? Hadn't he given half his private fortune, back twelve years ago, to these same workers to start their hospital fund? No factory workers in the world, he believed, had things as easy as these men who now stood before the Goodyear gates barring his way into his own factory.

He turned savagely on the pickets, feeling no pity for their exhaustion, not impressed by their long agony. It never once struck him as strange that men as happy as he believed his factory hands to be, should risk their jobs and risk food for their children in order to picket hour after hour in weather so terrible big men wept from the cutting wind.

Paul Litchfield waited impatiently, tapping his foot on the icy street, while the pickets decided whether or not he should enter his factory. He did not know how close he was to danger, because he never thought of these workmen as individuals with adult emotions of rage and adult notions of revenge. Finally, the more level heads on the picket line won. "Let the old guy in," a muffled man growled. The strikers stood silently aside. In the now rapidly graying day, Litchfield stamped up to the gates, and the guards hastily opened the steel-barred doors. While the pickets listened with narrowed eyes and mounting rage, Litchfield berated the company guards and the Akron policemen. He demanded that they should allow "his" workers to enter. He shouted that the majority of "his" men wanted to work. He ordered the gates left open.

No men came for the six o'clock shift. A few foremen approached the gates, but turned aside when they saw the number of the pickets. No marching army of "loyal" Goodyear workers appeared to sweep aside the "Reds" lined up at the factory gates. Instead, hundreds of half-frozen tirebuilders and pitworkers shuffled stolidly along the sidewalk.

At seven o'clock the picket-captain said, "O.K., fellows. Get some breakfast and warm up."

Now a certain order emerged from the noisy confusion at the Goodyear union hall. Committees sprang up almost by themselves. Picket-captains and their crews got regular "shift" assignments for six-hour turns. A soup kitchen developed out of the sandwich- and coffee-making crew.

Men, exhausted from a fourteen-hour stretch on the picket

line, formulated hasty strike rules. The union decided to close off East Market, the main street of East Akron, and re-route the streetcars. A squad left the union hall to notify the streetcar company. The union planned to close all the liquor stores in the whole district.

A big map of the company's property was tacked up on the bare wall of the union hall. Picket-captains checked gates. It appeared that nearly eighteen miles of company property required policing. Men, slouched in wooden chairs, still wearing caps, put dirty fingers on the location of key gates. "Here's a tough spot," a passing striker would say, interrupting the seated strategists.

By noon these informal early-morning conferences had brought a hasty but efficient discipline. Traveling automobile crews of picket-line supervisors surveyed the vast Goodyear plants. A loud-speaker truck turned up at street meetings followed by a motorized canteen service for frost-bitten pickets.

Goodyear rubberworkers, men famous for skill and strength, organized for a long tough strike. Accustomed to order, to precise machinery, to a pattern of work-life in which every detail fitted and no second of time was lost through mismanagement, they set about applying this discipline to their own strike.

The talk in the union hall no longer centered on speedup and wage cuts. By a kind of tacit agreement, the rubberworkers crowding the big bare room left aside the oratory with which they had begun their revolt. Instead, they talked strike strategy. Every few minutes the loudspeaker blared: "Fifteen men wanted for Post Number Five; fifteen men, right away." Rangy pitmen leaned over the desks of exhausted officials and snapped, "We need more men for the airdock. They'll try to ship the tires they got stored out there."

In the streets, the strikers built picket shacks—little shanties of tarpaper and old tires—right over the streetcar tracks. The crew on the Plant Three main gate started the idea and by noon it had spread to every picket post. Men rushed home, returning with old boards, canvas tents, pieces of automobile fender. Open fires flared, and picket crews warmed their stiffened, frozen faces and numbed hands, and then went back to the work of building shelters.

While the strikers brought order out of enthusiastic confusion,

The Goodyear Tire and Rubber Company considered its position. All its great factories in Akron were empty and silent except Plant One. Inside the largest plant were nearly three hundred office workers, foremen, Flying Squadron men, company officials, switchboard girls, and private secretaries. Litchfield himself had gone in prepared for a long stay.

A tunnel ran under the street, connecting Plant One with Goodyear Hall. In the building where Goodyear workers had been given free French lessons and free basketball instruction, the office workers slept on cots and the Flying Squadron men drilled. Food and supplies had been laid in to feed the small army for a long time. True, no "production workers" ran the machinery or built tires. Mr. Litchfield believed they waited somewhere in Akron, dismally anxious to work and prevented from doing so only by a band of lawless Communists at the gates. But, from anybody's point of view, they weren't inside the factory, and the vast acres of machinery lay quiet and dead.

The girl secretaries and the switchboard operators didn't get in on some of the more interesting activities of the interned foremen and Squad men. Many of them, veterans of Colonel Johnston's gas-bomb training squad of the year before, checked over the piles of ammunition freshly stored in the plant and called up the sheriff to see if his new supplies had safely arrived.

Since January, The Goodyear Tire and Rubber Company had spent the sum of $13,063 on gas bombs and $2,640 on guns and bullets. Some of the deliveries had been to the plant, for use of the uniformed company guards in case of trouble; many more to the worthy sheriff and his trusty aide, the beefy Colonel Johnston, now comfortably installed in the sheriff's office at the county jail.

However, the company's strike moves on the second day were not confined to making preparations for a siege. Outside the plant, Goodyear moved quickly and ominously on two fronts. Before noon, a crowd appeared at City Hall. When Mayor Schroy greeted them, they yelled, "We want our jobs at Goodyear. We want law and order." They went away after a while, held a meeting, called themselves "Non-Strikers," and elected a company foreman as chairman of their organization.

303

At the same time, in a thick-carpeted lawyer's office, a group of men sat around a conference table drawing up an injunction petition. The injunction would straighten out this business of peaceful picketing. Both the Mayor and the sheriff refused to use force to break the picket lines. Peaceful picketing, they kept saying over and over, almost hysterically, was allowed under the Ohio law. They wouldn't put themselves on the spot, busting strikers' heads or using tear-gas bombs, not so long as the law was on the strikers' side.

The Goodyear lawyers planned to straighten out this detail. The injunction would prohibit mass picketing, and then the Mayor and the sheriff would be *forced* by law to attack the picket lines and open the gates. Once the picket lines were broken, the company could bring in foremen and other sympathizers, and the strikers, seeing others getting jobs, would be frightened and return to work.

While the Goodyear lawyers wrote the injunction petition, the union broke into the papers with another statement. This time the union stressed the fact that the company would not meet with the strikers to settle the controversy. The company replied icily that it looked to the forces of government to allow it to operate.

Late Wednesday the picket-captains met again. Exhausted from hours of exposure to the bitter cold, they stood in an empty storeroom and talked and argued, finally agreeing on an "immediate" program.

The first thing, they decided, was to make the strike a legal U.R.W.A. strike. Next, they must get all the strikers to join the union and grant them full voting rights. Third, they must force negotiations with the company on the basis of the demands decided on yesterday—six-hour day, signed agreement, and so on. Fourth, picket lines must hold no matter what, injunction or no injunction. Fifth, they must win public opinion by putting the case of the strikers more strongly before the community.

Just after seven o'clock, most of the men, wrapped in layers of blankets, went back to the picket shanties to spend the night talking to the new night-shift picket crews. By midnight strikers were nodding their heads in agreement—they'd hold the line no matter what until they had a signed agreement for the six-hour day and no speedup.

The temperature stood at three below zero. Men's faces bled in the cold. The picket line marched steadily before the Goodyear gates. Inside the plant, company guards slept on cots and Mr. Litchfield went to bed in the handsomely equipped company hospital.

That was the second day.

The Third Day   *February 20, 1936*

The Goodyear Tire and Rubber Company officially closed the gates of its Akron factories today and ordered its "loyal" employees to stay home until "law and order could be enforced."

"Our decision," said the statement, "to close our gates follows two days of futile hope that law-enforcement agencies would provide means whereby our employees who wished to work might reach the plant without undue danger. . . . We are unwilling to subject our employees to further risk. Some of them have already been injured in their efforts to get past picket lines."

Goodyear now expressed a sudden willingness to discuss the immediate issues of the strike. "Numerous Akron citizens have asked us to define the issue involved in the present situation. We find it difficult to arrive at such a definition unless it be the issue of orderly processes versus mob rule or minority dictatorship."

The statement touched on the famous sitdown, and claimed that the seventy layoffs, now an Akron legend, were caused by a drop in anticipated production.

Although not mentioning the eight-hour-day policy by name, the statement remarked: "In recent months we have been endeavoring to readjust our working personnel so as to give our older employees a greater total earning. Our objective was to give in 1936 an average of thirty-six hours per week as compared with an average of thirty-two hours per week worked in 1935. Without a marked increase in our business this policy would naturally call for a certain number of layoffs and rehires from time to time. . . .

"Having carried a more than fair share of the burden during

the leaner years, we felt justified in endeavoring to revise this situation so that our older employees could be relieved of this burden."

The statement ended: "We do not presently see the end of this difficulty. Probably it will not come until there has been time for the public to digest and act upon the real facts. In the meantime, we will do our utmost to avoid violence."

This pronouncement presented the great Goodyear corporation in the pathetic light of a sinned-against innocent. The eight-hour day, it appeared, was but a device to pay higher wages to the "older" employees. The company closed its doors rather than provoke violence. It was all very, very sad.

And somewhat startling. For in the same edition of the newspapers was a headline story announcing that Goodyear officials had demanded that Mayor Schroy call in the National Guard.

Old Mr. Stillman, the white-haired Goodyear vice-president, called on Mayor Schroy, who was flanked by the sheriff.

"Law and order," thundered Mr. Stillman with great asperity, "has broken down."

"It has not," snapped the nervous Mayor. "My policemen have protected lives and property."

Not only Mr. Stillman spoke for the National Guard. The "non-strikers" turned up again, also yelling for more protection, specifically, the National Guard. They offered their services, too, as "special" deputies to the sheriff, who was advised by frantic politicians to say nothing.

The Goodyear statement also seemed somewhat less than complete in view of other news which the local papers trumpeted. It appeared that two Federal mediators were in town trying to get Goodyear to negotiate with the union. The corporation flatly refused. Spokesmen said coldly that Goodyear would talk to the men when they went back to work, and not before.

While Mr. Stillman, dignified and furious, demanded the National Guard, both newspapers had their say about the strike. Both, on sober thought, opposed the strike. Both argued for mediation. Both, somewhat regretfully, reminded the public of the famous Fact-Finding Board and suggested that the company might be slightly wrong about the eight-hour day. Both decided that the union did not have the majority of Goodyear workers enrolled and so could not speak for the company employees. Both were against violence.

The *Beacon Journal* went so far as to hazard that The Goodyear Tire and Rubber Company was on "poor ground" in its refusal to negotiate. With rather remarkable logic, this paper blamed the strike, in part, upon the Social Security Act. The *Beacon Journal* was an anti-Roosevelt paper.

The *Times-Press*, nominally the "liberal" paper, infuriated the union by stating that from 10,000 to 12,000 Goodyear workers were "members" of the Goodyear Industrial Assembly.

Both papers, however, took care to print as much union news as company news. The statements of company and union were displayed side by side. The remarks of the non-strikers were quoted next to union officials who denounced them. The reporters covering union headquarters were allowed a pretty free hand to describe the courage and determination of the strikers, and reporters allowed inside the Goodyear plant wrote generously about the courage and determination of the besieged company men.

On the whole, the Akron press allowed its readers to make up their own minds about the strike. While, editorially, both papers were against the strike, the opposition to the strikers was somewhat judicial in tone, and not without a hint of fence-sitting.

This really remarkable record, a true phenomenon in provincial newspaper history, was accounted for by the unusual circumstances of newspaper ownership. The *Beacon Journal,* the largest paper in Akron, owned and published by John Knight, represented great wealth and power, but the paper was not owned by rubber interests. Mr. Knight, while a large holder of real estate, a former bank director, with a finger in nearly every political and business pie, was still primarily a newspaper publisher. He had a healthy interest in circulation figures, and a labor boycott could ruin him. The strike would be over soon, and rubberworkers, once in the habit of buying the *Times-Press*, might keep on remembering any too obvious favoring of the company in the *Beacon Journal* news columns.

The *Times-Press*, part of the Scripps-Howard chain, was edited by Walter Morrow, a genuine liberal. He had a personal code of fairness in news columns, and would have resigned his job rather than have used his paper for strikebreaking. He had largely imported his talented and youthful staff, which was enthusiastically pro-strike, from out of town. Mr. Morrow had some difficulty restraining his more eager employees who regarded The Goodyear Tire and Rubber Company as their personal opponent. This, coupled with the necessity for the *Times-Press* to stay more liberal than its opposition (which stubbornly refused, in the opinion of the gentlemen of the Scripps-Howard paper, to show its true "reactionary" colors), left the *Times-Press* wide-open to the strikers.

Few important strikes in American labor history have been fought out in a town where the newspapers actually published both sides of the story. The Goodyear Tire and Rubber Company, amazed by what it considered "unfair" treatment by the local press, reconsidered its publicity program. The union, much cheered, made plans to use the forum offered by the town's newspaper editors.

The battle for public opinion was apparently to be fought in the open. The union cheered, and Goodyear gnashed its teeth.

Fog rolled over the Akron valley late this third day. Far out on Springfield Road, the vast bulk of the Goodyear airdock, where once the *Macon* and the *Akron* had been built, rose above the mist. Two red lights burned on the top of its huge roof. A railroad spur ran from the street, nearly a quarter of a mile away, to the egg-shaped airdock.

At night, Akron sweethearts used to drive out to park in the deserted neighborhood. A few houses were scattered around. Near by stood the buildings of the airport proper, where mail-planes landed. Usually only two or three watchmen spent the night near the airdock, guarding the great piles of stored new tires piled high in the huge workshop.

On this evening, fires flamed in the fog. Here, miles from the uproar and excitement of union headquarters, were the farthest outposts of the Goodyear strikers. In the cold damp, rubberworkers sat, surrounded by a gray backdrop of fog that shut out the world. They had made themselves comfortable with a little lean-to, equipped with blankets. Now and then one of the pickets went out from the fire into the fog to gather more wood.

They talked endlessly. The picket-captain on the post, one of those who met every night, said, "Yeah, so we're doing O.K. so far. But tomorrow them bastards is going to get an injunction and get Schroy and Flower to bust the picket lines. We got to fight it. We got to decide not to obey the injunction no matter what."

The men sitting around the campfire nodded their heads. They glanced now and then toward the vast black airdock filled with stored tires, and huddled a little closer against the cold gray fog.

"You said it," one of them replied. "The main thing is to hold the picket lines, and then stay out until we get this here agreement for the six-hour day and no speedup, like you said yesterday."

They talked at Picket Post Number One too. Picket Post Number One, across the street from the union hall, was always the center of some excitement. Union officials dropped across the street to talk to the boys. Reporters asked questions. The coffee wagon stopped here first, and a man could get warmed up in the restaurants near by. It was O.K. as picket posts went.

"We got to get our side in the papers more," the picket-captain said, out of the fog. In the quiet street where no streetcars ran now, the strikers listened carefully.

"Of course today House comes out against the Industrial Assembly, and that's good, but we ought to get in the papers with a broad statement—the six-hour day, and no speedup, and all that."

"Yeah," one of the pickets said wearily. He had worked a full shift at Firestone before he turned up for picket duty.

"The main thing," the picket-captain said, "is to hold our lines now. These bastards are going to get an injunction tomorrow probably and then yell about law and order. Well, we got to bust that injunction, see?"

"What's an injunction anyway?" someone asked.

The picket-captain hesitated. The fellow at the meeting had explained it real good, but he didn't know if he could quite make it clear.

"Well," he said dubiously, "it's like this. The Goodyear outfit

309

goes into court and gets the judges to order the Mayor and sheriff to bust up the picket lines."

"Yeah," the striker returned, "but I thought the law said we was allowed to picket."

"Well, it does," the picket-captain returned, "but you can bet your last dollar that they ain't going to let no law interfere with them."

"That ain't right," another striker said slowly, in the voice of a man struggling with thought. "We got a right to strike and picket; the law says so. Well, it ain't right for a bunch of judges to say it's against the law."

"You said it," the picket-captain replied gratefully. "And we got to make up our minds we ain't obeying no injunction, and tell everybody else we see."

The men on Picket Post Number One agreed. The picket-captain added, "We got to get fellows to make up their minds not to obey this injunction, so's they won't be discouraged when the judges pass it, because they're sure to do it, all right."

"Yeah," a striker said. "My old lady is always saying it: forewarned is forearmed."

The picket-captain felt a glow of satisfaction. If all the fellows were doing their talking right, this injunction couldn't hurt the strike.

At midnight the fog was very thick. The coffee truck pulled up way out at Plant Three, and a dozen men stepped out of the gray mist to get their sandwiches.

"Jesus," a man on the truck said. "It's sure lonely at this damn post."

"Yeah," a picket replied, gulping down the hot warm stuff. "We've been talking, though, and singing a little. Mostly talking. What's going on at headquarters?"

"Oh, the fellows is all steamed up about this injunction, I guess," the coffee truck driver answered. "There ain't been much about it in the papers yet, but boy, the fellows is sure against it. The talk is that they ain't going to stand for it."

"That's what we've been saying," the striker answered. The truck drove away in the fog.

That was the third day.

310

"The Company will not agree to meet with the strikers' representatives while the plant is blockaded."—The Goodyear Tire and Rubber Company in the Akron newspapers.

All six Summit County Common Pleas judges nervously took the bench to hear The Goodyear Tire and Rubber Company pray the court to enjoin mass picketing at the gates of its Akron plants.

No single judge cared to sit on Case Number 144974, and at the last moment, no group of three judges would take the ticklish assignment. For the second time in Summit County history, the entire Common Pleas bench, hoping that in union there would be strength enough to carry the next election, faced an explosive community question. The other six-man act of the local judges was for the bank-reopening case.

The injunction hearing got away to a dramatic start. Most of the defendants cited in the Goodyear petition could not fight their way into a dangerously jammed courtroom. Crowds milling around the buckling doors overflowed the wide corridors, and policemen fought to keep excited rubberworkers from falling down airshafts and elevator wells.

While strikers bundled up in sweaters and old hunting caps struggled with politely dressed Firestone and Goodrich company representatives to battle their way into an already completely packed courtroom, the six judges finally let E. E. Zesiger, attorney for the union, ask for a continuance.

Mr. Zesiger said that he had been given the case late the day before. He hadn't had a chance, he told the court, to confer, except briefly, with the defendants.

The Goodyear legal talent brushed aside Mr. Zesiger's argument. Picket lines were preventing men from returning to work. Goodyear needed action—now.

The union lawyer pleaded for a postponement until The Goodyear Tire and Rubber Company had an opportunity to meet with the strikers and begin negotiations.

Rubber lawyers were shocked. Strike mediation had nothing to do with whether the law was being broken or not. They asked the court to hear the injunction petition at once.

The union demand for a continuance was denied.

Feeling refreshed by this opening victory, the Goodyear lawyers began their case by reciting horrid details about the strikers' picket lines. Men were being prevented from going to work. Food was being kept out of the factory. The Goodyear Tire and Rubber Company was sustaining untold damage.

"The number of pickets and their conduct is a threat of physical violence and is unlawful," cried attorney L. M. Buckingham.

He stated that his clients did not deny that men had the right to strike; they merely wished to suggest that workers also had the right to work.

Mr. Buckingham cited cases where Ohio courts had permitted a limited number of pickets at a selected group of factory entrances during strikes. "In a word," Mr. Buckingham declared, "that's what we're seeking."

The union reply to the Goodyear case got a bad black eye when John House, president of the U.R.W.A. local, said on the witness stand that the strike was not a U.R.W.A. affair. The union was interested in the "demonstration" only because numbers of its members were involved.

Mr. Zesiger told the court that an injunction might mean violence and loss of life. He prayed the court to consider the community welfare.

The six judges picked up their papers and filed uneasily out of the courtroom, their minds made up.

The Central Labor Union, with every accredited delegate present for the first time in its history, met tonight to consider ways and means of helping the Goodyear strikers.

First order of business was the passage of a resolution stating, "We will take all measures within our power to defeat the issuance or enforcement of injunctions."

A fifteen-man defense committee was appointed to collect money, organize squads of pickets, and "otherwise help to bring the Goodyear strike to a successful conclusion."

President Wilmer Tate told a cheering audience: "Organized

labor in Summit County stands behind the Goodyear strikers one hundred per cent. Onward to victory!"

The Fifth Day   *February 22, 1936*

Mass picketing at Goodyear company gates was prohibited today by a sweeping blanket injunction ordered by the full bench of Common Pleas judges.

Sherman Dalrymple, president of the United Rubber Workers of America, replied: "It has been demonstrated by action and word of mouth that the men will resist the injunction if attempts are made by authorities to enforce it.

"Opposition and unwillingness of the company to meet with their workers' representatives has been the chief cause of the shutdown at Goodyear.

"Present indications lead me to believe that if any attempt is made to enforce an injunction there will be an industrial paralysis affecting the entire city."

Mayor Lee D. Schroy announced that the enforcement of the injunction was up to Sheriff Jim Flower.

Sheriff Flower asked for twenty-four hours' grace. He said he would not attempt to open the plant on Sunday anyway.

Goodyear "non-strikers," 2,500 strong, met in the armory, offered their services as "special deputies" to the sheriff, and sent President Paul Litchfield a message affirming their loyalty.

The company said: "We have not changed our minds in our decision that for us to negotiate with this minority mob would constitute cravenness in the face of outlawry and a breach of faith with our loyal employees."

The Sixth Day   *February 23, 1936*

The C.I.O came into town today to help the working people of Akron take up the injunction challenge and win the Goodyear strike.

John L. Lewis and his Committee for Industrial Organization

313

brought up their big guns to aid the Akron rubberworkers keep the six-hour day. By Sunday morning, Adolph Germer, United Mine Workers' organizer, old-time lion of strike struggles and Leo Krzycki, from the Amalgamated Clothing Workers, were sitting in on U.R.W.A. meetings. John Brophy, executive director of the new C.I.O., was expected hourly.

It was the first C.I.O. strike—and the out-of-town labor leaders brought money and advice—both badly needed by the young United Rubber Workers.

Germer started the ball rolling by telling excited President Dalrymple and other U.R.W.A. officials that now was the time to organize—the whole town was ready to sign union cards. "Organize everybody in the shops, regardless of crafts," he suggested.

The wires burned with that bit of advice and in Washington, President William Green bumbled, "The jurisdiction of the United Rubber Workers as set up in its charter is unchanged. The union must leave to craft unions the machinists, maintenance men, electricians, and the like."

Dalrymple replied placidly, "I don't care to get into any controversy with the A. F. of L., but we are accepting as members any men working in the rubber shops who care to sign up."

The C.I.O. brought national encouragement, but the rubberworkers hardly needed to be told to support the Goodyear strike. Anxious officials of the Firestone and Goodrich locals asked their members to stay on the job until they were needed on the Goodyear picket line. Both locals promised to tax themselves until it hurt to pay for soup kitchens and loudspeakers.

The C.L.U. defense committee met for ten hours straight, sending telegrams to hundreds of unions throughout the country asking for support. General-strike talk dominated the meeting, but no definite plans were made. Tate told his committee to wait and see what the sheriff did or tried to do.

W.P.A. workers, some thousands strong, pledged a complete shutdown of projects in case of a violent attack on the Goodyear picket line.

The Goodyear U.R.W.A. local met briefly, took a legal strike vote, and asked assistance of the U.R.W.A. executive board.

Dalrymple summoned all the members of the national executive board to Akron.

And all day crowds milled around the Goodyear picket posts cheering, talking, marching.

"Nobody's busting up any picket lines in this man's town," the strikers growled, and their friends replied, "You said it."

The Seventh Day   *February 24, 1936*

A jittery town was out of bed early this Monday morning. Streets near the Goodyear factory were jammed with pickets long before Sheriff Jim Flower turned up to read the injunction order.

The strikers listened to Flower intone the legal phrases. Three times the sheriff ceremoniously addressed pickets, once at the union hall, once at the main plant entrance, once at Plant Three. Three times the strikers screamed at him: "Are we going to obey it? No!"

The sheriff went thoughtfully back to his office at the county jail, where, newspapers said, he made plans to "enforce the injunction at some time in the immediate future."

Both newspapers printed editorials urging no force and violence on the part of the strikers. "Obey the injunction," the papers told the pickets.

The *Times-Press* went the *Beacon Journal* one better. Painting the strike in hopeless colors, the editorial urged The Goodyear Tire and Rubber Company to have mercy on the union men and give them back their jobs, "if work can be found for them."

Both papers suggested that if the strikers violently resisted the sheriff, the National Guard might have to be called. The *Beacon Journal* wound up its editorial with a plea that Edward McGrady, flashy Government strike settler, come to town.

Sherman Dalrymple, president of the United Rubber Workers, called the extraordinary meeting of the new executive board to order.

"The main and only business of this meeting," he said slowly, in his quiet, hesitant way, "is how to win the Goodyear strike."

Brophy spoke first. "Akron has been famous for many things, but now it is famous for its revolt against despotism. This is a fight for the right to organize."

When the meeting broke up, Dalrymple announced to waiting reporters that the U.R.W.A. executive board had not only officially sanctioned the strike, but had voted to "broaden it in the industry if necessary."

The Eighth Day   *February 25, 1936*

Job Hendrick's alarm clock went off at 5 A.M. His wife rolled over on the lumpy mattress and stretched out a hand in the darkness to quiet the clamor. One of the kids in the next room cried out in a startled voice, "Ma?" and sank back into sleep.

Job dressed quickly, putting on two suits of patched woolen underwear and a frayed sweater under his shirt, vest, suit coat and lumberjacket. He glanced out the bedroom window once and saw the fog rolling under the street light.

When he came down the creaky stairs Missus Hendrick had a cup of coffee ready for him. Still sleepy, her hair uncombed, an old woolen shawl over her flannel nightgown, Missus Hendrick was not very beautiful in the early morning. But Job looked at his wife with tenderness and as he gulped the coffee, he patted her gaunt shoulder.

"Don't you worry, Ma," he said shyly.

"I ain't." The quaver of her voice belied her words.

"Maybe nothin's goin' to happen. You can't tell," Job said slowly.

"It'll happen."

"Yeah, I guess it will," Job answered heavily. "Are you sore at me because I'm goin'?"

"Sore?" Missus Hendrick's face broadened into a smile. "You dope, Job Hendrick, do you think I'd live with a man who wouldn't stand up and fight when there's fightin' that's got to be done?"

Job grinned. He put his long arms awkwardly around his wife's shoulders.

"If you was a-seekin' out this fight," his wife went on, her face now sad and drawn, "I would say different. I would say you got kids and have no right to go about crackin' heads. But you ain't seekin' it out."

"If they should bust the picket lines at Goodyear," Job half argued with himself as he went to the kitchen broom closet, "we would get the eight-hour day at Goodrich in a month, and I'd be back on relief."

Job's wife watched her husband carefully reach behind the old broom and the carpet sweeper to take out a short length of iron pipe. One end of the heavy club was freshly taped. Job had worked on it for an hour before he went to bed last night.

"Well, good luck, old man." Missus Hendrick went out on the porch with her husband.

"Tom's waiting for me up the street."

"Yeah. Well, get along."

Job Hendrick turned back to his wife and hugged her.

"Oh, Job," she said, and ran into the house. Her husband walked slowly down the porch steps and then his step grew brisk as he marched up to the corner.

Tom Gettling was impatient. "You're five minutes late," he began as Job came out of the white mist.

"What've you got?" Job answered mildly, and Gettling let him get the heft of a piece of garden hose he carried under his arm.

"Say," Job asked with open admiration, "what's in that damn thing?"

Gettling was proud. "I got a nice chunk of old iron tied up at the tail of this here snake. Some old deputy sheriff is goin' to be real surprised when I belt him one with this."

"Yeah. Maybe we're goin' to be surprised when they start showerin' machine-gun bullets an' tear-gas our way."

Gettling walked faster.

"Lookit what they did in Barberton."

"I brought along one of the kid's cowboy handkerchiefs," Gettling said. "They say you should tie a wet handkerchief over your nose and mouth."

"I dunno," Job said slowly. "All we guys want is a job and

317

enough to feed the kids, and them rich guys got to give us machine-gun bullets and gas. This is one hell of a country."

Gettling's voice came out of the darkness, gruff with passion. "Well, there's a lot more of us than there is of them. And, believe me, this is our country as much as it is them rich babies'."

"Yeah."

"Why, my folks and yours has been in this country since way before the Revolution."

"Yeah."

"Tom," Job said after the men had walked in silence for blocks along the dimly lighted city streets.

"Yeah."

"I'm hoping you don't get a bad—" his voice hesitated—"a bad wallop. You been a good friend, and don't think I don't remember how you got me back at Goodrich last fall."

"It was nothin'."

"This sort of reminds me of that time we went down to City Hall to get jobs." Job's voice hesitated.

"Aw," Tom replied quickly, "this ain't the same at all. This is different. This time we know what we're doin'."

"Yeah."

The men turned into East Market Street, walking fast.

"We've gone a lot of places together, Tom." Job touched his friend's shoulder.

Tom laughed. "I was rememberin' how you fought me when we was kids back home. You said I swiped your BB shooter."

"You were one hell of a scrapper."

In the distance, above the mist, the Goodyear tower clock shone faintly. After another block, Job muttered, "I can make out the shops."

Gettling strained his eyes. The heavy mass of factory buildings were black against the slowly graying sky. "There's a lot of the fellows there already. See 'em standin' around the fires?"

"Yeah. It's awful quiet, though."

"The cops has taken all the cars away and roped off the streets for a mile," Gettling remarked. "They're sure gettin' ready for a big battle."

"Nice of 'em," Job chuckled, "clearin' the decks for us."

318

"Or them."

Pete Lamphrey at Picket Post Number One saw Job coming. "Hey, come on over and get a load of what's goin' on."

Job mumbled to Gettling. "He's one of them picket-captains I was telling you about. He's got the lowdown on the strike. They have meetin's all the time. Maybe you know him. He was from Elkins."

Job and his friend settled down around the fire. Men kept arriving out of the gray dawn—tall men wreathed in fog until they stepped into the firelight. Every man carried a piece of taped pipe, or a length of rubber hose weighted at the end, a baseball bat nail-studded at the tip, or a bowling pin.

"I hear every piece of pipe the size a man can get his fingers around, and every inch of garden hose, and every baseball bat in town is sold out of the stores," a man said, chuckling. The deepening circle around the bonfire laughed.

"A bowling pin," somebody drawled in reply, "ain't such a bad thing to wallop a cop with."

"Fellows!" Pete began, and the chuckles died away. "We got word on just exactly what the sheriff is aimin' to do. I ain't sayin' how we got it, but we got some friends in this town, and anyway the sheriff ain't even tryin' to keep it secret."

Pete's audience sat tense.

"He's got about thirty deputy sheriffs and about a hundred and fifty cops."

Job snorted.

"Yeah, not many guys," Pete replied, "but they got gas, machine-guns, riot guns, k.o. gas. And if they ever get near the company gates, there's all them company guards inside and the Squad men, and they been drillin' for days, and besides they got plenty more of what it takes to polish off a few thousand dumb cluck strikers."

The men around the bonfire moved uneasily and clasped and unclasped their baseball bats and bowling pins.

"The sheriff is aimin' to get his men together down at the foot of the hill, see. Then he starts them up to the picket lines in wedges. In between each wedge is a cruiser. The idea is to pile the guys they arrest into the cruiser which is right there handy, see?"

"So what do we do?" Job asked impatiently.

"I'm comin' to that. Now the idea is, we don't start nothin'. We just stand up here on top of the hill, as many of us guys as we can get. We don't say nothin'. We just stand here."

"Scare 'em, huh?" somebody said from the back of the circle.

"Maybe. Just maybe. If we're lucky."

"And if we ain't?" It was Job, asking what the others wanted to ask.

"If we ain't," Pete said, "if they come up that hill, shootin' their guns and throwin' their teargas bombs, then some of us is goin' to get killed. But not all of us. There'll be enough of us left to beat the living hell out of them cops and deputy sheriffs and hold our picket line. They ain't breakin' this strike today."

In the heavy silence, Job's voice sounded loud. "You said it, Pete."

The sheriff's office was a nervous, jittery bee-hive at eight o'clock. Uniformed deputies banged in and out of doors, breathless with self-importance. Out-of-town strangers in frowzy overcoats, sporting a day's beard, threaded in and out of the crowd, hoping for a job in case of trouble. Reporters badgered Sheriff Flower every time that nearly hysterical gentleman put in an appearance.

At 8:10 A.M. an excited deputy left the door to the sheriff's private office wide open for a fatal second. There in plain view sat the famous Colonel Johnston. He slammed the door as excited newspapermen yelled questions.

The sheriff finally explained irritably, "Johnston? Why, the Colonel has a perfect right to be here. Goodyear's payin' him to help me."

"Oh," said the reporters.

The Colonel proved quite a help. He sat—cozily out of reporters' sight—at the private wire between the Goodyear plant and the sheriff's office alternately barking orders and looking wise.

Shortly after nine the sheriff announced that the injunction had been officially broken. The strikers had refused to let a four-car supply train into the factory. Deputy sheriffs had taken pictures of the pickets blocking the engine. The sheriff had the legal evidence to proceed.

A few minutes later the jittery sheriff added that thirty deputies and one hundred and fifty policemen had assembled in military order on the edge of the strike zone.

"Zero hour," Sheriff Flower stammered, "is at ten sharp. The advance begins on the dot."

Job stuck close to Tom Gettling. He didn't want to lose Tom in the dense crowd. He wanted to look out for Tom.

"You stay by me," Gettling said to his friend. "I gotta answer to your old woman for you."

Job looked a little dashed. "There must be ten thousand fellows here."

Tom was judicious. "Well, not right on this spot, but I guess if you figure in all the guys out at Plant Three and at all the other gates, there must be ten thousand fellows out on these here picket lines."

"Fellow said just now hardly any of the departments at Firestone and Goodrich is workin' this morning. All the guys is down here on the line."

The blare of the loudspeaker drowned out Job's reply. "Meetin' in union hall for as many of you guys as can get in," the enormous voice shouted.

Gettling and Job and nearly two thousand others jammed into the damp wooden hall. Outside thousands more stood quietly while the loudspeaker trumpeted the voices of the speakers within.

By nine-fifteen uniformed deputies and policemen stood clustered down the hill around a dozen cruisers, fingering guns. In the Goodyear tower, President Paul Litchfield watched the crowd through binoculars. At the factory windows company guards and Squad men pressed noses to the glass.

Paul Williams, a mill-room employee at Plant One, and a West Virginia lay preacher, mounted the platform in the union hall. "Let us pray," the loudspeaker blared and President Litchfield in his tower, the policemen at the foot of the hill, watched thousands of men sink to their knees and grab off old felt hats and battered caps.

Job and Tom Gettling bowed their heads as Williams began, "Almighty God! I ask thee to bless our cause in this critical situation."

The union hall, and the street outside, grew silent. Williams's voice gathered strength, grew clear and loud.

"We think of Him," Williams prayed, "and of the time when Jesus died on the Cross for every man on each side of this picket line."

Job gulped. He heard the sound of men weeping.

"We ask that we do nothing contrary to His will. We know we are fighting for our rightful due."

Tom wiped the tears from his eyes.

"Amen," Williams said.

Thousands of men picked up lengths of pipe or baseball bats as they clambered to their feet. A sigh passed over the crowd. John House shouted into the loudspeaker, "Good luck, fellows!" Somebody started to sing, "Onward, Christian Soldiers," and Job bawled, "For-ward in-to ba-atul, see-e-ee his ban-ners go!" as he tramped out of the union hall.

The rubberworkers of Akron, having prayed, faced the army at the foot of the hill.

The phone rang in the sheriff's office at 9:25 A.M. Colonel Johnston, sleeves rolled up, collar open, grabbed the receiver. "It's the Mayor, for you," he barked at the sheriff.

"Yeah?" the Sheriff said into the mouthpiece. As he listened, his big face reddened. Colonel Johnston bent close, and he could also hear the excited voice of Mayor Schroy.

"Now you listen," the voice rasped. "For God's sake, stop this crazy plan you got. It's suicide, and murder besides. They got thousands of men up there. They just got through praying, thousands of them."

Johnston nudged the sheriff. "Tell him you got to enforce the injunction. Law and order."

The distracted sheriff said into the phone, "I got to enforce the injunction, law and—"

The mayor hung up.

At 9:30 A.M., Chief Deputy Anderson called. "Everything's all set!"

"O.K.," Sheriff Flower barked. When he hung up he started to bite at his thumbnail.

"Re-lax," Colonel Johnston snorted, picking up the phone. "Everything's all set," he reported to the Goodyear chief-of-guard. "The men got their orders. Ten o'clock on the dot is zero hour. They're all down at the foot of the hill now. Look sharp!"

At 9:50 A.M. Chief-of-Police Frank Boss called the sheriff. "Listen, you!" his voice boomed over the telephone. "This plan of yours may be great military tactics, but it's damn poor policing."

"Tell him you got to enforce—" urged Colonel Johnston. The sheriff ground his strong white teeth.

"I got to enforce . . ." he began.

Chief Boss shouted, "It's foolhardy to send police in there, like sending them into a slaughterhouse. For God's sake . . ."

"Law and order," the sheriff screamed. "I got to . . ."

The police chief hung up.

At 9:58 A.M. Police Chief Frank Boss zoomed out of the station house garage in his official car.

"Drive like hell," he muttered to the uniformed chauffeur.

The siren drowned out his voice. The car with the license plate "Chief, P.D." screeched around the corner into East Exchange Street, missed a bus by a bare inch, skidded between two oncoming cars. Chief-of-Police Boss shut his eyes and wiped a nervous hand across his nose and mouth. The siren shrilled in his ears.

One hundred and fifty uniformed policemen standing in loose formation at the foot of the hill heard the siren from far away. Their backbones prickled. A deputy sheriff vomited over a cruiser tire. A man could stand just so much excitement.

"It's exactly 9:59½ by my watch," Chief Deputy Anderson announced through a megaphone. "Stand by for orders to advance."

The policemen shuddered. The sound of the siren drowned the shouts of the strikers on the hill. Chief-of-Police Frank Boss's car rounded the corner, and the driver smacked on the brakes.

"Men!" Boss cried. "The attack is all off as far as you're concerned. I'm giving orders from now on. We ain't attacking any picket line."

The pickets heard the policemen yelling, "Hurray!" but they couldn't see the blue-coated cops trying to slap their chief on the back, couldn't see them all but dance in the streets. Chief Deputy Anderson shouted, "What's the idea? The cops was supposed to take orders from my office."

Chief Boss snorted. "Call up that sheriff of yours and tell him we're keeping the peace, and that's all."

"O.K.," he said to his men. "We're going up the hill like peaceable men. When we get up there, we scatter to the various gates."

He started ahead. Walking behind him, not in military formation, but single-file, grinning, the Akron city police approached the vast picket line. The strikers waited, puzzled, tense. Boss shouted, "This ain't no attack, boys. My men is scatterin' to the various gates, if you'll let 'em."

"Attaboy, Boss!" a striker screamed. Thousands of men echoed the cry. The cops threaded through the pickets, shaking hands with friends, laughing, clapping strikers on the back. The crowd reached out friendly hands to touch the arms of the policemen. The loudspeaker blared, "Chief-of-Police Frank Boss has withdrawn his men from the attack. Give him a cheer, fellows!"

The cheer rattled the windowpanes of the Goodyear factory. The officers took their places at the factory gates. "I wasn't goin' to attack you guys, anyway," one cop shouted. The crowd lifted him from his feet, carried him on their shoulders around and around in a dizzy dance.

President Paul Litchfield left the Goodyear tower. The deputy sheriffs, alone at the foot of the hill, got a telephone order to come back to the county jail. Thirty men couldn't attack half the town. The strikers had the field to themselves.

"Thank you," John House said into the loudspeaker, and his voice trembled. "Thank you! You men have saved the Goodyear strike!"

He paused for the deep cheer.

"Go home now, fellows. Show 'em we got discipline. Show 'em we can assemble ten thousand pickets and then disperse 'em and

324

nothing damaged at the plant, nothing in the whole neighborhood touched. Go home peacefully! And thank you!"

Job cheered and cheered again. Then he and Tom Gettling started home.

"They can't bust our strike," Job said.

Two reporters sprawled on old wooden chairs in the deserted sheriff's office. A deputy sheriff, his neat collar unbuttoned, his hands shaking, burst out of the private-office door. The newspapermen were on their feet.

"What the hell's goin' on in there?" one of them shouted. "You guys got a nerve keeping us out. What's Johnston doing? What's Flower say about Boss taking the cops out of the attack?"

"My God." The deputy sheriff's voice quavered. "Listen! The sheriff don't know what's coming off. You guys know more than he does. Nobody tells him nothin'. Johnston is sore as a boil, believe me."

"Well, the sheriff had better have a statement. I got a deadline in four minutes. He'd better say something, or this town will be . . ."

"He is sayin' somethin'." The deputy pulled two sheets of paper from his pocket with quiet deliberation. "This here is a ver-ba-tim record of what Flower just said to the governor's office."

The reporter from the *Times-Press* grabbed. "Hey," the deputy sheriff said. "I gotta explain it. The sheriff asked for the National Guard, see, but the Governor wasn't there, and he's got to call back, and . . ."

"Christ!" The *Times-Press* reporter snatched the paper and ran for the phone.

Five minutes after newsboys rushed the damp papers to the downtown street corners, the sheriff's phone rang. The sheriff turned respectful when he heard the voice. The Republican Party howled, "The National Guard! Are you crazy? Throw that Johnston guy out of your office if he's going to melt down your brains!"

"Why, what do you . . ."

"Don't talk," screamed the Republican Party. "You've been doing too damn much of that already. Listen."

"I got a right to call the . . ."

"A right!" the Republican Party howled. "You got a right to commit suicide too. I suppose you don't read the papers? I suppose you don't know that the rubber union had announced it will strike every plant in Akron and the C.L.U. will close down every business in town if the National Guard comes in."

"Ah," said the sheriff.

"And I suppose you don't know they had ten thousand men out there this morning. This whole town would rise up to a man if the National Guard got within twenty miles of Barberton."

"So," said the sheriff.

"Yeah," said the Republican Party. "Kindly let Goodyear pull its own chestnuts out of the fire. Even voters will remember the màn who called in the National Guard."

"Ah," the sheriff replied as he hung up.

At noon the sheriff announced to a large press conference that a newspaper in Akron had made an error, a serious error. "I never said I was going to call in the National Guard," Sheriff Jim Flower declared stoutly. "It was all a mistake, boys."

"It sure was," a reporter said under his breath.

In the office of the United Rubber Workers, Sherman Dalrymple, just to be on the safe side, announced once again to reporters that should the National Guard come to Akron, no rubber plant in town would operate.

The sheriff read Mr. Dalrymple's statement carefully.

In the evening men snapped on their radios to hear President Paul Litchfield plead the cause of Goodyear before that mysterious entity, The Public.

"Citizens of Akron," the deep pleasant voice began. Men in silk lounging robes and leather slippers hitched deep armchairs nearer to polished radios. Stocking-footed strikers in much-washed flannel shirts turned up the power on cheap little sets.

"For more than a week now," the voice said, "the plants of The Goodyear Tire and Rubber Company, your largest industry, have been closed, and approximately 16,000 employees have been for-

326

cibly prevented from engaging in their usual occupations by a group of men violating the laws of the city and State and defying the order of the court."

Strikers snorted. Some switched off their radios and shouted "son-of-a-bitch" to empty rooms. But the lawyers, the chemists, the well-to-do folk on West Hill nodded in satisfied agreement and bent forward to catch every word.

President Litchfield began his address with a skillful description of the founding of the Goodyear Industrial Assembly, "to bring more democracy into the management of industry." He declared wages in Akron rubber plants, Goodyear included, were higher than in any other major industry in America. He gave his version of the sitdowns that led up to the strike.

"The question of the number of hours has been raised," he said, to the amazement of even the listeners on West Hill. "Many misstatements have been made that the company was to put everybody back on eight-hour days, although this has been emphatically denied by the management."

This was the first emphatic denial of Goodyear's announced intention to install the eight-hour day. President Litchfield expanded, coming presently to the tell-tale remark, "We feel that the emergency is past and that our employees should not carry an undue share of the burden [short work-week]."

Passing from this remarkable version of the eight-hour-day policy, announced in November by Cliff Slusser, President Litchfield took up the immediate problem.

"The present issue at stake is one of the defiance of duly constituted government to protect a man in his right to work. . . . The suggestion that management confer with representatives who take this means [strike and picketing] of enforcing demands would be a surrender of the rights of citizenship and a recognition of mob violence as a means of negotiation as against the processes of duly constituted government.

". . . As a citizen of this community and as the head of this corporation, I cannot be a party to any recognition of the theory that government stability has collapsed and that the seat of constituted authority has been forcibly removed from the city hall and

327

the courthouse to the center of the mob that mills before our gates."

The Goodyear Tire and Rubber Company had answered the namby-pamby people in town who thought that President Litchfield should at least sit down around a conference table with union officials.

The word was "no quarter."

That was the eighth day.

The Ninth Day   *February 26, 1936*

A high wind blew sheets of ice-cold rain into picket shanties. Strikers huddled under flimsy canvas roofs watching the near-sleet beat down on the high iron gates and brick walls of the factory. Now and then a man struggled out of his lumberjacket to wring the water out of the heavy blanket cloth. His friends had to help him pull the sodden coat back over his rain-drenched shirt.

At four o'clock, the picket-captains on nearly every post, from the lonely station at the Goodyear airdock to the famous Picket Post Number One across from the union hall, left their comparatively cozy shanties to brave the howling wind and the smashing sheets of rain. They crossed deserted streets, half ran along empty sidewalks, to arrive at their meeting shuddering with cold and wet.

The strikers met now in an empty storeroom, bare and dusty. A big handsome fellow who kept a prosperous grocery store near by, had turned the place over to his friends the picket-captains somewhat apologetically. There were no electric lights, no stove. But the strikers were delighted because a grocery-store-keeper wanted the union to win, and at least it was a roof over their heads.

The room was filled with shadows when the first picket-captains arrived, and by 4:30 the rain-soaked shivering men sprawled cross-legged on the dusty floor in nearly complete darkness.

"I'm waiting for one of the fellows to bring in a kerosene lamp," Bill began, "so's I can read some stuff I got here. In the meantime, though, I guess we can have some reports from you fellows on the floor."

The picket-captains struggled to their feet, one after another, and in the gathering blackness described the morale of the strikers on their posts, repeated questions, assured their listeners that "the men is standin' firm for the signed agreement on the six-hour day and union recognition."

The door swung open. A striker brought in a lamp swaddled in an oilcloth raincoat. Bill's matches were wet, soaked by his dripping coat. A tall lean picket produced a cigarette lighter and volunteered to hold the lamp for Bill while he spoke.

"Nothin' can stop us now," Bill began, his long angular face shadowed on one side, lighted softly on the other, "unless we don't do our part. There's more ways than one of killing a cat, and certain people in this town, the *Beacon Journal,* and a couple of councilmen and no doubt the Mayor and some others, think they've got a pretty slick way to break this strike, or as they put it, put men back to work and then negotiate."

The lamp illuminated the front rows of the audience. The men frowned.

"I'm talking about this guy McGrady."

The picket-captains murmured. One sang out, "Who is he, anyway?"

"I'm comin' to that," Bill said. "First, I hope you guys noticed that he rode into town on enough publicity to make a movie star. The *Beacon* had an editorial about what a great guy he was, and a cartoon about McGrady's plan is the way to end the strike peaceably, and then a bunch of stories on the front page about what a human dynamo he is. That's what they called him. Here's a headline from today's *Beacon:* 'Successful, Nervy, Active, Persistent'— that's McGrady."

Bill snorted. He stuffed the newspaper clipping into a pocket and shuffled some papers in his hand. The striker held the lamp closer.

"First, about what kind of a guy he is. He used to be an A. F. of L. organizer—like Claherty."

The picket-captains stirred, muttered to each other.

"Then the Government took him on. He goes around the country doing what the *Beacon* calls 'settlin'' strikes. I call it breakin' them. In San Francisco, McGrady was there all the while they

329

were trying to bust up the longshoremen's and sailors' strike. In Toledo, McGrady was on hand when the boys *failed* to get a signed agreement with General Motors. And not long ago McGrady 'settled' a strike in Cleveland." Bill's voice was richly ironic.

"After the strike was settled, as John Knight would write it, the entire executive committee of the United Textile Workers was tossed out of their jobs at the Industrial Rayon Company. Some strike settlement!"

Bill paused and drew out a penciled sheet of paper from his coat pocket. He squinted at it in the lamplight.

"That's the fellow certain people in this town is trying to sell to the strikers as a great little guy."

He paused, studied his notes again. "Now this here Toledo plan the *Beacon* talks about is a sort of fancy arbitration system which always screws up the working-guy's chances because of course the arbitration board always has a lot of ministers and people on it who are sure to feel sorry for the poor old broken-down company or something.

"But that ain't terribly important right now. The Toledo plan always comes afterwards, to prevent more strikes. Right now we got to see how McGrady works in a strike situation like this one.

"His plan of operation—get this straight, fellows—is always the same. He gets the strikers to agree to go back to work, 'pending negotiations.' The company promises to negotiate, see, and the union goes back to work."

"Well, anyway, the company negotiates, don't it?" came from the back.

"Sure it negotiates," Bill said. "Boy, does it negotiate! For weeks and months. Until all the guts is worn out of the strikers. Until the company spies put a finger on all the leaders and the company fires them for breaking machinery or not working good or something. Then the company says politely that, having negotiated, it regrets that it cannot grant any of the union demands. And that's that. The strike's busted and the workers are back where they started from. And this ain't guesswork, either, because that's what's happened in nine out of ten of the strikes McGrady has settled."

"If the company is going to negotiate, it should negotiate now. Nothin's stoppin' them." The drawl from the back of the storeroom made the picket-captains laugh.

"Yeah, you got the idea," Bill said, glancing up from his papers into the half darkness.

"Now there are a couple of important points for us fellows to get in our heads," Bill began after another pause. "I ain't going to waste time on any oratory about holdin' our picket lines and savin' the strike. I only want to say that this McGrady plan is dangerous, and one reason it is, is because maybe some of these union fellows in here from the outside will fall for it. I ain't sayin' they will, and we all know Dalrymple himself is a swell guy, and they don't make 'em any honester than he is. But just the same, some of the outside guys might just think that the strike ain't strong enough to last and they better settle quick, for anything."

"Dal ain't goin' to let us down," a striker shouted.

"I never said he would," Bill replied sharply. "Don't get me wrong. I only want to warn you guys that unless the union leaders feel damn sure of the strike they might think they *got* to settle on the McGrady plan. It's our job to show 'em we want to hold out for a signed agreement, six-hour day, union recognition. See?"

The picket-captains nodded.

"A union leader ain't no tougher than the guys on strike, and usually not as tough," Bill said. "He can't be. It's up to us, by voting at meetings and all that, and talkin' around the union hall, to let the guys know we don't want McGrady."

"What's the other thing you got in mind, Bill?" the man holding the lamp asked quietly.

Bill looked up from his papers. "Well, this is the toughest angle. The way I figure it, Goodyear probably won't go for the McGrady plan at first either. Litchfield's probably still hoping he can get the National Guard and bust the strike by violence.

"That would suit him better. But if he can't get the National Guard, then he'll fall back on McGrady, the next best thing. So I wouldn't be surprised if the papers came out tomorrow and said Goodyear turned McGrady down. Then McGrady will probably shoe it out of town fast. The *Beacon* will slap Goodyear on the

331

wrist, naughty-naughty, for not agreein' to McGrady's plan. Some guys will be fooled and think that if Goodyear don't want McGrady's plan, it must be good.

"That's where we got to be careful. Because as soon as Goodyear sees it can't get the National Guard, and I don't think it is going to get it either, McGrady will hotfoot it back to Akron, and this time they'll put the heat on for sure to send the men back to work while negotiations are going on." Bill stopped to get his breath.

"Some of you guys talk now," he said abruptly.

A thin mill-room worker came up to the pool of lamp light. "Brothers," he said earnestly, "I think we ought to thank Brother Bill for his fine talk. It would have been bad if we hadn't found out who this guy McGrady was."

The men hunched up on the floor clapped loudly. A man passing by on the rain-swept street looked up, startled.

"Now the way I see it," the picket-captain continued, "is what are we going to do to lick McGrady? I think there's just one way of beating him—that's to talk the McGrady plan to death. The newspapers is goin' to be for it. The fellows on strike won't know what to make of it. They never heard of McGrady before, just like we hadn't until Brother Bill told us about it.

"The newspapers will butter the McGrady plan up until it would melt in your mouth. The fellows on strike will be all mixed up. So the way I see it, is we got to talk, talk, talk about McGrady until we're blue in the face. Tell everybody on every picket shift. Talk it in the union hall. Get the facts on McGrady. All we got to do is to let the fellows know who McGrady is and what's happened other places—we don't have to convince 'em they're against McGrady. They'll be against him as soon as they know."

He sat down, breathless.

In the back, among the shadows, a picket-captain said, "What did McGrady do in Toledo? I forget what you said."

Bill squinted at his papers. "Well, I hear he went in there when the General Motors strike was on, and just as the fellows had all the other General Motors plants shutting down for lack of supplies, and the fellows had the strike about won, see, they accept this 'plan' for going back to work. Dillon got them to accept it, in fact."

"Dillon?" the picket-captain asked. "Oh, yeah, I remember that. O.K."

"Here's a little leaflet the Communist Party put out about Mc-Grady," Bill added. "I guess they're going to distribute it tomorrow. I got some copies here. It's got all the dope written down about McGrady. I know some of you fellows don't go along with these Communists, but that's all right, this leaflet is just about McGrady. The Communists know about McGrady, see. They watched him work in other towns."

The millworker who had made the speech took one of the leaflets a little gingerly. The other men watched him.

"It's got that stuff about the Cleveland strike in it," he remarked casually. Hands reached out. Men said, "Gimme one. I never can remember names of companies and stuff, and I got to have the facts about McGrady to tell the boys."

"Brothers and sisters," a man said, reading the leaflet in the lamplight, "if your job is dear to you, if your family is dear to you, if you want union security on the job, you must vote No! on McGrady's proposal."

"That's good stuff," picket-captains murmured. They stuffed the leaflet carefully away before they stepped out of the bare storeroom into the pouring rain.

The Tenth Day   *February 27, 1936*

Edward F. McGrady, Assistant Secretary of Labor, conferred with Goodyear and union officials in a series of secret meetings.

The union and The Goodyear Tire and Rubber Company started a pitched battle for public opinion. The corporation led off with a full-page ad labeled, in huge black type, "They're giving us this space to say *our* say." The text of the ad began, "For nine days we non-striking Goodyear men have been held away from our jobs. We don't like it. We want to work."

C. W. Seiberling went on the air in the evening. J. Edward

333

Good introduced him as "a friend of the workingman—a man everyone loves." Mr. Seiberling said he believed most of the Goodyear employees were not on strike and wanted to go back to work.

Sherman Dalrymple followed the "man everyone loves." Mr. Dalrymple stated, "Almost without exception, in labor disturbances, the rich have looked upon the agencies of government as their private instrument to protect and defend them in their raids upon labor's rights. . . . We are now, as we always have been, ready and willing to sit down with Mr. Litchfield or his representatives to discuss the issues involved."

Lyle Carruthers, chairman of the non-strikers, went on the radio too, getting in his licks in the war of words.

Mr. Carruthers said his committee had visited Governor Davey and shown him pictures of the injunction being violated, "although we did not ask the Governor for the militia."

"Enforcing the injunction is still Flower's job. If he doesn't do it, the job won't be done, and if the job isn't done and done quickly, then God help Akron."

The tenth day ended with weary citizens snapping off radios, surfeited with words.

The Eleventh Day   *February 28, 1936*

The union scored a decisive victory in the please-be-on-our-side-Mr.-General-Public battle.

"Is This a Democracy or a Dictatorship?" a full-page advertisement in both papers trumpeted in huge type. "Shall an arrogant management deny to workers the right to have a voice in their own working conditions?"

The Goodyear publicity department gulped at the text of the message that followed, for the C.I.O. had sent its best publicity experts to help the beleaguered rubberworkers.

"WAGE CUTS," the text of the advertisement began. "In the face of increased profits in 1935, the company has begun a program of wage cuts on piece-work—and this in spite of the increased cost of living which is making it harder and harder for us to support our families even with wages staying as they were."

This simple tone, this disarming use of the first person plural, this reference to rising prices which every housewife in town understood, made the Goodyear officials blink with surprise.

"LAYOFFS. Before the Fact-Finding Board from the Department of Labor last fall," the advertisement continued, "the Goodyear management openly admitted that they had installed a plan which called for gradual reduction of productive workers. This plan means laying off twelve per cent of the force, or about one thousand workers. What does this mean? It means that these workers will be an added burden on the relief rolls, and the taxes they would have paid will not be paid. The layoff of several hundred workers precipitated this strike. . . .

"SPEEDUP. FAVORITISM," the message continued, "FEAR. The result of these company policies has been that no worker feels secure in his job. Any day his wages may be cut. He may be laid off or fired. As he gets older and less able to stand the terrific strain of the factory, he will be discarded. . . ."

"IS THIS A MOB?" the advertisement asked. "No. . . . If no violence is resorted to by the company, the workers will remain absolutely peaceful.

"IS NEGOTIATION UNREASONABLE?" the message went on, reaching the deadliest part of its argument. "Is it unreasonable that we should ask Mr. Litchfield to sit down quietly and talk things over? We don't think so. Would you, Mr. Small Business Man, refuse to talk over hours of work and wages with your employees? Would you, Mrs. Housewife, refuse to discuss such matters with the girl working for you? It is universally accepted that negotiation is a reasonable right which workers should be granted. They ought not to have to fight for that right.

"WE ASK YOUR SUPPORT in this fight for democratic privileges. The small businessman with whom we trade, the doctors who care for our children, and everyone else in the community will profit if this strike is settled peacefully through negotiation. If thousands of workers are thrown on the relief rolls, the small taxpayers must foot the bills. In Akron's present situation, this would be a civic catastrophe. We ask you—we urge you—to support us in

335

our efforts to obtain a conference and peaceful settlement with the company in this dispute. THIS ADVERTISEMENT WAS NOT PAID FOR OUT OF COMPANY FUNDS! . . . UNITED RUBBER WORKERS OF AMERICA and SUMMIT COUNTY CENTRAL LABOR UNION."

Goodyear replied, somewhat lamely, with a full-page advertisement of its own. The town's newspapers carried the two broadsides on succeeding pages. The public could judge for itself.

"A WORD IN BEHALF OF GOODYEAR MEN," the Goodyear message was headlined.

"I am especially concerned," the text started off, "that the people of Akron do not misunderstand the role of Goodyear men in this strike.

"By Goodyear men, I mean not the company department heads, or office workers, so much as the rank and file of the Goodyear plants.

"For thirty-six years I have worked with these men.

"I want to say now that nothing in my whole business experience has made me more grateful than their superb conduct during these troublous days.

"What a lesson their demeanor has been!

"When they met in popular assembly—some 4,000 strong representing thousands of others—to consider the question at issue, they met thoughtfully, as self-respecting citizens of the community in which they live. . . .

"In these days since, they have found themselves affronted with insult, threat, violence. . . .

"So, when you read or hear about the Goodyear 'strike'—and of disorder or lawlessness there—make a sharp distinction.

"Draw a line between those defying the court and the majority of Goodyear men. . . .

"These Goodyear men are not 'out' by choice—they want to be back at work, and we want them back, when they can be back *safely*.

"I take off my hat to them, because they so well deserve it.

"P. W. LITCHFIELD
"THE GOODYEAR TIRE AND
RUBBER COMPANY, AKRON, OHIO."

The town pored over these two advertisements, debated them, quoted them, clipped them out of the papers to read the arguments aloud at dinner tables.

The union had gotten off to a poor start in the race for public approval. The confused statements of the union officials the first few days of the strike were duck soup for the Goodyear publicity experts. But the findings of the Government board, which the union trotted out in such impressive fashion, gave Goodyear a black eye that no hearts-and-flowers messages from President Litchfield could cure. The small businessman, the doctor, and the housewife agreed with the union that negotiation seemed "reasonable."

The rubberworkers had public opinion fighting beside them on the picket line. The newspapers, the Mayor, and the sheriff took note.

Lisle M. Buckingham, attorney for The Goodyear Tire and Rubber Company, stated in a letter to the county prosecutor today that the failure of the sheriff to call the National Guard into Akron made him "guilty of a most flagrant violation of official duty which cannot be too severely condemned."

Mr. Buckingham wrote furiously, "The mere fact that the sheriff is confronted with a large number of individuals disobeying the law does not excuse him, because he may employ military forces which are available to him at his command whenever he requests them."

"Edward F. McGrady, ace U.S. conciliator who flew into Akron to settle The Goodyear Tire and Rubber Company strike, left on a bus, his plan unaccepted by the Goodyear management." —*Beacon Journal*, in its late afternoon editions.

The C.I.O. sent Powers Hapgood, miners' leader, John Owens, president of the Ohio district mineworkers, and Miss Rose Pesota, of the International Ladies' Garment Workers, into Akron to supplement the C.I.O. staff already in the field.

Strikers at an evening meeting booed a tentative attempt to ballot on McGrady's back-to-work-while-negotiating plan.

337

Union leadership, said in the newspapers to favor acceptance of the McGrady proposals, hastily backed down when faced with angry strikers.

C.I.O. officials were amazed by strikers' familiarity with the Government conciliator's scheme. Rubberworkers crowded into the union hall, burst into boos at the first mention of McGrady's proposals. Impromptu speeches from the floor indicated that the rank-and-file knew even details of McGrady's strike record.

"How about the Industrial Rayon strike in Cleveland?" tire-builders yelled.

"We-want-a-signed-agreement!" parts of the crowd chanted. Other bands of pickets chorused, "We'll-hold-out-for-the-six-hour-day!"

While John House sat quietly on the platform, paler than usual, the pickets sang, "Let's hang Ed McGrady to a sour-apple tree-e-ee."

Ushers made no attempt to pass out the hurriedly printed ballots on which strikers were to have indicated a yes or no vote on the McGrady plan.

After a wild fifteen minutes, the meeting was turned into a strike pep-rally, with songs, speeches, and cheers.

The Twelfth Day   *February 29, 1936*

The biggest armory meeting in Akron history, with hundreds standing in the aisles and thousands milling outside the doors, heard Sherman Dalrymple, president of the United Rubber Workers of America, declare, "The Goodyear strike is making labor history!"

Wilmer Tate, John Owens, Rose Pesota, and Powers Hapgood made speeches to a wildly enthusiastic crowd.

In the evening Frank Grillo, secretary-treasurer of the union, went on the air to charge, "We have been reliably informed that underworld characters are operating in our community just as they did last year during the strike scare, and they are lending aid and encouragement to the group that calls itself the 'loyal employees' of The Goodyear Tire and Rubber Company."

This was the fourth successive night the union used the radio to carry its side of the controversy to the public.

The Thirteenth Day   *March 1, 1936*

The section organizers of the Communist Party in northern Ohio settled down in a District Committee meeting to hear Jim Keller report on the rubber strike.

Men squirmed on hard folding chairs while Keller stood behind a plain wooden table, his faint cough betraying a slight nervousness. His audience, comrades from Youngstown, in steel; from Canton, in steel; from the Cleveland flats, in steel; from East Cleveland, in auto; from Bedford, in auto; from the lakeports, in marine; and from downtown Cleveland, in light industry; stared at the pictures of Browder and James Ford on the wall while Keller shuffled his notes.

"Comrades," he began, "a struggle of major dimensions, a conflict involving vital issues for American labor, is now taking place in Akron. If successful, this strike will result in the organization of an important mass industry."

"Comrades," Keller repeated, his voice very low, "the organization of the rubberworkers into a powerful industrial union is bound to have a far-reaching effect upon other still unorganized industries."

His voice sharpened. "Particularly in steel and auto."

"The Goodyear strike is of vital concern to all labor, and the importance of the struggle is also fully recognized by Goodyear, other rubber companies, and big industry in general. They also are girding for a showdown. They know if the present strike can be defeated, it would mean a telling blow against the influence of the union and its further growth in the rubber industry. They know it would mean the effective retarding of union organization in steel and auto. . . .

"The Goodyear strike did not come as a surprise." Keller's

339

voice dropped again. "You will recall the sitdown in the Firestone plant. . . ."

He recited the events leading up to the Goodyear strike. The comrades in steel and auto bent over notebooks as he talked.

"The sitdown is an extremely effective organizational weapon. But credit must go to Comrade Williamson for warning us against the danger of these surprise actions. The sitdowns came because the companies refused to bargain collectively with the union. Now we must work for regular relations between the union and the employers—and strict observance of union procedure on the part of the workers."

The comrades in auto scribbled rapidly.

He paused for a gulp of water. The audience stirred, glancing around the bare room.

Keller outlined the rubberworkers' grievances, the beginning of the strike, the defeat of the injunction, the U.R.W.A. moves to legalize the walkout. "One thing is very clear—because of the magnitude of the issues involved, the rubber companies will mobilize their maximum strength to defeat the strike. For this reason, in order to win the strike, two conditions are essential—first: maximum mobilization of the picket line and rallying of the broadest support for the strike both locally and nationally; second: a firm stand by the leadership of the U.R.W.A. and of the Goodyear local."

Keller reached for the glass of water. Johnny Williamson, the District Organizer, glanced at the comrades. "I suggest a two-minute rest to stretch legs. These chairs are plenty hard."

The thirty-odd men yawned, looked out the window into the Cleveland streets, checked over notes they had written.

"Comrades," Keller started again, promptly on the two-minute mark. The murmurs died away. "Up until the coming of McGrady the leadership of the U.R.W.A. on the whole had been splendid. They corrected their tardiness in coming to the support of the strike; they took steps to rally maximum forces behind the strike; they took measures to counteract the poisonous publicity of the Company.

"But McGrady succeeded in dealing a heavy blow to the second condition necessary for winning the strike—the firm stand of the leadership. It is easy to see why the union leaders accepted McGrady's proposals. They wanted to put Litchfield into an unfavorable position by having the union accept McGrady's 'peace' plan—and then if Litchfield refused to do the same—they put him in bad before the public.

"But whether Litchfield accepts or rejects McGrady's proposals, the position taken by the strike leadership considerably weakened the strike. They forget that the thing Litchfield wants above anything else is to have the picket lines called off and to get the strikers back to work without any definite guarantees. They forget that while Litchfield still feels high and mighty and can only be shaken through the mass strength of the strike—how really high and mighty he will become if the workers go back inside the plant without an agreement."

He paused for a moment, looking at his audience. "It is a high tribute, comrades, to the strikers that they booed and rejected the plans to vote on McGrady's proposals and thereby defeated the move to entice them back into the plant."

The men from auto and steel wrote fast in their notebooks. "The stand of the Party is that no return to work take place until a satisfactory agreement is reached.

"We shall spread support for the strike and strengthen its picket lines until a minimum agreement is reached.

"We shall do everything in the power of the Party to connect the movement for support of the Goodyear strike with the grievances of the workers in other rubber plants and to use this excellent opportunity for the union organization of the rubber industry.

"In the immediate situation, our line is to demand a meeting of the union for discussion of minimum demands, and of the McGrady proposals.

"We feel certain that the Progressive forces in the Goodyear local will fight the fatal McGrady plan to the last ditch, but the strike leadership doesn't seem to be fully aware of its dangers. Every effort must be made to forewarn the union officers as well as the strikers.

"The eyes of all rubberworkers as well as the workers in the

341

auto, steel, and other industries are now focused on the Goodyear strike. With proper mobilization of labor's State and National forces the union leadership will be able to turn the present setback in the strike into a smashing counter-offensive. Let us hear the loud voice of the trade unions in Cleveland, Youngstown, Canton."

"Comrades," Johnny Williamson said, "we all agree Comrade Keller has made a brilliant report. I want to hear proposals on mobilizing support for the strike. . . ."

Goodyear's first nibble at negotiations collapsed after conferences held all day in the luxuriously furnished private dining rooms in the Mayflower Hotel.

L. E. Judd, public relations director, explained the fiasco to the public in a radio address. "Mr. Litchfield did not enter into these negotiations because of any change in his conviction that an approach on his part to the leadership of the law-defying movement which has completely paralyzed the orderly processes of government does not square with the highest duty of an American citizen," Mr. Judd stated, thus scotching rumors that The Goodyear Tire and Rubber Company, unable to break picket lines by force, was at last ready to try to grab off a victory around the negotiation table.

Mr. Litchfield consented to talk to union leaders, Mr. Judd declared, because a committee from the Goodyear Industrial Assembly begged him to do so.

The Goodyear Tire and Rubber Company then offered the forces of lawlessness and disorder at their gates a truce, as follows:

All freight to go in and out of the factory; production to be stopped by the company; two pickets at each entrance; all office workers allowed in the plant; all maintenance men to go past the pickets.

During the truce the company agreed to negotiate on wages, hours, and seniority with a committee of members representing the Industrial Assembly; the union; and Goodyear.

Mr. Judd reported in hurt tones that the union refused to accept the company's terms for the truce. It appeared that the union wanted no freight to pass; the injunction to be vacated; five

342

pickets at each gate; and finally that the negotiations include working conditions and be conducted between the union and the management, with the concession that the company could select two Industrial Assembly delegates to sit on its side of the table if it chose.

"This attitude on the part of the union," Mr. Judd declared, "meant only one thing—an immediate termination of the efforts in this direction. It is the feeling of the management that we have fully discharged our obligations [on the matter of negotiating with the union]."

A joint committee of the Central Labor Union and the United Rubber Workers of America called upon Mayor Schroy today to inform him that in the event of a violent attack on the Goodyear picket line 35,000 members of 105 Akron unions were prepared to walk out in a general strike.

The Mayor, flanked by the chief-of-police and other city officials, listened to Wilmer Tate explain that a C.L.U. vote taken Saturday had already been ratified by scores of locals. More planned to vote Monday.

"The locals are voting unanimously for a general strike," Tate said. "The C.L.U. vote was unanimous. Plans have been completed for clearing and shutting down the Firestone, Goodrich, and other rubber plants in town within an hour's notice.

"Akron will be shut up tight as a drum the minute police, deputy sheriffs, National Guardsmen or paid company hoodlums attack the picket line."

Mayor Schroy thanked Mr. Tate and his committee for their formal call.

That was the thirteenth day.

The Fourteenth Day   *March 2, 1936*

"The Goodyear Tire and Rubber Company will not sign an agreement with the United Rubber Workers of America under any circumstances."—President Paul Litchfield as he emerged from his two-week self-imposed exile in the Goodyear main plant.

343

Mr. L. M. Buckingham, lawyer for Goodyear, wrote the following personal letter:

"DEAR MR. SHERIFF:

"This is the third week of the Goodyear strike. East Market Street is still obstructed with picket shanties. There is still open and defiant violation of the law.

"It was suggested that Goodyear get an injunction. That was done. It was suggested that Goodyear indicate a willingness to negotiate. That was done, and on a basis obviously fair.

"Everything has been in vain. In the opinion of the company and of a very large part of the community, this situation has arisen because of the lack of positive action upon those charged with the enforcement of the law.

"Goodyear wants you to name the date upon which it may open its plant for production so that these employees now forcibly kept therefrom may return to work.

"Signed."

Sheriff Flower received this letter with public groans to the press. "I'm cussed if I do," he complained, "and I'm cussed if I don't."

The plaintive sheriff added that he had been forced to revoke Colonel Joe Johnston's commission as a special deputy.

"It was the only way to squelch a lot of absolutely untrue rumors about Joe going around enlisting a head-cracking crew to break the strike. I only used Joe one day in my office during this strike, but that only shows you how unfair people are."

Reporters clucked sympathetically. "People call me up day and night," Sheriff Flower continued sadly, "and the union fellows tell me I'd better not try anything, and the Goodyear guys tell me I'd better hurry up and break the picket line, or else."

"It's a tough life, sheriff," a reporter said.

Sheriff Flower sighed deeply.

Edward F. McGrady, United States Government conciliator, returned to Akron stating that he planned to "start all over" in his attempt to settle the Goodyear strike.

344

He began by going into a prolonged and secret conference with union officials.

James Keller, secretary of the Akron Communist Party, broadcast a scathing attack on Edward F. McGrady, Government conciliator, over WJW, local station, this evening.

Mr. Keller read letters written to McGrady by the wives of union men who had lost their jobs after a McGrady strike settlement in Cleveland.

Keller quoted McGrady's replies to the desperate women: " 'I have no further part in the controversy because I rendered a decision and have no power to compel anyone to accept it.' "

Keller concluded, "We feel it our duty to point out that any break in the picket lines or a return to work before a settlement is made and definite guarantees are secured—will mean defeat for the strike."

The Fifteenth Day   *March 3, 1936*

Edward F. McGrady, Government conciliator, left Akron after a second fruitless attempt to settle the Goodyear strike. Union officials made no comment.

Attorney Charles E. Smoyer, candidate for the Republican congressional nomination, said in a speech to the Veterans of Foreign Wars, "The time is near at hand when veterans' organizations and other public-spirited citizens should demand, forcibly if necessary, that these men and women who have come here for the purpose of fomenting strife and agitating trouble be invited to get out of town."

Mr. Smoyer referred, he said, to "Communistic" C.I.O. officials.

The union and the company waged a bitter word-duel over local radio stations. Industrial Assembly representatives spoke for the company.

345

"It is the duty of the mayor so to administer the affairs of this city that not only the interests of the strikers, the non-strikers, and the Goodyear management are protected, but that the interests of all citizens and businesses are not jeopardized by some act of the administration which would bring about violence and a general strike."—Mayor Schroy.

The Goodyear management made a major concession to strikers. The Flying Squadron, long a sore point in the factory operations, was stripped of its extra-seniority privileges. The college boys being trained for foremen's positions would no longer stay on the job when employees with longer service records were laid off during seasonal drops in production.

The union, which considered the Flying Squadron a strike-breaking force of company spies, had demanded its complete abolition.

Announcement of the concession was made over the radio by an Industrial Assembly delegate.

"Granting such a concession to the Assembly, which never even raised the issue," Thomas Burns, vice-president of the U.R.W.A., declared, "is just one more evidence that Mr. Litchfield is using the Assembly as a servile and docile tool."

"The Governor wants blood on the streets before he sends troops in," Sheriff Flower reported after a conference in Columbus.

"He said I would have to start something and if the situation got out of hand, he would send in troops.

"The National Guard leaders are sorry they ever went to Toledo. They are facing a couple of suits from the tear gas they used. They want the liability to be placed on the sheriff instead of the State."

The union scheduled meetings open to the public as well as strikers three times a day in a theatre near by the picket lines.

Speeches, songs, skits, appeals to still unorganized workers to sign union cards featured the three-a-day meetings.

"The steel trust and the auto magnates are bringing pressure to bear on President Litchfield to break the union," Adoph Germer, C.I.O. leader, declared at the opening union rally.

"Wall Street realizes that the success of the Goodyear strike will be a tremendous impetus to the labor movement elsewhere. The settlement of the strike depends very much on who has the most pressure—Wall Street or local people."

Wilmer Tate, head of the C.L.U., announced to the big audience that the general strike vote taken among Akron locals was nearly complete. No negative votes had been recorded. Akron labor would quit work if a violent attack of any kind were made on the Goodyear picket line.

To the tune of "Old McDonald Had a Farm," strikers wound up the meeting shouting out a new strike song:

"Old Man Litchfield had a shop—
    E-i, E-i, O!
And in this shop he had some scabs—
    E-i, E-i, O!
With a rat, rat here, a rat, rat there,
Here a rat, and there a rat, and everywhere a rat, rat,
Old Man Litchfield had a shop—
    E-i, E-i, O!"

The Seventeenth Day   *March 5, 1936*

The Goodyear Tire and Rubber Company delivered copies of the *Wingfoot Clan*, its house organ, to every front door in Akron.

The radio war, with the two local stations carrying hours of programs from both sides, continued.

The *Times-Press* carried a long dull editorial which carefully said nothing. Strikers noted that the Scripps-Howard paper no longer felt their cause hopeless. The editor had retreated from his last week's plea to President Litchfield to have mercy on the strikers, but this time he felt a general strike, or even the threat of a general strike, would wreck the Akron labor movement.

The Eighteenth Day *March 6, 1936*

Pickets lolled in the balmy weather beside their comfortable shanties waiting for the coffee crew to bring sandwiches and idly discussing the strike situation.

Union officials, touring the picket lines, reported increased determination to hold out for a signed agreement.

Relief authorities stated that the charity load in the city had tripled since the Goodyear strike.

The Nineteenth Day *March 7, 1936*

The day-picket shift came on duty just before seven o'clock. Sleepy strikers who had watched the great Goodyear gates through the chill night shook hands with the new crew, yawned, went into union hall for breakfast, and started home.

The streets near the Goodyear plant glistened under a bright spring sun. The picket shanties near the gates were almost deserted. The new shift was still at union hall, checking in, drinking coffee, passing the time of day before they went out to the company gates.

The union picket lines were at the daily low ebb. Strike strategists expected no trouble at this hour when the whole town was turning off alarm clocks or eating ham and eggs.

A rumble of heavy trucks in the distance made the few pickets sweeping out their shanties and tidying up their "front lawns" prick up their ears. The strikers in union hall rushed out just in time to see a force of fifty city street cleaners, guarded by thirty cops, rattle up to picket lines in garbage trucks.

"We're clearin' off these shanties, boys!" a police lieutenant shouted.

348

"Hal-looo!" the pickets screamed, by way of reply. "Help! Hey! All out!"

Inside the union hall an excited striker grabbed the phone. A moment later the truck-tire department at General, a mile out on East Market Street, was down, the conveyor belt shut off, the tirebuilders running for the door.

The first hasty battle-line fought it out in a series of wrestling bouts with the police. The street cleaners stood stolidly. Thirty of their number had been fired an hour earlier for refusing to do "scab work."

The cops managed to beat the strikers back past the first picket shanty. The street cleaners demolished it. Fighting hard, the pickets fell back beyond the second picket shanty. A policeman raised his club to sock a striker—his superior officer caught it as it descended.

The word spread. The auto tire department at General was deserted. Company foremen threw up their hands as their workers rushed the doors.

Goodrich men shut the power off their machines. "We're standing by," union delegates snapped, "for further orders. They may need us."

"Oh," the company foremen gulped.

The streets leading to the Goodyear main plant clogged up with old cars. Fourteen men jammed into a single 1926 Chevy. Wind whipped the coat jackets of rubberworkers riding precariously on running boards, hanging on to a windshield with one hand, grabbing a club with the other.

The tide turned as the pickets retreated to the third picket shanty. The reinforcements took up their stand behind the Goodyear strikers. Swinging their clubs, the pickets went into action. The policemen retreated, first slowly, and then in full flight. A police lieutenant rode a garbage truck into the third picket shanty, and found himself in enemy territory. He hastily retreated in his lumbering vehicle.

At eight o'clock the Goodrich tirebuilders resumed work. "Everything's O.K. at the picket line now," the union delegates snapped.

"Oh," said the foremen.

349

The Twentieth Day   *March 8, 1936*

The Goodyear Tire and Rubber Company and the United Rubber Workers of America met in a secret conference.

The Twenty-first Day   *March 9, 1936*

President Paul Litchfield infuriated union leaders with whom he had been negotiating by broadcasting, over both Akron radio stations, terms of a proposed secret peace settlement.

The Twenty-second Day   *March 10, 1936*

John House, Goodyear local president, replied to Mr. Litchfield's general peace proposals with a radio statement of union aims. His counterproposal included straight six-hour day for all departments; straight seniority; notice of wage cuts to union committees; recognition of union shop committees; and termination of financial support for the Industrial Assembly.

The Twenty-third Day   *March 11, 1936*

The Goodyear Tire and Rubber Company made public the amended peace proposals it offered the United Rubber Workers of America.

"To all employees of The Goodyear Tire and Rubber Company," the memorandum began.

"I. All employees of The Goodyear Tire and Rubber Company as of February 12, 1936, shall return to work without discrimination or interruption of service record.

"II. Management of the company will meet with any and all employees individually or through their chosen representatives.

"III. Notice will be given to representatives of the employees affected of changes in wage rates before they are posted.

"IV. In the tire division, the company has adopted the thirty-six-hour week, six-hour shifts. Any change in these hours per week or per day below thirty hours or above thirty-six hours a week will be by arrangement with the employees in the departments or divisions affected.

"V. Lists of contemplated layoffs will be made in duplicate by the department foreman—one copy will be retained by the foreman and the other copy will be kept in the office of the labor department; both lists will be available for inspection."

The Twenty-fourth Day *March 12, 1936*

The United Rubber Workers of America announced a union meeting to be held Saturday, March 14, in the armory, to ballot on the peace proposals made by The Goodyear Tire and Rubber Company.

The Akron *Times-Press* carried a long editorial entitled, "Time to Go to Work."

"Mr. Litchfield," the editorial said, "is a sincere, wise, and generous man. The proposal dealing with representation of the workers to the management covers everything. It should satisfy any reasonable person or group. . . . The public is sick of the strike . . . the proposals should be accepted. Everything that can be settled on a restricted front has been settled, and there remains nothing to do but accept the proposals and restore the income of thousands of workers who have been off their jobs for a month.

"It is time to go to work."

The Akron *Beacon Journal* headlined a front-page editorial, "We've Had a Belly Full." The article began, "Akron has its belly full of the Goodyear strike." The *Beacon Journal*, more subtle than the *Times-Press*, did not argue directly for acceptance of the management proposals. Instead, the editorial suggested that Goodyear might move its business out of town if the strike were not settled soon, and urged "both sides" speedily to end the industrial conflict.

351

The Twenty-fifth Day   *March 13, 1936*

Relief authorities announced that 1,683 families averaging 4.6 persons each have been placed on relief rolls as the result of the Goodyear strike.

The Akron section committee of the Communist Party came somewhat haltingly to order. Bill sat in the Kellers' neat, bare little kitchen gulping coffee and chewing furiously on a thick sandwich. He still wore his heavy lumberjacket, although the night was mild, and his frayed cap stuck out of his pocket.

Mrs. Keller stood in the bedroom talking to Mrs. Holland about her little boy Stevie. "He won a prize for being the best in history," Mrs. Holland said and came to the doorway, her broad face beaming, to repeat, "Hey, Bill, did you hear that? My Stevie won a school prize. Pretty good, huh?"

Bill grunted. He didn't look up from a battered, coffee-stained sheet of typescript he had propped up on the sugar bowl before him. "Let me make you something else to eat, Bill," Mrs. Keller said.

Bill waved a vague arm. "No, no, this is plenty. Many thanks." He pushed back the chair impatiently and took two long steps into the little parlor. "O.K., Jim, let's get going."

The bustle in the crowded room died away. Mrs. Holland hurried in from the bedroom and settled down in a straight, stiff oak chair. The men wedged into the long, frayed horsehair davenport got out pencils and scraps of paper. Bill fidgeted, cross-legged on the floor. Keller walked over to the big oak table by the window, and glancing at the eleven solemn members of the section committee, began quietly, "Comrades, this is about the most important meeting of this section committee in its history, I think. Will somebody move to dispense with the minutes and all other business so we can get down to discussing the Saturday meeting at the armory right away."

"Ah so moo-ve." Jack Peterson's voice was nervous. Mrs. Holland wet her lips. Bill unwound his long legs and crossed them again.

"The Goodyear strike has reached its most critical point,"

352

Keller said. "The armory meeting will decide whether the first great effort of the rubberworkers to make their lives and working conditions bearable is to end in failure or go on to success."

"They'll vote the company proposals down—to a man!" Peterson's excited West Virginia drawl made Mrs. Holland stiffen on her chair. "I know. I've been talking to the boys on the picket lines. They ain't goin' to take those lousy five points of Litchfield's. They're goin' to win this here strike."

"Talk like that's what we're afraid of, dope!" Bill scrambled to his feet. "Jesus, if we just vote down the Goodyear offer we'll be in hot water. The whole town will say the union is pig-headed, and jist tryin' to prolong the strike, and . . ."

"Comrades!" Keller's voice was sharp. "You'll have a chance to talk. Let's have some order here."

"Yeah, but he can't tell us to vote yes on them proposals, why, the guys would just laugh at us, and us supposed to be Communists, and besides . . ."

"Comrade Peterson, you'll have a chance to express your opinions later on."

Peterson subsided, muttering. Bill leaned against the faded wall-paper. Under the glaring over-head light, the faces of the members of the section committee looked white and tired. Keller picked up a note-book. "I'm going to just go over the situation, comrades," he said evenly, "and after that, Bill's going to read a proposal and then the floor will be open for discussion. That means you, Comrade Peterson." Peterson grinned sheepishly.

"The present situation," Keller began, "is messed up because while the union was so damn anxious and pious to observe secrecy about the negotiations, Litchfield took the bull by the horns and announced the company's five points over the radio, putting the union entirely on the defensive."

Keller leaned over to sort his scrambled notes. "With regard to the proposals themselves. Of course they're very bad. It stands out that the company carefully omits mention of the union and will refuse to commit itself to anything that would mean open recognition of the union. It's my opinion that this point should be conceded, as this is not the time to press the fight to the point of recognition. That comes later.

353

"However, the union has a memorandum signed by the company attorney and two of the management which recognizes the right of the union committees to negotiate on the questions of hours and wages, this right being extended to the union president although he is not an employee."

Bill slid down the wall to the floor and wrapped his legs into another knot. Mrs. Holland took notes on the back of a grocery handbill. "Outside of this memo, the company proposals represent no actual concession from the position of the company when the strike broke out."

Keller's listeners sighed. "Comrades!" Keller's voice was loud. "The position of the union is very strong. The plant is closed. So long as public opinion stays behind the strikers, the company can't use armed force to break the picket lines. The spirit of the men is very high. The union can win this strike—the union must reject these proposals."

Peterson clapped, the sound heavy and explosive in the crowded, small room. Keller held up his hand. "But there is something else we must consider. There are sinister things happening in this town. Hysteria is being whipped up—look at the editorials in the papers yesterday. Our comrades have reported well-known industrial thugs seen on the street. We have information on guns being shipped in here. The union must step very carefully, or public opinion will turn against it. And then anything can happen. The union simply *must not* be put in the position of flatly rejecting these proposals." Keller paused and then repeated, "Comrades, I can't put this too strongly. The union must not be made to look bull-necked and unreasonable to the city of Akron."

Keller nodded to Bill, who struggled up from the floor, peeled over his lumberjacket. "I guess I should say right away," he began, "that the picket-captains, of which I'm one, are in favor of this proposal. The idea of it is simple. Instead of just votin' no on Litchfield's offer, why, we accept some of the points, the harmless ones, and the others we reject. Then we adopt a resolution saying that the committee should go back to the Goodyear guys and talk it over some more. That way the newspapers will say in their headlines, 'Union Wants More Parleys,' or somethin' like that. Akron will think that sounds sensible, see, and the union

354

won't be blamed for prolongin' the strike after the company, according to the *Times-Press*, was so nice and reasonable."

The men and the two women in the room stirred, nodded. Bill went on, "I'll just give you the gist of the actual resolution. The union agrees to the company Point I about taking men back to work, except that a clause be added that the men return to work within seven days.

"The union agrees to Point II and Point III as written. Those are the ones about the management meeting with representatives of workers; and about the notice being given of change in wage rates. On the company's offer of a six-hour day in the tire divisions, the union asks a straight six-hour day in all divisions. On the company's offer to make layoff lists in duplicate, the union asks the lists to be triplicate, one copy to the union.

"Plus these replies to the company offers, the union instructs its negotiating committee to go back to Goodyear and demand that the financing of the Goodyear Industrial Assembly be ended; and that a straight seniority policy be instituted throughout the plant."

Bill stuffed the copy of the resolution back in his shirt-pocket. "That's all, comrades. Only I want to sort of emphasize what Comrade Keller said. This is a tough spot for our union to be in. We know the company is cookin' up some vigilante business in town. They're just waitin' for the union to pull a false move and vote down the proposals and then they'll be out in full force. Well, if we can let the common, ordinary man in town know that we're reasonable and only askin' for our due, Goodyear will never be able to bust our picket lines—this town won't let 'em. But if we can't sell the public on that—well, it'll be tough."

Keller said, "All right, Comrade Peterson, it's your turn now."

Peterson got up slowly. "Well, I see it sort of different now. I hadn't exactly thought about what the people would say if the union guys just went ahead and voted no. All I can say now is, God help us if we can't convince the men at the meeting Saturday and put this across. It ain't going to be easy, because the guys is all in favor of just slamming this thing back in Goodyear's face."

He started to sit down and then hesitated, straightened up, and said in a loud voice, "This strike means everything to me and to every rubberworker. We just got to lick Goodyear. Otherwise the union will be busted and it'll be a hell of a long time before there'll be another. We waited for this strike so long, and things have been so tough at home, you know how it is. We just gotta win." He sat down abruptly.

Mrs. Holland fell into step with Comrade Peterson on the way home from the meeting. "It'll come out O.K.," she said gently, "I'm sure of it."

"It's just got to," Peterson replied somberly.

The Twenty-sixth Day   *March 14, 1936*

"Mine eyes have seen the glory of the coming of the Lord!"

Four thousand Goodyear workers, jammed inside the bleak armory hall, lifted up their heads and sang. Hundreds more standing patiently in the drizzling rain outside heard the solemn chant and picked up the melody.

"He is trampling out the vintage where the grapes of wrath are stored—"

The man at the piano on the big armory stage sounded a deep chord. The huge audience rustled to its feet.

"My coun-try, 'tis of thee-ee!" the rubberworkers sang in a deep bass, "sweet land of liberty, of thee we sing!"

The strikers outside followed the melody. "Land where our fath-ers died, land of the pilgrim's pride."

Men wiped tears from their eyes as the strikers thundered, "From eve-ry rock and rill, LET FREEDOM RING!"

"O.K.," John House said into the microphone, "while we're waiting, let's sing something funny."

He hesitated. "No, No, a Thousand Times No!" came from the audience, and the crowd took it up. House looked surprised. Over and over, the crowd bawled its version of the old ballad. "I'd rath-er DIE than say yes!"

"All right," House said finally. "The meeting is called to order. Now on the strike settlement . . ."

"No, no, a thous-and times NO!" the crowd chanted.

House waited for silence. His speech was noncommittal. He

356

introduced the secretary of the negotiating committee, George Hull, who reported that the company was hard to deal with. The proposals under consideration, Goodyear said, were final.

Hull sat down amid heavy silence. House cleared his throat nervously. Then he recognized Bill Ricketts, picket-captain. Bill got a big hand. The strikers liked Bill.

"I want to make a resolution on the company's proposals," Ricketts began. "I move we accept Point II and Point III, that we amend . . ."

The meeting was short. The *Times-Press* caught its last base-ball extra with the streamer headline:

"TWO POINTS OF PEACE PLAN ARE ACCEPTED BY STRIKERS."

The subhead read:

"COMPANY'S TERMS ARE PARTIALLY MET AT ARMORY MEET."

"Goodyear strikers," the bulletin began, "sent their negotiating committee back to the management."

"Of course, the company will try to say the union just turned down the offer." Keller's voice was quiet.

"Yuh old crepe-hanger!" A striker thumped him on the back. "Waiter, another cup of coffee. Boys, I'm feelin' good. Everything went off like clockwork. Ricketts made a swell speech. We're sittin' on top of the world."

Laughing, the men crowded closer around a greasy wooden table in the dark little hamburg joint on South Main Street.

Keller grinned. "When you guys get over congratulatin' yourselves we might talk about what comes next."

Bill said, "Aw, lay off, Jim. Things are lookin' good. The company's goin' to have to negotiate on our resolution and we'll win the strike by Wednesday."

"You said it!" The strikers waved exultant forks.

Keller's voice cut through the celebration. "What makes you guys think the company has to negotiate now? They still got tricks up their sleeves. All right, the meeting went off fine, but you got other things to do than clap hands for yourselves. If you think Litchfield's goin' to take this lying down—"

The strikers sighed. "Well, what next, Jim?" Bill asked.

"First," Keller said, "you got to get our point over to this town, that you didn't break off negotiations."

Bill got out his notebook. "Yeah, go ahead."

Paul Litchfield, President of The Goodyear Tire and Rubber Company, met late this evening with James Tew, President of The B. F. Goodrich Company, and John Thomas, President of The Firestone Tire and Rubber Company, to discuss the formation of an organization entitled "The Akron Law and Order League."

The Twenty-seventh Day   *March 15, 1936*

Headline from the Sunday *Times-Press:*

"COMPANY CHARGES
STRIKERS' ACTION
IS FULL REJECTION"

"Immediate plans," the *Times-Press* front-page story said, "for reopening the strike-blockaded Goodyear plants were laid by the company last night after the strikers refused to accept the whole of the company's 'final' peace proposal. . . . The management announced that it considered its final proposal rejected and withdrew its offer to take all employees back without discrimination or loss of their service records."

The Central Labor Union made public final tabulation of votes for a city-wide general strike in case of a violent attack upon the Goodyear picket line. The general strike vote was virtually unanimous, the statement declared.

Ex-Mayor C. Nelson Sparks announced the formation of the Akron Law and Order League. He said he personally founded the organization when a group of Goodyear non-strikers asked him to lead the aroused Akron citizenry in a movement to restore law and order in the Goodyear strike.

"As a citizen and a firm believer in American ideals, I consider the request the Goodyear non-strikers made of me the finest tribute I have ever had.

"I am entirely in sympathy with their perturbed state of mind, and I believe every true lover of the principles of liberty, justice, and majority rule upon which our Republic is founded, understands, as I do.

"It is deplorable, no, it is absolutely unbelievable, that any group of men, large or small, can, through threats and violence, place themselves above the constituted and legal processes of law and order in an American community such as ours.

". . . I believe it is my duty and the duty of every law-abiding citizen of this community to gang up upon the out-of-town radicals and Communist leaders who have brought to our city the threat of a reign of terror.

"The Law and Order League will co-ordinate public opinion. We want to back up the 13,000 men who are going back to work at Goodyear."

Ex-Mayor Sparks carried his message of law and order to the people of Akron in two radio broadcasts Sunday.

"There isn't any case here involving the rights and privileges of a decent union organization or decent union leaders," Mr. Sparks remarked in his evening radio speech.

"It is this handful of miserable chiseling leeches, labor agitators, radicals, Communists, Red orators, flocking in here from all over the country, like jackals around a carcass, that deserve repudiation. They can't be called citizens, and it is stretching a point to call them Americans.

"While these men were trying to enlist your sympathy with soft words over the radio, their henchmen, these outside agitators, were busy arming pickets with revolvers.

"The outside agitators came into Akron determined to make the rubber city a hundred per cent union or wreck the industry."

Mr. Sparks also declared that he would tell the "plain unvarnished truth about the union." He thundered, "At this moment the union is bringing in gas and firearms to create a reign of terror.

"Samuel Gompers never built the A. F. of L. through such frightfulness."

The Ex-Mayor ended his speech with an appeal for members in the Law and Order League. "Help us to gang up for constituted law and order in this wonderful city through this Law and Order League. Let us say to those thousands of men and women who want to go back to work, 'The City of Akron is back of you and the Law and Order League is back of you and those who dare to stop you will have to take the consequences.'

"Help us to make this Law and Order League so representative of public opinion that we can say to these out-of-town radical leaders who have lighted the fires of disorder, violence and discontent in this city to get the hell out of here and we are not too much interested in the dignity of their going. Good night, all."

The $15,000 donation that The Goodyear Tire and Rubber Company generously—and secretly—gave to the Law and Order League paid for Mr. Sparks's radio time, among other items.

Wilmer Tate, president of the Akron C.L.U., followed Mr. Sparks's last broadcast.

"The Akron labor movement deplores the efforts of Akron's former chief executive to bring about strife and bloodshed," cried the red-headed labor chief. "If anything happens it will be upon the conscience of this man who professes to be a friend of the workingman." Tate denied that union men were armed with tear gas, revolvers, or anything else.

Tate's speech reached a fiery climax: "In my experience in the labor movement I have sometimes heard incendiary speeches. Never have I heard a more direct incitement to lawlessness and disorder than that uttered today by Ex-Mayor Sparks. . . . There is talk of lynching parties and ganging-up buzzing around the lobby of the Mayflower Hotel. Organized labor wants to settle the Goodyear strike along peaceful and sensible lines and in an American way. There is no need for enlistment under any private flag. Akron is still the United States."

The Twenty-eighth Day   *March 16, 1936*

Sheriff Jim Flower, one of the first recruits of the Akron Law and Order League, presented Ex-Mayor C. Nelson Sparks with a commission as a special deputy sheriff in a pleasant little ceremony at the Mayflower Hotel early this morning.

The Akron *Beacon Journal* published a front-page editorial in all editions, headlined, "NO ROOM FOR VIGILANTES!"

"The most ominous note yet sounded in the prolonged Goodyear strike," the editorial began, "is the call for recruits to a 'Law and Order League.' The name is a misnomer."

"Resort to organization of a 'citizens' vigilante' to open the Goodyear company plants is an open invitation to rioting and violence. It is deliberately provocative and inflammatory. It will produce the opposite of law and order.

". . . Violence provokes violence, and this community wants none of it. It will not tolerate ruthless guerrilla warfare. And that is what plans of the vigilante will mean.

". . . The speeches of former Mayor C. Nelson Sparks over the radio Sunday were unfortunate and ill-advised. He talked loosely of driving leaders of the strike out of town, implying that typical vigilante mob methods might be involved.

"He is calling for the services of trained soldiers. That means he wants men accustomed to the handling of arms. No interpretation is left other than that he is looking toward a time when the use of arms will be ordered.

"The Sparks move, clearly endorsed by the Goodyear company, has evoked a warning from the strikers that violence would be met with violence. . . . Any man who stopped to weigh the present tense situation would have known that the counter-threat was inevitable.

"Many strange things have happened during the long strike period, but the strangest of all was the statement of Mr. Sparks that Sheriff Jim Flower was among the first to enlist in his projected vigilante group.

"There could be no greater mockery of the processes of law and order than this, a sheriff abdicating his office and lending support to an abortive, unauthorized and illegal group employing force.

"If the Law and Order League does not at once abandon its stupid and dangerous program, then Akron can prepare itself for a bath of blood. . . .

"We cannot believe that it is too late to appeal to the law-abiding citizenry of Akron to discourage this unwise movement. . . . Appeals for membership in the league should be met with blunt refusals. . . .

"In the face of all this talk of violence, we renew our appeal for sanity and right thinking. We are thinking in terms of human lives. The idea that any group of citizens can take the law into their own hands cannot be tolerated for a single minute."

Sheriff Jim Flower suggested that city law enforcement officers and a committee from the Law and Order League join him in an appeal to Governor Davey to send the National Guard into Akron "to maintain peace and see that the court's order is carried out."

Thirty telephone operators stationed in an office at the Mayflower Hotel spent the day recruiting members for the Law and Order League over three trunk lines hastily installed for their exclusive use.

"Fifty-two hundred organized vigilantes under command of one hundred and sixty-eight captains stand ready to serve where needed," Mr. Sparks announced. "Every civic body and luncheon club in the city has pledged its aid to the movement."

Officers of several of the luncheon clubs immediately denied that their organizations were enrolled in the Law and Order League, but Mr. Sparks was not dashed. Shortly after four o'clock, he announced that membership in the Law and Order League had grown to twenty-five thousand, a figure which, he said, did not include the fifty-two hundred "vigilantes" and their hundred and sixty-eight captains.

Both newspapers in the city mentioned, without confirming, the spreading rumor that Goodyear planned to open its gates and break the picket line Tuesday, the following morning.

Union ex-service men were sent home for their old uniforms and assembled at union hall. Union leaders at the Portage Hotel were placed under heavy guard by picket-captains.

The Twenty-ninth Day   *March 17, 1936*

"Attention! All union men and women! Attention! All United Rubber Worker members! Attention!"

Frank Grillo took a deep breath, stepped closer to the radio microphone.

"Do not turn your radio off! This program, broadcast by the United Rubber Workers of America, will continue all night. We are on the air to save the union movement of Akron, to save the jobs, to preserve the well-being of the working people of Akron.

"Goodyear strike leaders have reason to believe a violent attack may be made on the picket line sometime this morning. The company has refused to continue negotiations. The company has declared it will open its plant by force. The Law and Order League hoodlums are said to be planning an attack on the Goodyear strikers this morning.

"We call upon every listener to stand by us. We have a telephone line open to the Goodyear picket line. At the slightest sign of trouble you will have an instant report. Do not leave your homes for the picket line now. The call will be broadcast from this station, if call there need be. Stand by! O.K., take it away."

The C.I.O. publicity expert began, "Well, I think we'll have a little music now. We're going to have a radio play in a little while, just as soon as I get through writing it. Frank here is going to play the villain. O.K., this is 'I Like Mountain Music,' an old favorite around here."

"We have a bunch of records here," he said as the music whanged to a finish. "Just call us up and say which ones you want to hear. Let us know what you're doing at your listening-in parties. Here's a message from a lady who says she has six men— two of 'em her sons, and the other four friends of theirs—sitting around her living room listening in. Good for you! Now we'll hear 'The Old Oaken Bucket.' "

"It's exactly 2:30 A.M.," Frank Grillo said presently. "Attention! All union men and women! Do not turn your radios off. If you have a group of men at your house, take turns listening in while others sleep. Keep somebody at the radio at all times. This program will go on until the threat to the picket line is over. The Goodyear picket line cannot be broken!"

"That was Frank Grillo," the union announcer said, "and he may not sound sleepy, but he looks it. But he's just had four cups of black coffee, that ought to keep him from sleeping for a week. Now at this time we will hear from Leo Krzycki, a vice-president of that great brother union of ours, the Amalgamated Clothing Workers. Mr. Krzycki will speak on 'The Right to Organize.'"

Frank Grillo's voice was hoarse as he said, "Attention! The time is now 4:45 A.M. We have a report from the Goodyear picket line. Everything is quiet. Do not turn your radios off. Be prepared for a sudden call. Attention! Union men and women! Do not turn your radios off. You may be needed."

Grillo finally took the microphone again. "The Goodyear picket line will not be attacked this morning. Everything is quiet at the Goodyear gates. It is now exactly 8 A.M. This has been the longest broadcast in the history of the city, and in the history of the union labor movement. The United Rubber Workers of America wishes to thank the many thousands who have stayed up all night listening to this program ready to answer a call for help. Your vigilance prevented a violent attack on the Goodyear picket lines by Mr. Sparks and his hoodlums. Again, we thank you with all our hearts. This is the United Rubber Workers of America signing off the air after a nine-hour continuous broadcast. Good night! and Good morning!"

The Thirtieth Day   *March 18, 1936*

The Goodyear Tire and Rubber Company resumed negotiations with the United Rubber Workers of America.

364

The Thirty-first Day   *March 19, 1936*

The Goodyear Tire and Rubber Company announced that a private poll made through the mails showed that 11,000 Goodyear employees wanted to return to work.
    Union leaders laughed.
    Negotiations continued.

The Thirty-second Day   *March 20, 1936*

The U.R.W.A. announced an armory meeting for Saturday, to consider Goodyear's latest peace proposals.

The picket-captains settled down on their familiar orange crates. Strikers filled the old storeroom. Men sprawled on a dusty counter in the back, and squatted shoulder to shoulder on the floor.
    "O.K., fellows," Bill said. "This meeting is hereby called to order." The soft burr of mountain speech died away.
    Bill hesitated. He swept a big hand across the side of his face, fingered his nose nervously.
    "Now you have voted to hear what Jim Keller, the secretary of the Akron Communist Party, has to say about this here settlement that's going to be voted on tomorrow at the armory. Some of you guys were against having Keller come here, but I know you ain't going to object after a big majority voted for him to speak to this meetin'. I know you're going to show him every politeness."
    Bill paused. "Bring him on!" a striker near the store-front window yelled.
    "O.K., fellows," Bill said loudly. "I introduce to you my good friend, and the best friend the Akron working class ever had, Jim Keller."
    Some of the strikers clapped very loudly. The other picket-captains stared silently at the dark-haired man who climbed on the orange crate that served as speaker's stand.
    "Friends," Keller began in a very low voice.
    "Louder!" strikers demanded.

"I want to congratulate you," he said, in a stronger tone. "You men have won a great victory! The settlement is a glorious step forward for the Akron working class, yes, and the working people everywhere in America. I have seen a lot of strikes, but I have never seen men who went on the picket line in the worst blizzard in the history of northern Ohio and stayed there for thirty-two days in cold and rain and against threats of violence until they won a great victory. The Communist Party congratulates you! The Communist Party is proud of you!"

The strikers were surprised. They looked at each other. A man clapped. Then wild applause swept the crowded storeroom. But out of the hilarious din a great voice thundered, "I thought you guys was against the settlement? I got a leaflet here where you Reds call this a sellout."

The applause stopped instantly. In the tense silence men leaned forward, straining to hear every word.

Keller answered quietly, "I am glad you asked that question. I was going to take it up at the end of my speech, but I'll begin with it now. I have a copy of the leaflet you are talking about. The Communist Party did not issue it. The Communist Party considers this leaflet a betrayal of the Akron workers—in the same class as the Law and Order League. This leaflet was issued by Trotskyites."

"What's the difference?" The questioner was on his feet, a big handsome tirebuilder. His voice was angry, his chin had a belligerent tilt. "Ain't you Reds all the same, except for maybe who's the Pope of your outfit?"

"Well, I'll ask you a few questions now," Keller replied pleasantly.

"Ask 'em."

"Did you ever hear of union spies?"

"Sure."

"How do they work?"

The striker paused, frowning. "Well, they usually git inside the union and pretend they're red-hot union men."

"How do you know they're spies?"

The crowd murmured, following the questions carefully.

"Well, you mean how do we spot 'em?"

Keller nodded.

The striker considered. "Well," he said slowly, "usually it's them guys that start to get real enthusiastic in sitdowns and want to tear up the machinery or beat up the foreman or somethin' like that—stuff that would look bad for the boys sittin' down."

"O.K.," Keller said. "Now suppose somebody came along and yelled, 'Listen to that guy talking about tearing up machinery. Union men are all a bunch of rats.' "

"I'd answer that the punk doing the talkin' was a lousy spy!" the striker shouted.

"Sure, and suppose the guy said, 'Aw, you union men are all alike!' "

"Listen," the striker yelled. "A spy is a guy who works for the company. The company pays him. He ain't a union man."

"And a Trotskyite," Keller said deliberately, "isn't a Communist. He works for the company."

The striker, still on his feet, nodded slowly. "Ah, I git it." Around the crowded storeroom men nodded after him.

"Them sons-of-bitches," the striker growled. He sat down on the floor, crossing his long legs. "Excuse me," he shouted, his voice friendly. "Go ahead with your speechmakin'."

"No excuse needed," Keller smiled. "It was a good question. I don't want to take up much more of your time with this thing because we got better things to talk about—a great victory and what comes afterwards. But I think I should discuss this leaflet just a little."

He pulled a mimeographed sheet of paper from his pocket. "How many of you fellows have seen it?"

Three hands waved.

"They're not very good distributors," Keller observed. "However, poison like this is dangerous. The idea of the leaflet is that the settlement you're supposed to vote on tomorrow is no good."

Keller paused. "Now everybody in this room knows that the settlement isn't perfect. The Trotskyites say we didn't get complete union recognition, a signed contract. That's true. But we say we got an agreement that allows union shop committees to discuss wage rates and speedup with the management. You fellows work in the shops. What will that mean to you?"

The answer was a triumphant shout. "Boy! When we get union committees workin' in there, we'll tell the boss either you put the rates up on this tire, or we're sittin' down."

Keller grinned. "I see I don't have to go on with answering the leaflet. We didn't get a perfect settlement. We got one that's a lot better than what they offered last week. There's such a thing as dragging out a strike too long. A strike should end with everyone on the picket line feeling full of fight and ready to carry the picket line back into the factory. In our judgment, the Goodyear strike is at its high point in morale and enthusiasm right now. Any settlement, a signed contract or not, depends on whether or not the union is strong enough to enforce it. When the Goodyear strike started, the U.R.W.A. local had a few hundred members. Now it has many thousands. Goodrich and Firestone locals have fifteen times as many members now as they did when your strike started. That's the answer to whether the settlement is a good one or not!"

"You said it!" Excitement mounted in the old storeroom. Men clambered to their feet.

"Let's see exactly what the company's peace proposal is which the union will vote on tomorrow—and accept, I know. First—" Jim held up his index finger, in the characteristic gesture of a Communist speaker. "You got no discrimination on return to work."

"Two." The fingers went up again. The men in the storeroom stared at the fingers, their lips moving after Keller. "You got the right to negotiate with the company. Third. You got a guarantee of notice before changes in wage rates. Four. You got the six-hour day in the tire department and a forty-hour week in all other departments. That's the key of the settlement, you won the six-hour day, boys."

A man clapped, the sound loud and excited. "Fifth. Lay off notices to the union. And sixth. More important than anything. Union shop committees have the right to negotiate with foremen on wages, hours, working conditions. That may not be union recognition on paper, but as I said, that's the real McCoy."

Keller paused. Then his voice flickered with emotion. "The Goodyear strike is the beginning of a new world for the rubber-

368

workers of Akron. Yes, and it is the beginning of a new world for workers all over America. They're waiting in steel, and in auto. When they hear you've won, they will be on the march!"

The audience crowded around Keller. Faces worked. Men licked their lips nervously.

"Forgive me if we Communists take a sort of fatherly pride in your victory. Many of you sitting in this room had your first taste of organizing to fight for your rights in the ranks of the Unemployed Council. The unemployed movement in Akron was the very beginning of the rubberworkers' union—a sort of prophecy of this very day.

"Goodyear will say, after the strike is over, that the union was defeated. Companies always say it. Sparks will say you were defeated. The Trotskyites will say you were defeated. But the Communist Party congratulates you on the greatest victory in modern labor history."

Keller smiled wryly. "Communists never make predictions. It isn't what we call Marxist—but just the same—I hereby predict that if—and I know you will—if you fellows take the picket line back to the tire machines and the mill room, the Goodyear strike will be America's new declaration of freedom. Your strike, which you fought so bravely, was the first page of C.I.O. history."

The strikers waited. Keller hesitated. "It will not be," he said, a little shakily, "the last. You are the new pioneers."

The Thirty-third Day   *March 21, 1936*

Job Hendrick waited on the armory lawn. He ran a finger under his collar. "I'm sweatin'," he announced. "I'm so goddamned worked up. You think they won?"

Tom Gettling said yes. "You don't hear 'em singing 'No, No, a Thousand Times No,' do you, like they did last week?"

"I don't hear anything."

Tom said, "Listen!"

"They're cheerin'!"

Job flung his arms around Tom Gettling. "They won. Listen to 'em yell. They won! My God, Tom, they won."

The armory doors opened. Strikers poured out of the meeting hall on a wave of delirious cheers.

"Get a flag," someone screamed. "We're havin' a parade."

Job darted across the street, flung open the handsome bronze doors of City Hall, snatched the beautiful flag from its fine standard in the marble foyer, shouted breathlessly to amazed attendants, "I'll bring it back," and raced to the howling strikers.

"We won! We won!" The paraders were too intoxicated at first to sing. They shouted, making vague, wild, happy sounds. Traffic stopped completely on Main Street. Motorists didn't complain. They blew the horns of their old cars. Streetcars creaked to a jolting stop. Passengers jumped off, got in line, began to yell along with the strikers, "We won! We won!"

The cops didn't try to solve the traffic jam. The police radio station broadcast, "Calling all cars! Calling all cars! The Goodyear strike is settled!"

The parade wound past the Mayflower Hotel. "Boo-o-o-o!" The sound rolled back over the thousands in the line of march.

"Come on out, Sparksie!" strikers screamed. "Yoo-hoo, Litch! Look at us! We won! We won!"

Job marched in front carrying the great flag proudly. Its folds fluttered over his squared shoulders.

As the parade passed the Goodrich plant, Job sang, "Glory, Glo-ry, HALLELUJAH!" Tom Gettling took it up, and the marchers behind him echoed the tune.

"Glory, Glo-ry, HALLELUJAH!" the rubberworkers sang. "Glory, Glo-ry, HALLELUJAH! For his soul goes marchin' ON."

AND THREE YEARS AFTER

Akron set the pattern for industrial America. The rubberworkers were the first to fight their way to freedom. A year after Job Hendrick tramped proudly down Main Street shouting the brave words of "The Battle Hymn of the Republic," the steel workers and the auto workers had joined the march.

The working class of America came of age in 1937. Seamen and subway workers, girls in textile mills and boys in the great radio factories, clerks behind busy department-store counters, garment workers, fruit pickers, electrical workers, men and women in mills and mines, factories and fields, enrolled in the organized labor movement. Akron, a brave but lonely outpost in 1936, had become by the summer of 1937 only one of many C.I.O. cities. The United Rubber Workers of America, 70,000 strong, stood side by side with the 200,000 organized auto workers, the 250,000 steel workers, the millions in newly organized unions.

The story of Akron is not exceptional; it is significant only because it proved completely typical. The auto workers of Detroit also saw their city welter in blank misery in 1932, the banks close in the winter of 1933. They too joined the A. F. of L. Federal unions after the N.R.A. was passed in the summer of President Roosevelt's first administration. William Green led the auto workers' first attempt at organization to dismal failure. Increasing, back-breaking speedup, threatened wage cuts, forced auto workers to search for a cure. In Detroit, as in Akron and Pittsburgh and in a half a hundred American cities, the C.I.O. was not the invention of wild-eyed radicals, not the inspiration of one man alone.

The C.I.O. was an organic growth in Akron; it developed out of mass unemployment, bank failures, wage cuts, speedup. John L. Lewis is a hero in Akron today not because he was a Man on a White Horse to workers—but because he supplied courageous leadership to the forward surge of the labor movement.

373

Strong unions in mass industries do not flower overnight. The Goodyear strike launched organization in rubber. From March, 1936, to the Firestone strike in March, 1937, the U.R.W.A. struggled to organize Akron factories. Sitdown followed sitdown as the employers made desperate efforts to stem the tide. Some months rubberworkers staged as many as thirty separate—and successful—stop-work protests, mostly against anti-union provocation.

The workers' patience was finally exhausted by the guerrilla warfare. In the seven weeks' Firestone strike they battled it out for signed contracts and complete union recognition. Harvey Firestone made none of Goodyear's mistakes. He shut down his factory, refused to ask for the National Guard, carefully courted public opinion. But his peaceful gestures served him little; in the end, the U.R.W.A. emerged with its first contract and a notable victory.

The rubberworkers carried all of Akron with them. Suburban Barberton went one hundred per cent union. Main Street's stores bloomed with placards: "This store has a C.I.O. contract," or "Workers here are 100% organized in the C.I.O." The ten-cent-store girls, the bus drivers, the department-store clerks, won union contracts, sometimes after strikes, sometimes merely on the threat of one. W.P.A. workers, with the assistance of the U.R.W.A., built a strong union of the unemployed, the Workers Alliance local.

William Green tried to split the Akron labor movement. He demanded that the C.L.U. throw out the rubberworkers. He sent an organizer into the rubber shops, attempted to recruit members for an A. F. of L. rubber union.

But Akron labor stood solid. Wilmer Tate, the fighting president of the C.L.U., three times defied Green's attempt to break up the central labor body. When the C.I.O. unions withdrew to form their own city council, Tate set up a local co-ordinating committee between the A. F. of L. and C.I.O. In spite of William Green the A. F. of L. printers and mechanics would not forsake or be forsaken by the rubberworkers. Fifty thousand union men, C.I.O. and A. F. of L., side by side, marched in the Firestone strike parade.

William Green attempted to destroy the U.R.W.A.; but the Akron rubber companies tried even harder. An organization called the Greater Akron Association suddenly appeared to woo the aroused working class with soft and "reasonable" words. In dozens of radio speeches, in countless full-page ads in the newspapers, the Greater Akron Association told the workers that the rubber city was a land of milk and honey. The Greater Akron Association walked softly but carried a big stick in plain view. The great rubber companies threatened to move out of Akron, lock, stock, and barrel, if the rubberworkers didn't watch out.

"Don't kill the Golden Goose!" the Greater Akron Association trumpeted. "Stop the sitdowns!"

The rubberworkers defeated the more subtle attacks of the big companies, just as they won their big strikes and smaller sitdowns. Sometimes they had set-backs. Sometimes they were discouraged. But, by the fall of 1937, Akron was a solid union town. Union organization had proved no fly-by-night dream. It was a fact, for the future as well as the present. The U.R.W.A. leaders, Sherman Dalrymple and the others, seasoned, able, honest, faced the opposition sure of their strength. Allan Haywood, the C.I.O. lieutenant, came to Akron for a year to help the new union through its toughest months.

The rubberworkers had their union. What did it profit them? And what did it profit Akron?

The U.R.W.A. put a ceiling on the speedup; forced the rubber companies to maintain the six-hour day; increased wages. The union brought more jobs, more money, escape from the worst part of the speedup to the workers of Akron. The plaintive cries of the rubber-company presidents, from Litchfield down, proved what the rubberworkers knew from experience—the union made working conditions in the factories at least bearable. Annual company reports complained that labor in Akron factories was less "productive" than in the good old days; production costs had gone up. The rubberworkers agreed—wages were higher and speedup less since the organization of the union.

In a one-industry town, the U.R.W.A. was a prop for the merchants, the small businessman, the real-estate holder, the city and county governments. If the rubberworkers had lost their fight

375

against the eight-hour day, permanent unemployment would have deluged the city, ruined the average small businessman, sent real-estate values down a toboggan slide from which there could have been no return, closed most of the motion-picture houses, put the department stores in bankruptcy. Akron would have been a ghost town but for the rubberworkers' union.

When the recession hit Akron in the late fall of 1937, neither the city nor the workers collapsed before the economic crisis—1937 was not 1931. The Workers Alliance battled for more W.P.A. jobs, and the rubber union kept up the wage level. The rubber companies moved up their big guns; The B. F. Goodrich Company threatened to move thousands of jobs out of Akron unless the union agreed to a blanket pay-cut.

But the U.R.W.A. rallied the Akron working-class. Forty thousand pledged to defend wage standards at the greatest mass meeting in the history of the city. Firestone signed a new union contract immediately after the mass meeting. Goodrich neither cut wages nor moved jobs out of town. Goodyear made a sudden foray against the union, but skillful leadership frustrated its plans to bring in the National Guard and blast the C.I.O. out of rubber.

The rubberworkers bore the brunt of the first depression. But the union saved them from feeling the full force of the second economic crisis. The U.R.W.A. meant, to the workers, food on the table, clothes for the children, a movie ticket now and then. To the doctors, the candy-store keepers, the dry-goods merchants, the U.R.W.A. was a dike against the flood waters of economic disaster.

The C.I.O. was first a bulwark for the working people of Akron and, after them, for the small businessman who was dependent upon their wages; but beyond that, union organization taught the rubberworker pride of class. Americans do not live by bread alone. Mass industry has not crushed the spirit of the free-born. Rubberworkers, no matter how skillfully they work on the conveyor belt, are not robots. A membership card in the U.R.W.A. is the rubberworker's declaration of freedom. The union is the answer of American workingmen to the impersonal dictatorship of a faraway Board of Directors.

The Goodyear strike was hardly over before the rubberworkers began to fumble towards political action. Labor's Non-Partisan

League came into Akron for the 1936 Roosevelt election. Factory managers put up pictures of Landon on their gates, distributed Landon literature in pay envelopes. The campaign turned into class war. Rubberworkers tore down the Landon posters, scoffed at the half-concealed threats they got enclosed in pay envelopes. On election day, every ward in Akron except West Hill gave Roosevelt an enormous majority.

Labor's Non-Partisan League had been able to teach rubberworkers the necessity of voting on labor's side in a national election. But, although its leaders made an alliance with middle-class liberals in the 1937 municipal election, Lee Schroy, "liberal" Republican, beat the labor candidate, because feeling that the workers' vote was in the bag, he turned to Red-baiting in an attempt to show West Hill that he was "safe." Schroy ran with a more or less clean labor record. Less than a year later, he sent Akron policemen into a violent attack on a Goodyear picket line. Rubberworkers watched Mayor Schroy and then turned to Labor's Non-Partisan League to organize a Defeat-Governor-Davey movement.

The Ohio primary fight in the summer of 1938 developed into a contest for control of the Democratic party, with labor and the small middle class on one side, and machine politics backed by steel, auto, and rubber barons on the other. Governor Davey, loud-mouthed enemy of the C.I.O., stood on his strike-breaking, union-smashing record. He boasted hysterically during weekly campaign broadcasts that his administration had broken the back of the Little Steel strike. He defied John L. Lewis to defeat him. He called on "decent" citizens to renominate him for Governor and save the Commonwealth for reaction. The Democratic machine bosses, fed on state patronage, supported Governor Davey. The great industrialists poured money into his campaign. Reverend Gerald K. Smith of Louisiana appeared mysteriously in Akron with headquarters at the expensive Mayflower Hotel. Reverend Smith called on all Akron rubberworkers, in the name of Jesus Christ, the Saviour, in the name of their red-blooded 100% American ancestors, to defeat the atheist, Jewish, foreign C.I.O.—and to vote for that great patriot, Governor Martin L. Davey.

But Labor's Non-Partisan League overwhelmed Governor Davey and his friend, Reverend Smith. Ward by ward organiza-

377

tion in Akron brought thousands of workers to the polls on primary day. An honest, careful campaign of education won the votes of the middle-class. The rubber union responded to Reverend Smith's "religious" crusade by bringing preachers, rabbis, and priests to its huge labor day celebration. Tireless work by thousands of volunteers, new to politics but rich in enthusiasm, outweighed Governor Davey's expensive campaign for renomination. Labor's Non-Partisan League scored a great victory—Governor Davey, nationally famous as a strike-breaking foe of the C.I.O., lost the primary election.

The New Deal started its 1938 by-election campaign under a handicap, however. The Democratic party was still split after the bitter primary. Governor Davey, disgruntled by his defeat, openly sabotaged his party's campaign. The Republicans, with two able candidates, Robert A. Taft for Senator and John W. Bricker for Governor, had learned a lesson from Davey's defeat. Reactionary aims were concealed; open labor-baiting was discouraged. Labor's Non-Partisan League made a bold stand, but the downstate farmers, usually Republican in an off-year, gave victory to the opposition. Senator Robert J. Bulkley, the New Dealer, and his running mate, Charles Sawyer, carried Cleveland, Youngstown and Akron by large majorities. The labor vote went solidly New Deal.

But Labor's Non-Partisan League, in spite of the Democratic defeat in Ohio, emerged from the 1938 elections with new-found strength. For labor had found itself politically. In the short space of two years, workingmen had learned to unite with the city white-collar workers behind progressive candidates. Until the C.I.O. organized workers in the great industrial valley of Ohio, the labor vote had been largely inarticulate, exploited. But the 1938 elections proved that the new union men understood the need for political expression of their economic aims. With one great achievement behind it, Labor's Non-Partisan League began the task of making political alliances with the downstate Ohio farmers—hoping to break the hold of Republican machine politics in the rural areas of the state. After two brief years of experimentation, the Akron rubberworkers and their allies in Cleveland's auto and steel shops and Youngstown and Canton's steel mills, marched confidently forward on the political front.

All horizons, not only the political, widened for the rubber-workers with union organization. The C.I.O. jolted the Akron worker out of his provincialism. Swept up in a great national movement, rubberworkers contributed money to the east-coast seamen's strike, to the auto workers, to the steel workers. Men from the southern mountains, once fair bait for the savage program of the Ku Klux Klan, applauded the speeches of Jewish garment workers, cheered the advance of Irish Catholic transport workers, sat side by side in union meetings with Negro workers.

The world opened up for the people of Akron. Two thousand men wearing U.R.W.A. buttons packed an auditorium to hear four young Spaniards tell the story of the Fascist invasion of their country. Sherman Dalrymple led the list of speakers at a great "Save China: Boycott Japan" meeting.

The new union members were eager for knowledge. They flocked to lectures; they planned reading clubs. The U.R.W.A. organized classes in economics, history, public speaking. Every local had a lending library. The rubberworker reached out for learning, for life.

Once the people of Akron were meat for any demagogue. They flirted with Coughlin, they watched Huey Long.

The C.I.O. taught the rubberworker to understand and hate Fascism. Akron spewed out Reverend Smith; the rubberworkers crushed Mayor Sparks and a fly-by-night vigilante movement he tried to organize for the 1938 elections. The U.R.W.A. stood in the forefront of the Akron movements against the Fascist invasion of Spain, the Japanese attack on China, the Nazi terrorization of the Jews. The men and women of Akron march side by side with the people of Pittsburgh and Detroit, New York and San Francisco, in the brave army of Democracy.

In the past seven years, the rubberworker has learned how to defend liberty. In his hands, and in the hands of his friends and allies everywhere, lies the future of our country.

379